True Allegiance
(Book 3 of the Halberd Series)

John J. Spearman

DEDICATION

For Alicia, who has made my life so wonderful.

OTHER BOOKS BY THIS AUTHOR

Halberd Series

Gallantry in Action
In Harm's Way
Surrender Demand

Pike Series
Pike's Potential
Pike's Passage

FitzDuncan Series
FitzDuncan
FitzDuncan's Alchemy
FitzDuncan's Enlightenment

ACKNOWLEDGMENTS

I'd like to acknowledge my readers. They are the whole reason to do this. If you enjoyed this book, please consider leaving a favorable comment on amazon of goodreads. If you are interested in learning more about my other books, please visit johnjspearmanauthor.com.

1

Jonah was oblivious to everything in the outside world. He lay in a stasis pod in a medically-induced coma while his body slowly healed. What thinking he did in this state was limited to recurring nightmares of a beautiful woman being killed before his eyes, a friend dying as he held his hand, and bodies being sucked into a vacuum from what seemed to be a starship's bridge. It was neither pleasant nor restful. Outside of the stasis pod, a variety of events swirled.

Remington and Winchester, members of the King's Own, had arrested the would-be assassin who had sabotaged the stasis pod he thought was Jonah's. The assassin was a paid professional. Upon questioning, he involuntarily revealed who had hired him to do the job. Armed with this information, the Office of Naval Intelligence, working with the Commonwealth's MI-5 agency, tracked his connection back to the Sanies Corporation.

The full weight of the government descended upon the company. Overnight HM Revenue & Customs invaded the company and seized control of all documents and operating systems before they could be altered or deleted. The investigators found carefully concealed ties to the Johanssen family. The Johanssens owned one hundred percent of Sanies, through a smokescreen of shell companies. The investigators also found links between Sanies and the intelligence services of both the Rodinan Federation and the Chinese.

Negotiations had begun between the Rodinan government and the Commonwealth on ending their seven-year war. Representatives of the Rodinan government had reoccupied their former embassy on Caerleon. King Edward had placed himself in charge of these talks. Jonah's girlfriend, Amy Davidson, was a key member of the Commonwealth team. She had been surprised when one of the leaders of the Rodinan group, Admiral

Belyaev, had asked if he could visit Jonah in the hospital. He was disappointed to learn that Jonah was still in a coma.

On the medical front, Jonah's recovery was accelerated once King Edward demanded to know why the use of medical nanites had not been approved for Captain Halberd. When the king learned that the request to use nanites had been rejected by a minor functionary, he exploded in a white-hot fury that no one had ever seen from him before. The director of the Commonwealth Health Service, as well as the First Space Lord and director of the Naval Health Care Administration, were given a tongue-lashing so severe they thought their ears would blister.

In short order, the latest generation of medical nanites, which included upgrades incorporating Edoan nano-tech, were injected into Jonah's bloodstream. Regrowth of Jonah's missing forearm and leg had already begun. The nanites speedily repaired the other damage, commonly referred to as space hickeys, caused inside and outside of Jonah's body due to his exposure to the vacuum of space.

Eight days after administering the nanites, the doctors felt it was safe to bring Jonah out of the coma state of medical stasis. Amy and others had requested to be present for this, but the doctors advised against it. Patients who had been placed in medical stasis for a long period, particularly those who had suffered severe trauma, often experienced temporary memory loss. This memory loss and accompanying disorientation typically cleared up within 72 hours.

The doctors felt Jonah would be under enough stress and that Amy's presence would add to it unnecessarily, especially if Jonah did not immediately remember who she was. With the king now taking a very aggressive and personal interest in Jonah's health, the doctors assured her that he would receive the best possible care. They promised to call her, day or night, as soon as Jonah asked for her.

Jonah returned to consciousness completely befuddled. He had no idea where he was or what had happened to put him there. The bright lights overhead hurt his eyes. His throat hurt, and his mouth was dry. His left arm and leg itched like crazy. He saw a woman in a white coat and guessed she was a doctor or nurse and that he was in some medical center.

Noticing he had awoken, the woman asked, "Captain Halberd?"

Jonah's mind raced. *Captain Halberd...sounded familiar...Halberd, yes, I think that's me, but captain? She seems to think I am so...* "Yes?" he croaked.

Golly, he thought, *that made my throat hurt. Do I really sound like that? That didn't sound like me, I think.*

"Captain, you're in the Royal Navy Medical Center on Caerleon. How are you feeling?"

Caerleon, Jonah thought, *capital planet...how do I feel?* "Throat hurts."

"Not surprising. You've had a ventilator tube stuck down it for nearly three months."

The woman pressed a button and the back of the bed raised. When Jonah's torso had been brought up to a 45-degree angle, she held a glass of water with a straw up to his mouth. Jonah took a sip of water and swallowed. It hurt, but his mouth was less dry. He took some more.

"Still hurts," he commented, his voice sounding more normal to him.

"It will take a couple of days," the woman counseled. "I'm Dr. Starn, by the way. I've been assigned to you since you arrived."

Jonah nodded. He noted he could not see out of his right eye. He then figured out that he couldn't move and looked down to see why. He saw straps holding him to the bed. He noticed an odd-looking tube attached to his left forearm. His eyes darted rapidly as he tried to make sense of it.

"Prisoner?" he asked.

The doctor smiled and shook her head. "Goodness, no. You're a hero."

"Then why...straps?"

"To hold you still," she explained. "You've been in a stasis pod in a medically-induced coma for over eleven weeks. We removed you from the stasis pod this morning to bring you back to consciousness, but as your coma lifted, you started to thrash around. Bad dreams?" she asked.

Jonah remembered the things he had seen. He nodded slightly. His mind struggled to wrap around what she had said. Stasis pod and coma felt to him as though they belonged together. His thoughts whirled. "Injury," sprang to his lips.

"Yes, captain," the doctor responded. "You were injured severely."

Jonah pondered with a frown on his face. "Don't remember."

"That's normal," the doctor reassured him. "Patients who have been put into comas often experience a temporary memory loss. It usually clears up in two or three days. The feeling of disorientation you're undoubtedly experiencing usually goes away within the first twenty-four hours."

"Mhm," he grunted. "How bad?"

Dr. Starn had prepared carefully for this moment. "How much do you remember of who you are?"

Jonah shook his head. "You called me captain," he suggested, fishing for more information.

"So, you don't remember," she stated.

Jonah frowned and shook his head slightly.

"Then I suggest you just relax for now, and we'll talk about it more later," she said, pressing a button on a stand next to the bed, lowering him flat. She dimmed the lights as she left. Jonah drifted back to sleep quickly.

When Jonah woke again, he was less confused than the last time. He knew he was in a medical facility and that he'd been injured dramatically enough to have been put in a stasis pod. He had some understanding that stasis pods were used for people with severe injuries. His throat still hurt, and his left arm and leg still itched abominably.

The lights were still dimmed and there was no one else in the room. He took a moment to try to self-assess what he knew. The doctor had called him captain and he was in a Royal Navy hospital, so he understood he was an officer. That meshed with some of the nightmares he had been having. For some reason, he was sure his name was Jonah. He lay in bed, puzzling things out for a short time. He was coming up with more questions than answers. The itching was a damned distraction.

The door opened and Dr. Starn came in, accompanied by a man in a similar white coat. As they entered, the lights came up. Behind them came another white-coated woman, pushing a cart with a tabletop on it. "Good morning, captain," Dr. Starn said.

"Good morning, doctor," Jonah replied, his voice once again raspy and unpleasant sounding.

The doctor raised his bed again while the woman pushed the cart to the side of the bed. Jonah looked at it. There was a glass of water with a straw, and what looked like a bowl of…his mind spun, searching for the right description…oatmeal. He was pleased with himself for remembering.

After pushing the cart to his bedside, that woman left. Dr. Starn then introduced the other man as Dr. Doyle. She explained that Doyle was his cognitive therapist who would assist him in restoring his memory. She put into plain words the fact that his brain had been asleep for almost three months and it needed to be woken up.

She also told him that the oatmeal would be the first solid food to enter his digestive system in three months and apologized if it was somewhat bland. She asked if he would like to try to feed himself. Jonah nodded.

Dr. Starns raised the bed even more and Doyle pushed the tabletop of the cart almost to his chest. Jonah was a bit confused. The table was mostly on his left side, but his left arm had a strange tube on it, so he couldn't use it. He reached with his right hand and was bothered that he couldn't see out of that side, needing to turn his head.

Picking up the spoon felt familiar, though. He dipped it into the bowl of oatmeal and lifted it. It shook a little. When he brought it near his mouth, he smelled it. It didn't have much of an odor. He wondered if it were hot, so brought it near his lips to judge. It seemed warm, not hot, so he put the spoonful in his mouth. The doctor hadn't lied. It was bland. He rolled it over his tongue, tasting and feeling it. It was not unpleasant, but he decided it would have been better if it were hot and not just warm. It needed some flavor too. For some reason, the idea of maple sugar popped into mind. "Maple sugar," he mumbled.

Dr. Doyle smiled. "I wish we could give you some, but your diet will be restricted for a few days until your digestive system has had a chance to wake up too. You're right, though. Growing up on York, you would have put maple sugar on your oatmeal."

Jonah worked his way through the oatmeal manfully. He understood it would be good for him, even though it didn't taste that great. By the time he finished the bowl, his stomach felt full. His mind continued to gnaw away at things. His home was on York, or it had been at one time. He knew York was a planet.

When he finished, Doyle pulled the table over to the side. Dr. Starn asked, "Captain, do you remember any more about who you are?"

"Is my name Jonah?"

"Yes," she confirmed.

"Good," he grunted, then tried to explain. "My mind is racing. I can't seem to settle on any one thing."

"That's why I'm here," Dr. Doyle stated. "I'm a cognitive therapist and I'm going to help you work through that confusion."

Jonah nodded. "I have questions, though," he said.

"Go ahead."

"Why can't I see out of my right eye?"

"You lost your right eye due to an injury nearly two years ago," Dr. Starn shared.

Jonah absorbed this information. While he didn't have the sense of 'knowing' that, it didn't seem 'wrong' either. "Why are my left arm and leg in these tubes and why do they itch so terribly?"

"Your arm and leg were sheared off by a powerful laser blast when your ship was attacked. You were also exposed to the vacuum for a time. There was damage to your lungs as a result and other internal damage because of microscopic air bubbles in your bloodstream. You were put into a medically-induced coma so your body could repair that damage. Your healing was accelerated recently when we injected medical nanites into your system. Your arm and leg itch because your body is regenerating, or growing, a new arm and leg for you."

Jonah processed this news. It explained some of the nightmares he had been having. Regenerating a body part puzzled his mind. On one level, he thought it should seem strange, but again there was no sense of 'wrongness' to it. "Why does it itch?"

The doctor smiled sympathetically. "It itches because your body is growing new nerves in your new arm and leg. It's a false sensation—just random signals in the new nerves. I'm told it is the worst part of the regeneration process, even though it is a positive sign that your nervous system is growing back. The good news is that you are almost halfway through the process and only have a little more than three months left before your new arm and leg will be fully useable. The itching sensation will only last another four or five weeks."

"Ugh, it's driving me nuts," Jonah groaned. "Or maybe I should say, 'more nuts' since I'm already out of my mind."

The two doctors smiled. "A sense of humor is a definite sign of good mental health," Doyle commented. "That you can find something funny about your state of confusion tells us that you'll be back to normal quickly."

With that, Dr. Starn said her goodbyes and Dr. Doyle pulled out a computer tablet that he placed in front of Jonah. He began with a series of random images, asking Jonah to identify what he was seeing. The process fascinated Jonah.

2

On her way into the meeting, Amy received a message from Doctor Starn telling her that Jonah had come out of the coma but was suffering memory loss and disorientation. His vital signs were strong, and the doctor expected him to recover his wits in the next couple of days. That was as good as Amy had hoped, so she entered the meeting in a good mood.

Negotiations with the Rodinan government had begun only two days before. The war had ended with a cease-fire ten weeks earlier when the Rodinan military arrested and replaced the Federation government. It had taken them some time to establish a new governmental structure and to send their representatives to their former embassy on Caerleon. None of the Rodinans had been involved with previous diplomatic efforts before the war.

The Rodinans were led by Admiral Belyaev of the Rodinan Navy and Colonel Krupnikov of the Rodinan Army. The rest of the Rodinans seemed to be merely staff officers reporting to Belyaev and Krupnikov. The previous two days were spent establishing the framework for discussions. The meeting the day before had ended after King Edward had delivered a powerful opening speech.

The king had stated that the Commonwealth would demand no reparations from the Rodinans and explained why. It was clear that the Rodinans had suffered greatly as a result of this war, and equally clear that the fault for the war could not be blamed on anyone in the room. The previous Federation regime had started the war and the team representing the Rodinan government now had removed that regime.

For much of the previous ten weeks, Amy was busy negotiating with the German government and the government of New Delhi regarding reparations. The Rodinan Federation had attacked both and had held the planet of New Bremen for three years. The king acknowledged his 'no reparation' policy did not apply to them and any peace treaty they developed with the Rodinans was outside the Commonwealth's authority. He did 'hope' that the two non-aligned systems would be satisfied if the Rodinan government established favorable trade agreements instead of cash reparations.

Amy was placed as the lead representative for the Commonwealth Foreign Service in the talks with New Delhi and the Germans. This was a significant career step for her, and, at the beginning, both looked to be doomed to fail. It was some of the most complex bargaining Amy could ever imagine. Both the Germans and the planet of New Delhi suffered significant damage and financial hardship at the hands of the Federation. Initially, both were intent on demanding cash reparations.

After riding out the storm of their desired vengeance, she was able to redirect the conversation to desired outcomes for all parties. She demonstrated how favorable trade agreements would generate nearly equal financial rewards for the Germans and New Delhi while strengthening their core economies—something that cash reparations would not do to the same extent. The trade agreements would also benefit in rebuilding the economy of some of the Rodinan planets, which would promote the stability of the new government and help promote a longer-lasting peace.

She finished those talks only a few days before the conference with the Rodinans began. On top of that, she knew Jonah was due to be brought out of his coma and wanted to be there to support him during his convalescence. During the difficult beginning of the deliberations with the Germans and New Delhi, she had spent many nights pouring out her woes to an unresponsive Jonah as he lay in a coma. Though he had no idea she was even there, the ability to talk through her problems had kept her calm and helped her sort out her priorities.

Today they planned to begin discussing fleet and ground forces dispositions and numbers. In the king's opening speech, he had announced his desire that fleet and armed forces levels be capped at current levels. This meant that each fleet would be frozen at the current number of ships within each class and ground forces would be limited to the same number currently enlisted. He had also proposed capping military spending at the same percentage of GDP as the Commonwealth in the last pre-war year, which was three-point two percent.

Amy expected some significant opposition to both these proposals. Capping fleet numbers would give the Commonwealth a perpetual advantage over the Rodinans. Limiting military spending would further restrict the Federation, as their economy was neither as large nor as robust as that of the Commonwealth. In exchange, Amy had the carrot of trade resumption to offer, which would benefit the Rodinans more than the Commonwealth.

She did not know at this point whether the new Rodinan regime in place would be continuing the strict governmental control of their economy that had been in place or whether they would be moving to more of a free-market system. Resumption of trade would be a bigger carrot in a free market system, so she would need to try to determine their leanings.

Entering the meetings, knowing that the two lead negotiators for the Rodinans were military officers, likely high-ranking members of the group that had taken over the government, Amy had expected them to display a bit more ego and be somewhat defensive. So far, she was pleasantly surprised to find that both appeared to be far more pragmatic than ego-driven. Their candor up to this point was unexpected. Both stated their goal was to reach an agreement that would help them restore peace and prosperity for their people.

Amy wondered how much of what they showed to this point was genuine and how much was a false front developed for these meetings. One of her strengths was her ability to read people well, so she would be paying close attention. Talking about fleet and armed forces numbers would be a subject that might drive a crack in their façade.

They had not progressed far in the day's discussions when the meeting hit a snag. The Rodinans were reluctant to share their current fleet disposition. Amy possessed a set of figures prepared by Naval Intelligence, but the analyst's notes indicated that they could not account for eight capital ships: three superdreadnoughts and five battlecruisers.

Exasperated, Amy decided to share what she knew. "Admiral Belyaev," she began, "let's not play games. My Office of Naval Intelligence has given me a report on your current fleet disposition. I'm sure your intelligence people have provided you with a similar report on where all our ships are. The Commonwealth is not trying to hide anything, but it seems you are. Roughly fifteen percent of your fleet is hiding somewhere, and we would like you to tell us where they are."

Belyaev looked down at the table. He glanced over at his counterpart, Colonel Krupnikov. The colonel shrugged his shoulders as if to say, 'you're on your own.' Belyaev frowned, then nodded slightly as though to himself, then looked at Amy.

"It would be best if we request an adjournment of the meeting until tomorrow," Belyaev replied noncommittally.

"Is there a particular reason why?" Amy asked, troubled.

"We need to consult with our intelligence services," Belyaev answered, adding, "Please. By tomorrow I will have better information to share with you."

The meeting broke up shortly afterward. That evening over dinner with her boss, Brian Stewart-Crosland, the foreign secretary, she asked him about it.

"Is there a threat I'm missing?" she asked. "Has part of their fleet gone rogue and is lurking, waiting to attack us?"

Brian gave a slight smile. "My guess is that we are in no immediate danger. I'm willing to guess that a portion of their fleet has gone rogue, as you phrased it, but it is too small to mount a serious attack on the Commonwealth."

"What could they be doing?"

"I think we will learn that tomorrow," the Foreign Secretary answered.

The next morning the meeting reconvened. Admiral Belyaev immediately asked to speak. "Ms. Davidson, thank you for allowing us to adjourn yesterday. I was not trying to avoid answering you. I needed more information than I had. Unfortunately, I have learned little more than I knew yesterday. The truth is, we don't know where those ships are. We have some ideas."

Amy cocked her head slightly. She forced herself to react no more than that. She waited for more explanation.

Belyaev looked glum. "When we replaced the former government, we had control of almost the entire Federation military. There was one task force where we had not been able to gain cooperation under Admiral Denisov. They left the Federation using this corridor." Belyaev activated the holographic astrogation display, showing where.

"So, you do know where they are," Amy countered.

"Um, no," Belyaev admitted, accompanied by a heavy sigh. "From there, they could have gone in a variety of directions. As far as we have surveyed, from that system, they have at least three ways of reaching Chinese space, one way of getting to the Commonwealth, and one set of corridors would take them to Patagonia.

"In all cases, the transit times are absurdly long, with the quickest route back to a civilized system being nearly six months to reach the Chinese. We sent some patrol boats to look for them, but by that time, we were not able to pick up any traces of their trail in the nearest systems. Because of the number of corridors, the number of possible routes available to them increases geometrically and we did not have the resources to extend the search further."

"You can supply me a list of those ships?" Amy inquired.

"Yes." He glanced at Colonel Krupnikov, who nodded. "They also have with them a complete troop transport unit—18,000 men and all the equipment and heavy weapons for them."

"Do you have any idea what their intentions might be?" she pressed.

Belyaev gave a small shrug of his shoulders. "We have been trying to guess what they hope to do. They have enough supplies to last for quite some time. One of the support ships they took has a small cloud scoop and refining equipment, so they will never run out of fuel. The only limiting factors are food and crew morale. They have enough food to last years."

"What about crew morale?"

"Admiral Denisov was unlike all the other officers we replaced," Colonel Krupnikov broke in. "He actually knew what he was doing and was not merely a political hack. The men and women under his command are very loyal to him. Because of that loyalty and his lack of political clout, the Politburo did not trust him and kept him away from the action and with what we would have called a reserve unit.

"We tried to recruit him to our cause, but he refused our advances. He had no love for the former government, though. We honestly have no idea what he intends to do."

"The earliest we expect him to appear in or near a civilized system would be four months from now," Belyaev added, "if he appears in the nearest Chinese space. It would take him three weeks longer to reach Commonwealth space and about the same time to arrive at Patagonia."

"If you don't mind," Amy asked, "I'd like to bring in our navy at this point to discuss this. I suggest we adjourn for the day."

After the Rodinans left the room, Amy spoke again to her boss. After a brief discussion, he suggested she head over to the Admiralty. He would meet her there and they would go see Admiral Lothes.

When she arrived, they were expecting her, and she was shown into Admiral Lothes' office where the foreign secretary was already waiting. They were looking at a large and complicated three-dimensional projection of the star systems where the rogue force led by Denisov could have traveled. Amy noticed there were four different systems highlighted. After exchanging greetings, Admiral Lothes invited her to sit. Another woman in uniform was also there, introduced as Commander Douglas.

Douglas began the briefing. "As you may have guessed, these are the star systems that Denisov has access to. As the Rodinans mentioned in your conference, Ms. Davidson, and as you can see from the complexity of the maps, they have a journey of at least six months to reach the system adjacent to Chinese space." With that, Douglas made the highlighted system begin to flash.

"What would make the journey take so long?" Amy inquired.

"All the different routes involve passing through systems with neutron stars and, in one case, a magnetar," Douglas told her. "Neutron stars have extremely large heliospheres—areas where travel is limited to sub-light speed—that must be crossed. A magnetar is a huge neutron star. In addition, the gravitational pull from these stars is huge. This requires a ship to take a carefully plotted curved course from one corridor to the next instead of a straight-line course; otherwise, the ship would go too fast due to the pull of the star's gravity and end up imploding. In addition, these stars pulse, so the heliosphere can expand, so it is safer to drop out of hyperspace well before reaching the last plotted boundary. This adds to the transit time."

"What are the other systems you have highlighted?" Stewart-Crosland requested.

"This system," Douglas replied, making another highlighted area flash, "is the one adjacent to the Commonwealth. The only way to access the Commonwealth is through the next system, which is the one with the magnetar. The magnetar system alone would take over nine months to cross.

"Then this system," making another flash, "is adjacent to Patagonia. From where they left the Federation, it would take them eleven months to reach Patagonia. The last system," she made the last highlighted system flash, "is uninhabited as far as we know. We're not supposed to know about it. The Rodinans found it a couple of decades ago but have kept it quiet. It's a 'Goldilocks' world. In ONI, we call it the Hermitage."

"Why haven't they settled it and begun to exploit it?" Lothes queried.

"It's about a seven-month trip to get there from the rest of the Federation," Douglas stated. "Just far enough to make it not economically attractive. It's a shame, too, because the terra-forming expense would be minimal."

"Why would that be?" Amy asked.

"One of the biggest problems in terra-forming is the presence of native life forms," Douglas informed her. "The more evolved the native life forms are, the greater the problems with determining whether any of those are hostile to terrestrial settlement. Then there is the problem of introducing terrestrial species while maintaining habitat for the native species. There has to be a careful balance.

"In the case of the Hermitage, because there are massively thick Van Allen belts surrounding the planet, almost all solar radiation other than light is prevented from reaching the planet. This solar radiation is what fuels evolution. On the Hermitage, we understand life has not advanced beyond single-celled organisms. It would be no problem to terraform. We suspect they have already done so, and that the planet could already be fit for human habitation.

"Humans evolved on earth because the Van Allen belts were thin enough to allow enough radiation through to cause random gene mutations but thick enough to keep the radiation to non-lethal levels. The planets we have settled in space have thick Van Allen belts. The thick belts prevent evolution. The more complex the organisms are on a planet, the less likely we would terraform it."

"Does ONI have an opinion on which destination is most likely?" Lothes asked, getting back to the main thread of the presentation.

"Since we just learned of this development when you did, sir," Douglas responded, "no. My personal opinion is that the least likely destination is the Commonwealth due to the length of transit. I'm sure the analysts both here and at MI-6 will be diving into this and will respond as soon as possible."

Douglas was dismissed and Lothes was left alone with Amy. "Miss

Davidson, the current proposal in your negotiations to limit fleet numbers to the same number and type of capital ships represents a problem for the Commonwealth. We have a project underway to refit some mothballed ships, as we did for Captain Halberd's last command. The problem we face is they are of an older class that is currently not in either fleet.

"We understand the Rodinans are reluctant to agree with this proposal as it stands. We would like to suggest a compromise that we believe both sides can live with. Set the cap as the number of capital ships in each fleet, without regard to class of ship, as of before the Rodinan attack of Roosevelt. Insisting on the three-point two percent of GDP cap on military spending will ensure that neither side ever reaches that level. You should also include an 'out clause' to the spending cap in the event either party finds itself at war with another power."

"I will need to think about these ideas some more," Amy replied, "and I have others who will need to approve them before I move further. When you say 'another power,' you, of course, mean the Chinese. Do you suspect the Chinese will attack either the Rodinans or us?"

"I have no evidence the Chinese are planning an imminent attack on either of us," Lothes replied. "At the same time, I have no certainty that they will not do so. The Chinese have been an extremely interested bystander for the last seven years. If they believe that either the Commonwealth or the Rodinans have been weakened enough by the war to present them with an opportunity for gain, I am certain they will consider it."

"I understand, admiral. I will communicate your concerns to the leaders of my team. I'm sure they will wish to discuss the issues further."

"I took the liberty of typing up my suggestions beforehand. If you would like a copy?" Lothes said, handing the paper to Amy.

3

When he woke up the third morning after being roused from his coma, Jonah realized he felt...normal. After two exhausting and sometimes frustrating days working with Dr. Doyle, something happened while he slept. He knew who he was, he could remember his life, and he felt, well, normal. It was a huge relief. He pressed the call button to summon an attendant.

The next two days were a whirlwind of visitors for Jonah. First on the list were his mother and Amy, who stopped in on her way to the next day of meetings with the Rodinans. His reunion with both was tearful and tender. King Edward and Queen Celeste came to see him, as did many former shipmates. At the end of the second day, Dr. Starn put a stop to the constant stream of visitors.

"We need to begin physical therapy, captain," she explained. "While the stasis pods try to keep your muscles active, there is no substitute for actually using them."

Jonah began a limited set of exercises to work on his right side and his core. He was disappointed to learn how weak he had become and how quickly he became exhausted. During the same period, he was able to progress from the oatmeal, soup, and porridge diet to begin eating solid foods. Amy stopped by every evening, which was Jonah's favorite part of each day.

A week later, he was greeted by Admiral Lothes one morning, who told him he was going on a 'field trip' to the Admiralty. The nurses dressed him in an undress khaki uniform, modified to accommodate the regen tubes on his left arm and leg. He hopped into a hoverchair and was taken to the Admiralty.

Once there, he was taken to a conference room where the director of Advanced Warfare, Albert Niven, was waiting to greet him. Niven, though quite young, was responsible for incorporating the latest technological advances into a refit of three mothballed ships. Those three ships, led by Jonah, left a swath of destruction through the Federation, helping to bring about the change in government and subsequent peace talks. After exchanging pleasantries and inquiring about Jonah's progress through rehab, Admiral Lothes turned to Niven and asked him to get started.

"We want to discuss the next logical steps in capital ship development," Niven began. "Based on what we have learned from your excursion through the Federation, we have improved the Swordfish missile defense system further."

Jonah cocked his left eyebrow. "That would be hard to do."

Niven almost blushed. "Thank you. Nevertheless, there were a few small improvements we were able to make to both the software and hardware. We also took your idea of firing anti-matter warheads at the pre-positioned banks of enemy missiles and developed a new weapon. We have created a new missile that is purpose-built for that task. Our preliminary computer modeling indicates that it would be over eighty percent effective in destroying pre-positioned banks of missiles like those you encountered. Its effectiveness drops off when the enemy scatters the missiles over a larger area, but that makes them easier for the Swordfish system to pick off. But we are not here to discuss those.

"As effective as these developments have been, and no matter how tight our security, it is only a matter of time before the Federation and the Chinese come up with systems similar to Swordfish. Look how quickly the Federation was able to implement towed missile pods," Niven added.

Niven paused while Jonah pondered this. "You're saying it's only a matter of time before they have the same capability," Jonah confirmed.

"Well," Niven smiled briefly, "I'd like to think that ours will still be slightly better, but fundamentally, yes."

"Two forces, lobbing missiles at one another," Jonah said, thinking out loud, "with neither side able to inflict much damage unless they run out of defense missiles. Despite what happened to us, that's not likely to happen…" Jonah paused. "I'd say we're back to photon cannons then."

"Precisely," Niven agreed. "If neither side can damage the other by means of missile attacks, then the most efficient option is to use artillery."

Jonah shook his head with a bemused smile. "It wasn't too long ago that I was of the opinion that photon cannons had no place on a modern warship." He chuckled. "So much for my ability to predict the future."

"Then thank heavens," Admiral Lothes interjected with a smirk, "that we have young Niven here to look out for us."

Niven did blush this time. "Technically, they're not photon cannons," he amended. "While we were developing Swordfish, we realized that, if it were successful, missiles would no longer be effective, and we would need some sort of artillery. We began developing a 'next generation' artillery weapon.

We wanted to improve on the current ability of photon cannons. We have engineered a particle burst weapon that has three times the wallop of a photon cannon and fifty percent longer range."

"What size ship would it take to mount those?" Jonah asked.

"Big," Niven responded. "The power draw of the new weapon is enormous. We have taken another look at powerplants and have come up with a tweak to the current reactor design that increases power output by fifteen percent. Even so, we need a minimum of six reactors to power the PBGs."

"PBGs?"

"Particle Burst Guns. Not too original. I apologize," Niven shrugged.

Jonah tilted his head in dismissal. "You'd need a superdreadnought then to mount them."

Niven looked to Admiral Lothes, who took over the thread. "Not exactly," she said. "There are a lot of moving parts right now, captain. While Parliament approved the ship-building campaign some time ago, we haven't laid down a single new keel for a capital ship. Given recent technological developments, we didn't want to spend money on a ship that would be obsolete before she was finished. We have been building frigates and light cruisers as quickly as we can, though.

"Add to that the current peace talks and King Edward's proposal to cap spending at pre-war levels. That means the money will disappear soon, so we needed to move quickly on this before anything to do with capital ship development gets bogged down by a treaty."

"I'm guessing," Jonah said with a smile, "that Director Niven has been busy out at the Twelfth of Never." The Twelfth of Never was an unoccupied system where the Commonwealth Navy kept its mothball fleet of obsolete ships. Advanced Warfare also had what Director Niven called a 'skunk works' to develop new weapons and systems.

"Yes," Niven confirmed, "yes, I have. We actually started working on *Severn* and *Murray* immediately after we finished the refit of *Pallas* and *Euryalus*. HMS *Severn* is due to be completed and ready for trials in five months."

"Which is when the doctors tell me," Admiral Lothes added, "that you will be cleared to return to the bridge of a ship. We would like you to take her."

"Thank you, admiral, director," Jonah replied. "I'd be proud to take her. What kind of a ship is...was...she?"

Niven activated the holographic display, showing three-dimensional views of HMS *Severn* before and after the modifications. "As you can see, she's—" he began.

"A *Columbia*-class dreadnought," Jonah interrupted. He chuckled, shaking his head.

"You find this amusing, captain?" Lothes asked.

"Well," he confessed, "a little. *Achates* was a *Viceroy*-class battlecruiser before you modified her. A *Columbia*-class dreadnought is a generation or two older than that. I guess I'm a bit tickled that you keep finding uses for these old ships."

"We chose the *Columbia*-class partly for the same reason as we chose the *Viceroy*-class for *Achates*," Niven stated, "structural integrity. The frames of the *Columbias* are not quite as overbuilt as the *Viceroys*, but compared to more modern construction, they give us a huge advantage."

"The refit is not quite as ungainly looking as *Achates*; I'll grant you that," Jonah offered.

"It's a bigger ship, to begin with," Niven explained, "and we decided the payload of Vulcan missiles could be reduced. As you can see, we expanded the rear half of the ship to accommodate the missile hold and doubled the size of engineering. There are six of the new reactors, in sets of three, mounted radially as in *Achates*. The EM drives are new and make her as responsive as a *Dakota*-class battlecruiser. The entire hull has been replaced with AT-38 alloy armor. She's 964 meters long, 111 meters dorsal to ventral and 146 meters port to starboard. Crew is 497, with a 'long' company of 216 Marines added to that.

"She has 48 Vulcan missile tubes and 120 Swordfish tubes. In addition, she can tow 12 missile pods with nine missiles each. She has two of the new 155mm particle burst guns, one above and one below. You can only use one at a time. We put two on because we wanted redundancy. One of the drawbacks of the new weapon is that there is a minimum 30-second cycle time to charge the weapon. There are also 20 of the standard 155mm photon cannons.

"Her computer system is the same Edoan system as on *Achates*. She has all the latest bells and whistles—all the electronics have been replaced. Her chief vulnerability is the electrical conduits powering the particle burst weapons. Plasma shielding along those areas of the hull has been strengthened, and the conduits themselves are encased with AT-38 alloy inside the ship."

"She sounds like an interesting command," Jonah admitted. "Do you have any sort of a mission planned for us?"

Lothes shook her head. "No," she confessed. "As a matter of fact, we would like to keep her existence as quiet as possible. I know you're used to being in the thick of things, captain—"

Jonah held up his hand to stop her. "I could use a break from that if it's all the same to you," he said, nodding at the tubes on his left arm and leg.

Lothes smiled ruefully. "I suppose you could. In any case, with the outbreak of peace, there is no mission planned for you at this point. We will be testing *Severn* in various exercises once she is re-commissioned, but those will take place far from the public eye."

Niven picked up on her thread. "We know the perception of Advanced Warfare is that we're a bunch of spotty-faced teenagers playing at war games, captain. To a certain extent, at least as far as playing war games, it's true. Our people are continually looking at the 'what if' scenarios. Playing at war games led to the development of *Achates* and now to *Severn*.

"I mentioned early that structural integrity was one reason we chose a *Columbia*-class dreadnought for this project. There's another reason. Our initial designs always start with a 'purpose-built' ship of new construction. One of the handicaps in designing this ship is that it needed to be large enough to hold the powerplants necessary to make the particle beam weapon work.

"We conducted a great number of computer simulations, pitting our initial design ideas against a wide variety of possible opponents. We analyzed what tactics were effective for the 'captain' of the new ship. We then fed those back into the computer to see if they resembled similar sets of tactics in our databases. We were surprised to learn that the closest tactical matches were old Terran air-breathing fighter planes and early Commonwealth carrier-based interceptors. The designs of both the fighter planes and the interceptors placed a premium on speed and maneuverability.

"With that in mind, we tweaked our designs. We wanted to put the particle beam weapon in the fastest, most maneuverable ship possible in the short window of opportunity that we have. Starting with our 'purpose-built' design modified to enhance speed and maneuverability, we then look for things in the mothball fleet that are similar. This modified *Columbia*-class is darned close. Its only problem is that we feel it needs more firepower. We're already working on that."

"Director Niven and his people have compiled hundreds of hours of simulations," Admiral Lothes added. "You'll be spending the remainder of your convalescence studying those and then conducting new sims yourself to prepare yourself for this new command."

4

After the bit of kerfuffle when the Rodinans admitted that an entire task force escaped, which required a suspension of the peace talks while the Admiralty decided what to do, things had gotten back on track for Amy. The Admiralty decided that the Commonwealth was the least likely destination for this rogue element. The logical destination for the task force was the planet the Commonwealth designated as the Hermitage. In the negotiations, the Commonwealth issued only the demand that the Rodinans deal with it themselves.

Amy had taken Admiral Lothes' suggestions to the foreign secretary, who shared them with King Edward. A series of quiet meetings took place immediately following, but Amy was not included. Her boss, the foreign secretary, was apologetic for not including her, but it did involve a discussion at the highest level of security clearance to which she was not yet read in. After these meetings, Amy was instructed to offer to the Rodinans the compromise which Admiral Lothes suggested. The Rodinans received the compromise positively.

It was eclipsed in importance the same day when the Rodinans, in discussing returning each other's prisoners, notified them that during their takeover of the government, they arrested all the personnel involved with the camps where Commonwealth prisoners were held. Admiral Belyaev freely admitted that the Federation's treatment of prisoners was awful. They arrested those responsible and were holding them, prepared to turn them over to an international tribunal to be prosecuted for war crimes, in accordance with the Interplanetary Concordat of 3009. Prisoner exchange had already been set in motion.

In addition to the talks proceeding smoothly, Amy had another reason to be happy. Jonah had quickly regained his memory and their relationship was undamaged. That first morning she was able to see him, he greeted her by saying, "What you said." That had been the last message he sent to her before being severely injured. Earlier, she complained that he never acknowledged the danger he was facing, and the rather awkward messages he sent her on the eve of battle were incredibly understated. She suggested a flowery and melodramatic alternative, to which he replied, "What you said."

She began laughing and crying at the same time and he joined her. They clung to one another for a half-hour until the nurse shooed her out. She had stopped by every evening and every morning since. In one more day, he was going to be released.

Since she returned to Caerleon, she had been staying at the palace. Because of her being kidnapped while on Edo and the recurring threats on Jonah's life, she was still under the protection of the King's Own. They insisted on her living in the most secure environment possible, and Queen Celeste graciously invited her to stay there. When Jonah was released, he would be joining her there. Even better, it would be the weekend.

At the end of the day's discussions, Admiral Belyaev asked Amy if he could speak with her on an unofficial matter. She agreed and waited for the others to leave. Belyaev stated, "Miss Davidson, would you please allow me to accompany you on your visit to Captain Halberd this evening?"

Belyaev had made this request before. Amy thought it odd but was willing to go along with it. "Let me ask my minders," she said.

Amy checked with Agent Thompson, who was accompanying her. He asked if Belyaev had any bodyguards of his own. Amy signaled Belyaev to come over.

"Admiral," she asked, "do you have any bodyguards of your own?"

"Normally, yes," he replied. "But I will leave them behind if you can protect me until I return to the embassy."

Amy look to Thompson, who nodded in agreement. Thompson then murmured, almost to himself, through his subvocal microphone. He heard a response and stated, "If you can wait a few minutes, we can escort you both."

While they waited, Amy's curiosity got the best of her. "If you don't mind my asking, admiral, this seems important to you. Why?"

"Captain Halberd and I have met," Belyaev replied with a warm smile. "I'm responsible for him losing his eye."

"Oh," she gasped, "you're that captain."

"Um, how much did he tell you?"

"Enough to know why I did not know your name," she answered slyly. "I am very grateful to you, though, and I'm sure he will be happy to see you."

Shortly after, Thompson indicated they were ready to leave. He escorted them to a groundcar where Remington and Sauer were waiting. The drive to the Royal Naval Medical Center was brief. Thompson and Sauer escorted them inside and accompanied them to Jonah's room. Winchester was outside the door.

Jonah was seated in a hoverchair when they walked in. As he saw Amy, he grinned. When he saw Belyaev behind her, his mouth gaped open in astonishment.

"Captain!" Jonah exclaimed, saluting, then noticing his uniform, corrected himself. "Pardon me, I mean, admiral."

"Captain," Belyaev replied wryly, returning the salute. "Jonah—" he said, offered his hand in greeting.

"Max," Jonah replied, shaking the offered hand. "My god! What brings you here?"

Belyaev looked over at Amy. She shrugged her shoulders and murmured, "We haven't talked about work much."

"I'm part of the new Rodinan government," Max explained. "I'm one of the two leaders of our delegation here."

"I'm thinking we have some stories we could tell each other," Jonah said.

"But now is neither the time nor place," Max replied.

"Tomorrow, I am being released," Jonah explained. "For security reasons, I will be staying at the palace. I will ask if you can visit me so we can have that conversation."

5

The days and weeks of the next three months flew by for both Jonah and Amy. Jonah was busy poring through the computer simulations that Advanced Warfare had compiled and working on his physical therapy. Amy was shepherding the peace talks to their conclusion. They had just reached the point where all the major issues had been decided. It would be the task of lower-level functionaries to work out the details that remained.

Two weeks before, the king had announced two events. The first would be a ceremony awarding Jonah a second Victoria's Cross. The second was a ball in honor of the signing of the treaty with the Rodinan government, formally ending the war.

One week earlier, the doctors had removed the last of the regen devices from Jonah's left arm and leg. He had been working hard even before that to build up strength in the new limbs. He was having difficulty with his coordination, though. He was making progress, but his left knee was still unsteady. He wanted to stand on his own to receive the Victoria's Cross. At the ball, he hoped to be able to share at least one dance with Amy.

He had just finished putting on his dress uniform. His medals were arranged properly, his sword was fastened to his side. He took a seat in the waiting hoverchair and called to Amy to let her know he was ready.

Amy came out of the bedroom, fastening an earring. She was wearing a pale gray floor-length dress. It was understated, but she looked amazing in it. She opened the door to their suite, where Winchester was waiting. He accompanied them to the anteroom, where they waited to be ushered into the Throne Room.

The Royal Seneschal came and opened the door. Jonah stood and placed his right arm on Amy's forearm in case he needed it. Winchester followed close behind.

Jonah advanced slowly. His left knee was not entirely cooperative. Twice it tried to buckle, but Jonah was moving carefully enough that he was able to keep his balance, thanks to Amy. As they turned right to go down the center aisle, Jonah saw that the king and queen were not sitting on their thrones. Instead, they were standing, waiting for him at the end of the aisle. Together he and Amy moved until they were three paces short of the king and queen, where they stopped. Jonah bowed, and Amy curtsied.

"Ordinarily, we would call for Captain Sir Jonah Edwin Halberd to advance and be recognized," declaimed King Edward, "but due to the injuries he received on our behalf, we prefer not to ask him to climb those steps just yet. It has been over a thousand years since the Victoria's Cross has been awarded twice to the same person, so allowances can be made."

The crowd murmured appreciatively. The king waited for the buzz to die down, then opened a scroll and began to read:

> It is our great pleasure to award the Victoria Cross for conspicuous gallantry in the face of overwhelming odds to Captain Sir Jonah Edwin Halberd of His Majesty's Ship *Achates* of the Royal Navy of the Commonwealth. This man, with complete disregard of his personal safety, led a small force of three ships through a fearsome gauntlet of enemy firepower, enduring barrages of thousands of ship-killing missiles. His leadership, innovative tactics, and brilliance enabled this small force to return to Commonwealth space safely. Along the way, they destroyed five battleships and four battlecruisers, and other assets significant to the Federation's war effort. As a result of putting himself in harm's way, again and again, he influenced the course of the war, which we will end when we sign a treaty of peace with the new Rodinan government later today. His extraordinary heroism and gallantry in action were in keeping with the highest traditions of the Royal Navy of the Commonwealth and reflect great credit upon himself and his service and serve as an inspiration to us all.

The king took the medal from a small wooden box that the seneschal had given him discretely. He draped it around Jonah's neck. "Thank you," he whispered in Jonah's ear.

When the king stepped back, Jonah saluted him. As he dropped his salute, the crowd burst into cheers. Jonah did not know what to do next. In the previous ceremony, he backed down the steps. Here, he didn't know whether to begin backing away or wait for the king and queen to climb back to their thrones.

While Jonah was wondering, the seneschal came up behind him and quickly draped a red robe trimmed with white fur over Jonah's shoulders, then went to Jonah's front and tied the robe with a black silk ribbon. On the right side, two stripes of fur edged with gold lace were positioned horizontally, but his right arm was left free.

As the seneschal was tying the robe, a herald called out, "Their Majesties command Sir Jonah Edwin Halberd to present himself to them that he might receive this fief from Their Majesties' hands and swear his solemn affirmation."

Jonah had no idea what was happening. The king stepped forward with a sly grin on his face and announced, "We, Edward and Celeste, being well pleased with you and ever concerned with the health, welfare and wishes of Our subjects, are minded to invest you as Baron, and grant unto you the Barony of Somerset, on the planet of York, to hold as fief from Our hands for the rest of your life. Will you accept this charge?"

Jonah was stunned. The seneschal whispered very quietly, "Yes, Your Majesties." Jonah blinked and blurted out, "Yes, Your Majesties."

"Will you swear your Solemn Affirmation and pledge your service to this charge and to Our Crown?"

"Yes, Your Majesties," Jonah answered on his own this time.

The herald then spoke, "I, Jonah Edwin Halberd — "

Jonah repeated, "I, Jonah Edwin Halberd,

"—do solemnly, sincerely and truly—

"—declare and affirm—

"—that I will be faithful and bear true allegiance—

"—to Their Majesties King Edward and Queen Celeste—

"—their heirs and successors, according to law."

When Jonah completed the Affirmation, the king spoke. "Wear now this circlet, Baron Somerset, as a reminder of your Affirmation."

The king placed a silver circlet with six balls on Jonah's head. The herald announced, "The Right Honorable Jonah Edwin Halberd, Baron Somerset."

The king stepped forward, took Jonah's right arm, and placed it on his own forearm, and had Jonah turn with him to face the crowd. Queen Celeste did the same with Amy. When Jonah turned, the crowd erupted.

The king leaned towards Jonah as the applause continued. "I do love surprising people."

"This is the second time you've done it to me," Jonah replied, "but I'm not complaining."

"We broke protocol, you know," Edward commented. "Ordinarily, you're supposed to bend the knee to get your circlet, but Celeste and I think there's only one person you should get on one knee for."

Jonah had to turn his head to look at the king, who had a smirk on his face. Jonah then looked over to see Queen Celeste smiling at the king's quip. The applause died down, and the king and queen turned Jonah and Amy back around, then proceeded up the steps to their thrones. The seneschal whispered, "You may process out. Don't worry about turning your backs since you're already down the steps."

Amy crossed to Jonah's right and offered her arm, which Jonah took gratefully. They walked down the aisle carefully, with Jonah mindful of his balky knee. As they processed, people clapped politely.

When they reached the anteroom, the doors were closed. Waiting for them were Jonah's mother and Lord and Lady Thorner. As they were being congratulated, a page came to collect Jonah's robe and circlet, informing him that this regalia would be stored with his other ceremonial dress. Jonah sank into the waiting hoverchair with a sigh, and the five then went to a small dining room where lunch was waiting for them.

The lunch was brief. The ladies excused themselves quickly, informing the two men that they needed to leave to prepare for the ball that evening. Jonah and Geoff could not linger much longer either. They had been invited to attend the ceremony of signing the peace treaty formally ending the war.

The treaty signing was blessedly brief. It was more of a photo opportunity for the news media who wanted to capture this historic moment. Admiral Belyaev and Colonel Krupnikov signed for the Rodinan government, King Edward for the Commonwealth. After it was over, Geoff pushed Jonah in the hoverchair back up to the suite where he was staying.

Along the way, Jonah tried to quiz Geoff about what the ladies had planned for the evening, but Geoff pleaded ignorance. Jonah had no sooner taken off his formal dress uniform when a knock on the door announced the arrival of his physical therapist, Jude. Jude was an imposingly large black man who seemed to fill the entire doorway.

He would not allow Jonah to use the hoverchair to get to the exercise facility. Jonah tried to use the argument that he needed to save himself for the dance that evening, but Jude just laughed at him. For ninety minutes, Jude put Jonah through a series of exercises both to build the new muscles in the parts of his left arm and leg that had been regrown and to restore Jonah's control over those muscles. They finished with a special exercise that Jonah had requested. Jude made Jonah repeat it again and again until he was satisfied. When they were finished, he made Jonah walk back to his room.

Jonah spent the remainder of the afternoon going through the combat and maneuver simulations prepared by Advanced Warfare. At 4:30, his comm unit chimed, reminding him of a call he had scheduled. The call took almost an hour.

6

Jonah had time to shower. When he got out of the shower, he found his dress uniform had already been cleaned and pressed, with his new Victoria's Cross affixed in its proper place. After donning his uniform, he had only a few minutes before there was a knock on the door, signaling him it was time to head to the ballroom.

Jonah stood and buckled on his sword. He patted his pockets to make sure he had everything. He looked at the hoverchair and decided to leave it behind. Tonight, of all nights, he did not want to seem like an invalid. He walked out, mindful of his balky knee, and found his way to the vestibule outside the ballroom. As people entered the ballroom, the herald called out their names.

When it was Jonah's turn to enter, the herald cried, "The Right Honorable Jonah Edwin Halberd, Baron Somerset." Jonah almost laughed out loud. That was quite a mouthful, he thought. He didn't suppose he would ever get used to it.

He crossed the room carefully to pay his respects to the king and queen. They teased him slightly, insisting on addressing him as Lord Halberd. The king twitted him further, telling him not to bother looking for his assigned table since he would be sitting with them. The king then told him, "Turn around. I think you're going to want to see this."

Jonah turned carefully just in time to see Lady Thorner, his mother, and Amy enter the ballroom. While his mother and Lady Thorner were the epitomai of glamorous elegance, once again, Amy looked simply stunning. Jonah noticed voices quieting as she crossed the room.

She was wearing a dress that was mostly a becoming shade of light blue. The light blue fabric was wrapped around her torso under her breasts on a bias, covering one hip and flowing to the floor. Where that fabric didn't cover, there was a thin, gauzy material in the same shade, completely transparent but covered with sprays of light blue flowers in lace. One leg and hip were mostly exposed, as were her breasts, with the sprays of flowers strategically positioned to avoid too much exposure. One shoulder was bare, while on the top of the other shoulder, the transparent material changed back to the light blue fabric, which fell down her back on the same side as the covered hip. Her hair was pulled up, and she wore earrings that appeared to be dangling strings of diamonds.

"Miss Davidson certainly knows how to make an entrance," Queen Celeste commented wryly. "Close your mouth, dear," she teased the king.

That reminded Jonah to do the same as he stood speechless. He thought she looked like a goddess out of mythology. He hadn't realized he'd spoken that thought aloud until the queen agreed, saying, "She certainly does."

The three women paid their respects to the king and queen. Queen Celeste told Amy, "Dear, you look amazing! That dress is magnificent!"

Amy blushed prettily and replied, "It's all Laura's doing. She found the designer who dreamed it up."

"She's actually local," Laura explained. "A young, up-and-coming designer named Megan Cavendish."

As Lady Thorner and the queen chatted about designers and fashion, Amy crossed to Jonah's side. "We decided you look like a goddess," the king commented, "or at least Jonah did. We agree."

"You're so beautiful it almost hurts to look at you," Jonah murmured.

Amy gave him a quick kiss on the cheek. Jonah noticed others coming to greet the king and queen, so he discretely guided Amy off to the side. They found their seats at the head table. Jonah was relieved to learn he was not sitting at the king's immediate right. The place card for Admiral Belyaev showed that he would be. The next place card indicated a Captain Pavlishcheva, then Jonah and Amy. Lord and Lady Thorner were on the other side of the table. Having finished her discussion with the queen, Laura came over to join them. Geoff materialized with Marian, Jonah's mother, and the five of them chatted, remarking as people came to greet the king and queen.

Once again, the room quieted, and Jonah looked to see who had entered. First, they saw Colonel Krupnikov in the dark green formal uniform of the Rodinan ground forces. Behind him, they saw Admiral Belyaev in the black dress uniform of the Rodinan Navy. He was accompanying a beautiful blonde woman, tall and slender, in a form-fitting black gown. Her hair was almost white, it was so pale, and it fell absolutely straight down her back like a silken brush to just below her shoulder blades.

After greeting the king and queen, Krupnikov, Belyaev, and the woman joined the little group with Jonah and Amy. Max introduced the woman as Second-rank Captain Raisa Pavlishcheva. Jonah introduced the Rodinans to Lord and Lady Thorner, who quickly asked to be called Laura and Geoff, and to his mother. Before they had a chance to dive into conversation, a bell tinkled, indicating everyone should find his or her seat. Apparently, the Rodinans, as guests of honor, had been the last to arrive.

King Edward and Queen Celeste came to their seats and waited until the hubbub of everyone finding the proper place died down. "I'm pleased to welcome you all on this joyous occasion," began the king, raising his wineglass in a toast. "Tonight, we welcome our guests, and we celebrate the signing today of a treaty between the Rodinan government and the Commonwealth. We hope to be partners in peace and prosperity for generations to come."

Cries of 'hear, hear' were heard from the crowd as people lifted their glasses to join in the toast. The queen sat down, followed by the king, which was the signal for everyone else to sit. Waiters in palace livery appeared from everywhere as if by magic and served the first course.

Jonah quickly found himself the center of attention between the two women flanking him. Raisa, he learned, was a doctor in the Rodinan Navy. She out-ranked her older brother Nikolai who had been the flight surgeon on the battlecruiser *Pyotr Velikiy*. It was he who had treated Jonah when he lost his eye. She had met then-Captain Belyaev several years ago through her brother. She and Belyaev had been involved ever since.

She asked about Jonah's injuries and how his rehab was progressing. She and Amy then got into an involved discussion about the difficulties of dating naval officers. Amy complained to Raisa about how unsatisfactory Jonah's messages were when he was heading into danger. Raisa shared that Max was just as bad. The two found so much to talk about that Jonah switched seats with Raisa after the third course so they wouldn't have to talk over him.

The king noticed and pointed out to Max and Jonah, "I think you gentlemen are in trouble now."

The king had been discussing with Max his hopes for the trade agreements that were included in the treaty just signed. Jonah found the topic interesting, and soon Raisa and Amy wanted to be involved too, so he ended up trading seats again. Soon the dinner was finished, and the orchestra began to play. The king and queen rose and began to dance.

About halfway through the first song, Lord and Lady Thorner got up and joined them. This was the sign that everyone could dance. Max offered Raisa his hand and invited her to dance. Jonah did the same for Amy. He made his way around the table carefully, hoping his knee did not betray him.

"Please don't expect too much," he whispered. "I'm just hoping I don't fall down."

Amy giggled and gave him a hug. They moved slowly, cautiously. It was enough for Amy to have her lover in her arms. It was almost enough for Jonah, as he felt the warmth of her embrace and luxuriated in the smell of her perfume. Almost enough because he wanted more.

After the first song, the orchestra did not immediately begin another tune. Jonah let go of Amy and gently lowered himself onto his left knee. This was the special exercise Jude had helped him practice. He reached into his pocket and removed a small box covered in blue felt. He opened it and took Amy by the hand as he offered it to her. With the realization of what he was doing hitting her, Amy gasped. A spotlight winked on, focusing on the two of them in the middle of the floor. The crowd had cleared space around them, and everyone had fallen silent.

"Amy, love of my life, darling of the foreign service, though I have flown into battle many times, this is the scariest moment of my life. I love you with all my heart, and the greatest treasure in my life has been the time I've spent with you. Will you make me the happiest, luckiest man in the universe? Will you marry me?"

Amy's eyes glittered with tears. "Yes," she rasped, in a voice choked with emotion, then, "YES!" she shouted for the crowd as she pulled Jonah to his feet. The crowd cheered as Amy threw her arms around his neck and kissed him passionately. The spotlight winked out, and the orchestra began to play an up-tempo song.

Jonah and Amy stood in the middle of the dance floor, embracing as people danced and whirled around them, offering congratulations or best wishes. The two of them clung to one another, both sobbing. When she caught her breath, Amy whispered in his ear, "You are so getting lucky tonight."

They made their way off the dance floor. Amy realized she had not even looked at the ring. Once out of the crowd, she held her left hand out, indicating Jonah should put the ring on. It was a huge diamond, with an equally large sapphire on either side on a platinum band covered with smaller diamonds. Jonah slid it onto her finger.

"Oh," she breathed, "it's beautiful! And it fits perfectly!"

She embraced Jonah again, burying her face into his shoulder as she cried. When she pulled away, she looked at Jonah. Tears and mascara were running down her cheeks. Jonah offered her his handkerchief, which she took. A look of horror crossed her face after she used it. "Oh, I must look a mess!"

Before Jonah could reassure her that she was by far the most beautiful woman in the room, Laura and Marian stepped in. Amy embraced them both, and the tears started all over again. The two women gently steered her away to fix her makeup as she held her left hand out so they could see her engagement ring.

Jonah was quickly surrounded by well-wishers, led by the king and queen. Queen Celeste gave him a quick hug and kiss on the cheek. Geoff pumped his hand and beamed. Admiral Belyaev smiled and shook his hand.

When Amy returned, she was surrounded by people wanting to see the ring. The band continued to play, so Jonah danced gingerly with his mother, then Laura, and then, to his surprise, Raisa asked for a dance. By the end of that song, the group around Amy had thinned, and he went to her. When the orchestra leader noticed Jonah and Amy dancing again, he signaled to the musicians and changed the tune mid-song to an old familiar romantic ballad. Once again, the spotlight blinked on, finding them on the dance floor. Everyone pulled away and let them dance all by themselves. When they finished, there was polite applause. Amy blushed, and Jonah grinned.

7

At the end of the evening, Amy and Jonah returned to their suite. Amy's beautiful dress slid to the floor with a whisper, leaving her in just her heels. She crawled on the bed and lay there seductively, admiring the ring on her finger.

"It's not fair," Jonah complained, struggling to remove his uniform as he sat on the edge of the bed.

Later, after they satisfied their passion, with Amy resting her head on his chest, she said, "Okay, spill the beans, buster."

Jonah pretended not to know what she was talking about. "What about?"

"Don't give me that, you little schemer. You had the whole thing choreographed. I want details."

Jonah sighed. "Where do you want me to start?" he asked.

"At the beginning. When you decided."

"I decided the third day after coming out of the coma," Jonah explained. "The morning I woke up feeling normal. They let me see you that morning for the first time."

"I remember. So…after you saw me, you decided."

"No. Before I saw you. As soon as I remembered, I decided. I knew I'd almost made a terrible mistake because I should have asked you before that."

"Great minds think alike then," Amy concurred. "I was so afraid—"

"I'm sorry," Jonah apologized. "All my fault. I knew I had to fix it. When I figured out that I hadn't gotten you anything for Christmas too—"

"I already forgave you for that. You were in a coma, after all. As far as not asking me sooner, apology accepted," Amy said, kissing him. "Now tell me all the fun parts."

"The next time Laura came to visit me, I asked if I could speak to her alone, so she shooed Geoff out. I asked her if the Armontrout jewelry people had measured your ring size back on Lutetia, and she said they had. I told her that I was going to propose to you. She told me I was an idiot for not doing it sooner. I told her that I had an idea in my head of what I wanted the ring to look like and described it to her. She met with her jeweler and sent me some different designs they worked up, based on my description. The one I chose is exactly what I had pictured. Do you like it? Would you like something different?"

"Good God, no! It's fabulous! I love it!" she exclaimed, giving him another kiss, this one quite passionate.

When they caught their breath, Amy asked, "Then what?"

"Then it was a question of waiting for the right opportunity," Jonah said. "When Edward announced the ball to celebrate the treaty signing, I knew that was it. My biggest worry was being able to do it properly. Jude worked with me so I could get down on one knee without falling on my ass."

Amy laughed at this. Jonah continued, "Two days ago, I was pretty sure I'd be able to do it. I asked Celeste if it would be okay to ask you at the ball. She's the one who arranged for the spotlight and the break in the music. All I had to do was stumble around on the dance floor in such a way that we ended up near the middle. Then, this afternoon, I called your father and asked his permission. I was on the call with your folks for almost an hour. You're supposed to call them tomorrow, by the way. After that, I only had to worry whether you would say yes."

"Did you have any doubt?"

"I had high hopes, but," he admitted, "there's a part of me that thinks you'd have to be crazy to want to marry me."

"I'm crazy about you," she quipped. "Does that count?"

"Good enough for me," he said, then kissed her.

"You asked my dad for my hand in marriage?" she queried.

"Yes, I did."

"That's very old-fashioned of you," she commented. "Kind of romantic too. Did he grill you?"

"No, he and your mom did that before, when they were here. But he did give me his permission."

"Good. I liked the way you asked me. So much better than your usual."

"Tell me about the dress."

"You like it?"

"Mhm!"

"Laura arranged the whole thing," Amy confessed. "I've been so busy with negotiations I didn't have time for anything. Laura told me she'd found this designer. I never even saw a sketch. Laura just said, 'Trust me,' so I did. I saw the dress for the first time when I put it on."

"It was unbelievable," Jonah told her. "You could hear the room grow quiet as you walked in. Everyone stopped to look. Celeste told Edward to close his mouth."

Amy giggled. "So, when are we going to do this?" she asked.

"Whenever you want, dearie. Where are we going to do this?" Jonah asked.

"That's probably the bigger question," she admitted. "If we were normal people, we'd get married on the beach on Carolina near where my folks live. That's where I always wanted to get married. When I married the jerk, we did it at the courthouse. I should have known it was doomed."

"The beach sounds nice. What's wrong with that?"

"In case you hadn't noticed," Amy said somewhat exasperated, "we're hardly normal, Lord Halberd."

"That's 'my Lord' to you," Jonah cracked.

Amy was about to smack him in response when she stopped. "Does that mean I become Lady Halberd?"

"It does."

"Cool. Good thing I said 'yes' then." She snuggled back down on Jonah's chest.

A few minutes later, she murmured, "I'd better ask Elaine."

"Ask Elaine what?"

"Tell you tomorrow," she mumbled as she drifted off to sleep. Elaine was Captain MacLeod of the Navy's Office of Public Affairs.

The next morning when they woke, they found a paper slid under the door. Queen Celeste had handwritten a note inviting them to brunch. She had noted: "This is a command performance, but dress is casual." Amy laughed when she read it.

Waiting for them was only a small group. The king and queen, of course, Jonah's mother Marian, Geoff and Laura, and Amy's boss, the foreign secretary, Brian Stewart-Crosland, and his wife, Joanna. The engagement was the topic of conversation. They were asked when the wedding would be and replied they hadn't set a date. They were asked where they would be getting married, and Amy answered that they had not decided.

Queen Celeste picked up on Amy's internal struggle and asked, "What's the matter, dear?"

With a sigh, Amy explained her confusion about location. "I'd always figured I'd get married barefoot on the beach back home on Carolina, but—"

"What's wrong with that?" Celeste asked. "That sounds lovely!"

Amy sighed again. "Well, I'm marrying a public figure, and I think there are certain compromises that one has to make."

"Dear," Celeste pointed out, "you're a public figure in your own right. Did you happen to see the media coverage of the ball? As far as they are concerned, you were the 'belle of the ball.' And no one has to tell me about the compromises you have to make when you marry a public figure."

"I'm sorry," Amy apologized. "I don't mean to complain, least of all to you. I just want to do the right thing."

"Nonsense!" Celeste exclaimed. "You're the bride. Whatever you want is the right thing!"

"But you did it," Amy countered.

"Because I'd always dreamed of a fairy-tale wedding," Celeste responded. "By marrying Edward, I got to have the wedding I always wanted."

"That's what makes it so hard," Amy admitted. "Having a fairy-tale wedding would be fantastic too. It's just different from what I—"

"Get married on the beach, dear," Celeste affirmed. "And if we're invited, we'll be happy to stand with our bare feet in the sand along with you."

8

When the next week began, Jonah was summoned to the Admiralty into Admiral Lothes' office. Leaving in a groundcar with Thompson driving, Jonah noticed the throng of reporters at the gate was larger and more aggressive than usual. "What's going on, Agent Thompson?" he asked.

"You are," Thompson replied laconically.

"What do you mean?"

"Since you came out of your coma, captain, the press has been swarming wherever you are. You didn't see it, but while you were in the hospital, there were scads of them camped outside. Here at the palace, there's always a bunch of them, hoping to see the king or queen or to track the comings and goings of other VIPs, but a few more since you came. With you being made a Lord and all and then proposing to Miss Davidson at the ball, you're the top of the news. Congratulations, by the way. We all think the world of Miss Davidson."

"Thank you. So do I."

Jonah just shook his head in disbelief at all the commotion. Reporters shouting questions all at once, only reluctantly giving way as the groundcar advanced. Once they were through it, he put it out of his mind.

"The medical folks tell me you are making good progress," Admiral Lothes commented, "and are ahead of schedule. In less than six weeks, you should be cleared to return to command. It's time we started filling out your crew. I've made some preliminary assignments but wanted to share the files with you to see if you had any suggestions or objections."

She sighed, pushing her hair back from her temples. "Personnel questions have consumed me the last six weeks, captain. Moving to a peacetime navy…already we're seeing some of our promising junior officers and senior non-coms jumping to the private sector. That will continue for the next year or two. With the fleet frozen at whatever the number ends up to be, young officers think the path to promotion is blocked. Plus, there isn't the allure of serving during peacetime that there is when there's a war on. I need to put some of the more senior officers 'on the beach' so to speak, in order to open up promotional paths for the promising younger officers, but in peacetime, it becomes so much harder to do that."

"Just curious," Jonah ventured, "what sort of officers are you looking to 'put on the beach'?"

"For the most part," she sighed again, "perfectly competent ones. The incompetent ones we weed out as we go. Only a few bad apples hang around, usually because of politics. That gets worse in peacetime, as you can imagine, and the higher up the ladder, the more difficult it becomes to move them aside. No, the ones I need to move aside are decent commanders, but they're the ones we feel have reached the limit of their potential. They haven't done anything wrong. Usually, their performance has been above average, but they're not going to take the next step."

Jonah could think of a number of captains who fit her description. "I understand," he said, nodding.

"You're probably wondering why I'm complaining to you like this," she confessed.

"Well, everyone needs to vent sometimes."

She smiled. "Venting to a subordinate would be extremely unprofessional. What I'm trying to do, in a roundabout way, is set the stage for the bad news I have to give you."

"Bad news, sir?"

She leaned forward. "Jonah, if ever there were a 'fast track' to flag rank, it would describe your career. You have excelled at every step along the way. There is no one, and I mean no one, in the whole damn Commonwealth Navy more deserving of a promotion to flag rank than you. Everyone knows it, from King Edward on down. I simply don't have an open position right now, and I couldn't even begin to guess when I will. All I have to offer you is command of *Severn*, even though you deserve more. I'm sorry."

"Sir," Jonah began, trying to order his thoughts carefully, "when I came to your office today, the last thing I was expecting was a promotion. That's not because I lack ambition, as I believe you know. Beginning when I served under Admiral Von Geisler, I have enjoyed the postings I've been given and have never looked too far ahead or focused my attention on trying to grasp the next rung of the ladder. I'm pleased with the trust you and others have put in me and do my best to continue to merit that trust.

"If you hadn't mentioned flag rank today, I would not have been disappointed. I would not have felt slighted or frustrated. I'm looking forward to taking command of *Severn* and working with you and Director Niven to see what she can do. I guess what I'm trying to say is that I appreciate your concern, but you've given me an interesting assignment, and my focus has been on that…well, not entirely on that, as I'm sure you've heard."

Lothes smiled in relief. "I think the whole Commonwealth and every civilized system has heard about your engagement by now, Jonah. Congratulations."

"Thank you," Jonah replied. "I'm a lucky man."

"And I'm not surprised by your reaction to my bad news, but I will admit to being relieved. Now, to the business at hand…please review those personnel assignments and get back to me in the next 48 hours. In addition, Director Niven will be uploading some new sims for you to take a crack at. His people have been studying what you've been doing and have come up with some new wrinkles. As far as *Severn* is concerned, they plan on tuning the new drives about the same time you will be cleared to return to duty. Until then, review those files, play with the sims, and continue to work on your rehab. If you decide to leave Caerleon during the next few weeks, just let my office know where you'll be."

Jonah next stopped by Advanced Warfare to check in with Director Niven. Niven complimented him on what he had done with the existing simulations. They had a new batch that were being finished by the afternoon that he would upload. Since it was time for lunch, they ate together in the commissary.

When Jonah returned to the palace, the same swarm of reporters was still outside, still shouting questions. Once out of the groundcar, he forced himself to walk back to the suite. His left knee was still shaky, but he knew he would have to answer to Jude in a few hours. When he reached the suite, he found Amy waiting for him.

"Honey, I'm home," he called out playfully.

"Good," she answered, "we have a lot to talk about."

"Sure. What's up?"

"Well, I talked to Elaine this morning. She called, actually, to congratulate you on getting your head out of your butt and proposing to me. I asked her, from a public affairs standpoint, where we should have the wedding."

"I thought Celeste suggested to have it wherever you wanted?"

"She did. So did Elaine."

"Okay then," Jonah suggested.

"It's not that simple," Amy protested. "Elaine also pointed out that no matter where we get married, it's likely to be a media circus. The tabloid press is already calling it the 'Wedding of the Century'."

"Huh," Jonah grunted. "Wasn't the 'Wedding of the Century' those two actors who got married a few years back?"

"Yes, and before that, it was when Edward and Celeste got married," Amy responded. "But that's not the point. What Elaine was saying is that having a small, intimate wedding is probably going to be impossible."

"Based on what I just saw outside, I'm inclined to agree with her."

"And we've been lucky because we've been staying here at the palace," Amy added. "Can you imagine how awful it would be, living in an apartment and having to run that gauntlet every time you went out or came back? Anyway, Elaine's point was that there's not much we can do to prevent it if we have the wedding on Carolina. I mean, sure, the agents can make them stay a certain distance away, but we'd still know they were there. That's not to mention how they would harass our guests."

"Ugh," Jonah groaned, envisioning the unruly mob of reporters crowded onto the beach and people being pestered every time they left the hotel. "So, what do we do?"

"Well, although Elaine said we can't prevent it, she did say that there are ways to manage it by restricting access. We can't restrict access to a beach unless we go to a private resort somewhere."

"Okay. Let's do that then," Jonah offered.

"Oh God," Amy said almost to herself, "you're going to think I'm such a pain in the neck." Speaking up, she said, "That's not the point. I wanted to get married on the beach, but not just any beach. I wanted to get married on my beach—the beach where I grew up. That's what made it special."

"No, I get it," Jonah reassured her. "Damn."

"Yeah," Amy agreed. "After she and I talked, I took a little time to process it, then I called her back."

"What did you decide?"

"Elaine's advice about 'managing' the situation is what got me thinking," Amy explained. "Going home to Wilmington—it's only a small city. They'd never be able to handle all the hoopla, all the reporters, all the fuss, not to mention the security problems. So, I started thinking about where we could manage all that. The best place where we can manage security and media access and not get run over by the media in the whole Commonwealth is right here. Then I decided to talk to Celeste. I mean, who do we know who has more experience in dealing with that kind of attention?"

Jonah shrugged his shoulders and nodded in response.

"She came up and listened to me and gave me a shoulder to cry on. We talked it out, and I think we came up with a pretty good Plan B."

"Which is?"

"We're going to be married here on Caerleon, in Glastonbury Cathedral, on Boxing Day at 6:30 in the evening."

"Wow!" Jonah breathed. "Are you sure?"

"I'm going to let my mind chew on it a little more, but the more I think about it, the more I like the idea."

"Oooookay," Jonah said uncertainly.

"I asked Celeste how she deals with it—the constant pressure from the media. She said that she learned early on not to fight it. She said, 'Never wrestle with pigs, Amy. You both get dirty, and the pigs enjoy it.'"

Jonah laughed.

"She suggested that instead of fighting all the attention, we should embrace it to a certain extent. That's when what Elaine said about managing it really clicked. We can't fight being the 'Wedding of the Century,' and we shouldn't even try. We should try to enjoy it and have fun with it."

Jonah nodded. "That makes sense in a weird sort of way."

"I know," Amy agreed, smiling and shaking her head. "Then Celeste and I got a little silly with the whole 'Wedding of the Century' idea…what would it look like, where would it be, what time of year, what time of day, how many guests, the reception…that made me stop for a moment, thinking about asking my father to foot the bill for all that, but Celeste read my mind and said she and Edward would cover all the expenses—as our wedding present. I started to cry again, I hate to say."

"It's darned generous of them," Jonah agreed.

"That's what I said, too," Amy confirmed, "but Celeste said she thought that ninety-nine percent of the Commonwealth would feel it was a justifiable expense, so we shouldn't worry about it. Then we went back to being silly—at least a dozen bridesmaids, a sword arch, the archbishop presiding, having it during the holidays, in the evening so its formal dress—"

"Why Boxing Day?" Jonah asked.

"Christmas is on a Friday this year, so Boxing Day is Saturday."

"That's only seven months from now. Will that be enough time to pull the 'Wedding of the Century' together?" he asked.

"If it were just me and my mom and Marian, no way," Amy admitted. "But I've got Celeste and Laura to help me. That reminds me—I have to call her and let her know. Oh, one more thing."

"What?"

"I heard through the grapevine that you don't have much to do the next few weeks."

"Oh, you did, did you?"

"Yup. I've got connections," she said smugly. "And Brian told me not to even think of coming into the office for a month. I took the liberty of making some arrangements."

"Really," Jonah said, bemused. "What sort of arrangements?"

"We're going to Aries to hang out on the beach for a couple of weeks. We leave Thursday. It's already been cleared with the Admiralty, and the agents, and everyone else. Jude is even drawing up your therapy schedule—he thinks walking on the sand will help you."

9

Jonah completed his review of the personnel files from Admiral Lothes without difficulty, and he and Amy embarked on their trip to Aries. They were accompanied by agents Remington, Browning, and Sauer. During the eight-day journey to Aries, he and Amy enjoyed traveling in their first-class cabin. They drew up a list of bridesmaids and ushers, ending up with a dozen of each, and had a blast calling them and inviting them to take part. Amy instructed her secretary before she left to forward any inquiries about the wedding to Lady Thorner.

Lady Thorner was already alerted by Queen Celeste before Amy called to ask for her help. Very quickly, she and Amy decided the colors for the wedding would be the traditional red, green, and white of the Christmas season. Within a few days, she was receiving design ideas for Amy's wedding dress from all the major designers, competing to see who would dress the bride for the 'Wedding of the Century.' Laura insisted that the designers also agree to furnish the bridesmaid dresses too. Florists were also contacting her.

Queen Celeste placed herself in charge of the reception, which she insisted on being held at the palace. She pulled together the menu and also arranged for an orchestra to provide music. She lined up the archbishop to conduct the ceremony and made sure Glastonbury Cathedral would be available. She also arranged for the rehearsal dinner to be held at the Admiralty.

Anne Davidson had only the job of ordering the wedding invitations. Marian Halberd had only to approve the menu for the rehearsal dinner and order her own invitations. Laura and Celeste helped them with both of those. The only job Amy and Jonah had to attend to was helping develop the guest list for the wedding, but even that would be reviewed by Laura and the queen, with the additional assistance of Captain MacLeod. Amy laughed, saying that the 'Wedding of the Century' was turning out to be far less work for her than planning the small ceremony which she planned originally.

By the third day of their stay at the exclusive resort on Aries, Amy's skin was tanned and her hair lightened. Jonah had to be a bit more careful, particularly on the new skin of his left forearm and left leg. On the second day, noting how the other female guests were attired, she left her bikini top in the bungalow whenever they went to the beach. She made Jonah remove his eyepatch to avoid getting a tan line.

She proved that she was, as she had described, a 'water-rat.' She went kiteboarding, which Jonah was not ready to attempt, and the two of them went sailing and swimming every day. Jonah kept the exercise schedule that Jude prepared and found that walking in the sand did indeed help.

After twelve days of sand, sun, and surf, they boarded the liner to return to Caerleon. Amy would be heading back to take over as trade attaché on New Delhi. Jonah would be heading to the Twelfth of Never to take command of HMS *Severn*. It was likely they wouldn't see each other in person until just before the wedding, six months away.

Indeed, immediately upon their return, the whirlwind of their lives whisked them apart. Amy left the next day to take up her post. Jonah was medically cleared to return to active duty the same day and boarded a courier boat that evening. Though sad to leave Amy, Jonah was excited about returning to the bridge of a ship. He had reviewed the personnel files that Admiral Lothes had prepared to try to get to know his new crew as much as he could before he arrived. The engineering staff was already aboard, and the rest of the crew would be following right on his heels.

The org chart of his new command was different from what he knew. *Severn* would carry a chief gunnery officer with two assistants. Jonah wondered how many decades it had been since officers carried those titles in the Commonwealth Navy. The chief gunnery officer was a maverick, promoted from the ranks, Lieutenant Commander Samantha Boger. Her two assistants were Lieutenants Alice Marshall and Chauncey Depew. All had extensive backgrounds in engineering.

His new executive officer would be recently promoted, Commander Joe Jacobs. Jonah encountered Jacobs only briefly, but his reputation was somewhat legendary. One of Jonah's officers on a previous command was in the same class with Jacobs when they attended the boot camp required after graduating from an ROTC program. She had many amusing stories to tell about him. He was known as having some of the highest performance ratings in boot camp history and accumulating the most demerits of anyone who graduated due to his strong sense of mischief. Jonah was sure he would like him.

One good piece of news was that the ships *Pallas*, *Euryalus* and *Achates* would be arriving in the system soon to have their photon cannons reinstalled. Jonah had asked Captain Delhomme of *Pallas* to be his best man.

Delhomme had taken over as the commodore of the small force when Jonah had been injured. Thornton Mellon captained *Euryalus* and Fred MacMurray had stayed in place as captain of *Achates*.

Jonah asked Director Niven if he could take advantage of their presence in the system to have their crews act as OpFor, or Opposing Force, in a set of simulations. Niven thought that was an excellent idea. He did point out that Captain Mellon would be turning over *Euryalus* to Sarah Donan once they reached the system, as Mellon was slated to take command of HMS *Murray* when her refit was completed. Jonah was pleased for both of them.

Jonah connected to *Pallas* and was put through to Captain Delhomme. "Mon Capitaine," he said, using an obviously fake French accent, "I am calling to fulfill another of your age-old longings."

"Argh!" Delhomme pretended to scream in horror, "Someone, save me! He's going to make another horrible request I cannot refuse!"

"Au contraire, Monsewer Crapaud."

"What is it this time, you one-eyed Lordling?"

"Hey! That's 'my Lord' to you, cheeky peasant…or is it 'pissant?' I can never remember with you."

"Sorry, milord, Baron Somerset," Delhomme replied with mock humility, tugging his forelock.

"That's better," Jonah sniffed snobbishly. "Anyway, how would you and your ragtag collection of scurvy sailors like to be OpFor against me when you get out to the Twelfth of Never?"

Delhomme looked up and clasped his hands together as if in prayer. "Thank you, God. I promise I'll never doubt you again." Then, looking at his fingernails, pretending disinterest, he replied, "um, sure, buddy, whatever you want."

"Ha!" Jonah exclaimed. "You forget I know all your tricks! I know you're as giddy as a little boy on Christmas Eve! Admit it—you've always wanted to be blown out of the heavens by me!"

"Hardly likely, old man," Delhomme replied with an aristocratic drawl, still pretending to inspect his fingernails out of boredom. "We both know that's highly unlikely."

"We shall see, Capitaine Crapaud. Young monsewer Niven and his team of wonder-spods are setting the whole thing up for when you arrive."

"Ooooo—now that does sound good," Delhomme admitted. "Ok, you talked me into it. We'll do it."

"Excellent. Au revoir, Mon Capitaine."

"Back at ya."

10

When Jonah arrived on board *Severn*, there was no one to greet him. That suited him just fine. He could do without the pomp and ceremony. He found his way to his quarters and activated the palm lock. His quarters were even more spacious than his quarters had been on *Achates*, which were the biggest he had seen. Like *Achates*, there was a wooden desk and hardwood floors, and outside in his ready room was an enormous table of polished wood. He dropped his bags and then went to find engineering.

Severn's chief of engineering was Commander Vicki Gruber. He had not met her yet but read her file and her impressive record. When he walked into engineering, all the workstations were manned, and it was a hive of activity. After a moment, someone noticed him and shouted, "Captain on deck!"

Jonah barked, "As you were!" before anyone could lift their butts out of their seats. He hadn't come to disrupt their work. An attractive blonde woman of about fifty straightened up from where she was helping one of the techs and came to introduce herself. Jonah recognized her from her file pictures.

"Captain Lord Halberd," she said, saluting.

He winced slightly while returning her salute. "Commander Gruber," he replied, offering his hand to shake.

"Please," he asked, "can I just be 'captain' or 'skipper' or 'skip'? I'm not used to this 'Lord' stuff."

"Works for me," she answered easily.

"Please spread it around. How's it going?" he asked.

"Way better than it should," she grinned.

"I read your report on tuning the drives. Seriously? Five hours and change?"

"I couldn't believe it myself, skipper," she answered. "I like skipper for you, by the way. Balances out the effect of the eyepatch. Anyway, I tested 'em forward, backward, and sideways after that, just to make sure I wasn't dreaming. They're running sweetly. I'm planning on taking all the credit, by the way," she smirked.

"Go right ahead," Jonah offered. "What do you have your people doing now?"

"Learning the new systems. They give us monitoring capability I've only ever wished for. My people are finding new things all the time."

"I have good news for you then," he said. "*Pallas*, *Euryalus* and *Achates* are due in system in a couple of days. I know Commander Patel personally, but I'm sure all three heads of engineering will be happy to share everything they know. One word of warning, you can't tell them about our new weapons yet."

"I wasn't planning to," she replied, "but I would love to pick their brains."

"In addition, Captain Mellon is turning over *Euryalus* to Captain Donan, who is moving over from *Pallas*. Mellon will be taking over *Murray* when she's ready. I'm planning on borrowing him to help train the bridge crew, but I'll make sure he's available to you also."

Jonah had her introduce him to the engineering staff. When he finished, he returned to his quarters. He put his things away and activated the comm console and sent a message to Admiral Lothes formally requesting that Captain Mellon be assigned to *Severn* for a couple of weeks to help train the crew on the new computer systems.

The next morning, he noted that Lothes approved his request. Commander Jacobs arrived shortly after, and the two of them developed duty and training schedules. He, too, addressed Jonah as 'Captain Lord Halberd' and, like Gruber, decided to call Jonah 'skipper' when Jonah offered the choice. Before the end of the week, the entire crew of 497 was finally aboard *Severn*. Jacobs conducted the first general quarters drill almost before the most recent arrival stowed her duffel. Jonah waited until the drill was over before reading his orders appointing him to take command of the crew.

The bridge crew heard Jacobs addressing Jonah as 'skipper,' and soon it was all through the ship. Jonah enjoyed it. The last time his entire crew had called him that was on his last frigate command, HMS *Essex*. That had been a wonderful command. He felt the nickname was a good omen and a strong step towards a happy ship.

Captain Thornton Mellon reported aboard the next day. He met with Jonah and Commander Jacobs and jumped right into beginning to train the bridge crew on the aspects of the new computer system with which they were unfamiliar. Their first simulation would take place the next day, pitting *Severn* against the combined crews of *Pallas*, *Euryalus* and *Achates*. Director Niven had shared none of the details with them.

At 8:00 am the next morning, the general quarters alarm sounded. It was at this point that the details of the simulation were given to them. *Severn* had been in stationary orbit around the fourth planet of a K-class star. Three Chinese capital ships, a 527-type superdreadnought and two 461-type battlecruisers entered the system 27 hours before. *Severn* had tried repeatedly to hail the Chinese with no response. *Severn* had been clawing its way from deep in the gravity well after sling-shotting around the star while the Chinese were taking an intercept course. They were now fifteen minutes away from missile range and another seven minutes from the range of the PBG.

Jonah had a hunch. He looked at the astrogation map of the system quickly. "Joe," he ordered, "lay in the course for the seventh planet and begin immediate braking so we can use it to turn around. If you can do both of those at the same time, so much the better. Weapons—don't fire until they fire on us but roll pods in—" he checked the clock, "— six minutes. Aim them all at the 527. Guns, aim for that 527."

"What's going on, skipper?" Jacobs asked, after acknowledging the course change.

"We're preparing to fight a battle in a post-missile universe," Jonah told him.

"We'll be in range of the PBG for one minute, forty seconds," Jacobs affirmed, "but then we'll both be in range of photon cannons for two minutes, thirteen seconds. Pretty close to their max range too."

"Skipper," Lieutenant Commander Boger spoke on the bridge comm from her station in what used to be the secondary bridge, now the tactical center on *Severn*, "we can only get four shots off with the PBGs because of the cycle time. We'll have the same window for the photon cannons as they do."

"Then make those shots count, as best you can, Guns," Jonah replied.

The minutes ticked away until sensors announced that the Chinese had fired missiles. "Two hundred and forty-four 'Shark' missiles inbound, skipper," came the announcement from the tactical center, which the crew had taken to calling the TAC.

"One hundred and fifty-six Vulcans outbound," called weapons.

For the next seven minutes, the two forces launched missiles at one another as fast as the automatic reloaders could cycle.

"Firing PBG…now," announced Boger.

"Holy shit!" Jacobs exclaimed. "I think you got a hit, Guns!"

Indeed, the tactical display indicated a sensor bloom on the Chinese superdreadnought. Along with that were the streaks indicating the Chinese missiles targeting *Severn* and the Swordfish defense missiles streaking to intercept them, and the Vulcan missiles aimed at the Chinese, with what appeared to be their own version of Swordfish rising to meet them."

As the groups of missiles met, sensor blooms from the explosions merged into one another. Almost escaping notice in that orgy of destruction were two small blooms appearing on the Chinese superdreadnought.

More missiles were announced as they launched from the Chinese ships.

"Let 'em," Jonah answered. "Weapons, don't fire any more missiles."

Both forces had now closed to within photon cannon range of one another. The Chinese SDN disappeared from the astrographic projection.

"We got two hits out of four shots, skipper," Boger announced. "The PBG must have blown their shields. Photon cannons did the rest."

"Switch PBG targeting to the 461s," Jonah ordered. "Damage control?" he then asked.

"Not much to report, skipper," Jacobs confirmed. "Shields holding. A few brownouts."

None of the missiles from the salvos survived. Swordfish missiles were already on their way to eliminate the latest salvo of Chinese 'Shark' missiles. Within seconds none of the missile tracks remained on the screen. One of the Chinese battlecruisers winked out on the display.

"Out of photon cannon range. PBG has time for three more shots," Jacobs called out.

When they passed out of range, Boger reported, "We got two more hits, skipper."

"Sensors," Jonah commanded, "I want a damage assessment on that 461 as soon as you can."

Less than two minutes later, Jacobs announced, "Sensors reports damage to the EM drives on that 461, skipper. The other two ships are destroyed. The 461 is having trouble. They're too close to the primary and have no way to slow their acceleration. Computer estimates they will exceed $0.3c$ in twelve minutes."

Jonah watched the clock. Not long after the twelve-minute mark, the icon on the display for the remaining Chinese battlecruiser winked out. "Skipper, the 461 just disappeared. Sensors seems to think it imploded."

Just then, the displays read: Simulation Terminated.

The bridge crew cheered.

"Nice shooting, guns," Jonah called on the bridge comm. "Debrief in the TAC in 15 minutes."

11

The Governing Council of the Chinese Republics was in heated debate. Wang Zhu, the chairman of the council, called once again for order. "The chair recognizes the premier of Cǎodì!" he called over the tail end of the grumbling that was winding down.

"Chairman," she responded, "the request made by these Rodinans could not come at a better time. If we supply them with the new technologies, we give ourselves a chance to see how well they work at no risk to ourselves. It commits us to no further course of action. Of course, I will not deny that we might influence them to provide us with an excellent opportunity, but at present, the council should consider it along the lines of field-testing these new weapons."

The premier of Hǎiyáng, Si Pengyu, interrupted. "Premier Dong, we all know your desire is to go to war. You and your friends think the Commonwealth is weakened by their recently concluded war. You think they are weak enough that we can take advantage and now achieve for the Republics the position of dominance we have long sought. The council just tabled a motion on that very subject. We will examine it further in due time."

"In due time!" Dong spat.

"In due time," Si repeated. "If the Commonwealth is weakened by the war, they will be weakened further still by peace. We do not need to move precipitously. How does it serve the interests of the Republics to provide these Rodinans with weapons and technology far beyond their own? These Rodinans are a stateless group at present. In time, their new government will either bring them to heel or destroy them. Why should we help them when helping them delays outfitting our own fleets and adds to the already considerable expense?"

"It adds an element of uncertainty and some chaos into the state of the relationship between the Rodinans and the Commonwealth," she responded.

"Uncertainty and chaos that could provide the Republics a real opportunity to advance our interests. The expense is minimal compared to what we have already invested in upgrading our technologies. The delay in outfitting our own fleets is likewise minimal. It would be some months before these Rodinans would be able to act on our behalf in any capacity, in which time I would hope the council would come around to a better way of thinking than at present. If the council does not change its opinion regarding the opportunity history has presented us, arming these Rodinans commits us to no course of action."

Chairman Wang allowed the debate to continue, with other parties joining in to advance one side or the other. As the afternoon wore on, it became clear that Dong's side had gained the upper hand. At last, he called for a vote. The premiers representing the 23 planets of the Chinese republics cast their votes electronically. Thirteen sided with premier Dong. The council had agreed to arm the fleet of Admiral Denisov with their new technologies.

Back onboard HMS *Severn*, they were in the middle of the debrief of the first simulation when the general quarters alarm sounded again. This caused more of a scramble, as most had taken off and stowed their ship suits before coming to the debrief. It took nearly two minutes before everyone was at his station.

"What do we have, Joe?" Jonah asked.

"Three *Gagarin* superdreadnoughts, lying in wait just outside the hyper corridor," Jacobs responded. "Looks like we exited the corridor 30 light-minutes short. We're traveling in-system at 0.23*c*. Looks like they've triangulated the normal exit. Pulling up the plot...now."

The holographic astrogation map appeared, showing the location of the hostile ships, the planets, and the star at the center of the system. There were five planets, with the closest to *Severn* being the fourth, a gas giant. There was an asteroid belt between the first and second planets. The fifth planet and the first planet were on the other side of the star. The plot showed that the three hostile ships were centered on the course *Severn* would take if it headed for the fourth planet.

"Stay on course, maintain current speed. You're going to need to rotate the ship when we're in range—I don't want them to get a shot up our skirts. Once we're out of range, keep adjusting course for that gas giant and lay us into an orbital insertion."

"Course looks like...this," Jacobs affirmed, keying the changes in. The new plot showed as a blue line, arcing up to the right and then down.

"Factoring in their predicted course change in response..." he added. "Looks like, worst case, we'll be in PBG range of the closest ship for three minutes, twenty seconds before we reach photon cannon range. We'll be in missile range of all three ships for a long time. Those numbers will change depending on how aggressively they react to our course change."

Jacobs cut his mike to the bridge comm and turned to Jonah. "Gotta say, skipper, this feels weird."

"How so?"

"Completely disregarding missiles and focusing on guns," he responded. "I mean, cannons weren't much of a threat or a weapon. Missiles would decide the battle, and cannons seemed kind of useless."

"It takes some getting used to," Jonah admitted. "I started working on sims like this a couple of months ago, so I have a head start. A couple of months ago, I thought cannons were pretty useless too, but not anymore."

Turning his mike back on, Jacobs commented, "Hostiles are reacting to our course change. Looks like they're taking a downrange intercept and pursuit plot. We'll actually overtake them when we're in missile range."

Jonah studied the plot for a moment, entering some data on his console. "Monsieur Crapaud is a quick learner," he murmured.

Jacobs turned his head. Jonah remembered to cut off his bridge mike and told Jacobs, "Captain Delhomme. He and I go way back. It's one of my nicknames for him. He's set his course to avoid what happened this morning. If he loses his drives, he won't accelerate into the primary."

"Gotcha."

"Joe, take a look at what we need to do to use the planet to slow as much as possible, then head for the second planet and swing around it to try to catch them as they pursue, then tuck us into the asteroid belt," Jonah requested.

"Give me a minute, Skipper," Jacobs answered. "Ok. Here's our current course, and here—" he brought the course revision up on the display, "—would be the new course to come around the second planet. Beyond that, there are too many variables to figure our exit from the second planet's orbit."

"And the new course slows us down?" Jonah queried.

"Yes," Jacobs confirmed. He turned off his bridge mike. "This still seems weird, skipper, like you want them to catch us."

Jonah turned off his mike to respond. "I do, but not all the way. I want to close the range to between 8 and 12 million kilometers for as long as possible."

"Let me play with some numbers, skipper," Jacobs suggested, "there might be a different way."

"Have at it," Jonah agreed.

A few minutes later, Jacobs spoke. "I think this'll do it. Take a look."

He showed a new course plot that changed *Severn's* angle of approach to the nearest planet and swung them around. The new plot also showed the vectors that the hostile ships could take depending on how they reacted.

Jacobs explained, "If we come all the way around the planet on this course, it gives us a window of between five minutes twenty seconds and six minutes, ten seconds where we're in that range. We'll be in missile range a helluva long time, though, skipper."

"That is better," Jonah agreed. "Make it happen."

"Aye, aye, skipper," Jacobs said, shaking his head.

They watched the navigation plots for the next hour and a half as the distance closed. When they were seven minutes from missile range, Jonah commanded, "Weapons, roll out missile pods. Guns, you should have time for many shots with the PBGs at the nearest *Gagarin*. I doubt they'll let us hit their drives again, so pick a spot midship and pound it with the PBGs. Maybe we'll get lucky and force them to eject cores. If we do enough damage, switch to the next one. Just to warn you, when we're in their photon cannon range, I'm going to roll the ship."

"Appreciate the heads up, skipper," Lieutenant Commander Boger responded.

The three hostile ships waited until all three were within missile range and staggered their launches so that missiles from all three would arrive at the same time. Unlike Jonah's recent experience with Rodinan ships, none of the missiles went off-course. *Severn* launched her own initial salvo of 156 missiles, all targeted at the nearest hostile vessel.

Lieutenant Commander Garrity, manning sensors in the TAC, reported, "Three hundred and twenty-four Sokols inbound. Swordfish have already launched in response."

The holographic display showed all the inbound and outbound missiles. Blooms showing explosions in space lit up as *Severn's* Swordfish missiles destroyed the attacking Sokols and the Rodinan defense missiles eliminated the Vulcans fired at them.

It was almost eight minutes before they reached the range of the *Severn's* big gun. A small bloom showed on the nearest Rodinan superdreadnought.

Jacobs called, "Looks like the PBG got a hit."

Attack and defense missiles continued to intercept each other, perishing in cascades of explosions. None of the Sokols or Vulcans survived to reach their targets. More sensor blooms appeared on the Rodinan SDN.

"Switching targets," Jacobs announced. "First SDN has dropped shields."

The first Rodinan ship had dropped shields in surrender. It seemed as though it had lost power and was drifting. It did not fire any more missiles. Sensor blooms appeared on the second Rodinan ship.

"Coming into photon cannon range," Jacobs called out.

"Roll ship," Jonah responded. Rolling the ship during an artillery attack was done to avoid having one section of the plasma shielding take the full brunt of an attack. It had been standard practice over a hundred years before but had been done only seldom recently due to the reliance on missiles. Jonah hoped that his opponents had forgotten that maneuver but wasn't counting on it.

"Second SDN has dropped shields," Jacobs reported. "Shifting targets."

The remaining SDN disappeared from the holographic projection less than four minutes later.

"Third SDN destroyed," Jacobs announced. "Looks like the PBG got multiple hits on all three ships. Damage assessment will take a minute. We have a shield out on the port side and some brownouts elsewhere. Master Chief Loree is already sending out crews to replace the blown units."

The display changed to read: Simulation Terminated. The bridge crew cheered again.

"That's a wrap, people," Jonah called. "Review your logs tonight and prepared for a working breakfast at 06:30 in my ready room. Commander, you have the bridge."

12

Jonah returned to his quarters and stripped off his ship suit. He was about to undress and take a shower when his comm console indicated an incoming call. He checked the display, which read: Captain Delhomme, HMS *Pallas*.

"Capitaine Crapaud," he began, using his fake French accent, "zis is an unexpected pleasure to hear from you."

"Go ahead and gloat, cyclops," Delhomme commenced, "yuck it up. Call your fiancée and tell her all about it, you one-eyed freak. I should have known a regenerated monster snatched from the jaws of death itself would have some dastardly trick up his sleeve."

"Why, Monsewer Crapaud, you sound zo hangry!"

"What did Niven give you and whose butt do I have to kiss to get one?" Delhomme asked.

"I could tell you," Jonah answered, "but then I'd have to kill you…oh, wait a minute…I already did! Twice, if I counted right!"

"Damnit, when Niven gave me a version of Swordfish to use, I was sure I'd be able to roast you. So, go ahead, have your fun, you one-eyed freak."

"I'm just *lord*-ing it over you," Jonah cracked, then pretended to wince. "Sorry, that was really bad. I apologize. I really don't think I'm cleared to tell you, but Niven should be. Since you're helping us out, he probably will. As far as getting one yourself, I don't think anyone knows the answer."

"I just hate the fact that you've got one, whatever it is, and I don't," Delhomme said with a pout and pretending to whine.

"Oh, I have lots more things you don't," Jonah quipped, "good looks, charm, style, wit, panache, a smoking hot fiancée—"

"I concede the smoking hot fiancée, but the rest of your claims are still in dispute," Delhomme countered.

"Alright," Jonah said laughing, "I'll settle for that."

"She's way more than you deserve," Delhomme reminded him.

"Don't I know it," Jonah agreed.

"You sure you can't tell me?" Delhomme asked.

Jonah shook his head.

"Ok then. Gotta call Director Niven. See ya."

Jonah went and took a shower. After dressing, he began checking the logs from the simulations. The PBG had a hit rate of just over fifty percent. Considering the distance and the evasive action the enemy was taking, Jonah felt that was acceptable.

The rest of the week was full of other scenarios. One thing that became apparent was that the days of fly-by missile barrages were over. In fact, given the opportunity to plan his entry to a hostile system, Jonah had slowed to $0.08c$ before entering the hyperspace corridor. Towards the end of their week of exercises, when the other captains had the opportunity, they would approach *Severn* as fast as possible to minimize the time exposed to the big gun before they could respond with photon cannons. If they could escape, they attempted to do that. Jonah begged Director Niven to allow Captain Mellon to join them, as though *Murray's* refit were complete, but the director refused.

At the end of the week, *Pallas*, *Euryalus*, and *Achates* departed, their photon cannons reinstalled, to join the Home Fleet. *Severn* began her actual ship trials and shakedown cruise. Captain Mellon joined them for the first legs but jumped ship near Lincoln and headed back to the Twelfth of Never. HMS *Murray* was due to tune her new drives and then begin crew training.

With her shakedown cruise finished, *Severn* was ordered to return to the Twelfth of Never to 'tighten up the bolts' as Master Chief Loree put it. Once that bit of work was done, Jonah received orders to report to the Home Fleet, based on Caerleon. Admiral Lothes admitted she did not have any particular assignment on tap for *Severn* and that the ship would just settle into boring station duty.

Jonah had stayed in touch with Amy throughout this whole period. She had settled in the eponymously named capital city New Delhi. By the time Jonah and *Severn* reached Caerleon, it was late October, and the wedding was only two months away. Amy kept him up to date on the status of various wedding-related things. He and Amy had figured out a guest list and submitted it to Lady Thorner, Queen Celeste, and Captain MacLeod. It came back to them less than a week later with over 300 names added. When Amy protested that she and Jonah didn't know any of them, Laura shot back that they would likely get to know them and having VIPs being grateful to them wasn't a horrible thing.

As the calendar drew closer to the Thanksgiving holiday, Jonah received an invitation to visit Lord and Lady Thorner for the long weekend. Jonah declined, choosing to stay aboard ship so that other members of the crew could have a break. He would be taking leave just before Christmas and for the three weeks following for his honeymoon. He wanted others to have the chance to see friends and family as well.

The honeymoon promised to be fabulous. The king and queen had offered them the use of their residence on the beach on the planet of New Wales. The beaches there were reputed to be even more beautiful than the famous beaches on Aries. They would also be given the use of the Royal Yacht, *Griffin*, to travel to and from New Wales.

After seven years of war, Jonah was finding peace boring. He tried to keep the crew's morale up and their edge sharp, but as time went on, it became more difficult. He found himself wishing that something would happen and immediately regretted those thoughts when he had them. He forced himself to remember the friends he had lost during the war. He would go look in the mirror with his eyepatch removed to remind himself that he didn't really want anything to happen.

He did take advantage of the dull period over Thanksgiving weekend to get started on his shopping. In addition to a Christmas present, he also needed to get Amy a wedding present. As usual, he hadn't the faintest idea of what to get. Once again, he turned to Lady Thorner for assistance. She was expecting him to call, but she admitted she was surprised to hear from him so early—she teased him by telling him she thought he would wait until almost the last minute.

She already had the solution. Once she, Queen Celeste, and Amy had chosen the design of the wedding dress (which they had kept secret from Jonah), Laura had contacted jewelers to develop accessories to go along with it. Laura had three designs of earrings. Two were of diamonds, one was diamonds and sapphires. The diamond and sapphire set matched the engagement ring he had bought.

When he saw that one, he exclaimed, "That's it! My God, it's perfect!"

"Good choice, since that's the one I ordered for you. That's your Christmas present. Now let me show you your wedding present."

She sent him a picture of a beautiful silver circlet. "When you marry, Amy becomes Baroness Somerset and is entitled to wear the circlet. All you need to do is call your broker and pay for it. This way, you have a present for Christmas and a wedding present."

"Call my broker?" Jonah inquired. "Don't you just need my account number?"

"Not for this, dear," Laura informed him, "unless your credit limit can handle £2.5 million."

"£2.5 million?"

"And a bargain at twice the price," she continued. "Don't worry. You can afford it."

"If you say so," Jonah said uncertainly.

"Oh, Jonah," she laughed, "I know so. And while you're at it, they have a beautiful pearl necklace you can get Marian. She needs a better string of pearls for the wedding."

Jonah gulped. As so often happened with Laura, he felt like he was in over his head. Just say yes and thank you, he thought. "Thank you, Laura," he said with sincerity. "I'll have my broker contact you."

Jonah hadn't paid attention to his finances for some time. As a frigate captain, he had won some significant prize money. On the advice of his former captain (now Admiral) Karl Von Geisler, he had hired a broker to invest the money. His broker mailed him regular statements and handled his taxes, but Jonah hadn't really looked at his statements for years. He looked up on his comm unit how to log into his account and checked. He was surprised at how large his investments had grown. He sent a message to his broker and asked her to contact Lady Thorner to arrange payment for the jewelry, indicating it was in excess of £2.5 million.

He hadn't needed Laura's help to figure out what to get his dozen groomsmen. He had ordered each of them a watch from a universally recognized manufacturer. Though no one had needed to wear a watch for hundreds of years, they were still popular. He had also bought joke T-shirts for each of them, planning to hide the watches in the box with the T-shirt.

The days crept by until December 22 arrived, and he went on leave. He was excited and apprehensive. Very few of the guests invited to the wedding had declined. There would be over 1,200 people at the wedding and reception. The rehearsal dinner alone would be nearly 300 people.

Amy and her parents, Mark and Anne, had arrived the evening before. Jonah's mother Marian had arrived a week earlier and was staying with Lord and Lady Thorner. Jonah was met as he disembarked by Agent Remington, who escorted him to the shuttle that would land on the grounds of the palace.

When he arrived at the palace, he began to head for the suite he and Amy usually were given but was stopped by a page. The page led him into a different part of the wing and to a suite that was far larger. Amy was not there, but he could see her belongings. He would be staying there for three nights, but Christmas night, he would stay at the Admiralty.

13

Standing above the transept in Glastonbury Cathedral, looking out at the hundreds of guests (and hundreds of reporters who had crowded in), Jonah felt oddly calm. He had expected to feel nervous but instead felt quietly happy. His groomsmen, led by his best man, Captain Pierre Delhomme, looked handsome in their formal dress uniforms or white tie and tailcoats. The guests were attired in formal dress. Candles were lit all over the cathedral, softening the light. The musicians began playing Pachelbel's Canon in D, and the bridesmaids began to process down the long aisle of the cathedral.

Their dresses were rich red silk, attractively cut. The women wore their hair up and carried sprays of white flowers. Captain Elaine MacLeod gave Jonah a big wink as she approached. Lady Thorner gave him a smile.

The music changed to Handel's 'Air.' Mark Davidson appeared with Amy on his arm. This was the first Jonah had seen of her wedding dress. A tight-fitting bodice was topped with lace covering her shoulders, with a V dipping down to her cleavage but stopping discretely short. The skirt was full and poufy, with a train following on the ground. Her face was covered by a veil, and she carried red roses. Her hair was pulled back.

A grin crept onto Jonah's face—he couldn't help it. As she walked closer, he could see Amy smiling too. When her father handed her over to him, and he looked in her eyes, his heart soared. They turned to the archbishop, and the ceremony began.

The ceremony itself flashed by. When told he could kiss the bride, he and Amy gave each other a sweetly romantic kiss. Before leaving the cathedral, they were pulled aside into a vestibule to allow all the other guests to process out.

With such a large number, it took a few minutes. When all had exited the cathedral, they were sent out to climb into the horse-drawn carriage that would take them to the palace for the wedding reception. Waiting for them was the traditional navy sword arch. They walked under the swords. At the end, Admiral Von Geisler and Captain Delhomme were waiting and lowered their swords to prevent Jonah and Amy from passing.

The custom was not to release them until they kissed, and Jonah did not disappoint. He clasped his new bride and gave her a smooch filled with all his love and passion for her as the crowd cheered. Satisfied, Von Geisler and Delhomme raised their swords to allow them to pass. As Amy came even with him, Delhomme gave her a substantial backhand swat on the butt with the flat of his sword, telling Amy, "Welcome to the navy, Lady Halberd."

Amy yelped in surprise, then giggled. Jonah helped her climb into the carriage. Lord and Lady Thorner were sharing the ride to the palace with them. Laura helped Amy remove her veil. It was then that Jonah presented Amy with her circlet. "Lady Halberd," he said with a twinkle in his eye, "now that we're married, you're missing an important item."

Amy gasped when she opened the box and saw it. Laura helped her place the circlet on her head. Then both Amy and Jonah joined in thanking her for all her help in arranging everything for the wedding.

With so many guests, they had decided weeks ago that a receiving line would be impossible, so they went immediately to the head table. When Amy sat, it was the signal for everyone to take a seat. Queen Celeste had insisted that 'wedding protocol' take precedence over 'royal protocol' for the reception.

Captain Delhomme, as best man, gave an extremely witty toast, staying away from 'in' jokes and focusing on aspects of Jonah's life that everyone knew while poking gentle fun at the couple. The dinner was sumptuous. The orchestra began to play a recently popular romantic ballad that Amy especially liked. Jonah and Amy rose and headed to the dance floor after fastening the train of her dress to a loop around her wrist so it wouldn't drag on the ground.

As they began to dance, they were slightly startled to hear the words to the song being sung. They looked over to the orchestra and saw that Billie Robinson, the singer who had made the song a hit, was herself singing the ballad. Amy gasped and looked over at Queen Celeste, who was grinning at the surprise she had managed to arrange for Amy. Recovering quickly, Jonah and Amy continued to dance. Amy put her cheek next to Jonah's and whispered, "Best. Wedding. Ever."

Others joined them in dancing, including the king and queen. Billie Robinson stayed to perform through the evening, her beautiful voice adding an extra dash of romance and sensuousness to the music. Jonah and Amy stayed on the dance floor, in high demand as dancing partners. He did not have the chance to stand by her side again until it was time to cut the wedding cake with his sword. After a brief respite, the music started again, and they rejoined the crowds on the floor.

An hour later, Lady Thorner and Queen Celeste came to collect Amy, to accompany her to change into her 'travel clothes' in which she would make her departure from the reception. The music continued, and Jonah was dancing with Captain Renee Fung when he was interrupted by a worried-looking Admiral Lothes. Looking past Lothes, he could see Admiral Von Geisler and Captains Delhomme, MacMurray, and Donan, all with glum looks.

Lothes asked Jonah, "Please come with us. We need to talk quickly."

He followed them out of the ballroom and into a smaller room off to the side. Admiral Von Geisler shut the door, and Admiral Lothes announced, "The missing Rodinans have turned up."

Jonah took a deep breath, trying to prepare for what he suspected would be unpleasant news.

"The entire task force, including the transports, just appeared above Patagonia," Lothes disclosed. "They issued a surrender demand which our embassy recorded and transmitted to us. The Rodinan Navy is responding and has asked for passage through Commonwealth space to cut transit time. The Rodinans also specifically requested your assistance, Jonah. Admiral Belyaev apologizes for interfering with your wedding, by the way.

"We're sending *Achates*, *Pallas* and *Euryalus* along with *Severn*," she said, turning to address the other captains. "Your ships have the most advanced weaponry in the Commonwealth Navy, and we want to help the Rodinans put a quick end to this. You need to depart immediately, I'm afraid. Your crews have all been recalled from liberty and are on their way back to their ships. I apologize, Jonah, but your honeymoon will need to be postponed. Lady Halberd is being informed about this right now as well.

"We want to handle this as discretely as possible because of the huge media presence here. They'll find out about it eventually, but we would rather that it be later than sooner. We would like you to depart the reception as though you are going on your honeymoon. Captains," she said, addressing MacMurray, Donan, and Delhomme, "I need you to make your way to the shuttle quietly right now. Captain Halberd, please stay behind for a moment."

With sympathetic nods and gestures, the three captains left the room. When the door closed again, Admiral Lothes resumed speaking. "Captain, you're in command of this task force. Destination orders are being cut at this moment. More detailed orders will follow shortly. You're to depart as soon as possible and head to Lincoln, where you will rendezvous with Admiral Belyaev and the Rodinans. You'll exchange kewpies there. In the meantime, all communication with the Rodinans will be routed through the Admiralty and the Rodinan embassy. I can't even begin to tell you how sorry I am to have to do this. The whole evening has been magical, and now I feel like the wicked witch."

Jonah didn't know how to respond. He felt anger, frustration, disappointment, fear at how Amy would react and, underneath it all, slightly guilty at the small sense of excitement growing within him. He couldn't come up with the right words to say, so he merely nodded in acknowledgment.

Admiral Lothes nodded in response and departed, leaving Jonah with Admiral Von Geisler in the room. Karl patted Jonah on the shoulder in sympathy. Jonah said, "Give me a second to compose myself."

He took a couple of deep breaths, then nodded he was ready. Karl opened the door, and Jonah walked out with a smile as though the gathering had been some form of teasing to which his navy colleagues had subjected him. Sure enough, a reporter spotted him and shouted, "What was that all about, captain?"

"Just some friends giving me a hard time," Jonah answered casually, adding a smile he didn't feel.

He crossed the ballroom to wait for Amy to appear. When she did, she looked chic in a cream-colored jacket and skirt 'traveling suit.' When people saw her appear, they scrambled for the exit, preparing to shower the couple with birdseed. Jonah offered her his arm, and she smiled serenely. For a moment, Jonah wondered if she knew, but then the strength with which she clasped his arm gave it away. When they reached the doors of the ballroom, they scurried outside under a hail of birdseed thrown by the guests. They reached the shuttle and ducked inside.

The door closed immediately. Captains Delhomme, MacMurray, and Donan were huddled at one end of the shuttle to give Jonah and Amy some space. The three of them had such guilty looks on their faces that it acted to cheer Amy up. Jonah started to say something, but Amy shut him up with a kiss.

After the kiss, she turned to Delhomme. "Welcome to the navy indeed, you cheese-eating garlicky-smelling cheeky sod!"

His head snapped up with a more hopeful expression, hearing her berate him in terms Jonah would typically use.

She turned back to Jonah. "I'm not mad, honey," she told him. "It's who you are and what you do. I knew all this when I allowed myself to fall in love with you. The timing is lousy, and it's going to throw my work schedule completely out of whack since I have to lay low until word gets out, so I can't go back to New Delhi right away, but I know you'll make it up to me when you can."

"You're taking this really well," Jonah commented. "Maybe better than I am."

"Jonah," she said kindly, "don't kid yourself. I read you like yesterday's news, in case you didn't know already. You're upset because this interfered with our perfect wedding. You're afraid my feelings are hurt, and I'm going to be mad. You're disappointed that we're not going to be fucking like bunnies having wild honeymoon sex for the next month. But secretly, you're excited about a new challenge and maybe even feeling guilty about that excitement."

Jonah gulped, then cleared his throat. "That about sums it up."

She clasped his hand tenderly. "Relax. Our wedding was perfect. It was a fairy tale come to life, and I enjoyed every single second of it. My feelings aren't hurt, and I'm not mad at you. I'm disappointed about having to postpone the wild honeymoon sex too. Now, get your head on straight and spend the rest of this shuttle flight telling me all the sweet nothings you should tell me before we say goodbye."

"Okay," Jonah replied, turning to face her and clasping both her hands. "Here goes. Amy, Lady Halberd—"

"Oh, I like that," she commented. "Keep going."

"Lady Halberd," he repeated. "Love of my life, darling of the foreign service—"

"You're learning," she quipped. "Continue."

"You made me the happiest, luckiest man in the universe by marrying me today. You were the most beautiful bride I could ever imagine."

He paused, thinking of what to say next.

"Every minute we're apart will be an agony," Delhomme whispered, feeding him a suggestion.

"What he said, but unspeakable agony," Jonah embellished.

"No help from the peanut gallery," Amy warned, looking over her shoulder at Pierre.

"A woman as smart, as talented, as beautiful inside and out as you could have any man she chose," Jonah continued.

"Damn right," she interjected, "and don't you forget it!"

"I am honored and blessed that you chose me. As I head off to face my dastardly foes—"

"Good one," Sarah Donan commented. "I like dastardly foes."

"Last warning, peanut gallery," Amy admonished.

"As I head off to face my dastardly foes, please know that I long to return to the safe haven of your arms. I will do my best to come back to you quickly—"

"With no more missing body parts," cracked MacMurray.

"Silence, peasants!" Amy commanded.

"With no more missing, or wounded, body parts, except my aching heart, which only you can mend," Jonah finished.

"You're getting better," Amy remarked, "even though you did need the peanut gallery's help."

"I didn't need their help," Jonah protested.

Amy looked back at the three and smiled with a sarcastic nod, "Sure."

Jonah reached up with his hand and gently turned her head back to face him and kissed her. At first, sweetly, but with growing passion.

"Ugh. They're doing that kissing thing again," Delhomme complained like a little boy. "Make them stop. It's gross."

Amy broke off the kiss briefly to turn and stick her tongue out at him, then turned back to Jonah and resumed kissing him, being sure to make it wet, sloppy, and noisy. A small bump and a click, followed by the beep of an alarm, let them know they had arrived at Caerleon Station.

Delhomme, MacMurray, and Donan stood and exited without delay, giving Jonah a real chance to say goodbye. He and Amy stood and embraced one another. "You did make me the happiest man in the world, Lady Halberd. I will miss you and will do my best to come back soon, in one piece. I love you with all my heart and soul."

14

Jonah immediately went to his quarters to change. He logged onto this comm console and read the orders directing them to head to Lincoln and placing him in charge of the task force. He headed to the bridge where the ship's third officer, Lieutenant Commander Sheila Garrity, was sitting in the command chair.

"All crew have been recalled from liberty, skipper," she reported, "and are in transit, due before the top of the hour. We've topped off the tanks and will be ready to go as soon as they arrive."

"Thank you," Jonah responded. "You're relieved. I'll take the bridge."

Jonah sat and keyed in the contacts for Delhomme, Donan, and MacMurray. He transmitted copies of his orders to them and asked when they would be ready to depart. Within minutes they responded that they were in the same state of readiness as *Severn*, waiting on crewmen who were already in transit, due back imminently. Jonah set a time for departure and shared that with the Admiralty.

During the nine-day transit to Lincoln, Jonah was in regular contact with Amy, who let him know that the media caught wind of Jonah's hurried departure almost immediately. She shared with him some of the more outrageous headlines and stories that appeared in the tabloid press. Her favorite was a picture taken of her crying when Jonah proposed but cropped to show only her face in tears, with the headline, "Wedding of the Century Over in Hours. Heartbroken Bride Abandoned by 'Hero' Husband."

After seeing that (and other stories equally awful), Elaine had called and organized a press conference to set things straight. Amy laughed in recounting it, telling Jonah how she used onions to make tears form before heading out to face the reporters and hamming it up, pretending to put on a brave face while choking on emotion. The king and the Admiralty both supplied some good quotes, and the same media outlet's next headline was:

"Duty Calls. Hero Husband Torn from Beautiful Bride." Jonah said that one was his favorite.

Jonah also established contact with Admiral Belyaev to discuss the situation they would be encountering and to go over tactics and formations. The Rodinan force was made up of five superdreadnoughts and six battle cruisers, along with a number of escort warships and supply vessels. Along the way, Jonah was given clearance to share limited details of the capabilities of the Swordfish defense missile system and worked with the other captains of his task force to determine the formations where the four Commonwealth ships could provide an umbrella of protection for the entire combined force. Belyaev knew of Swordfish, having seen the logs transmitted by the Rodinan ships that had faced it.

They shared more mundane details, like communications protocols. Jonah agreed to shift the clocks on the Commonwealth ships to match the time on the Rodinan fleet, which meant an adjustment of six hours. They also settled on a name for the group. Delhomme had suggested the "Commonwealth-Rodinan Action Patrol" because he liked the acronym CRAP, but they settled on calling themselves the Unified Action Force.

The last updates they had received from Patagonia had stopped within two days. The government had capitulated, and the rogue force was landing their troops in the capital. The Rodinan embassy had reported their suspicion that Admiral Denisov was negotiating with Patagonian ground forces commanders to secure their cooperation. The Patagonian space forces had surrendered without a shot being fired. They wouldn't have been able to survive any sort of a conflict with the rogue fleet, as the biggest ships they could muster were two obsolete heavy cruisers purchased out of mothballs from the Chinese over four decades earlier.

When they reached Lincoln, Admiral Belyaev's force was already in-system, having arrived a few hours before. The two groups met near Lincoln Station and traded kewpie pairs among themselves to enable ship-to-ship communications. The kewpie took its name from the Quantum Particle technology, which made them work. They were communication devices that made possible communication of data in real-time without regard for distance.

From Lincoln, it would take another three hyperspace jumps and seven days in total to reach Patagonia. Before the last jump, they had a final conference with Admiral Belyaev. Jonah shared his experience, pointing out that Admiral Denisov likely positioned stealth drones to alert him to their arrival. Jonah warned that they should expect banks of missiles to be waiting for them at or near the normal corridor exit, with Denisov's three superdreadnoughts and five battlecruisers immediately behind. Jonah suggested exiting the corridor 30 light-minutes early and using a much slower entrance speed than the usual $0.23c$. Belyaev agreed with no dissent from his captains, who all knew that Jonah's experience, along with the experience of the other three Commonwealth captains, was worth heeding. They established targeting priorities of the enemy ships.

Before entering hyperspace, Jonah had one important message he needed to send.

"Dear Amy, love of my life, darling of the foreign service, Lady Halberd, Baroness Somerset—I'm not very good at this, as you have experienced, but I'm willing to try to improve. We are about to enter hyperspace and will be arriving where we expect our enemy to be waiting. We've put together a plan that I'm confident will succeed, but there's risk. If something bad should happen, I don't want to leave anything unsaid. I love you with all my heart and soul. The few hours I spent with you as your husband before being pulled away were probably the only time I ever experienced what it means to be truly content. I hope to be able to send you a happier message soon and return to the dry wit you appreciate so much. Love, Jonah"

The Unified Action Force entered the hyperspace corridor at Jonah's suggested speed of $0.08c$ and exited after a transit time of 17 hours and 31 minutes. They re-entered real space 30 light minutes short of the usual corridor boundary. When he felt the flip in his stomach that indicated they had transitioned out of hyperspace, Jonah called out, "Shields up, sensors hot."

Almost immediately, the TAC called out, "Missiles inbound, skipper. System shows 2,774 Sokols inbound. Swordfish is responding."

"Roll Swordfish pods as you're able," Jonah commanded.

Damn, he thought, he made too much of a habit of exiting hyper corridors at 30 light-minutes early. Denisov obviously picked up on it and was waiting. Denisov's ships were less than 30 light-seconds behind the missile gauntlet he had prepared. The Unified Action Force was within missile range of both the gauntlet and the ships. Between the four Commonwealth ships, the Swordfish system could likely have handled the incoming missiles if they'd had time to prepare, but Denisov caught them flat-footed. With the missiles on the way, it was too late to use Director Niven's new anti-matter dispersal defense missiles. Even worse, none of the Rodinan ships could roll pods to counterattack with anti-ship missiles. They would be limited to what they could fire from their tubes.

"Return fire," Jonah commanded, "Target priority alpha."

Jonah watched the missile tracks appearing on the holographic display. "Are any of the in-bound going astray, Joe?"

When Jonah had last encountered the Rodinans, roughly forty percent of their missiles went off-course, fooled by Commonwealth electronic countermeasures or ECM. This was because the missiles were flying 'blind' and not being updated by ship sensors that were better able to detect ECM.

"All 2,774 running hot and true, captain," Jacobs reported.

Damn, Jonah thought. Somehow Denisov upgraded his computer systems beyond what the rest of the Rodinans have. He keyed numbers into his console quickly.

"Joe," he asked, "let me know how many Swordfish pods we and the other three are going to be able to roll before it's too late.

Jacobs queried the other Commonwealth ships, then answered, "Twelve total."

Jonah keyed the link to Admiral Belyaev. "Admiral, I apologize," Jonah began, "they caught us unprepared. Our Swordfish system will be able to destroy most of the inbound, but I estimate 194 of this initial salvo will get through. Make sure your point defense people are ready."

Belyaev nodded soberly. "He's changed command codes too, captain. We tried hacking the missiles to activate the destruct codes but without success. I'm guessing he's also programmed in Federation ECM protocols too. We'll do our best."

Jonah looked back at the display. He noticed lines rising from Denisov's ships to meet the 820 missiles the UAF had fired. "Joe, those new green lines," he asked, "are those what I think they are?"

"I think so, skipper. I think they have their own version of Swordfish."

"Damn," Jonah hissed under his breath. "Where the hell did they come up with that?"

Jonah studied the astrographic projection of the larger system on his console. Patagonia was a seven-planet system. The outer two planets were small frozen rocks. The fifth planet was a gas giant, which was fortunately located on the near side of the ecliptic. He took a deep breath to calm himself.

"Joe, let's head for the gas giant," he said. "Just like we've practiced, get us within PBG range of at least one of their SDNs and try to keep us out of cannon range."

"Aye, aye, skipper. I'll have it in a tick."

"Admiral," Jonah said, keying the comm link to Belyaev, "it appears as though Denisov has done a substantial upgrade to his computer systems. We're picking up tracks from defense missiles similar to ours."

"We see the same, captain."

"We have an artillery weapon on *Severn* that has longer range than photon cannons," Jonah explained. "We've actually practiced scenarios where the hostile force had missile defense like this, so we have some experience. My XO is plotting a course to take us in the direction of the fifth planet, bringing us within range of the nearest SDN but keeping us out of their photon cannon range as much as possible. We will be targeting that nearest SDN with all of the artillery that can be brought to bear. It will take roughly thirty minutes to come within range. With your permission, admiral, I'd like to suggest we follow that course."

"Send me the course when you have it, captain," Belyaev replied. "I'll let you know once I see it."

Jacobs had the new course, and Jonah sent it to Belyaev. Within moments all ships received the order to change course and to target the same SDN if their photon cannons were in range. Jonah turned his attention back to the display. The sensor blooms of defense missiles destroying attacking missiles were distracting, but Jonah was trying to study the targeting of Denisov's missiles.

"Looks like Denisov is focusing on the SDNs. What does the TAC say?" Jonah asked Jacobs.

"TAC confirms, skipper," Jacobs replied a moment later.

Jonah keyed to speak only to *Achates, Pallas,* and *Euryalus.* "Commonwealth ships, Swordfish is going to leave as many as 194 Sokols untouched. Rodinan ECM efforts will likely be ineffective. Anything we can do with ECM will help them out."

The three captains acknowledged. Jonah continued to watch the battle unfold on the display. He could now see the smaller Rodinan escort ships gliding into position to help boost the point defense effort.

The rogue fleet of Admiral Denisov began to accelerate in the same direction as the unified force. "Joe," he asked, "now that they've changed course, what's our time on target for the PBG?"

"Based on how they're responding to our course change, it lengthens the time they'll be in range of the PBG to eight minutes, twenty seconds for the nearest SDN," Jacobs responded, "until we are both within photon cannon range of each other. We'll be in photon cannon range for almost nine minutes. We're twenty-seven minutes from PBG range."

"Guns," Jonah called, "Drives first, then midships. You'll get plenty of shots. Let's take some out."

"Aye, aye, skipper," Lieutenant Commander Boger responded.

There was nothing for Jonah to do for a few moments now except watch. He magnified the display on his console. He began to see some of the incoming missile tracks go astray due to the Commonwealth's ECM. He started to see individual missiles disappearing as the Rodinan point defense network of lasers hit them. Swordfish continued to destroy others, but with five seconds until detonation, he knew Swordfish was done.

Of the 194 missiles Swordfish could not reach in time, 43 survived the point defense network to ignite their nuclear bomb-pumped x-ray lasers. Admiral Belyaev's ship *Kasparov* was relatively lucky, with only seven lasers aimed at her. Five expended themselves on *Kasparov's* shields, but two managed to penetrate the hull. One of his superdreadnoughts, the *Brezhnev,* had the misfortune to be the target of fourteen x-ray lasers, one of which hit the hull and triggered the ejection of the fusion reactors. Another x-ray sliced into the reactors just as they exited the ship, causing a massive explosion that blew *Brezhnev* into pieces. *Chernyenkov* and the *Yekaterina Velikaya* were each targeted by eight missiles. *Ivan Grozny* was targeted by only six.

Both sides launched their second salvos of missiles. Denisov's force launched 360 missiles. The UAF returned fire with 740. Salvos continued to fly as the unified force closed the range. None got through.

After the distance closed, the *Severn* was within range of her big gun. She had over eight minutes to fire without the rogue Rodinans able to respond effectively. The TAC reported as the PBG fired, tracking its success. The first rogue SDN lost her EM drives after the fourth shot. The second SDN blew up after the fifth time it had been targeted. The third SDN lasted through seven shots before it too lost its drives and power to accelerate. The five battlecruisers of the rogue force lowered their shields in surrender just before *Severn* reached photon cannon range.

After Jonah coordinated with Admiral Belyaev about having the Rodinan marines board and assume control of the rogue Rodinan ships, he returned to his ready room to begin the debrief meeting with his captains in order to prepare his after-action reports.

By the time Jonah reached his ready room, Jacobs already pulled up the sensor logs from the battle. He also had the plots of their current course and the projected plot of the enemy course in pursuit. Jonah sent a message to his steward, Gardner, asking him to bring coffee.

"What do we have, Joe?" asked Jonah.

"First, the good news," he responded. "Although the PBG missed on eight of the seventeen shots, the hits it made were devastating."

"Now the bad news," he continued. "Their computer system is seriously upgraded. They launched missiles from pods of nine—seven pods from each SDN, five from each battlecruiser. They launched 2,000 remotely deployed missiles and were able to control them all. They changed the command codes and programmed in the Rodinan ECM protocols, so Admiral Belyaev's ECM didn't do a thing.

"They also have their own version of Swordfish that was one hundred percent effective against our throw weight. Its cycle time is slightly slower at eleven seconds to our 7.5, but it's not enough to make a difference."

MacMurray jumped in, "Seems a waste of taxpayer money, shooting off all these missiles that won't get through."

Donan replied to him, "It's still SOP. Wouldn't want to go before a Board of Inquiry and try to defend that one."

"I don't want to put words in the mouths of my fellow captains," Delhomme said, "but I feel like 'tits on a bull'—is that the right expression, Fred?"

MacMurray chuckled and nodded. Delhomme continued, "It looks like our role in this is limited to missile defense while you pop away with the PBG. I'd like to change that, by the way, to BFG."

Jacobs laughed. "That's what the enlisted are already calling it."

Tim McQuillin, executive officer on *Achates*, asked, "BFG?"

"Big...Gun," Jonah explained.

"Whatever you call it," MacMurray added, "I want to get me one of those."

No one had any further ideas. Jonah wrote up his after-action report and went to bed after a long day.

15

His comm console woke him up a few hours later. Admiral Lothes was calling. He rubbed the sleep from his eye, put on his eyepatch, and sat down in front of the unit.

"Captain Halberd," he reported as he answered.

"Captain, we need you and your task force to return immediately to Commonwealth space, least time transit," she began, without preliminaries. "Stop at Lincoln Station to rearm and refuel. By the time you get there, I may have additional orders."

"Yes, admiral," Jonah replied. "May I ask what's going on?"

"Admiral Denisov obtained his advanced computer systems and new technology from the Chinese. We are in crisis mode and expect an attack imminently—it may happen before your return. They already moved and seized Edo's unexploited system. Admiral Niimura put up a good fight and was just barely able to survive. Niimura shared with us that the Chinese ships had the same capabilities as you saw with Denisov. Right now, the only thing we have to stop them is the *Murray*, so we need you back here pronto."

"Understood," Jonah answered.

"Hours might make a difference. Lothes out."

Jonah rubbed his face in his hands. He contacted the bridge. The ship's fourth officer, Lieutenant Lucarelli, was on duty. "Lieutenant set an immediate course for the Commonwealth, least-time transit."

"Aye, aye, skipper," she responded, her eyebrow lifted in surprise.

Jonah informed the other three captains of their new orders. He contacted Admiral Belyaev and informed him of their immediate departure. Wide awake now, he saw Amy's picture on his desk and was reminded he needed to let her know he was safe, for now. He decided to take a shower first. After he dressed, he sat back down and began to write: "Dear Amy, Baroness Somerset, Lady Halberd, darling of the foreign service and love of my life, I survived our encounter with the enemy unscathed and as sound of mind and body as I was before. I have new orders, responding to a new crisis, about which I'm sure you know more than I. I'm guessing it will mean further postponement of our honeymoon but wanted you to know I'm safe and miss you as much as is humanly possible. Love, Jonah.

He hit send and was rising out of the chair when he noticed the error message. "Unable to send. Destination node offline."

Fearing the worst, he sent a text to Admiral Lothes: "New Delhi?"

He waited by his console for an answer, his heart in his throat. Twenty minutes later came the response: "Now under attack by Chinese." Jonah barely managed to make it to the head before he threw up. He fell back from the head, slumped against the shower door. He lifted his face and howled as though he were trying to expel all his heartbreak in one feral roar. He stopped when he ran out of breath.

He allowed himself to wallow in misery for a minute or two, then shook his head and took a deep gasping breath. He stood up slowly and checked in the mirror to make sure he had not soiled his uniform. He then rinsed his mouth and brushed his teeth again.

Jonah allowed himself to be reassured. Amy was a diplomat and enjoyed some protection as such. She would likely be repatriated with the other Commonwealth embassy staff, or else the Chinese would be in violation of the Concordat of 3009. After calming himself, he strode to the enlisted mess. The crew would have questions because of their quick departure. He likely didn't have the answers they sought, but he owed it to his people to share with them what little he knew.

After breakfast, he returned to his quarters to check for updates on his console. A bulletin from the Admiralty noted that the Chinese had seized Edo's unexploited system and was in the process of taking over New Delhi. While he was reading the notices, Pierre buzzed in.

"Jonah, old friend," he said, "I'm really sorry. She'll be okay. Don't worry."

"Thanks, buddy," Jonah replied. "I know she'll be okay."

"I'm guessing we'll be at war by the time we get back," Delhomme offered.

"If the Chinese have their entire fleet equipped the way Denisov was, we might not have much to come back to," Jonah said glumly.

"Think positive," Delhomme suggested. "Their entire fleet can't be fitted out with the new tech. They can't have started any earlier than we did."

"Yeah, but we did all their testing for them," Jonah pointed out. "Our big hang-up was the computer system, which is still a bottleneck. If they had already solved that before we did, then they could have put their Swordfish and the bigger missile pods in their whole fleet. This could be bad."

"Well, from what I read of Admiral Niimura's report," Pierre remarked, "they still don't have the BFG."

"Yet," Jonah cautioned.

"Yet," Pierre agreed. "They also don't have you and me, and that's gotta count for something."

Jonah smiled wryly. "Yup, there it is," he added with a note of finality.

"I do have some good news," Pierre allowed. "The Admiralty is demanding that the ships we just captured be handled by prize court. I'm guessing they want their share of the loot due to recent developments."

Jonah shook his head, chuckling.

"What's so funny?" Pierre asked.

"I quit paying attention to prize money back during my first tour in command of *Essex*," Jonah admitted. "The number got to a certain point that it didn't seem real anymore. Karl told me to get an investments guy and set me up with a broker who has handled it since then. She sends me quarterly statements and does my taxes. I just look at them, say 'yup, okay,' sign them and forget about it. I hadn't paid a bit of attention to it until right before the wedding."

"What made you check?" Pierre asked. "Redo your will? Or wanted to see if yours was as big as the other Lords?"

"Naw, before that," Jonah responded, ignoring Pierre's snarky comment. "I was buying Amy that circlet she wore at the wedding and needed to tap into my investments to pay for it. If it weren't for that, I'd still be clueless. What about you, you money-grubbing cheese-eater?"

"Ah, now I know you're cheering up because we're back to the insults," Pierre commented. "I'm in the same boat as you. When they put me in command of *Iphigenia*, we had some success, and Karl gave me the same advice. Probably hooked me up with the same person. The last time I looked was when I was back with Third Fleet a couple of years ago. I was so disgusted that I was going to retire and wanted to see if I could afford to. I haven't really paid attention since and just checked this morning when I heard about prize court."

"Well, I thank you for giving me the only piece of good news I'm likely to hear today."

"No problem. Talk to you later." Delhomme cut the connection.

Jonah went back to the reports. He read the portions of Admiral Niimura's report that were shared with the Admiralty. The Edoan Imperial Navy had the same Swordfish missile defense and detached missile pod systems as the Commonwealth due to a technology-sharing agreement Amy had orchestrated. Their battle against the Chinese task force that entered their unexploited system turned into an artillery duel, but the Chinese outnumbered the Edoans significantly, so Niimura withdrew to save his ships after suffering heavy damage.

He saw the notice that Admiralty was officially requesting that the captured Rodinan ships be administered by the prize courts. Jonah suspected there would be some disagreement over the issue to be handled by the diplomats. If the five completely intact battlecruisers were subjected to prize rules, his share of the proceeds would be an enormous amount of money.

The day wore on, and in the middle of the night, they entered the first of three hyperspace corridors on the journey back to Lincoln Station. When they emerged from hyperspace, Jonah accessed the Admiralty to get an update on the situation in New Delhi. The Chinese had invaded with an entire fleet and had brought an armada of troop transports along shortly after gaining control of the system. The Admiralty estimated that the Chinese had landed nearly a half-million soldiers on the planet. This was an astonishing number.

When they exited the second and longest of the three corridors on the return to Lincoln, Jonah's comm console began to buzz the moment he felt the twitch in his gut that signaled the shift back to normal space. All four captains were included on the call, with a haggard-looking Admiral Lothes on the other end.

"Captains," she began, "we are at war. The Chinese invaded the Hercules system about—" She checked the time. "Twenty-eight hours ago. They issued a declaration of war just as their ships entered Hercules. They took some losses entering the system due to Admiral Antonelli's foresight in pre-positioning 9,600 Vulcans at the entrance from the neighboring H2813. More ships followed."

Lothes took a deep breath and continued, "Second Fleet has been destroyed. Admiral Antonelli is dead. Hercules Station and Aries Station have been destroyed. The Chinese are continuing to Roosevelt. Admiral Sayyah will not be able to pre-position a substantial number of pods due to lack of inventory.

"Captain Halberd is hereby appointed rear admiral and assigned to command Second Fleet, or what's left of her. Your four ships, along with HMS *Murray*, will be the only capital ships in Second Fleet for the time being."

16

Wang Zhu was troubled. The premier of Căodì, Dong Li, succeeded in winning 15 of the 23 premiers of the Chinese Republics to her side. Not only did they provide the new weapons technology to Admiral Denisov, but they also convinced the rogue Rodinans to attempt a takeover of Patagonia.

The Commonwealth had sent to Patagonia the only ships in their fleet which were equipped with the Swordfish technology. This left Commonwealth space wide open to the Chinese attack. Everything was proceeding exactly as Dong Li had predicted.

New Delhi surrendered quickly and was in the process of being occupied. The Edoans were forced to retreat. The attack on Commonwealth space was so far wildly successful. It seemed likely that Dong Li's goal of destroying forty percent of the Commonwealth Fleet would be easily met. The Rodinans were unable to respond. They had neither the ships nor the technology. They likely had no will for a fight either.

Wang knew it was rare for a plan to remain unchanged after first contact with the enemy, but, so far, he had to admit the operation was proceeding like clockwork. With the Commonwealth rocked back on its heels, there would be nothing to stop the Chinese Republics from snapping up the non-aligned systems one by one. After New Delhi was brought under control, they would move next to Lutetia, then Rotterdam. After that, the German systems and finally, Edo.

Dong's plan was based on the amount of civilian resistance expected on each planet. Her goal was that the Republics would be able to add at least the first three populated systems by the earliest time the Commonwealth would be able to respond militarily. The projections from intelligence indicated that they might also be able to add two of the German systems as well.

When the Commonwealth rebuilt their strength and were able to oppose further efforts by the Chinese to expand their holdings, the Republics would open peace talks. They would drag these talks out as long as possible in order to consolidate their positions on the planets they had taken by force. By the time peace negotiations reached a meaningful point, they had planned to have eliminated any opposition to their rule on those planets.

If successful, Dong's plan would bring the Republics to near-parity with the Commonwealth in terms of numbers of populated systems. The Commonwealth would still have a slight edge in overall economic strength, but the gap would be much smaller. The Rodinans would fall behind.

This was the main thrust of Dong Li's argument and one that found many ears willing to listen. She stated that throughout human history on earth, the Chinese were almost always the dominant power, or at the very least, one of the two dominant powers. Since the colonization of inter-planetary space, however, the Chinese were a sometimes-distant third, behind the Commonwealth and the Rodinans. Her faction promoted the view that returning the Chinese to a position of dominance was in accordance with human history—returning things to their proper and normal alignment.

The Chinese were slower to begin colonizing space. During the destructive upheaval of the Second Great Intifada that involved so much of earth and driven the rush to colonize space, China was the least affected of the traditional earth superpowers. The United States and Russia both suffered more serious damage, adding urgency to their colonization efforts. China was content for a time to enjoy being the remaining superpower on an earth they did not realize was doomed. As a result, they were slower to begin interplanetary exploration and colonization.

When it became apparent that the future of humankind was no longer on earth, China found itself locked into third place behind the Anglo-American efforts that became the Commonwealth and those of the Russians. This was the status quo for hundreds of years now. It rankled people like Dong Li and her followers.

Wang Zhu survived as chairman of the governing council for thirty-seven years by knowing when to bend and when to stand firm. In the current circumstances, he bent. He did not want to be remembered like those leaders on earth who, content with China's position in a failing world, failed to pursue inter-planetary colonization. This could be an historic opportunity to restore the Chinese people to a position of dominance. Yet, he was not motivated by the historical arguments.

While so far everything was proceeding exactly as predicted and hoped, he did not believe this happy state of affairs would continue indefinitely. There would be setbacks—there always were. What troubled Wang was the risk involved in this effort. The citizens of the 23 Chinese Republics enjoyed a quality of life better than their earth-bound ancestors could ever have dreamed. If Dong's plans achieved success, the addition of the non-aligned planets to the Republics would further enhance the quality of life for all citizens. But if the current quality of life was threatened by the war, he would withdraw his support immediately.

He and his allies in the governing council were agreed upon this. Some voted to support Dong Li, and some voted against her plans, but all were keeping a wary eye on the progress of the venture. If things began to go badly, there would come a time to change tactics. His fear was that a turn in fortune would happen so quickly that there would be no opportunity to maintain control.

17

In the city of New Delhi, there was panic. Hours before, the government had broadcast news of the Chinese invasion of the system. The small force New Delhi had in space had been quickly destroyed by the Chinese. The invaders had been broadcasting a surrender demand, promising no one would be harmed if there were no resistance.

In the Commonwealth embassy, the entire staff was busy. Shredding documents, erasing computer drives, eliminating every bit of data possible before they were forced to leave the facility. They did not know whether they had hours or days. Agent Sauer had disappeared almost immediately but had sent a message to the ambassador to delay destroying his comm console and the passport and visa system. Ordinarily, the ambassador would disregard such a message, but she was well aware that Sauer was a member of the King's Own—the elite bodyguards who protected the king but who had also been assigned to assure Amy's safety.

Sauer returned within an hour, looking disheveled. She immediately found Amy and ordered her to her apartment on the embassy grounds. Sauer had a bottle of hair dye and ordered Amy into the bathroom to begin coloring her hair. She took care to instruct Amy to make sure she did above and below and not to forget her eyebrows. Amy was puzzled but knew that when the agents issued instructions, it was only for her personal safety.

Meanwhile, Sauer summoned her colleague Smith, and the two of them went through Amy's quarters thoroughly. They had piled most of her belongings on her bed. When Amy came out of the shower, her hair and eyebrows now blonde, she asked what they were doing.

"Removing any connection to Captain Halberd, ma'am," replied Sauer tersely. She handed Amy her personal comm unit and a data chip. "You'd better back up anything you want saved onto this chip, then we need to scrub the unit. Get dressed while you're waiting on that. We have to hurry."

Amy did as she was told. While she dressed, she asked what they were planning on doing to the things they piled on the bed. She saw framed pictures, some souvenirs, her black dress that Jonah had given her, most of her clothes and undergarments, her shoes, her purse and its entire contents, and some keepsakes from her youth.

"Have to destroy them, ma'am," Smith answered. "You need to disappear. Or at least, Amy Davidson, Lady Halberd does. I also need your wedding ring and engagement ring. I won't destroy those—they'll go in a diplomatic pouch along with the data chip backing up your comm. I'll return them as soon as I am able."

Amy nodded, suddenly afraid. She finished dressing and dried her newly blonde hair. Smith went to a small case he had brought. He opened it and pulled out two pieces of foam rubber.

"These are cheek implants," he noted. "Put them in. They change the lines of your face."

When she finished, he instructed her to lie down on the bed. He went to the bathroom to wash his hands. When he returned, he retrieved a small case with two circular compartments. He opened it carefully. "This is going to feel uncomfortable at first, but you'll get used to them in a few hours. Hold your right eye open with your fingers."

Using his fingertips, he lifted a thin spherical concave membrane from the small case. He positioned it and placed it over Amy's right eye. "Now the left," he instructed. He did the same for Amy's left eye. The membranes changed her eye color from blue to brown and could not be detected.

He then went to the bathroom again, running the hot water. When it was warm enough, he placed two semi-circular things under the hot water for a few seconds. He returned to Amy.

"Put this on your upper teeth and bite down hard and hold it for a count of ten."

When Amy finished, Smith gave her the other one and said, "Same thing for the lower. Bite and count to ten."

By now, Amy's comm unit had backed itself up to the data chip. Sauer took it and inserted a different chip. "Let me know when it's loaded," she instructed, and she gathered up the pile of materials from the bed, using the bedspread to contain them all.

Smith told Amy, "Stand against the wall for your passport photo." She did, and he snapped a picture with his comm unit. He inspected it on the screen and grunted approval. He closed his case. "Come with me," he said.

They hurried through the confusion of the embassy to the ambassador's office. They reached the office and blew past the ambassador's secretary. The ambassador looked up from his desk, surprised. "Sorry, sir, I need access to your console."

Smith put his case on the desk and opened it again. He extracted a swab and gave it to Amy. "Swab the inside of your cheek," he said. Amy did and handed the swab back to him. He put the swab in a small black device that beeped a second later. Meanwhile, Smith's fingers were a blur on the keyboard. He spoke as he typed.

"Ambassador," he instructed, "this is Amelia Clarke with an e. She's a GS3 who just arrived at the embassy to start work. The person you know as Amy Davidson left on a commercial liner three days ago at the request of the foreign secretary. Before the Chinese arrive, you need to instruct all your people that Amy Davidson left on that liner. What I'm doing now is registering her DNA to an existing passport with a visa for Miss Clarke. Earlier I hacked into the New Delhi passport control systems to show Miss Davidson's departure and Miss Clarke's arrival. The official embassy roster on file with New Delhi shows Miss Clarke started last week, and Miss Davidson departed. I'm also adding the correspondence from the foreign secretary ordering Miss Davidson to return to Caerleon."

Smith paused for a moment, waiting for a response on the console. He pulled another small box out of the case. "Put these on, please, Miss Clarke." He handed her a box containing false fingernails. They appeared to be garishly painted, with the lacquer chipped in spots. Amy did and reported that the chip had finished loading into her comm unit. Smith held out a hand for the chip, then swallowed it.

The console beeped, and Smith resumed work. After some furious typing, he pushed the chair back and stood. "Sir," he said, addressing the ambassador, "I need to watch you delete the passport control programs and scrub your console now."

The ambassador nodded and sat down to begin doing as ordered. Agent Smith looked over his shoulder to be satisfied it was done thoroughly and correctly. When the ambassador was finished, Smith said, "Thank you, sir. I apologize for ordering you around like this, but I take my orders from King Edward."

"Come with me, Miss Clarke," Smith instructed. He led her down to agent Sauer's quarters. There was a cheap, battered suitcase and a garment bag in the closet. "I need you to change into the clothes in that bag and suitcase. Lingerie, shoes, everything. I'll need the clothes you're wearing. What you don't decide to wear, pack back in the suitcase or garment bag neatly. I'll be in the hall. Come out when you're finished."

Amy looked in the garment bag and suitcase. The clothes were cheap, somewhat garish, and showing signs of wear. The lingerie was cheap. The shoes had heels at least two inches higher than Amy would ever wear and definitely looked worn. There were some accessories—plastic for the most part, with one very thin gold chain. Amy picked out an outfit and put it on. She looked in the mirror for the first time since the process began. She almost laughed out loud. The woman who appeared in the mirror was a low-level secretary, with clothing slightly on the slutty side for an embassy employee. Her face looked different, and her new teeth were slightly crooked.

She put everything back in the suitcase and garment bag somewhat neatly, but not perfectly. Amelia Clarke was slightly untidy, she decided. She gathered up the clothes, lingerie, and shoes she had removed and opened the door. Agent Smith took them from her. "Get the bag and suitcase and follow me."

Amy retrieved the two pieces of luggage and followed the agent. He led her to one of the staff apartments on the same floor. "This is your assigned quarters, Miss Clarke. You'll find toiletries in the bathroom. Please brush your teeth and brush your hair. We want your DNA on the toothbrush and some of your hair in the hairbrush in case they decide to check. Your purse is in the closet. I'll be back in a jiffy."

After Amy had brushed her hair and her teeth, Sauer and Smith returned. "Come with us."

Amy took the purse, a too-large cheap imitation of a designer bag. She looked in it briefly and saw the usual junk appropriate for someone like Amelia Clarke. She took out the wallet and looked inside. There were the customary ID cards, including her passport card. There was a tattered photo of an older couple sitting on a couch.

The ambassador had gathered all the employees in the lobby of the embassy. "I just heard from the New Delhi government. They have agreed to cooperate with the Chinese. I also spoke with the Chinese ambassador, who assured me that the entire staff would be allowed to leave tomorrow on a commercial liner. They will provide transportation for us to the spaceport at 07:00 local. From now until we board the bus to the spaceport, no one is allowed to leave embassy grounds. At the spaceport, we will board a shuttle and be taken to the liner. There will be other embassies on the same liner, so quarters will be cramped. Everyone will need to share a cabin, with some cabins holding three people. Please take with you only a suitcase and a garment bag.

"There is one more important detail I need to share with you. The person you know as Miss Davidson left to return to Caerleon three days ago. Please pay attention. Miss Davidson left three days ago. Now, though the timing is terrible, I'd like to introduce you to our newest employee, Amelia Clarke, with an e. Amelia just arrived last week as a GS3 to do secretarial work here in the embassy. Because she hasn't had time to settle in properly, she is understandably very scared and nervous. Please be kind to Miss Clarke and help her through this difficult time."

Most of the embassy staff was distracted, more concerned about how they would fit their belongings into a suitcase and garment bag. Some caught on to the announcement and gave faint smiles. Amy stood, clutching her purse with both hands, playing the role perfectly.

The meeting broke up. A few of the clever ones introduced themselves to Miss Clarke and consoled her on the bad timing of her arrival. When the lobby cleared, Sauer and Smith nodded at Amy, indicating she should follow. They went down to agent Sauer's quarters. Smith activated a field suppression device to counter any listening devices. Sauer invited Amy to sit.

"Sorry to push you around like this, Miss Clarke," Agent Sauer apologized. "We moved just in time, I think. By now, all the computer records on New Delhi show that Miss Davidson left three days ago, and you are officially on the embassy's rolls as of two days before that when you arrived last Wednesday. You're a smart person, so I'm sure you've figured out what we did and why. We're sure you still have questions, though."

"You think the Chinese would violate the Concordat of 3009 and try to detain me?"

"It would be a serious violation, to be sure, ma'am," Smith replied, "but we're paid not to take any chances. Because of who you are, they would be tempted."

"We created the Amelia Clarke identity for you some time ago but haven't needed to activate it until now," Sauer continued. "If you look in your wallet, you'll find all the usual things, including your credit access. Your credit is terrible, by the way. You only have £217.84 saved. You've had a series of low-level, low-skill jobs. You did not go to college. You're from Carolina originally, though."

"You think this will work?" Amy asked.

"We hope it will work," Sauer answered. "Based on the briefing we received, we expect one or two of the Chinese intelligence people from their embassy to be here tomorrow morning to check everyone out. One or two others will likely be at the Edoan embassy since they are already at war. The Rodinans, Lutetia, and Rotterdam will also get attention. The Germans, Patagonians, and Nyumbanians will get little scrutiny. There are only six people in the Chinese embassy who are intelligence that we know of. We suspect there are more since they've obviously been preparing to attack New Delhi for some time."

Smith picked up the thread. "Our hope that this will work is because people see what they expect to see. When Agent Sauer disappeared from the embassy a couple of hours ago, she went to access a secure terminal we had in a different location. She hacked into the government systems to alter their records. The Chinese intelligence agents have likely just pulled the rosters from the New Delhi government of registered foreign nationals and are examining them tonight. They will see that Miss Davidson departed, with appropriate documentation from passport control at the spaceport and a berth on the liner registered to Miss Davidson. That liner is currently in an empty system, and its next stop is Ithaca in the Commonwealth. They will see that Miss Clarke arrived in New Delhi, also with appropriate documentation in the system.

"When they look at Miss Clarke, they will see a typical Commonwealth working girl—attractive in a cheap and available sort of way, not bright, not ambitious, not successful. She looks like what anyone, especially a foreigner, would imagine a GS3 secretary looks like. The material on her personal comm unit includes hundreds of text messages to and from Amelia. Running the serial number on the unit shows it registered to Amelia Clarke. Her background checks out. If they really want to dig, though, it won't hold up."

"How long does it need to hold up?" Amy asked.

"We'll be on a Lutetian liner, scheduled to depart at 11:00 tomorrow," Smith confirmed. "Once we make it into the first hyper corridor, I'll breathe a little easier."

"The liner's first stop is Lutetia," Sauer added. "We'll head to the Commonwealth embassy when we get there. From there, we'll figure out how to get you home. In the meantime, go to your apartment here—the key card is in your wallet. Study what's on your comm unit and check out what's in your purse. We'll be ignoring you until we're in that first hyper corridor. As a just-arrived embassy employee, you wouldn't have any idea who we are."

Amy spent a mostly sleepless night. She ventured into the commissary for dinner and ate alone. The other diners were not in a gregarious mood. Everyone was maintaining his or her own space. She went through the purse and found the usual stuff someone like Amelia would carry around. The makeup was cheap, and she resolved to put it on just a little too heavily in the morning.

In the morning, she showered, put on the makeup, and stuffed everything into her suitcase and garment bag, trying to make it look like she had just unpacked and repacked in the space of a few days. At 06:30, there was an announcement summoning everyone to the lobby. She put her purse on her shoulder, grabbed her garment bag, and pulled her suitcase behind her.

She quickly studied the other embassy people already in line. Their expressions showed a lack of sleep, a bit of irritation, and a bit of fear. She tried to adopt those feelings herself. There were four Chinese there. A man and woman examining people's IDs and two standing by the door. The man and woman checked the identities against their comm units. Most people were whisked through quickly. A few were asked questions before being sent through.

When it was Amy's turn, she put on a blank look and kept her mouth slightly open. The woman checked her ID against the comm unit, then waved her on. Amy went out to the bus that was waiting on the curb. She stowed her suitcase and garment bag underneath as everyone else had done and climbed aboard. Now that she was past the first check, she was afraid they'd realize their mistake and come get her. When the last passenger climbed on the bus and they pulled away, she was able to take a deep breath.

At the spaceport, they again had to present ID and be checked against a comm unit. Amy adopted the same vacant look she'd used earlier. Like the others, she was cleared to board the shuttle up to New Delhi Station. She checked her luggage and boarded the shuttle. Once they arrived, the shuttle passengers were herded directly to board the liner. She was assigned to share a cabin with two other women, both older. One was from the Lutetian embassy and one from the German embassy. There were two berths and a sleeping pallet on the floor. As the last to arrive, she got the floor.

The liner departed on time. She pretended not to speak either French or German. The other two women were trying to converse in English and often asked Amy for help with words since neither of them spoke it well. Amy had fun being Amelia—when one of the women did not understand something Amy had said in English, Amy would repeat it speaking very slowly and loudly as if that would make it easier for them to understand. By the time they were called to dinner, both women had just about given up on Amelia.

They invited her to sit with them but out of courtesy and without enthusiasm. The dinner was bland and no longer warm. Amy forced herself to eat since she knew she had been burning nervous energy. After dinner, Amy stayed in the cabin. She was still expecting a knock on the door from a Chinese intelligence agent. She was too nervous to move until she felt the twitch in her stomach that meant they'd gone into hyperspace. The other two women returned, and they prepared to go to sleep. Amy stared at the ceiling until her stomach flipped. She relaxed and fell asleep.

18

Before leaving on their last jump to Lincoln, Jonah received three important messages. The first was terse: "Chinese continued to Roosevelt and eliminated Third Fleet. Admiral Sayyah is dead. Roosevelt Station is destroyed. Chinese do not intend to try to hold these systems. They are already returning to Chinese space. Third Fleet has a number of frigates and light cruisers out on patrol which survived, which will also be reporting to you. Lothes out."

The next was a burst transmission from the Admiralty containing a huge, compressed file. The last was the one he really wanted to see. "It read: Hi Darling—I'm safe. On Lutetia. The universe has gone to shit. Call me when you can. Love, Amy."

Jonah checked the clock—there were two minutes until hyper transition. He typed quickly: "Hi Sweetie—Glad you're safe. I am, too, for now. Going to be super busy. Love you with all my heart, Jonah."

He hit send and saw, to his relief, that the message went through. He then felt his stomach wobble as they went into hyperspace. He opened the compressed file from the Admiralty. There was a message confirming his promotion. His orders assigning him to Second Fleet were next. A copy of a confidential report from Mtumbo Sweedler, the director of Naval Intelligence, to Admiral Lothes was the third file. The fourth file was a confidential memo from Admiral Lothes to the admirals of Second, Fourth and Fifth Fleets. The fifth was a copy of a confidential memo from Director Niven of Advanced Warfare to Admiral Lothes. The sixth file appeared to be a personal note from Admiral Lothes and was marked 'read last.' The last file was the list of the ships that still belonged to Second Fleet: HMS *Murray*, *Achates*, *Euryalus*, *Pallas*, and *Severn*, eleven frigates and eight light cruisers, along with their duty rosters. There was a separate list of the ten frigates and seven light cruisers attached to Third Fleet with their duty rosters. They were now attached to Second Fleet. Along with all this was the official update from the Admiralty on the overall situation.

He looked first at his orders. He was to proceed with haste and due caution to the Hercules system. That was the system in his sector that had access to Chinese space. HMS *Murray* and freighters full of Vulcan missiles would be meeting him there, and he was to arrange disposition of remotely deployed missiles at the hyper corridor to defend the system and Commonwealth space. His priority was to defend the corridor.

He decided to read the general update next. The Chinese began to withdraw from the Commonwealth after destroying Second and Third Fleets. Nearly half the Commonwealth's capital ships were gone, and there were no keels currently laid to replace them. It would take three years minimum for replacements to come off the slips. The Chinese took an unexploited system from Edo and seized New Delhi. Lutetia and Rotterdam were begging for Commonwealth assistance, fearing they were next. Admiral Belyaev was returning from Patagonia, which was suffering an outbreak of civil war after the existing government capitulated so quickly to Admiral Denisov. The Chinese had not yet attacked the Rodinans, and opinions varied on whether they would. There was a reference file at the Admiralty that was linked, but Jonah could not access it from hyperspace.

Jonah next chose to read the ONI report. As he read, he shook his head in disbelief. The previous director of ONI was allied with the Johannsen family. The Johannsens used their power and position in a wide variety of illegal ventures. The venture that most concerned ONI was where operatives hired by the Johannsens obtained detailed information on the Swordfish missile system and the new-design missile pods and sold it to the highest bidder, who turned out to be the Chinese. Information from field agents about this and about a build-up in the Chinese fleet was suppressed by the previous director of ONI. This treasonous action earned the Johannsens billions, which they funneled through dozens of phony corporations that the previous director allowed to stay hidden. Now that Sweedler's forensic accountants found them, the Crown would be confiscating billions of pounds. The report also confirmed an obsession on the part of the Johannsen family and their vendetta against Captain Halberd. There was a link to a reference file entitled 'Dneiper Summary,' but again, Jonah could not access it while in hyperspace.

Jonah then read the memo from Lothes to the admirals of Second, Fourth, and Fifth Fleets, Halberd, DiGiovanni, and Von Geisler. The thrust of the memo was an assessment from ONI on the Chinese navy. Because of the losses that the Commonwealth suffered at Roosevelt in the attack by the Rodinans and the losses that the Rodinans took in New Bremen, Juno, Dneiper, Demeter, and Venera, ONI felt the Chinese navy had surpassed the Rodinans in capital ships and almost equaled the Commonwealth as of the start of this conflict. With the loss of Second and Third Fleets, the Chinese had a substantial advantage in capital ships.

Based on the timing of when the Chinese purchased the Swordfish and missile pod technology, ONI believed that less than forty percent of the Chinese ships had that capability at the moment, but that percentage was expected to climb. ONI postulated that the Chinese actually prioritized the refit of Admiral Denisov's ships over their own because Denisov agreed to turn Patagonia over to them if he could serve as governor. It was a bonus for the Chinese when Denisov's attack had pulled away the only Commonwealth ships that could have caused trouble for the Chinese fleet.

There was some good news. The outbreak of hostilities convinced the Edoan government to allow the Commonwealth to license the computer technology to build the systems in the Commonwealth. Computer system availability had been the logjam holding up introducing the new systems throughout the navy. Within weeks a refit schedule would begin, cycling the capital ships of Fourth and Fifth Fleets through the yards to get the new computers and Swordfish launchers, followed by the capital ships of the Home Fleet. ONI was confident the Commonwealth would complete this refit schedule before the Chinese would finish refitting their navy.

Finally, the memo stressed that defense of the borders of the Commonwealth must be the priority. The sensor data received from Admiral Antonelli before he was destroyed showed that a remotely-deployed missile pod defense could overwhelm the Chinese missile defense in part. A link to those logs and the logs of Third Fleet was attached, but Jonah could not access the Admiralty while in hyperspace.

Jonah was depressed after reading this far. It would take years for the Commonwealth Navy to recover, all because of the actions of a degenerate family of traitors. He felt angry and frustrated. He took some deep breaths to calm himself, then decided to open the memo from Director Niven of Advanced Warfare. He hoped it would cheer him up somehow.

As he read, Jonah's mood began to lift slightly. Niven started by stating that the transfer of equipment and personnel from the Aries and Roosevelt yards, along with licensing the Edoan computer architecture, would accelerate the refit schedule by a factor of ten. He stated that the suppliers of the new power plants and the AT-38 plating guaranteed they could meet or exceed the new delivery schedules. The revised schedule of the remaining *Columbia*-class refits was listed, with five more due to be complete in the next six months. Niven then thanked her for approving the *Regent*-class refits and included a schedule showing six to be completed, with the first two ready in seven months and the last complete in fifteen months.

Jonah had to look up the *Regent*-class on the computer. The *Regent*-class was the second class of superdreadnoughts ever commissioned by the Commonwealth, contemporary with the *Viceroy*-class battlecruisers. A total of twenty ships were built, with eighteen a part of the mothball fleet and two being used as museums. The *Regent* looked like a bigger version of the *Viceroy*, though Jonah knew that would change after Niven was done tweaking it.

An additional eleven capital ships returning to service in the next fifteen months gave Jonah hope that the Commonwealth would survive this war if they could make it through the next fifteen months. It didn't replace the losses they just suffered, but it would close the gap. Though the ships were ridiculously old, he knew first-hand their capabilities after one of Director Niven's refits. He'd just proven what one of them could do, even facing ships equipped with the new technology the Chinese obtained. The *Regent*-class would likely be even more powerful. He found himself secretly hoping he'd get one.

As instructed, he read the personal note from Admiral Lothes last.

"Admiral Lord Halberd—though the situation is dire, there is some hope. We have placed you where we feel the Chinese will aim the tip of their spear. The Commonwealth needs you to hold the line to buy us time to recover. We have given you the best ships in the fleet to do this, though it makes me shudder to think that our best is three old battlecruisers and two ancient dreadnoughts. I would like to remind you that an admiral cannot fight his own ship. I will endeavor to find you a good captain, though with our recent losses if you feel Commander Jacobs can step into the job, I will consider him. Lothes."

Jonah took a breath, then pulled up to the desk and began to type:

"Admiral Lothes—Commander Jacobs has my enthusiastic recommendation for promotion. He has demonstrated to me that he has tremendous potential. I would be delighted to have him as my flag captain if the Commonwealth chooses to assign that role to him. Halberd."

He pressed send. As soon as *Severn* returned to normal space in the Lincoln system, the message would be sent.

A few minutes after exiting the hyper corridor, Jonah's console announced an incoming message. From Admiral Lothes, it read:

"Admiral Lord Halberd—Commander Jacobs has been promoted to captain on your recommendation. He will not be your flag captain, however. A courier boat will meet you in Hercules to deliver your new captain and to take Captain Jacobs to his new command in Fifth Fleet. Also arriving will be your flag lieutenant and a new executive officer. Files attached. Lothes."

Jonah opened the attached files to see who his new captain would be. He grinned when he saw that it was John Blutarsky, recently promoted to captain. Blutarsky had been a lieutenant under Jonah a few years before on HMS *Cumberland*. Blutarsky had been the one to suggest the idea of remotely deploying missiles that became the missile pods. After *Cumberland*, Blutarsky had been promoted to lieutenant commander and served as the XO on a frigate, HMS *Boxer*. He had then been promoted again to commander and served as the XO on a *Dakota*-class battlecruiser, HMS *Indefatigable*. Blutarsky was a 'maverick'—someone who had begun his navy career as an enlisted man. His potential had been spotted, and he was sent to OCS to become an officer.

Blutarsky was outspoken, blunt, and brilliant—and a bit rough around the edges. Reading his fitness reports, his captain on *Indefatigable* seemed to be more concerned with Blutarsky's rough edges than his actual performance. Though Jonah was disappointed to learn that Captain Jacobs was leaving, he felt it was for the best. Jacobs had potential. He needed his own command not to be in an admiral's shadow. Blutarsky was an excellent replacement.

The new executive officer would be Catherine Hayes. Commander Hayes came up through the ROTC track. Her service record was solid, her most recent fitness reports uniformly outstanding. Admiral Von Geisler had written his personal recommendation for her.

The new flag lieutenant would be Jackson Colehower. Colehower was an academy graduate. As an ensign, he had served on a light cruiser, and his first posting as a lieutenant was on a battlecruiser. Digging into his file, Jonah discovered Colehower was Lord Thorner's nephew.

He sent a message to the other captains asking for a conference in fifteen minutes. He asked Joe Jacobs to come to the ready room before that. When Jacobs knocked and entered, Jonah stood and shook his hand, congratulating him on his promotion. Jacobs shared with Jonah that he would be reporting to Fifth Fleet to command a *Dakota*-class battlecruiser. When he told Jonah it was the *Indefatigable*, Jonah laughed out loud.

He explained to Jacobs that his replacement was coming from the 'Indy' as she was known throughout the navy, and that Jonah had read the previous captain's fitness reports and had concluded that the captain was a bit of a priss. Jacobs said he had heard from friends about the guy and that 'priss' was an accurate description and even a bit of an understatement. The rumor was the previous captain was being transferred to some sort of meaningless staff position within the Admiralty.

Jacobs complained about needing to buy new uniform insignia—that he had just bought his commander uniforms and hadn't gotten much use out of them. That reminded Jonah that he needed to order all the appropriate clothing for his new rank as well. He made a note to contact the outfitters in Lincoln Station.

At the appropriate time, the holographic projections of the other captains blinked into existence at the conference table. After congratulations were shared for the two promotions, Jonah got down to business. They would be stopping at Lincoln Station to refuel, rearm, and re-provision and head to Hercules without delay. HMS *Murray* would meet them there along with freighters carrying 5,400 Vulcan missiles in 600 pods of nine each. They would position the missiles at the corridor to the H2813 system and prepare for another Chinese attack. He informed them that Captain Jacobs would be departing at that time and Captain Blutarsky would be replacing him.

Jonah also shared with them that the Chinese had purchased the information for Swordfish and missile pods from a traitor within the Commonwealth. This news met with muttered curses. Jonah raised his hand, indicating they should stop, and then shared the more positive news. First, that the Edoans had allowed the Commonwealth to license their advanced computer technology, enabling the navy to refit and upgrade the remaining capital ships in the Home, Fourth, and Fifth Fleets. Second, that the Chinese had likely not equipped their entire navy with the new technology yet. Finally, before the Chinese attack, Admiral Lothes had the prescience or good luck to have ordered the transfer of most of the yard workers and a substantial amount of equipment from Aries and Roosevelt Stations out to the Twelfth of Never. Director Niven was putting these resources to good use and hoped to have as many as eleven capital ships refitted and restored to service in the next fifteen months.

"I cannot deny," Jonah said in summary, "that the situation we face right now is pretty desperate. We few, plus Captain Mellon and the *Murray*, are Second Fleet. I would not expect any reinforcements from the other fleets until their systems are upgraded. The other *Columbia*-class refits will likely be spread through the other fleets. That means we are probably on our own for at least six months.

"While they could attack Fifth Fleet from New Delhi, I believe they will have their hands full completing their conquest of that system. It's possible they could travel to Avalon to attack Fourth Fleet. Based on their success in destroying Second and Third Fleet, the path of least resistance into the heart of the Commonwealth is through us.

"My guess is that the Chinese will recall the technologically advanced ships that were sent to New Delhi and the Edoan system and merge them with the fleet that destroyed Second and Third Fleets. Then they will try to come through H2813 again and punch through us. From there, they will keep going and attack Home Fleet to try to force a quick end to the war on their terms. I expect this attack to come as quickly as they can muster the ships."

The meeting ended on a somber note. Jonah shared with them the logistical information about their upcoming stop at Lincoln Station, asked for questions, and then they adjourned. Jonah then turned his attention to the other far-flung ships of Second and Third Fleets. Scattered throughout the Second Fleet sector, he had eleven frigates, eight light cruisers, and three patrol boats. In the Third Fleet sector, there were ten frigates, seven light cruisers, and also three patrol boats. They were all on routine assignments, monitoring shipping lanes. Jonah confirmed to them that they were to continue with their current assignment until further notice, though he did recall one frigate, the *Bradley*, and one patrol boat, PB 429, ordering them to return to the Hercules system. Jonah turned his attention to the files he could not open while in hyperspace.

The first file was an assessment of whether the Chinese would attack the Rodinans. The author believed that the Chinese would prefer not to, avoiding a two-front war. He believed that the main focus of the Chinese was to force the Commonwealth to come to terms quickly and then deal with the Rodinans. The Rodinan navy had been decimated and was the least technologically advanced of the three major powers. As a result, it was of lesser priority for the Chinese in the short term. The file did note that once the Rodinans had the opportunity to examine the five battlecruisers just captured in Patagonia and which they had bought back in prize court, they would have access to the same level of advanced technology as the Chinese. They estimated it would take the Rodinans at least eighteen months to reverse-engineer a suitable computer system.

Jonah then read the 'Dneiper Summary' file. It was a report from the new director of ONI, Mtumbo Sweedler, to Admiral Lothes with all the evidence ONI had uncovered regarding communication to the Rodinans in advance of Jonah's mission the previous year. The report went into great detail, so Jonah skipped to the conclusion. Sweedler had found that the Johannsens were behind this. He had learned that, unlike the other information they had sold to the Rodinans, the Johannsens supplied this information at no charge. Sweedler concluded their motivation was to enable the Rodinans to set a trap that would destroy Captain Halberd.

19

Jonah pursed his lips and blew out a deep breath. Shaking his head, he was about to access the sensor logs transmitted to the Admiralty by Second Fleet before it was destroyed. His comm console alerted him to an incoming call from Amy. He immediately answered.

Amy's face appeared on screen. Jonah was taken aback by her now-blonde hair. "Hi, sweetie," he spit out.

Amy grinned. "Hey, baby. Like the hair?"

Jonah was thinking fast, trying to come up with the right thing to say. Amy interrupted his train of thought by bursting into laughter. "You should see the look on your face," she chuckled. "Don't worry, I'm going to change it back. I just wanted you to see it."

She recounted the whole adventure of leaving New Delhi and how agents Sauer and Smith transformed her into 'Amelia' to help her get off the planet. MI-6 later confirmed that the Chinese were disappointed to have not been able to detain her. As far as they knew, though, 'Amy Davidson' left New Delhi three days before their attack. The foreign secretary surmised that they would be furious if they knew she slipped through their fingers. She shared a picture showing her in full 'Amelia' get-up. Jonah was astounded at how effective the disguise was. Though he could tell after looking at the picture carefully that it was Amy, the hair, clothes, makeup, brown eyes, cheek implants, and crooked teeth of 'Amelia' made it difficult.

"Now that you've seen me, should I stay blonde or go back? I'm all blonde, by the way," she commented with a sexy smirk.

"Whatever you want, honey," Jonah replied, finally realizing what the correct answer was.

She laughed at him. "I'm changing back later today, don't worry. I can't go out in public yet anyway. All I have are 'Amelia' clothes. They had to destroy all my 'Amy' clothing."

"Crap!" Jonah blurted. "I never had the chance to tell you. You've been added to all my accounts. Just contact the bank, and they'll get you set up. After all, you're on Lutetia." Then with an aristocratic drawl, he added, "We do have certain standards to maintain, Lady Halberd., harrumph."

She laughed. "It still sounds so strange to hear that. Here in the embassy, it's "Lady Halberd this" and "Lady Halberd that," and I'm still slow in realizing they're talking to me. I did file all my change-of-name stuff, so I am Amy Halberd now. I'll contact the bank. I'd like to go shopping but can't leave the embassy until Agents Sauer and Smith work out getting more coverage from the DGSI. At least Gauthier and Fontaine have all my sizes on file, so I can order a few things to hold me over until I can get out."

"If they won't let you leave the embassy, they have their reasons," Jonah advised.

"Oh, Jonah," she sighed, "things are crazy right now. Lutetia and the other non-aligned systems except the Germans have all declared neutrality, but here and on Rotterdam everyone expects to be attacked any minute. Both Lutetia and Rotterdam have unexploited systems they own like Edo's."

"What about the Germans?" Jonah asked.

"The Germans have not declared war on the Chinese but have expressed solidarity with Edo and stated that they intend to honor all their obligations. Of course, the Germans are in the safest position with regard to Chinese space. Lutetia and Rotterdam are much, much closer astrographically to the Chinese. They have those unexploited systems that they simply cannot defend. Hell, they can't even defend their home systems against the Chinese. On an official level, my contacts are torn. They want to support Edo but are terrified of doing anything to provoke the Chinese.

"On an unofficial level, the mood here on Lutetia is bizarre," she commented. "I've never experienced anything like it. People are going through the motions of their regular lives, but underneath is an atmosphere of a sort of fatalistic hedonism—eat, drink and be merry, for tomorrow we die. On top of that, everyone knows that the Chinese had a number of politicians in their pocket. Though they exposed some of them, no one thinks they identified all of them. That's why Smith and Sauer won't let me leave the embassy. For the same reason, they can't let me leave the planet. They're afraid someone in the government will try to turn me over to the Chinese as a way of buying favor. They are being very careful, and I appreciate it."

"Why did you leave the liner at Lutetia then?" Jonah asked.

"It was a Lutetian liner," she responded, "and the Commonwealth was the last destination. The agents were worried that the 'Amelia' ruse would be discovered. They wanted to get me to the nearest embassy as soon as they possibly could. I'm far better off here than if I'd been detained on New Delhi. At some point, things may stabilize enough that I can leave but right now, no. Please tell me what you can about your situation."

"Good news or bad news first?" he asked.

"Good news, definitely. We all need some good news," she answered.

"The good news is that you're married to 'Admiral' Lord Halberd now," he said, though with a grim expression on his face.

"I'd heard a rumor," she admitted, "but am glad it's true. Congratulations. You don't seem too happy about it, though."

"Amy, you heard what happened, right?" he asked. When she nodded, he continued, "It's bad. And it's not over. I'm right where I need to be, but things are likely to get pretty scary soon."

She sighed heavily. "I've been briefed, and I've read between the lines for what the briefing didn't cover."

"If we can make it through this, though, I think we'll be able to turn it around," he offered.

"You'd better. Your note before Patagonia was much better, by the way. Still plenty of room for improvement, though," she said, trying to lighten the mood. "And you still owe me a honeymoon, buster, full of passionate, animalistic sex. I mean to collect."

"And I mean to deliver."

Amy looked as though she were planning to say something else but instead was silent as her eyes filled and a tear escaped, rolling down her cheek. Seeing this, Jonah's eye welled up with tears also.

"I love you, Amy," Jonah said in a voice choked with emotion. "I miss you. I will see you as soon as I can."

Sniffing through her tears, Amy replied, "What you said," and closed the connection.

Jonah laughed in the middle of a sob. He spent a few minutes getting his mind back on his job and the many things he needed to do. When he regained control of his emotions, he opened the file containing the sensor data from Second Fleet and Third Fleet.

Admiral Antonelli positioned 3,600 Vulcan missiles at the boundary of the hyper corridor. The Chinese had entered with seven 527-type superdreadnoughts and ten 461-type battlecruisers. To face them, Antonelli had every capital ship in Second Fleet: six superdreadnoughts and nine battlecruisers. The opening Commonwealth missile salvo overwhelmed the Chinese missile defense, destroying two of the 527-types and damaging one other. After that, without the Swordfish missile defense, the Commonwealth force was overwhelmed.

Even though the Chinese were not able to deploy missile pods due to the suddenness of Antonelli's defense, their first salvo of 900 missiles was nearly 150 more than the point-defense network of the Commonwealth fleet could handle. Four of the Commonwealth superdreadnoughts were destroyed in the opening exchange. With two more salvos, the Chinese eliminated the rest of Second Fleet.

The Third Fleet information was even more lopsided. The Chinese force was able to deploy missile pods and fired an opening salvo of 1,422 'Shark' missiles. Admiral Sayyah's fleet of five superdreadnoughts and nine battlecruisers was overwhelmed. All fourteen ships perished without landing a single blow against the Chinese.

After viewing the battle data, Jonah considered it a small mercy that the Chinese had chosen to pull back at that moment. They might have continued to the heart of the Commonwealth and attacked the Home Fleet. They were probably worried about more pre-positioned missile defenses and that Fourth and Fifth Fleets would have enough time to return and support Home Fleet. Their invasion force would have wreaked more damage but might have taken some significant losses.

That caused Jonah's brain to start churning. The unwillingness of the Chinese to risk this portion of their navy might mean that the ships of this invasion force, plus the ones that seized Edo's unexploited system, might be the only ones they had upgraded so far. The amount of force with which they could mount an attack might be limited now to a handful of superdreadnoughts and a dozen or so battlecruisers.

Jonah sent a query to ONI and copied Admiral Lothes: "Please estimate how many 527s and 461s in the Chinese navy have the advanced tech. Please estimate how many 527s and 461s were deployed to Edo and New Delhi and whether all had advanced tech. Want to estimate 'worst-case' scenario of what might come through system H2813 and earliest possible date. Please respond as soon as reliable numbers are available. Who is in command of Chinese that would come through H2813? Please send complete personality profile."

His comm reminded him to contact the outfitters on Lincoln Station. After he did, that reminded him that he needed to switch quarters. Since *Columbia*-class dreadnoughts were the most powerful ships in the navy when they were built, they included admiral's quarters. He summoned his steward, Gardner, and asked him to make sure the admiral's quarters were cleaned and dusted so he could move in.

Gardner informed him that the crew had already done so when they learned of their captain's promotion. Jonah ordered him to move his belongings to the new quarters and headed to the bridge. Out of habit, he headed for the command chair but stopped himself two paces short. There was a separate 'courtesy' seat where an admiral could observe the bridge. He spun and walked to that. After logging into the console, he saw a return message from ONI and another from Admiral Lothes.

"Estimate Chinese navy has no more than six 527 SDN and fourteen 461 BC upgraded to advanced tech at this time," ONI's message read. "They continue to bring ships in for refit, so those numbers may increase slightly in the short term. Capital ships sent to New Delhi were not of the upgraded type. Capital ships sent to Edo (2-527, 2-461) are remaining in occupied system. Repairs to 527 SDN damaged in Hercules estimated to be complete in seven days."

Admiral Lothes sent a related message. "Admiral—ONI estimates that the Chinese would be able to send in a week a force of 4 SDNs and 12 BCs, all upgraded. One SDN and 2 BC currently being upgraded and due to rejoin fleets in eleven days. Additional SDN and 2 BC per month following. Admiral Belyaev shared information from captured ships—defense missile stocks on board had been nearly exhausted immediately prior to surrender. ONI is trying to determine if on-board inventory is similarly limited for 527 and 461-types. Personality profile of Chinese admiral being compiled. Lothes out."

20

The visit to Lincoln Station was brief. Within hours all four ships had been restocked with weapons, fuel, and supplies. Last to arrive were Jonah's new uniforms.

Second Fleet headed immediately to Hercules. Passing through Aries, they were able to see the wreckage of what was Aries Station and the huge fleet shipyard. Jonah was pleased to see salvage tugs already in operation, towing sections of the structure back. How much they would be able to save was not as important to him as seeing signs that there was an effort underway.

When they reached the Hercules system, as at Aries, Jonah again saw salvage tugs towing sections of what remained of Hercules Station back into place. They were hailed by the logistics officer in charge of the freighters full of missile pods, the commander of the navy courier boat, and by Commander Raymond Wang, captain of the frigate, *Bradley*. He ordered *Bradley* to proceed to the entrance to the hyper corridor leading to system H2813. The *Bradley* was to scan for any stealth drones the Chinese might have left and to intercept if a Chinese patrol boat tried to enter the Hercules system. Once the *Bradley* determined that there were no drones in place, the freighters could begin positioning the missiles.

When the courier boat docked with *Severn*, Jonah had the transfer of command ceremony prepared. The entire crew mustered in the enlisted mess. When Captain Blutarsky entered, he was presented with full honors. The crew sang "God Save the King" and the chaplain read a short invocation. Master Chief Loree gave the command, "Parade Rest." Jonah made a brief speech, thanking Captain Jacobs and wishing him well in his new command. Jacobs then thanked Jonah and the crew and read his orders detaching him from *Severn*, finishing with, "I am ready to be relieved."

Blutarsky stepped forward and read his orders summoning him to take command of *Severn*. When he finished, he stated, "I relieve you, sir" and saluted.

Jacobs answered, "I stand relieved," returning the salute.

Blutarsky then turned to Jonah, saluted, and announced, "Sir, I have properly relieved Captain Jacobs as captain of *Severn*."

Blutarsky turned and addressed the crew, saying, "I am proud to be the captain of HMS *Severn*. I wish Captain Jacobs the best of success in his command of HMS *Indefatigable*. All standing orders, regulations, and instructions remain in effect. Lieutenant Commander Garrity, take charge and dismiss the ship's company."

As Captain Jacobs departed, he was given parting honors, accompanied by the bosun's pipe. It was at this point that Jonah noticed a young lieutenant and a commander standing nervously just inside the entrance of the mess. Blutarsky nodded them over. The two walked over briskly, saluting Jonah and offering him their orders. Jonah returned the salute and took their orders, acknowledging, "Commander Hayes, Lieutenant Colehower, welcome aboard. Please find Lieutenant Commander Garrity, and she will assign your quarters."

The two saluted, saying, "Aye, aye, sir," and turned neatly away.

When they left, Jonah offered his hand to Blutarsky to shake. "Welcome aboard, John. I'm glad to see you. I'll walk you to your quarters."

As they walked, Jonah asked, "What do you know about your XO?"

"Don't know her, heard of her though," Blutarsky. "She got stuck in Third Fleet under Johannsen but survived. Since she's been in Fifth, I've heard she's become a go-getter. Tell me about the ship? I mean, sheesh, a *Columbia*? I thought they were yanking my chain."

"No time right now," Jonah remarked. "But I'm issuing orders for a formal dinner in the officers' mess at 19:30. We'll talk after dinner. The short version is good crew, great ship."

Jonah returned to his quarters. Outside of his ready room was a small office. Lieutenant Colehower had already found it and had logged on the console. He started to jump up when he noticed Jonah. "As you were lieutenant," Jonah said before Colehower managed to stand completely.

Jonah leaned against the desk. "I have to tell you, lieutenant, I've only been an admiral for a few days, and I've certainly never had a flag lieutenant. Since my XO was promoted to captain the same time I was, our roles didn't change much, but all of a sudden, I got a lot more paperwork relating to the admiral thing. Having a new captain will help me switch into being an admiral, I hope. Having a flag lieutenant will help me stay on top of the paperwork. I guess your position is to be my XO on the admiral stuff. We'll work it out as we go. That sound okay to you?"

"Yes, sir."

"Alright then. Here's your first task. I'm issuing orders for the captains of the capital ships to a comm conference tomorrow morning at 08:00. I'll be in my ready room," Jonah said. "Let me know when you're done with that, and I'll likely have something else for you to do."

After dinner, Jonah and Captain Blutarsky moved to Blutarsky's ready room to sit and talk. Blutarsky asked his steward to get some coffee.

"That reminds me," Jonah said, "do admirals get stewards?"

"Nope," Blutarsky cracked, "you've got a flag lieutenant."

"Oh, he's going to love that," Jonah smirked.

"So," Blutarsky said, "I've been briefed but tell me what's important to know about *Severn*."

"Well, Director Niven at Advanced Warfare calls her the first ship of the post-missile age, and he's right. I'm going to suggest you review the logs of what we just finished in Patagonia right before the Chinese attacked. Our ships and the rogue Rodinans had a similar missile defense system. Admiral Denisov bought his from the Chinese who bought the information from a traitor in the Commonwealth."

"You're fuckin' kidding me!" Blutarsky interjected.

Jonah shook his head. "I wish I were. Both are one hundred percent effective. There are only two ways to beat these systems. You either fire so many missiles at once that they can't launch enough defense missiles, or you fire so many missiles that they run out of defense missiles. The Rodinans ended up being able to do both to me when I took that little trip through the Federation a year and a half ago."

"The key to the whole thing is the computer system," Blutarsky confirmed. "I read up on it."

"Right. Anyway, when both sides have it, neither side can hurt the other with missiles, except for the two ways I mentioned. That's where *Severn* comes in. Director Niven and his group also developed a new artillery piece—the Particle Burst Gun, or PBG, although Captain Delhomme calls it the BFG."

"I like BFG better," Blutarsky commented.

"You'll like Captain Delhomme. It has fifty percent longer range than photon cannons and three times the power. I haven't seen the analysis back from Advanced Warfare yet, but it seems to me it might cause more damage than a missile x-ray. Have you run any of the sims yet?"

"Yeah. Once I was given my orders and read into it, they gave me the sims," Blutarsky confirmed. "I haven't gotten the hang of it yet."

"Did they tell you it's like early interceptors?"

"Yeah, it is, and it isn't, though," Blutarsky confirmed.

"I agree. The whole point is to somehow match course and speed with the enemy, get close enough to fire the PBG — "

"BFG," Blutarsky suggested.

"Okay, get close enough to fire the BFG but not so close they can return fire with their photon cannons. Then hit them as many times as you can. And the whole time, both sides are firing missiles at each other that can't get through. In Patagonia, they were waiting for us at a dead stop thirty light-minutes short of the corridor entrance. I guess I made too much of a habit of exiting thirty light-minutes early, and they picked up on it. We entered the corridor slow, at only 0.08c. Since they were at a dead stop, it gave us the chance to get a long window where the BFG was in range, but their photon cannons weren't."

Blutarsky was thinking, envisioning the situation in his head. "Okay," he said after a minute.

Jonah agreed. "I wish I could say I had it all planned out, but that would be a lie. We just found ourselves in that situation and realized it was practically perfect."

"That actually helps me understand what I was doing wrong with the sims," Blutarsky confessed. "I was thinking speed and maneuverability, but it's more like using that to get in good position and then bashing them to death."

"I'm going to ask Niven to send us some sims so that you and Captain Mellon can practice."

"Sounds good," Blutarsky commented.

"One other thing," Jonah said. "I wanted to let you know I'm really happy to have you as captain of the *Severn*, but I'm going to announce tomorrow in our meeting that I'm transferring my flag to *Pallas*."

Blutarsky looked puzzled.

"I've been an admiral about as long as you've been a captain. Captain Jacobs was my XO. He's going to be a heckuva captain. But I realized this afternoon that if he stayed on *Severn*, it wouldn't have worked. You served under me on *Cumberland*. Mellon, Donan, and MacMurray have all served under me. It would be worst for you since I was captain of *Severn* until a few days ago. People would still come to me with things they should be taking to you. Plus, I'm worried that you would constantly be concerned about whether I agreed with how you were running your ship instead of just running your ship. Captain Delhomme never served under me. He won't give a rat's whisker worrying about whether I would run the ship the same way. Does that make sense?"

"I guess," Blutarsky replied glumly.

"It's not a slight to you or the ship, even though the crew might be upset," Jonah said. "I'll make an announcement explaining why I'm doing it. In a few days, they'll understand it better, though. The Commonwealth is going to need our very best soon, John. I'm going to need your very best—to be the best captain of *Severn* you can be. It will be easier for you to do that with me not on board."

Jonah returned to his quarters and placed a call to Captain Delhomme.

When Pierre answered, Jonah greeted him with, "Mon Capitaine, I am calling to tell you your wildest dream is about to come true."

"The one where Amy leaves you and comes running to me, and we spend the rest of our lives having wild and crazy sex?" Pierre responded.

"Even better," Jonah said, unphased. "Tomorrow, after the captains' conference, I'm transferring my flag to *Pallas*."

"Um, wow, I guess," Pierre responded, surprised.

"Try to contain your enthusiasm," Jonah commented sarcastically.

"No, it's fine," Pierre protested. "I can see why you'd want to move. Why not *Murray*?"

"You're making me feel as though you don't really want the honor of being my flag captain, Pierre. My feelings are starting to get hurt," Jonah said, screwing up his face, pretending as though he were about to cry.

"Okay. I get it now. Mel was your XO. So was Fred. Sarah also served under you, too. Makes sense," Pierre mumbled, almost to himself. Then, as if trying to talk himself into the idea, "Okay, Pierre…for the good of the service…lie back and think of England—"

Jonah laughed at the last crack.

"Sorry, Jonah," Pierre continued. "Me, personally? I'd love to have you, you know that. I'm just thinking of my crew. You do have the habit of getting your ships blown to shit your last few commands, you have to admit."

"We didn't get a scratch in Patagonia, and I promise I won't try to get your ship blown to shit on purpose, Pierre," Jonah responded. "And I promise I'll stay in my quarters and do admiral-ly stuff and won't come onto the bridge unless you invite me."

"Actually," Pierre said, "I would like to put you in the TAC when things get going if you promise to stay out of the way."

"I promise," Jonah said solemnly.

"Okey-dokey then," Pierre sighed. "I'll send my shuttle to come get you after the conference tomorrow."

"And my flag lieutenant," Jonah added. "Can't forget him."

After the call, Jonah sent a message to Director Niven, asking him to prepare simulations with specific parameters. He read a report from the *Bradley*, indicating they had found and destroyed a stealth drone near the hyper corridor. Jonah sent the command to the freighters to proceed to the corridor entrance and begin deploying the missile pods according to the plan they had given him.

21

In the conference the next morning, Jonah introduced Captain Blutarsky to the others. Then he announced his impending move to *Pallas* and explained why he was doing it. He also told the captains that they would begin running sims as soon as Director Niven sent them over.

After the conference, Captain Blutarsky summoned the crew to assemble in the enlisted mess. Jonah spoke to them and explained why he was moving to *Pallas*. In the middle of what he prepared to say, he noticed some gloomy faces in the crowd. He called one of them out by name, "Seaman Coons...Tom...you know me, right?"

Seaman Coons nodded.

"You all know me," Jonah continued. "We've become a great crew since we came aboard a few months ago. But I'm not the captain anymore; I'm the admiral. And if I stay aboard, you'll still think of me as your captain, even though I'm not. Captain Blutarsky is. You wouldn't do it on purpose, but as long as I'm here, it's going to be difficult for you to develop the same relationship with Captain Blutarsky that we," he waved his arm to indicate them all, "have. That's not fair to Captain Blutarsky, and it's not fair to you. Captain Blutarsky is a hell of an officer. He served under me and won the DSC. He's going to be a brilliant captain of *Severn*, and in a couple of weeks, maybe even sooner, you're going to be glad as hell to have him. I'm not going to *Pallas* because I'm disappointed in you or in Captain Blutarsky. I'm doing it because soon I'll need everyone to perform at his very best. My getting out of your way will help make that happen."

With that, the crew was dismissed. Jonah stayed and shook hands with many of them. Several of them told him that they understood and thanked him for explaining it to them. After a few minutes, Lieutenant Colehower approached and informed him the shuttle had arrived, and he already transferred their belongings onto it. Jonah ended his conversation and went to the shuttle bay.

He was greeted with full side honors when he arrived aboard *Pallas*. Captain Delhomme escorted him to his quarters. Because *Pallas* was a battlecruiser, it was built with admiral's quarters since battlecruisers were often flagships. His quarters on *Pallas* were not as large as on *Severn* but still spacious. He had a head, sleeping quarters, an office, and a ready room. Outside the ready room was a workstation for Lieutenant Colehower.

His belongings were brought within a few minutes, and Lieutenant Colehower arrived at the same time. Jonah would wait to stow his things. He went into his office to activate the comm console.

Three messages caught his eye. The first was notification from Lieutenant Commander Monica Gracia that PB 429 arrived in the Hercules system and would rendezvous with the flagship in fourteen hours. The second was from Director Niven with simulation packages attached, designed according to Jonah's requested parameters. The third was from Director Sweedler of ONI and was a personality profile of Admiral Xu.

Jonah asked Lieutenant Colehower to inform the captains that a simulation would begin at 13:00, with more details to follow. He forwarded the sim files to Colehower for him to load them onto the command-and-control net. Each captain would control his own ship, with Jonah in overall command of the fleet. The computer program would command a force of five 527-type superdreadnoughts and fourteen 461-type battlecruisers.

With three hours remaining before the simulation began, Jonah leaned back and began reading the personality profile of Admiral Xu. He wanted to get an idea of who he would be facing in the upcoming battle. He hoped he would find something in the man's background that would help him prepare for the battle to come.

According to what ONI had compiled, Admiral Xu was bright, personable, and diligent. His career progression was fairly normal, though rapid by Chinese standards. Xu was married with a daughter and was only six years older than Jonah. He was identified early in school as a student with potential and moved into accelerated classes. One of the psychologists writing the report commented that many of those selected to enroll in the accelerated programs in the Chinese system developed an elitist arrogance, but Xu apparently did not. After completing secondary school, Xu was given admission to the Chinese Naval Academy. He finished third in his class, but the ONI researcher commented that the administration at the academy was displeased with him because he had chosen to focus on the study of history instead of engineering or physics.

After a short break for lunch, Jonah went to his ready room to begin the simulation. He invited Lieutenant Colehower to join him. The hyperspace corridor from H2813 to the Hercules system took three days, one hour, twenty-five minutes and eleven seconds to go from one end to the other. When PB 429 arrived, Jonah planned to order her to travel towards H2813. She would drop from hyperspace outside the range of any Chinese' gravimetric sensors and go into full stealth mode, drifting through deep space into H2813. PB 429 would then be able to tell Jonah exactly when and at what speed the Chinese entered the corridor. Jonah would have nearly three days to position his forces. In the simulation, this was done at the beginning to save time.

He activated the three-dimensional holographic display above the conference table and established direct comm links to the fleet. The computer would determine at what speed the 'enemy' fleet would be entering hyperspace and share it with Jonah, as PB 429 would report it. The computer would decide whether its fleet would follow the hyper corridor until its end at the heliopause or exit it early, and at what point. Jonah would not know where the exit point was until the simulated Chinese fleet appeared.

Jonah was alerted by the programming that the enemy had entered the corridor at $0.23c$, which was usual. Jonah then entered information indicating that at the time of the expected enemy exit, his fleet would be positioned to be traveling at $0.23c$ at the normal hyper corridor exit, heading in-system to match course with the Chinese, with missile pods deployed. If the computer's 'Chinese' force exited the corridor earlier, Jonah would be in front of them. If the computer decided to go to the end of the corridor, he would drop into normal space right on top of Jonah's force.

He figured that the computer, and Admiral Xu when the real battle came, would exit the hyper corridor short of the entrance. How far short, he couldn't guess. The missile deployment plan he developed with the captains factored in an early exit. If the enemy returned to normal space at $0.23c$, even as much as thirty light-minutes short of the normal exit, their momentum would be such that they could not avoid the gauntlet of missile pods. The missiles would not be at maximum range, and the shortened distance would give the Chinese missile defense system less time to launch enough defense missiles. The Chinese system had an eleven-second cycle time. Jonah hoped it would make a difference.

With the information entered, the simulation began. Immediately, Jonah learned that the enemy exited hyperspace twenty light-minutes short of the corridor entrance. This information was captured by gravimetric sensors, which reported the arrival of five superdreadnoughts and fourteen battlecruisers. Within their effective range, gravimetric sensors had no time lag due to distance. Their capabilities were limited, though. They could report distance from, direction to, and the mass of bodies entering normal space from hyperspace. They could not report the course or speed of the enemy. Jonah's fleet would not be able to actually see the enemy until almost twenty minutes later. At that point, they would be able to determine whether the enemy fleet was adopting any course or speed changes and determine its formation.

Jonah ordered his fleet to cut acceleration to zero and drift on a ballistic course. Jonah cut acceleration to maintain contact with the enemy. If the enemy chose to accelerate, that would close the distance between the two fleets. If they chose to decelerate, it would widen the gap. Jonah's small fleet was much quicker to ramp up to full thrust, so he could overcome the delay in seeing what the enemy chose to do.

Jonah was pleased. He had the 'weather gage'—the advantage of position—as his childhood heroes Horatio Hornblower or Jack Aubrey would have termed it. Idly he thought of what it should be called in these circumstances. Time gage? Momentum gage? Regardless, he should be able to control the engagement between the two fleets.

When the time due to the light-speed lag elapsed, the simulation showed the enemy force began to accelerate. Jonah fed the numbers into his console to determine what he could do to close the distance and still not allow the enemy to overtake him. He then gave the order to his fleet to begin deceleration at eighty percent thrust and to change course for the hyper corridor that led deeper into the Commonwealth.

Over the next hour, Jonah monitored the behavior of the enemy fleet. It continued to accelerate, and it adjusted course to pursue his fleet. Jonah adjusted the deceleration of his fleet to allow the enemy to close the distance gradually. An hour and twenty minutes into the simulation, the distance between the fleets dropped to eight light-minutes. During the eighty-fourth minute, the enemy fleet reached the gauntlet of missile pods Jonah had prepared.

The enemy's course had drawn them to one side of the gauntlet. Missiles on the far side of the gauntlet would need to travel just over 50 seconds to reach their targets, but those on the side nearest the enemy would reach their targets in under 40 seconds. Those were the missiles Jonah felt would get through. All 5,400 Vulcan missiles were aimed at the superdreadnoughts. Part of the Commonwealth deployment included nine kewpie drones which connected the missile pods to the powerful computers on-board the ships.

When the sensors showed the data, nearly eight minutes later due to light-speed lag, they showed that none of the Commonwealth missiles had penetrated the enemy defense. Over the next fifty minutes, the distance continued to close. "Roll pods," Jonah called at seven minutes until missile range. When the range was closed, both fleets fired. The 'Chinese' fleet simulated by the computer fired 1,749 'Shark' missiles. Jonah's fleet fired 636 Vulcans in response.

The distance continued to close. Each side continued to fire missiles. No missiles penetrated the umbrella of the defense missile systems. As the two fleets neared the range of the BFG—as it was now known throughout the fleet—Jonah studied the two formations. The enemy was in a standard formation, with the SDNs in the center and the battlecruisers arranged around them in a ring.

Severn and *Murray* could remain out of range of the photon cannons on the Chinese superdreadnoughts indefinitely. The Chinese battlecruisers had the ability to close the distance and come within photon cannon range, though. The computer estimated it would take them less than nine minutes. It would give *Severn* and *Murray* enough time to shoot their big guns at least sixteen times before coming under fire themselves.

Both fleets continued to fire salvos of missiles at one another in the simulation. The Chinese were able to launch 804 each time their automatic reloaders cycled; the Commonwealth ships would return 204. None of the missiles breached the missile defense systems of either side.

The Chinese fleet drew within range of the BFGs. Three minutes later, two of the Chinese superdreadnoughts dropped off the display, indicating they had been destroyed. By the five-minute mark, two more of the big ships had fallen out of formation. The Chinese battlecruisers responded immediately, accelerating hard to come within range of the Commonwealth dreadnoughts. At the eight-minute mark, the last Chinese SDN disappeared from the display.

The fourteen Chinese battlecruisers closed within photon cannon range of the Commonwealth fleet. As they did, the Commonwealth ships rotated on a horizontal axis to present their noses to the advancing Chinese. The display showed *Murray* and *Severn* taking damage from the Chinese ships. The BFGs continued to fire, along with all the photon cannons on all the Commonwealth ships.

Two minutes after the Chinese reached photon cannon range, the computer simulation indicated that *Severn* had lost her ventral BFG due to damage. One, then two, then three Chinese battlecruisers fell out of formation due to damage. After another minute, the computer indicated that *Murray* suffered a hull breach and lost targeting sensors. Two more of the Chinese battlecruisers disappeared from the display, indicating they were destroyed, leaving nine still firing.

Four minutes after reaching photon cannon range, the computer indicated *Severn* had lost targeting and was suffering severe damage. Two more Chinese battlecruisers dropped away. The computer showed that *Murray* and *Severn* were out of the fight, and the Commonwealth battlecruisers were beginning to take hits. The three Commonwealth ships were focusing their fire on one target at a time but were taking heavy damage. One more Chinese battlecruiser disappeared from the plot, and one more showed serious damage, but then the three Commonwealth ships were knocked out of the fight. It left five Chinese battlecruisers relatively undamaged.

The computer simulation displayed: "Simulation Terminated."

Jonah presided over the debrief. Spirits were mixed. Captain Delhomme pretended at first to be glum. When Captain Donan asked him why, he responded, "Because I'm dead. You're not supposed to be happy when you're dead, are you?"

Though the Chinese lost all five superdreadnoughts and eight battlecruisers, five battlecruisers emerged unscathed, with one more damaged. All five of the Commonwealth ships had been destroyed.

"I got greedy," Jonah said. He activated the holographic display and moved it to the point where the fourth Chinese 527-type had disappeared. "If I had ordered *Murray* and *Severn* to go to max acceleration here, it would have given us a few more minutes to whittle down the number of battlecruisers before they reached photon cannon range."

"It would have left the one 527 still intact," Captain Mellon pointed out.

"But we would have whittled the numbers on the battlecruisers down by another four or five," Jonah responded. "They might have decided not to press home the attack."

"They took heavy losses in this sim," Captain Blutarsky commented, "and it didn't cause the computer to lose heart."

After the holographic meeting adjourned, Jonah wrote up his notes. He noticed PB 429 was nearing. He queried Lieutenant Commander Gracia about her supplies. Upon learning that PB 429 was well-stocked, he issued the orders for her to proceed towards H2813 to provide the fleet with data on the departure of the Chinese fleet.

Every day they conducted a simulation. The results varied. In most cases, the results were similar to the first, though the Commonwealth fleet was able to inflict substantial damage on the computer enemy in every case. Jonah wrote up the results and sent them in. After the fifth simulation, where all five Commonwealth ships were destroyed, allowing two 527-type superdreadnoughts and ten 461-type battlecruisers to advance deeper into the Commonwealth, Admiral Lothes sent news.

"ONI reports on-board inventory of defense missiles on Chinese ships larger than Rodinan, fewer than ours. In the latest simulation, all enemy vessels would have been easily destroyed upon entering next Commonwealth system. Lothes out."

Jonah's friendship with Captain Delhomme showed signs of strain. The few times they tried to engage in their usual light-hearted banter, it seemed forced. For the first time, they were not colleagues but superior and subordinate. It might not have been a problem if they were not in a direct reporting relationship. Jonah tried to stay out of the way as much as possible. Delhomme noticed. He appreciated what Jonah was trying to do, but there didn't seem to be the right words for him to talk to him about it.

Every day during those twelve days, Jonah checked with Lieutenant Commander Gracia, waiting for word of the appearance of the enemy fleet.

In the middle of the simulation that afternoon, his comm alerted him to an urgent message. Jonah spun around to access it.

"Six 527-type, fifteen 461-type, eight 348-type, twelve 270-type and nine frigates entered H2813. Proceeding on least-time course for corridor entrance. Expected ETA entrance 8:57. Gracia."

Well, Jonah thought, we know what's coming at least. He sent a message to the Admiralty informing them. He asked if ONI knew whether the Chinese had upgraded systems on escort ships to handle the new defense missiles. The answer came back quickly that they had only standard point-defense systems.

Jonah allowed the simulation to run its course. It was not one of the better ones. The Commonwealth fleet was destroyed, with two enemy superdreadnoughts and eight battlecruisers surviving. During the debrief, he told the captains that they had heard from PB 429 and gave them the numbers: six superdreadnoughts, fifteen battlecruisers, eight heavy cruisers, twelve light cruisers, and nine frigates. He reminded them that the escort ships did not carry the missile defense system. The additional missiles the escort ships would launch would not be enough to have any impact on the Swordfish system's effectiveness, and only the heavy cruisers carried photon cannons strong enough to damage the Commonwealth ships. He reminded the captains that, based on Gracia's report, the Chinese would be arriving near midnight, three days from now. Jonah requested that duty rosters be changed to make sure the bridge crews were well-rested in advance.

Jonah stayed up, waiting for Gracia's message that the Chinese had entered hyperspace. When she transmitted that the Chinese fleet jumped into hyperspace, he started the clock. She reported they entered at the customary 0.23c. Three days, one hour, twenty-five minutes and eleven seconds, or less, if the Chinese exited early until the climactic battle would begin. Jonah issued orders, and the fleet headed into deep space. He ordered the frigate *Bradley* to get away from the corridor exit and to retreat to safety. He ordered PB 429 to return to the Hercules system after the outcome of the battle was known.

22

Jonah found time to at least trade messages with Amy every day. She had changed her hair back to its normal color. Due to navy censorship issues, he could only tell her a very little. Even though Amy had a high enough security clearance that she was able to learn nearly everything he was doing, where he was, and what his mission was in general, he was forbidden by regulations to tell her directly. It made them confine their conversations to banal topics. She was perceptive enough to read between the lines, though, figuring out that Jonah's friendship with Pierre was suffering and offered her sympathy.

Jonah read the personality profile on Admiral Xu so many times he felt he could recite parts of it in his sleep. The morning after he heard from Gracia that the Chinese were on the way, he called Amy. The time difference was such that it was late at night for her, while morning for Jonah. He mentioned that he wished she could read the profile. Her insight was so much better than his; he felt she might be able to pull something from it. Amy calmly said, "Call me tomorrow, same time. I'll have read it by then."

"It's highly classified, Amy," Jonah protested. "I'm only getting to read it because of 'need to know.' I know you're the darling of the foreign service, but—"

"There are more things in heaven and earth, Jonah," she responded calmly, "than are dreamt of in your philosophy. Don't worry. If I find anything, I'll clue you in."

The next day Jonah called. Amy held up a copy of the report. Jonah was astonished.

"Remind me never to doubt you again, sweetie," he said humbly. "May I ask how?"

"It wasn't as easy as I thought," she admitted. "I thought Brian would get it for me, but he got nowhere. Then I called Laura. Did I ever tell you that I think Laura used to be a spook?"

"A spook?"

"A spy," Amy explained. "I'm pretty sure Laura was a spy. We can talk about that some other time. Anyway, Laura ran into a brick wall, which surprised her, she said. So, she called Celeste."

"She didn't!"

"Sure, she did," Amy responded matter-of-factly. "Next thing I know, I'm on a call with the two of them going over it. We had quite a little confab about your pal. We think we've got him figured out for you. The information is all there; you just need context. We have more context than you."

"More brains, obviously," Jonah said sincerely.

"No," she said firmly, "more context. I'm guessing that cultural appreciation is not a course offered at the academy?"

"No," Jonah answered, chuckling, "didn't make the catalog."

"Well, it's a big part of my training. Don't be embarrassed, honey, I wouldn't have the faintest idea of how to do things that you take for granted," she allowed. "I'm pretty good at what I do. Laura is maybe even better. And Celeste, even though she doesn't have the same training, is a natural talent. Anyway, context. Everyone is a product of his culture—that's context. He comes from a culture that values conformity. Edo has similar values. Are you with me so far?"

"I think so," Jonah said hesitantly.

"So, think about your guy," she counseled. "Is he a conformist?"

"I guess," Jonah said uncertainly.

"Mhm," Amy replied. "All the time? Never bucks the system?"

"Wait a minute," Jonah said, suddenly alert. "Wait. Not all the time. When he gets selected for accelerated studies, he breaks from the norm by not acting like a snob. And then, he studies history instead of engineering or physics. Reading between the lines of the profile, it kind of sounds like they were mad at him for doing that, so finagled the grades to keep him from graduating number one in his class."

"We agree," Amy confirmed. "About all that. Now let's add even more context. When he gets selected for accelerated studies, how old is he?"

"It said early in school, so eight? Nine?"

"Right around there," Amy agreed. "Everyone else in his group is arrogant and somewhat of a bully to those outside the group, but he chose to continue to be humble and nice."

"It would be tough to avoid going along with the group at that age," Jonah admitted.

"Yup. Probably cost him any chance at making friends, but he didn't change his behavior," Amy pointed out. "Probably a guy who fights quietly for what he feels is right."

"Then at the academy, he studies history when the norm is engineering or physics," Jonah added.

"Who usually studies history at our academy?" Amy asked.

"The guys who can't cut it...but this guy's brilliant—" Jonah trailed off, thinking.

Amy gave him a moment. "What's that tell you?"

"The guy loves history so much he's willing to go against the norm," Jonah stated. "Oh, wow! Amy, thank you. I think I can figure it out now, but I need time to think. I'll call you later if that's okay?"

"Happy to help. Laura and Celeste wish you the best of luck. Call me later—don't worry about waking me up."

Jonah closed the connection and started thinking about Admiral Xu in a new way. He spent the next half hour running things through his head. He then began to worry that he was going crazy and reading into things too deeply. Amy couldn't help him with this part. He reached for the comm but then pulled his hand away. After a minute's hesitation, he muttered to himself, "Damnit!" and called.

"Pierre—got a few minutes?"

"Yes, admiral. What can I do for you?" Captain Delhomme responded, wincing inside at how stiff he sounded.

"I really need to bounce something off you," Jonah asked. "I've got something I want you to read, and then I need to talk some things out. If you'd like, I'll meet you in your ready room."

"No," Pierre responded, sensing his friend really needed his help, "I'll come to your place. Need a cup of coffee?"

"That would be great, thanks."

Jonah waited eagerly. When Pierre arrived, he gave him the profile of Admiral Xu. Seeing the classified markings on it, he started to protest. Jonah interrupted him, saying, "It's 'need to know,' and I say you need to know. Or else you can't help me."

Jonah watched Pierre anxiously as he read the profile. When he finished, Jonah recounted the contextual points Amy had made. When he was sure Pierre understood, he started to explain what he was thinking, his excitement apparent.

"Okay, so Xu's a history nut, and he's willing to buck the system for things he believes in, right?

"I'm with you," Pierre confirmed.

"First attack, he goes by the book. Comes out at the end of the corridor, right into the missiles Antonelli positioned. Loses two 527s and a third damaged," Jonah recounted.

"Right," Pierre agreed, "but he still kicks the crap out of us."

"No question," Jonah said. "But he turns back after destroying Third Fleet. Here's where I think I'm getting squirrelly...I think he turned back because he was getting low on defense missiles, and he was worried that he'd run into another missile gauntlet, even though we didn't have one."

"I'd say that's a reasonable guess," Pierre shrugged.

"You would," Jonah concurred. "So would I. But that's because you and I lived through it a couple of times. Xu hasn't been in a shooting war. How would he know to suspect that there might be other missile gauntlets?"

"Because he studied what we…oh. I see where you're going with this," Pierre said, his excitement rising.

"Because he's a history buff," Jonah added, "and a diligent student. And since he didn't have experience of his own to fall back on, he made a decision based on what he studied. Being a student of history, he's likely also aware of what a pivotal moment this is for the Chinese to seize dominance. He knows opportunities like this don't come along except every thousand years or so, and he doesn't want to blow it. He pulls back. His superiors, who are all a bunch of engineers and physicists, are probably mad as hell at him for not pressing on. They want him to finish the job."

"He's studied us," Pierre said, nodding. "He knows this is a critical moment. He has to come back and finish the job. He did it by the book the first time and lost two SDNs."

"In the simulation today, which was our worst result, what did the computer do?" Jonah asked.

"Brought the Chinese out of hyper 30 light-minutes early," Pierre confirmed.

"And we had some of our worst results. Switching topics," Jonah stated, "what happened to us in Patagonia? We came out 30 light-minutes early, but Denisov was waiting for us. He guessed what we were going to do. Denisov bought his advanced tech from the Chinese. I'll bet he and Admiral Xu discussed us. One or the other of them picked up on my tendency."

"He's heading into what he figures is the climactic battle," Pierre summarized. "He knows he must not fail and wants to give himself the best chance of success. He studies who has been successful and what they did. That's us, and we exited the hyper corridor 30 light-minutes early. Hell, if he met with Denisov, he probably has copies of all the Rodinan sensor logs and probably saw what we did with the anti-matter missiles." Looking Jonah in the eye, he added, "You're not crazy, buddy."

"He's even bringing all the escorts with him to add to the traditional point-defense net," Jonah added. "He's not going to leave anything to chance."

"He's going to exit thirty light-minutes early," Pierre confirmed. "But we set up the missile gauntlet at the normal corridor exit. We don't have time to move it."

"I'm not going to. We'll make a new one here," Jonah responded, "where we expect him to drop in."

"Yup," Pierre agreed, picking up Jonah's train of thought without words, "use the ships' inventory. Based on what we saw in Patagonia and in the sims, they're useless in battle. At least out here, they'll have a chance of doing us some good."

23

With time running out, the Commonwealth fleet scrambled to set up a new missile gauntlet, using the stocks of Vulcan missiles on the ships. Each of the battlecruisers contributed 800 and the dreadnoughts 1,000. Each ship was left with 200 missiles. Jonah checked and double-checked the astrographic figures to determine as precisely as possible where the Chinese fleet would enter normal space if they dropped out of hyper thirty light-minutes early. The gauntlet created was narrower than the one at the regular corridor exit, and the missiles were not as well dispersed.

Flight time for the array of 4,400 Vulcan missiles would be roughly 34 seconds if the Chinese fleet exited precisely where the astrographic calculations indicated. Due to the margin of error in the calculations, Jonah did not dare to put them any closer. Each salvo of defense missiles from the Chinese would destroy 1,500 missiles. At 34 seconds, the last 1,400 missiles would detonate, one second after the Chinese' third salvo of defense missiles. With such a brief time for the defense missiles to reach them, some Vulcans might survive to unleash their deadly x-ray lasers.

Once the Commonwealth fleet offloaded the missiles, it proceeded further into deep space. The fleet stopped and turned back, accelerating to match the $0.23c$ speed at which the Chinese fleet would be traveling when it returned to normal space, thirty light-minutes short of the normal corridor exit. There was no time to spare.

With two hours remaining, Jonah went to his office and called Amy. It was mid-morning for her on Lutetia in the city of New Paris. When she answered, she held up her finger for him to wait, got up, and closed the door of the office she was using.

"Hey, baby," she greeted him when she sat back down, "normally, you just send me a lame text before you get in trouble."

"Hey," Jonah protested, "you said yourself that I was better in Patagonia."

"Okay, okay," she agreed dismissively.

"So," he started, after taking a deep breath, "here I am again."

Amy waited while Jonah struggled to find the words for what he wanted to say.

"We're as well-prepared as we're going to be," he explained, "but it's still going to be... crap... this is hard for me. I focus on what I can do, and I take things as they unfold and what happens, happens. It's how I've dealt with it and...but now, it's not just me. You're a part of me, and I owe you—"

"Jonah," Amy interrupted, placing her fingers on the screen as her eyes welled with tears, "I love you. I love that you're trying to reassure me. Don't worry about the things you can't control. Do what you do, take things as they come, and be who you are."

"Okay," Jonah said uncertainly.

"This was a really bad idea...you calling me," Amy remarked. "Let's go back to your lame text messages from now on, okay?"

"Okay. I love you, Amy."

"I love you, Jonah." She closed the connection.

Jonah took a minute or two to recollect himself. He put on his ship suit, then left his quarters. He grabbed a cup of coffee in the officers' mess and headed to the TAC. Since the TAC had originally been an emergency secondary bridge, it included an observation chair in case there was an admiral aboard. Jonah saw that Pierre had decorated the chair. There was a piece of red cloth draped over the back, embroidered in gold with a circlet and the words, "Baron Somerset" below. On the seat was a fat purple velvet pillow with gold tassels on the corners. He couldn't resist smiling and chuckling to himself. A weight he hadn't realized he'd been carrying lifted from Jonah's mind. The strain he had felt in his friendship with Pierre disappeared.

He removed the pillow, sat down, and activated the console. "Nice chair," he texted Pierre, "Thanks."

"Only the best for you, Lord High Muckety Muck," came the response.

As the seconds until the emergence of the Chinese fleet ticked away, Jonah started to worry whether he had guessed right, whether the Chinese admiral would exit where he hoped. Amy's advice to take things as they were helped calm him. It was too late to change things now anyway.

Instead, he focused his mind on what he hoped would be occurring shortly. If all went the way they planned, the Chinese fleet would exit right into the missile gauntlet he had prepared. His two Commonwealth dreadnoughts would be within range for their BFGs. If he were lucky, the first shots would hit as the Chinese shields were still coming up. They would then have a running gun battle through the second gauntlet of missiles.

Whatever happened to his fleet, though, Jonah at least had the satisfaction of knowing that they would greatly deplete the Chinese inventory of defense missiles. He hoped it would force them to turn back again. If it didn't, he was confident Admiral Lothes and Home Fleet could finish the job.

As the countdown clock approached zero, Jonah realized he was holding his breath. He forced himself to let it go just as the timer reached zero. A tick later, the icons for the Chinese fleet appeared on the huge holographic display in the TAC. Jonah allowed himself a moment of satisfaction before turning his attention to what was happening.

The 4,400 Vulcan missiles ignited, streaking for the six Chinese superdreadnoughts. Four of those 527-types were within range of the Commonwealth's big guns. The Chinese fleet launched its own missiles in response. Twelve hundred and forty-four Shark missiles flew at the five Commonwealth ships.

"Two hits from the BFGs," reported the chief petty officer manning sensors. "Substantial damage. Hull breach, bow-on."

The two big guns on the Commonwealth dreadnoughts had hit two of the Chinese 527s right on the nose. How much that would affect their performance remained to be seen, but Jonah felt it was a good start. The missile tracks of both fleets reached towards one another. Swordfish defense missiles rose to meet them from the Commonwealth ships. The Chinese defense missiles launched as well. Jonah caught himself musing on how rapidly things had changed. Three years ago, facing a salvo of 1,244 enemy missiles would have spelled certain death for his small force. Today, it didn't even concern him. He turned his mind back to the action.

"Enemy fleet is accelerating," called the astrographics officer. "Max thrust."

Jonah keyed into his command console, "Maintain current distance from enemy." The message was sent to all five captains.

"One hit," Sensors called out, reporting on the BFGs, "one miss. Different targets. No hull breach, but shields are gone on a quadrant of one of the 527s."

Thirty-nine Vulcan missiles survived the Chinese missile defense and point-defense net and detonated. Two of the superdreadnoughts lit up on the display. The CPO on sensors announced, "The two ships hit first by the BFGs are heavily damaged. Significant hull breach on the third where the shields were taken out. Spotty shield failures on the other three. Two have hull breaches but minor."

"The two heavily damaged SDNs are drifting, and the SDN with the hull breach is dropping behind," astrographics reported. "Out of range of the BFGs."

"Two misses," announced Sensors when the big guns fired again. "They must be doing some serious evasive."

Jonah keyed in a command to all captains, "Analyze enemy evasive action. Find the patterns. Don't fire Vulcans."

The Chinese fleet launched another salvo of Shark missiles. This time only 1,097 came out to attack the Commonwealth fleet. Sensors reported the launch and confirmed that the Swordfish system had acquired the enemy missiles and was responding.

"Eight enemy 461s are closing the gap with *Murray* and *Severn*," astrographics reported. "Forty-five seconds until they reach photon cannon range."

"One of the heavily damaged SDNs just blew up," sensors called out, as the icon marking it disappeared from the plot.

Jonah keyed, "*Murray* and *Severn*, disengage from 527s and maintain separation from 461s. *Achates*, *Euryalus* and *Pallas* prepare to support against advancing 461s. All ships, execute corkscrew when range is closed."

"The 461s are still closing the gap, sir," astrographics reported, "but more slowly. Time to range now two minutes plus."

"One hit on a 461, one miss," Sensors called out with results from the BFGs. "Significant hull damage—bow-on."

"Damaged 461 dropping back," came from astrographics. "Seven continue to advance. Time to range two minutes, ten seconds."

The Chinese launched another salvo of Shark missiles. The total number dropped to 1,072. When the dreadnought guns cycled again, sensors reported another hit and another miss. The second damaged battlecruiser also dropped back. On the next cycle, both shots from the BFGs missed. Astrographics reported the time to photon cannon range was now one minute, forty seconds.

"Two hits," Sensors announced. "Shield failures, no hull breach."

"Six 461s continue to advance," astrographics called out. "Time to range one minute, ten seconds."

As the clock ticked, the distance continued to close. When another thirty seconds passed, Sensors announced, "Two misses."

The enemy battlecruisers were now forty seconds from photon cannon range. Jonah said a silent prayer for the gunners. He sat, leaning against the restraints on the chair, waiting for Sensors to update.

Before the Sensors petty officer spoke, Jonah saw two icons disappear from the display. "Two hits, two 461s destroyed," Sensors confirmed.

"Four 461s closing," called astrographics, "in five, four, three, two, one…they're in photon cannon range. Second group of 461s accelerating—seven of them. Time to range is thirty minutes plus."

"We're getting some shield failures on *Murray* and *Severn*, with some minor hull breaches," the lieutenant on damage control announced. "Two on *Murray*, three on *Severn* so far. *Pallas*, *Achates* and *Euryalus* undamaged."

"One hit, one miss," reported Sensors. "Significant hull breach on the hit."

"All four 461s falling back out of photon cannon range," reported astrographics. "Second group of seven has slowed their advance. Second heavily-damaged SDN has broken up."

"More hull breaches on *Murray* and *Severn*," damage control announced, "including a couple of severe hits on both. Both ships losing atmosphere."

"Nine hundred and eighty-one missiles launched," Sensors reported as the Chinese fleet fired again at the Commonwealth fleet. "Swordfish is responding."

Jonah's console beeped with an incoming message from Captain Blutarsky. "Sensors report a shuttle flight from damaged 527 to undamaged."

Jonah acknowledged the message. He saw an icon disappear from the display. "Two hits," Sensors announced. "One 461 destroyed, one damaged—significant shield failure."

"The enemy has flipped!" the lieutenant at astrographics called excitedly. "They've flipped. Decelerating at max thrust! The damaged 527 and two 461s are slipping out of position."

"BFGs out of range," Sensors reported.

Jonah keyed into his command console, "All ships, reverse thrust, maintain current separation from enemy."

"*Severn* and *Murray* are asking to commence damage control EVAs," reported the lieutenant at the damage control station.

"Negative," Jonah responded. "No one outside the hull while the missiles are flying."

Jonah looked at the holographic display. The Chinese fleet would pass the normal hyper corridor entrance, even decelerating as hard as they could. It would slow their passage through the missile gauntlet, though, which would give their defense system plenty of time to eliminate all the Vulcan missiles that would fire. He wondered if that were Admiral Xu's intent or if he would continue to decelerate and try to return to system H2813.

"Nine hundred and eighty-one missiles inbound," Sensors reported. "Swordfish is responding."

He consulted his command console to see when the big guns on the dreadnoughts would be in range of the undamaged Chinese superdreadnoughts and where it would be in relation to the missile gauntlet. *Murray* and *Severn* were able to ramp up to full acceleration (or deceleration, in this case) more quickly than the 527-types. Jonah's command plot showed that the undamaged Chinese 527s would not come within range. Surprised, Jonah reviewed the fleet movements during the engagement.

"Oh, good move, admiral," Jonah commented under his breath, "but are you retreating or just slowing?"

The Chinese admiral had used the attack of his battlecruisers to allow the gap to increase between his superdreadnoughts and the Commonwealth fleet. He had cut thrust to zero. The increased distance made up for the slower response of his bigger ships. *Murray* and *Severn* would come tantalizingly close to being within range, within 1,000 kilometers, if the Chinese continued to decelerate and head back out of the system. If the Chinese were merely slowing to get through the missile gauntlet, the Commonwealth's big guns would have another chance.

Over the next two hours, Jonah watched as the Chinese fleet continued to slow as it approached the missile gauntlet. The three damaged Chinese ships and the two large pieces of the broken SDN had fallen away from the rest of their fleet. As each of the damaged ships approached the range of the Commonwealth dreadnoughts and their guns, they dropped shields one at a time and transmitted their surrender, though the broken ship had no shields to drop. Jonah ordered them to continue to decelerate as best they were able. He made sure the surrendered ships were removed from the targeting of the Vulcan missiles in the waiting gauntlet.

When the Chinese fleet reached missile range of the gauntlet, Jonah was strangely gratified to see Admiral Xu launch four dozen missiles. The missiles likely contained anti-matter warheads and were sent to cut down the number of Vulcans that would attack. Jonah had done the same thing a year and a half before against the Rodinans, so he considered Admiral Xu's use of the same tactic as a compliment. The Commonwealth missiles were more spread out than the Rodinans had been, but Xu compensated by firing more anti-matter warheads.

Xu's tactic eliminated over a third of the Commonwealth missiles, and his missile defense had no difficulty destroying the rest. Jonah watched carefully to see if Xu would continue to slow and reverse course back to the hyper corridor. When he was sure that was the case, Jonah issued recall orders to Lieutenant Commander Gracia on PB 429 to boost for the hyper corridor back to Commonwealth space.

The Chinese fleet eventually reversed their momentum and began heading back to the hyper corridor. Their adventure into the Hercules system had cost them two superdreadnoughts destroyed and one captured, along with three battlecruisers blown up and two captured. Most of their capital ships had taken some damage, and it appeared as though Admiral Xu had needed to shift his flagship in the middle of the engagement. Nevertheless, he escaped with three superdreadnoughts and ten battlecruisers.

Jonah's small fleet had suffered damage, with *Severn* and *Murray* hit the worst. Crews were on the hulls, and the ships were already under repair. He waited until the Chinese ships winked out of normal space, jumping into hyperspace at the corridor entrance. He then issued orders for the fleet to pursue the three Chinese ships that had surrendered and the pieces of the other and offer them all possible assistance.

Jonah pondered why the Chinese admiral had broken off the attack. If the Chinese had continued, they would have been able to destroy the five ships of his tiny Second Fleet. Granted, it would have cost them dearly, and they would have lost between two and three ships of their own for every Commonwealth ship destroyed, but they would have eliminated the only ships in the Commonwealth navy that could mount any sort of defense. Jonah could only guess that Admiral Xu did not know how total his destruction of the Commonwealth's capability would be and was unwilling to risk his fleet to accomplish the task.

Looking at the time, he decided to grab some breakfast before filing his reports. By the time he finished breakfast, the first report had come in from *Euryalus*, chasing the broken ship. There were life signs in both halves, and *Euryalus* would be mounting a search and rescue operation as soon as they closed the distance. Jonah sat down to write his after-action report. After he sent it, he sent a brief message to Amy.

"Long night, sweetie, but a happy ending. I've gotta sleep now, but I'll tell you all about it soon. Couldn't have done it without you. Love, Jonah."

24

"Congratulations, admiral," Admiral Lothes said. Her call to Jonah had awoken him after only four hours of sleep.

"Thank you, Admiral Lothes," Jonah replied. "It was a near thing. If they had pressed their attack, they would have destroyed us. Their losses would have been at least double what they took, but they would have been able to take all five of our ships out."

"Well, thank heavens they didn't. As it is, we believe you bought us the one thing we needed most," she commented, "time. We're still outnumbered and still back on our heels, but we hope we have a little breathing room now. Well done. The First Space Lord has decided to issue a Royal Unit Citation to Second Fleet. His office will be setting up a time to conduct the ceremony with you. They'll do over the comm, but it's going to be an 'all hands on deck' showing for the five ships."

"Seven, sir," Jonah corrected. "PB 429 and HMS *Bradley* also played their part and deserve to be included."

"Seven it is," Lothes agreed. "Now, to business. Transports are on the way to pick up your prisoners. Freighters are bringing fresh supplies and restocking your weapons. A fuel tanker is on the way to top up your tanks. Three salvage tugs will be coming to retrieve the enemy ships. By the way, Director Niven is strutting around like a proud new father. The damage the PBGs caused makes those ships look like tin toys hit by a baseball bat. Which reminds me, the official nomenclature remains PBG, not BFG. Even though the new acronym has gained widespread adoption throughout the service and even by the king, it has not yet been approved for official use. I'll be sure to notify you when that changes."

"Aye, aye, admiral," Jonah replied with a smirk, "it won't happen again."

"Second Fleet is to remain on station in Hercules. In reviewing your recent reports, I have a couple of questions," Lothes continued. "I agree with you shifting your flag to *Pallas*. How do you think things are going for Captain Blutarsky on *Severn?*"

"All I have is scuttlebutt, admiral," Jonah confessed. "I wanted to give him space to make the ship his own. I've heard a lot of good things through the grapevine about John and about his new XO. I think the ship is happy."

"That's my sense, too," she replied. "How is young Colehower working out?"

"The lad has been a godsend, admiral," Jonah admitted. "I didn't know all the crap you admirals had to deal with. He is all over that paperwork, and I love him for it, but I think he has more potential. He really wants to be a line officer, though, not staff. I'll be keeping my eye open for a suitable slot if one opens up in Second Fleet. If you learn of one sooner somewhere else, please let me know. I don't want to stand in his way."

"That's good to know," she confirmed. "I'll keep my eyes open for him and for a potential replacement. Now, last thing. I have to ask, how did you guess Admiral Xu would exit where he did?"

"My wife, sir," Jonah informed her.

"Your wife?"

"Yes, sir, my wife."

"How could she help?"

"My wife assisted me in interpreting the personality profile that ONI provided."

Lothes looked at Jonah sternly. "How did she obtain a copy of the report, admiral?"

"Not from me, admiral," Jonah replied, with a look of relieved innocence.

"That material was 'eyes only' admiral," Lothes said ominously. "If not from you, then from whom?"

"My wife has sources, sir," Jonah explained. "Sources in the highest places, but you'll have to ask her about it."

"We intend to," Lothes responded with a sly smile, "but I have a feeling from your remark that our inquiry might expire from lack of oxygen due to the altitude."

"That very well might be the case," Jonah said with a straight face.

"What insight was she able to provide?"

Jonah explained to Admiral Lothes the gist of Amy's thoughts about Admiral Xu. "I then took that information and speculated how it would influence his decision-making, admiral," Jonah recounted. "I believe his desire to escape and preserve his force also reflects that. I don't think he could believe that these five old ships are the full extent of the Commonwealth's defensive capability at this time."

"Interesting," the admiral commented. "Your wife has given me a good idea. We have psychologists analyze VIP profiles, but they have no more cultural context than I do. I'll have ONI start getting that kind of input in the future and will have them review the files of people we might encounter. There weren't the same cultural differences in fighting the Rodinans, so it didn't come into play."

Shortly after the call ended, Jonah received a message from the First Space Lord's office, establishing a date and time for the ceremony: Thursday at 09:00. Jonah forwarded the information to his captains, including Lieutenant Commander Gracia on PB429 and Commander Wang on HMS *Bradley*. Though he had hardly slept, by now, Jonah realized he might as well begin his day. He treated himself first, though, placing a call to Amy, catching her in the evening.

"Hey, baby," she greeted him, "I got your note. I was figuring you wouldn't be awake yet."

"Well, no rest for the wicked," he cracked. "I hate that I can't share details, but I know you'll get them soon if you don't already have them."

Amy chortled. "Already have them. Seems like you had everything figured out to a T."

"Sure did," Jonah agreed. "My boss called and woke me up a little while ago and wanted to know how I figured it out. I told her it was due to your help."

"Uh oh," Amy replied, "am I in trouble?"

"Well, my boss wanted to know how you got access to the profile. She thought I'd broken the rules, but I was able to convince her that you had your own sources—the highest sources. My boss seemed to think her inquiry would run out of oxygen before it climbed high enough to reach your sources. I didn't disagree with her."

"Okay, good. Thanks to you, I received some good news today, too. They're sending the diplomatic shuttle to come pick me up. I'll be back on Caerleon in eight days."

"They think it'll be safe enough?" Jonah asked.

"They do now," she answered. "I still can't go outside here on Lutetia, but they think we'll make it home safely. Your win has a lot to do with that."

"It wasn't so much a big win," Jonah said humbly, "as it was avoiding a big loss."

"No," Amy countered, "the prevailing view amongst the VIPs is that it was a *big* win."

"How do you hear all this stuff?" Jonah asked.

"I could tell you, but then — "

"Yeah, yeah," Jonah said in defeat. "Well, if the VIPs are happy, who am I to deny them that happiness?"

"Exactly."

"I'm glad you're heading home. I don't have a clue when I'll able to get away," Jonah sighed. "Probably going to take some time before we can go on our honeymoon. You mentioned passionate, animalistic sex, and that would be a great way to celebrate my 'big win'."

"We'll just have to be creative," Amy replied. "I did tell you I received a shipment from Gauthier, didn't I?"

"You hadn't mentioned it."

"Maybe that's because I was waiting to show you, baby," Amy said. She stood and walked away from the camera so that Jonah could see she was dressed in amazingly sexy lingerie.

Jonah made sure the door to his office was shut.

25

The next four months dragged by in a thankfully dull routine. One of the early highlights was the awarding of the unit citation by the First Space Lord. Once Lieutenant Commander Gracia had the chance to resupply following the ceremony, Jonah had ordered PB 429 to return to system H2813, proceed through the empty system H2896, and into the Chinese Múxīng system. It took PB 429 over a month since Lieutenant Commander Gracia was under orders to avoid detection. That required her to exit hyperspace well outside each system and look for Chinese ships.

According to ONI, the Múxīng system usually had little naval presence. The closest naval station and shipyard was one system further into Chinese space, the Límíng system. PB 429 was able to confirm that assessment. A battlecruiser and some escort ships were stationed in Múxīng, but there was no sign of the fleet which had tried to invade Hercules. PB 429 escaped the system, leaving behind a stealth drone. She also left a stealth drone at the hyper exit between Múxīng and system H2896.

Amy kept Jonah up to speed with things on the larger diplomatic front. Public unease had calmed down on Lutetia and Rotterdam. Jonah's ability to prevent the Chinese from wiping out the rest of the Commonwealth navy immediately had given them hope that their planets might be safe for now. Edo was still unable to dislodge the Chinese from the system the Chinese had seized. The Chinese were tightening their grip on New Delhi.

As far as the war was concerned, the Chinese navy still had an enormous advantage in capital ships. Both the Commonwealth and the Chinese were upgrading the rest of the ships in their fleets with the new computer systems that enabled the use of the Swordfish missile defense system (and its Chinese equivalent) and the ability to control large numbers of offensive missiles. Three more reworked *Columbia*-class dreadnoughts had been finished at the Twelfth of Never, *Yukon*, *Waikato,* and *Fraser*. *Yukon* and *Waikato* had joined

Fourth Fleet, *Fraser*, Fifth. Two more were due—one for Fifth Fleet and one for Home Fleet.

Jonah was reviewing logistic reports when he noticed he received an official communique from the Admiralty. These types of communiques usually contained official orders. Not expecting much, he opened it. He was stunned to learn that he was to board a Navy courier ship in three days and report to the Admiralty. He was to turn command of Second Fleet over to newly-promoted Rear Admiral Pierre Delhomme. He could hardly wait to give his good friend a hard time. Lieutenant Colehower would also be returning with him. The courier boat would be delivering a new flag lieutenant for Delhomme.

Once again, the ships within the Hercules system gathered their crews as the change of command ceremony was broadcast from *Pallas*. Jonah broke protocol and gave Pierre a hug after the formal salute. He had queried Admiral Lothes about what his new posting would be, but she had delayed, telling him he would find out once he returned.

It was a thirteen-day journey back to Caerleon. During the journey home, he asked Amy if she had heard anything about his possible assignment or the reason for his recall, but she stated that she had not. With no responsibilities, he was bored. He spent time exercising and reading. Colehower amused himself with video games. When Jonah showed him how to access combat simulations on the Admiralty net, Colehower was thrilled.

Jonah and Colehower were ordered to report to the Admiralty offices on Caerleon Station when the courier boat docked at the Navy section. Jonah walked briskly, carrying the two pieces of luggage he had. At the office, he was ushered in immediately. Jonah dropped his bags outside and entered to see Admiral Lothes behind the desk. Jonah saluted three paces in front of her desk. She returned the salute and waved at him to sit. She did not look happy.

"Admiral Lord Halberd," she began grimly, "I have been ordered...to send you on your honeymoon." She passed him his written orders with a grin she had been suppressing.

Jonah started to smile but held it in check. "Ordered, admiral?" he said, pretending to frown as he looked down at the orders.

"Yes, admiral," she confirmed, regaining her firm tone. "And before you start to question the merits of this posting, let me inform you that these orders come from high up the chain of command." She said this as though she disagreed with the orders.

"How high, admiral?" Jonah inquired.

"High enough that you would get a nosebleed," she said.

"Then I have no choice, admiral. I must obey my orders without question and do my duty for king and country and for the good of the service," Jonah stated solemnly.

"Indeed, Admiral Lord Halberd," she confirmed. "Please note you are to report to my office, planet-side, four weeks from today, at 09:00."

"Aye, aye," Jonah confirmed. "May I ask what has changed in the overall situation that makes it possible for me to leave?"

"You may," Lothes answered. "ONI reports there was turmoil within the governing council of the Chinese republics. There was a faction that wanted to continue to prosecute the war and seize the opportunity they have created. They wanted to press another attack immediately. It has been more than four months now, and this group still does not have the votes on the council to win the day. Admiral Xu's failure to punch through your defense cost them support. They blamed Xu for cowardice. He had been relieved of duty, though not arrested, as far as we know."

"What happens if this group gains enough votes?" Jonah asked. "Won't they launch an attack immediately?"

"ONI has studied the present disposition of Chinese assets," Lothes responded. "Even if the war party gains control tomorrow, which ONI believes is unlikely, they would still need at least two weeks to position the ships for an attack. If they did act, they would not find us so easy a target as they did before. Upgrades have been proceeding throughout the navy at the fastest possible pace."

"What about the group that currently controls the governing council?" Jonah inquired. "What are their aims?"

"Two weeks ago, we received word from the Rodinan trade attaché through his contact at the foreign office that the current group in power might be interested in beginning talks to end the war. This was all very unofficial and very much back-channel, which is, of course, the way these things typically begin. It will take some weeks before anything official will happen. For this reason, we believe we can spare you and your wife for the next few weeks. Now, I understand that the HMS *Griffin* is awaiting your arrival, and there is an agent waiting to escort you to her. Goodbye and good luck, admiral."

She stood, waited for him to stand, and they exchanged salutes. Jonah left her office and grabbed his bags. Agent Smith was waiting for him in the outer office. Smith escorted Jonah out of the Admiralty section of Caerleon Station, through the public portion of the station, into the small royal section, and onto the *Griffin*.

When Jonah entered the luxuriously appointed yacht, the steward took his bags. Amy, wearing what looked like silk pajamas, was artfully arranged on the sofa. "Hello, dahling," she said in an aristocratic drawl. "So good of you to join me."

Jonah shook his head in wonderment. "How in creation did you—"

She raised her hand to stop him and held it there as though swearing an oath. "I had nothing to do with it. As God is my witness."

"Okay," Jonah said affably, "tell me what happened."

"About three weeks ago, one of the tabloids—the ones with the boobies, I think—"

"That was my favorite as a lad," Jonah admitted.

"This tabloid led with the headline: 'Heartbroken Hero—No Hope for Honeymoon.' The others picked up on it. My favorite was: 'Bereft Bride Longs for Her Lonely Lord.' It picked up steam and appeared on the major news sites and was all over social media. Captain MacLeod, Elaine, made an appearance on the news with the whole noble sacrifice, duty to king and country theme. Her message went over well—polls showed it improved favorable opinions of the navy and the war effort, but still, it wouldn't die down." There was a clunk and a shudder as the yacht disengaged from the station.

"A couple of days later, the First Space Lord was asked about it in Parliament. He really screwed things up, saying the navy didn't make its decisions based on public opinion. That went over well, as I'm sure you can guess. That night he was called into the palace and ripped up one side and down the other. Edward was furious and reminded the FSL that positive public opinion was critical when there was a war on, and we are asking the taxpayers to foot the bill.

"The next morning, the FSL stood on the steps of Parliament and apologized for giving the wrong impression. The day after that, the Rodinan trade attaché mentioned to his contact that he had heard from a reliable source that the Chinese might be interested in opening talks with the Commonwealth."

"Admiral Lothes explained this to me just now. You've been holding out on me!" he complained with mock seriousness.

"Sorry, honey," she confessed, shrugging her shoulders. "If I'd told you, then someone would have had to—"

"Kill me. I know," Jonah sighed.

"Anyway," Amy continued, "that generated a lot of activity, as you can imagine. The consensus is that the communication was on the level, and a response was given to the trade attaché. Apparently, the king then seized the opportunity and demanded ONI's assessment of the likelihood of any offensive action by the Chinese in the near term. When they responded that they believed that there was little chance of that happening, he demanded that you be brought home on leave for your honeymoon.

"The First Space Lord trotted out the next morning to face the press. He stated the navy had a new assignment for you which would not begin for two months, but since a highly qualified replacement had just been found for you, they would bring you home early and grant you leave so you could take your honeymoon. I was told to keep it all a secret. Sorry, honey."

"That's okay. The story is so bizarre and twisted, it has to be true," Jonah commented, grinning.

"Laura told me that the FSL will be resigning soon to pursue other interests," she added.

"He's pretty dim," Jonah commented, "but then, so was the last one. I'm certainly not complaining. It got me home to you, it got Pierre a promotion which he's ready for, and I'm not in trouble with my superiors. A win-win-win. Where are we going?" he asked, changing the subject. "New Wales?"

Amy stood up languorously and said, "Right now? To bed. Wild, animalistic honeymoon sex, remember? Later, New Wales."

Amy and Jonah spent most of the trip to New Wales in their stateroom, physically reconnecting. When they arrived at the planet, they stayed at the royal residence on the beach. They had been told the beaches of New Wales rivaled those on Aries, but after having been to both, they felt New Wales was even more spectacular. They spent hours on the sand and water. Amy set the tone from the first day, wearing only the tiniest bikini bottom, accessorized with a thin gold chain around her waist.

Elaine and Laura sent identical messages within an hour of one another to the couple. A reporter with a telescopic lens had taken pictures of Amy topless on the beach and of the two of them canoodling on a blanket on the sand. Amy scanned the tabloids every day after that. They agreed their favorite headline was: Hunky Hero & Dishy Diplomat Snog on the Sand.

Within two days, her rich tan had returned. By the end of the two weeks, Jonah also looked bronzed. She taught him how to kiteboard. With Jonah's experience in sail racing, he grasped the concept quickly. Agents Smith, Sauer, and Lewis had joined them and kept a discrete watch over the two. At the end of two weeks, they boarded the *Griffin* and headed back to Caerleon.

26

As ordered, Jonah appeared at Admiral Lothes office at 09:00 on the morning of August 9. After exchanging greetings, she handed him his new orders. "Congratulations, Jonah, you are now in command of Third Fleet."

Jonah looked at her quizzically. Third Fleet had been destroyed. He wondered if she was having fun with him.

Reading his mind, she said, "That's not a joke. You're thinking I've given you a fleet with no ships. Technically that's true—today. But not for long. Six months ago, I gave you a schedule. In the schedule was the next project that Director Niven had—the *Regent*-class refits. Originally, we planned to refit six hulls over a fifteen-month period. We've been able to expand and accelerate that. We're now refitting eight *Regents*.

"When I pulled the personnel and equipment from Aries and Roosevelt, I did so because the refits we've been doing in the Twelfth of Never have proven to be the most cost-effective projects the navy has done in…well, maybe ever. They'd still be a bargain at twice the price. When the Chinese came in and wiped out Aries and Roosevelt, it made me look like a mind-reader, but I had no clue they were coming. Having those workers and that equipment in the Twelfth has been a godsend.

"We kept the *Columbia*-class refits on the original schedule. All the surviving fleets have two, except Home Fleet, which only got one. All those workers we brought in, and all that equipment, have since been focused on the *Regent*-class. The first two, *Centurion* and *Henry V*, begin tuning their drives next week. I'll let you pick either one for your flagship. The other six will come two-by-two over the next two months: *Edward I, Black Prince, Duke of Marlborough, Theodore Roosevelt, Eisenhower,* and *Elizabeth Regina*.

"Those eight ships will be Third Fleet, but you will not be assigned to the old Third Fleet sector right away. We are hoping to use Third Fleet as an offensive weapon in the short term. Given that the first steps are being taken towards peace talks, we want to give the Chinese governing council some incentive to speed up the process and possibly begin to even the odds we now face. You bought us time at the Battle of Hercules, as it is becoming known. We need still more time.

"There is little desire to rush the peace process with the Chinese. If we were to meet today, we believe they would insist on keeping New Delhi at a minimum. That is unacceptable to the Commonwealth for a variety of reasons. In the last six months, we laid down keels for six superdreadnoughts of the new *Defender*-class. We've also laid down keels for ten battlecruisers of the new *Retribution*-class. Parliament just authorized funding for ten more *Defenders* and fifteen more *Retributions*. Work in the Twelfth of Never will wind down when the *Regents* are finished, and we will be bringing all the workers and equipment here to Caerleon to work on the new ships. The Caerleon Yard is already being expanded.

"There is a determination at the highest levels of government to see this war through to victory. Public opinion also strongly supports the war effort—much more than the war with the Federation. We did not start this war, but we will finish it. It is up to us to provide that victory, even though we began at a disadvantage.

"Starting immediately, you have been assigned an office here in the Admiralty. You will begin reviewing personnel files immediately. Your new flag lieutenant is waiting for you. She was trained by Colehower before we transferred him to his new post. At the top of the pile that is already stacked up and waiting for you are the candidates who Admiral Von Geisler, Admiral DiGiovanni, Admiral Delhomme, or I recommend you consider for captains. Just after that is a group of files that BuPers has compiled of XO candidates, then files for Third, Fourth, Fifth, and Sixth officers and engineering officers.

"Today is Monday. You need to have selections made for all those posts by the end of the day Wednesday. After that, I have set up a meeting for you with BuPers to begin filling out the rest of the crew on Thursday morning at 08:00. Engineering staff has already been assigned to *Henry V* and *Centurion*, so that task is off your plate. You're going to be taking a large number of crewmen right out of boot—about one-third. The person you're meeting with from BuPers will help you select the right non-coms to bring them along."

"In your spare time, admiral," she said with a hint of sarcasm, "you need to study Director Niven's notes on the *Regent*-class refits. You're booked on a courier boat to the Twelfth of Never on Saturday at 07:00. There is office space for you on the station there, but you might find more peace and quiet on your new flagship."

Seeing the look of near-panic on Jonah's face, she added, "Welcome to the seamy underbelly of flag rank, Jonah. Don't just sit there looking dismayed—you have a pile of work to do and no time to do it."

Still feeling overwhelmed, Jonah followed an orderly to the office he had been assigned. At the desk outside was a lieutenant, who jumped up when she saw Jonah and saluted. "Welcome to Third Fleet, admiral," she said, somewhat cheekily.

"Thank you, Lieutenant—" Jonah glanced at her nametag. "Srp?"

"Yes, sir. Srp. First name, Martina," she confirmed. "It's Serbian. My family never anglicized it."

"Well, Lieutenant Martina Srp," Jonah said, "we have a ton of work to do and no time to do it. Come in and tell me what you've been doing so far."

She followed him into his office. "Lieutenant Colehower spent two weeks with me before he transferred out. Between the two of us, we reviewed the files provided to us by the Admiralty and BuPers. Based on the position they would be considered for, we sorted the candidates into three groups: Probably, Clarification Needed, and Red Flag.

"There is a Captain Gessert who was temporarily assigned to you last week who has reviewed the files of the engineering candidates. She also sorted them into three groups."

"Genevieve Gessert?" Jonah asked.

"Yes," Srp confirmed, "I believe that was the captain's first name. She works for Director Niven, and Admiral Lothes diverted her here for a week while she was returning from leave. She is the one who made the decisions on engineering staff for *Henry V* and *Centurion*. She is currently in transit to the Twelfth to oversee reactor start-up and drive tuning."

"That's going to be a huge help," Jonah admitted. "I have complete confidence in her judgment. Now, why should I have confidence in yours, lieutenant?"

"Sir, I spent the last three and a half years in BuPers," Srp replied. "I've reviewed tens of thousands of personnel files and FitReps. I know all the tricks and all the games of the human resources side of things. In addition, I was a psychology major in college. I wanted to work in ONI but was assigned to BuPers."

"Will you be happy in this position, lieutenant?" Jonah asked, cutting right to the point.

"I believe so, sir," she answered. "Until I am ready to take the next step."

"Which is?"

"Moving into a line position, as Lieutenant Colehower has done," she replied.

"Fair enough," Jonah allowed. "In terms of reviewing files, how far along are you?"

"I've reviewed the candidates down to the level of sixth officer," she responded. "Below that, it's a horde of green lieutenants and ensigns right out of school."

"I believe we'll begin with the candidates for captaincies," Jonah suggested.

She showed Jonah how to access the files on the computer. "These candidates are uniformly strong, sir," she commented. "I'll be just outside if you have any questions."

Jonah dove into his own review. Each of the four fleet admirals submitted two candidates for consideration. Jonah started with Second Fleet, figuring he already would know those candidates best.

The first candidate Admiral Delhomme selected was Commander Tim McQuillin. McQuillin served under Jonah and had shown great promise. Jonah quickly marked the file, "Approved."

The second candidate was Commander Catherine Hayes. Hayes joined *Severn* to take over as Captain Blutarsky's XO just a few months ago. She was not in the position long at all. Jonah was puzzled. He read Pierre's recommendation. He stated she was clearly ready for command. Jonah called Lieutenant Srp back in.

"Yes, sir. I suspected you would have questions about Commander Hayes," Srp began. "You'll see that her first posting as lieutenant was to HMS *Colossus* in Third Fleet while it was commanded by Admiral Johannsen. She was stuck in that position longer than normal. She was on leave when *Colossus* was destroyed in the Rodinan attack. After that, she returned to Third Fleet and served on Admiral Sayyah's staff. She requested transfer repeatedly before being sent to Fourth Fleet and Admiral DiGiovanni. Once she got out of Third Fleet, her career took off. She transferred to Fifth Fleet and took command of the frigate *Tinsdale*. Admiral Von Geisler recommended her highly for the XO slot on *Severn*. Her FitReps from Captain Blutarsky are outstanding. From looking at her performance record, I can see why Admiral Von Geisler and Admiral Delhomme have recommended her."

"Why do you think she spent so much time stuck at lieutenant?" Jonah asked. "She almost missed the promotion list. It doesn't match up with the rest of her record since then. Wouldn't that be a red flag?"

"It was," Srp admitted, "so I checked up on it. *Colossus* was part of Third Fleet under Johannsen. Her captain was one of the admiral's cronies, dismissed from the service after the debacle at Roosevelt. It's not in the file, but I strongly suspect Commander Hayes was the target of sexual harassment. The FitReps from that period are all bland and non-specific. That could be due to incompetent officers, which is also likely, or it could be due to a superior withholding a more positive review as leverage. Based on what I know of the officers on *Colossus*, I suspect the latter.

"When she returned to Third Fleet, Admiral Sayyah put her in a somewhat meaningless staff position, probably because he thought she was incompetent based on the uninspiring FitReps. Even though she was in a low-level staff position, you see her FitReps take a dramatic turn. After the positive FitReps accumulated, she was approved for promotion and transfer.

"Based on her performance since, I think the navy is lucky she stuck it out. Most people would have quit if they faced the same circumstances. It tells me that Commander Hayes is extraordinarily dedicated and probably bleeds navy blue."

"Thank you for digging into this, lieutenant," Jonah offered. "That explains a lot."

Srp returned to her desk. Jonah marked Hayes' file, "Approved." He then dove into reviewing the other candidates. As Srp said, the candidates were uniformly strong. He then needed to select one of them to be his flag captain. Other than Hayes, the rest of them followed similar career paths, and their progress up the ladder was regular. As he pondered them, he remarked to himself that the only one who needed to overcome any adversity was Hayes. He decided to contact Pierre to learn more.

He opened a comm to Admiral Delhomme.

"Admiral Crapaud," Jonah said in greeting.

"If it isn't the Right Honorable," Pierre answered, "to what do I owe the honor?"

"What?" Jonah protested, "Can't an old friend check up on how his buddy is adjusting to life without him?"

"Well, everyone in civilized space knows how you've been doing," Pierre commented. "The honeymoon pictures are very popular."

"Ouch," Jonah winced. "Actually, I do have an official reason for the call—"

"Commander Hayes, right?" Pierre guessed. Jonah nodded.

"Simply outstanding," Pierre continued. "I have to get her out of Second Fleet before she takes my shiny new Admiralty away from me."

"That good?"

"Even better," Delhomme confirmed. "She's got the whole package. Bright as hell, innovative, personable, and almost as good-looking as I am."

"You forget I met her, Pierre," Jonah cautioned, "she's got you beat on that by a wide margin."

"Says you. Anyway, between the two of them, she and Blutarsky put their own stamp on *Severn* within a couple of weeks. She was a happy ship with you and Joe, but she's even happier now. Giddy, almost. So much so that I decided to ruin the mood and make her my flagship when she came back from the Twelfth."

"You moved off *Pallas*?"

"Had to," Pierre nodded. "Hurt like hell, but—"

"Been there, done that," Jonah agreed.

"Yeah. So, back to Commander Hayes. I know you've already approved her for promotion because you have learned to trust my infallible judgment. Are you considering her for your flag?"

"Actually, I am."

"Do it," Pierre said emphatically. "Let me show you something."

Delhomme punched something into his console, and a video began playing on a split-screen. Jonah watched as *Commander Hayes' Greatest Hits* came up on the screen. The video showed the bridge of *Severn* during what appeared to be a battle since the holographic display was active. Commander Hayes shouted, "A hit! Take that, you big son-of-a-bitch!" then the video skipped forward in time to show her saying, "Another hit! No breach but we fried shields. *Murray* missed, those skiving bastards." Again, the video jumped forward in time. "We have missile impacts! Come get some, bastards!" The video skipped forward again. "A hit! Right in the kisser! Did that feel good, you bastard? Huh? Oh, can't take it, can you? One 461 dropping out of formation. *Murray* missed again. Get your shit together, guys!" Another jump in time on the video. "We missed?! Those bastards are juking like crazy, probably wetting their pants. Bastards can't dance forever."

"I've seen enough," Jonah said, laughing. "Who shot this?"

"Captain Blutarsky did during the Battle of Hercules," Pierre explained. "He used his personal comm, set it to 'record,' and leaned it up where it would catch her in action. I guess she was doing this from the first sims we ran. Some people might consider it unprofessional, but I love it."

"I do, too," Jonah agreed. "And she relays all the necessary information to her captain in a timely manner, so she's not in dereliction of duty. You convinced me."

"There's something special about her, even when she's not screaming at the enemy during a fight. Hard to quantify, but I know it when I see it. She's almost as good as John right now."

Jonah nodded. "John's doing okay?"

"He's fantastic," Pierre enthused. "You know Mel, Sarah, Fred—they're all terrific captains. John is better. He just looks at things from a slightly different angle. His crew loves him. I'm glad as hell I've got him. Now, was there anything else?"

"No, that was it," Jonah admitted.

"Well, the first one is free," Pierre commented, "but in the future, I'm going to need to charge you for these kinds of calls for advice."

"I'll keep that in mind, buddy."

"Thanks, pal. I'll be seeing ya," Pierre signed off.

Jonah called Lieutenant Srp back in. "The captain candidates are all approved, and I've selected Commander Hayes as flag captain. Please do whatever you need to do to get the paperwork moving."

"Which will be your flagship, sir?" Srp asked.

"I'm told that I can choose between *Centurion* and *Henry V*. I'm guessing that there's no difference between them," Jonah remarked.

"If I might make a suggestion, sir?" Srp inquired.

"Go ahead."

"*Centurion* doesn't have a nickname, so far as I know," she said, "but traditionally, ships named after King Henry V are always informally referred to as Hotspur throughout the fleet because that was Henry V's nickname. It's a cool name," she said, shrugging her shoulders.

Jonah smiled. "I wasn't aware of that tradition, but I like it. Let's take the *Hotspur* then."

Jonah returned to the apartment he and Amy were assigned on the grounds of the Admiralty. He was as mentally drained from reviewing files as he could remember. He and Lieutenant Srp reviewed and approved all the candidates for the position of captain. They followed that by reviewing the executive officer files and selected eight and assigned them to their respective captains. After that, they tackled the engineering staff.

Captain Gessert did a thorough job. She already selected the engineering personnel for the first two *Regent*-class refits. After reading the hundreds of files, Jonah and Srp endorsed her selections for the engineering staff of the remaining six. Then they returned to reviewing third officer candidates. They managed to eliminate the candidates that Lieutenant Srp identified as 'red flag' officers. It was nearing 18:00, and Jonah needed a break. Lieutenant Srp had done a tremendous job in reviewing and organizing the candidates. Jonah would have been completely overwhelmed without her knowledge and assistance.

He told Amy that evening about his transfer to take over Third Fleet, or rather, to recreate Third Fleet. He explained how he had spent the day and what a huge help Lieutenant Srp had been. He recounted his call with Pierre and how he commented on the photos of her that a sneaky photographer with a telescopic lens had taken on their honeymoon. Amy related that she was teased as well. While the agents of the King's Own confiscated the original digital files from the photographer, copies were all over the webs, and there was little they could do about it. Amy did admit she was keeping a couple of the files that the agents gave to her.

"Why?" Jonah asked.

"So that when I'm sixty and saggy and wrinkly, I can show the grandkids that I used to be a hot babe," she explained.

"I've seen your mom," Jonah quipped, "I don't think you'll have any problem convincing anyone that you're a hot babe." That earned him a smooch.

When they finished, they both started to speak. Jonah suggested, "You first."

"Well," Amy began, "I hate to rain on your parade, but I have some maybe not-so-great news."

He motioned for her to continue. She took a deep breath. "I head out at the end of the week to take over as consul on New Bremen."

"What do you mean?" Jonah replied, not unhappily. "That's great news.

It's the logical next step on the career path for you."

"That part I'm excited about," Amy admitted. "It's the leaving at the end of the week—"

"I am, too," Jonah confessed. "My courier boat leaves at 07:00 Saturday. That was what I was going to tell you."

"— and I have a boatload of material I need to read and review before I get there, starting now," she finished.

"Likewise," Jonah commiserated. "But at least we can be in the same room while we do it, for once."

They fixed a quick dinner, then sat down on the couch to each begin reviewing their assignments. It made Jonah feel very comfortable and content to have Amy on the couch with him, even though they were both engrossed in their work. Amy felt the same.

Jonah was reviewing the material Director Niven prepared on the *Regent*-class refits. As only the second generation of superdreadnoughts produced by the Commonwealth, the *Regent*-class was smaller than the current *Victory*-class SDNs. The *Regent*-class was built at the same time as the *Viceroy*-class battlecruisers like *Achates*, *Euryalus,* and *Pallas*.

The *Regent*-class had 56 missile tubes for Vulcan offensive missiles. The refit version had 120 Swordfish defense missile tubes as well. There were eight turrets with four photon cannons in each and, most interesting to Jonah, four of the new particle burst guns. The new guns could fire two at a time on the current 30-second cycle or one at a time on a short 15-second cycle.

The refit swelled the rear of the ship from its former graceful lines. The extra space was required for larger missile magazines, the installation of the Swordfish missile tubes, and the new reactor configuration. The entire hull was recovered in AT-38 armor plating. The reactors were replaced by eight of the newest generation powerplants, arranged radially in two groups of four. Two heavily armored electrical conduits carried power to the big guns. Massive new EM drives were fitted to the stern. She would be more responsive than any superdreadnought in service currently, though a shade less quick to the helm than the *Columbia*-class dreadnought refits. Until the new *Defender*-class ships were built, these refits of nearly 180-year-old hulls would be the most powerful ships in space.

She would have a crew of 699, with 70 of those being officers. She would also carry a short battalion of marines, led by a lieutenant colonel. Fortunately, Jonah thought, the marines would handle those personnel assignments. Tomorrow he and Lieutenant Srp would finish reviewing third officer candidates and move onto fourth, fifth, and sixth officers. With Srp's help, they had made tremendous progress today. Having the officer corps for Third Fleet selected by the end of Wednesday looked possible.

27

After a grueling week immersed in personnel decisions, Jonah and Lieutenant Srp departed on the courier boat for the week-long trip to the Twelfth of Never, the location of the navy's mothball fleet, where Director Niven of Advanced Warfare was working miracles with old, long-since retired ships. Srp and Jonah continued to work the entire journey. With the ships' crews selected, now they needed to attend to logistics.

The amount of detail involved in preparing a fleet astounded Jonah. The vast majority of the logistics was automated, but it had to be set up initially and set up correctly. Lieutenant Srp was a dervish, enabling the two of them to accomplish far more than Jonah believed possible. By the time they arrived, the 'heavy lifting,' as Lieutenant Srp had described it, was complete. *Henry V* was powered up, and the EM drives tuned before his arrival. A good portion of the crew already arrived, and the engineering staff was already on board. Jonah decided to move onto the ship rather than occupy an office on the station. His decision was made easier when he saw the station was crowded to overflowing with construction-related personnel.

Jonah's quarters were spacious—luxurious by his standards. Lieutenant Srp had an office just outside, with her own cabin attached. She, too, was very pleased. The officers' mess was not yet in operation, but Jonah couldn't resist taking a peek inside. Just as he had found on *Achates*, *Henry V* had its own china and silver patterns. The tablecloths and napkins were linen, and the glasses and stemware were cut crystal.

The next morning, Jonah met with Captain Gessert, who took him for a tour of engineering. Jonah thanked her for her help in selecting the engineering staff. The ship was ready to begin trials as soon as the rest of the crew arrived. When he returned to his ready room, he saw newly promoted Captain Hayes talking with Lieutenant Srp. Hayes just arrived and was about to stow her belongings in her quarters. Jonah asked her to join him when she finished.

She knocked on his door under an hour later. Opening it, she asked, "Admiral Lord Halberd?"

"Come in." Jonah got up from his desk and went into the ready room, and waved at her to sit.

"I'm far from a stickler for formality, captain," he started to explain. "The 'Lord' stuff still seems weird and unreal. On *Severn*, everyone just used 'skipper.' When it's just you and me, it can be "Jonah' if you like."

"Katie," she replied, "Jonah. Okay—that's a little too informal just yet. I'm more comfortable with 'admiral' for now."

"That's fine, captain," he replied.

"I'm going to have to get used to that, too," she admitted. "I have to say, I was surprised to be promoted and transferred so soon. I'd only been a commander and XO on *Severn* less than a year."

"You came with extremely strong recommendations from two people I have trusted with my life—Admiral Von Geisler and Admiral Delhomme. Pierre, Admiral Delhomme, said that between you and Captain Blutarsky, you took a happy ship and made her 'giddy.' Your credentials stood out, in a good way, from the other candidates—all strong candidates—who will be your fellow captains in Third Fleet."

"He didn't show you the videos, did he?" she asked, embarrassed.

"He did," Jonah said, chuckling. "I mean, someone could look at it and say it's unprofessional as hell. But I look at it and see genuine enthusiasm, and I don't know what to call it—your 'fighting spirit'? If I were on your crew, I'd rather have an officer like you than some robotic personality."

"Whew!" she sighed.

"I think the same sort of things during a battle," Jonah admitted, "but I don't let them out—maybe I should start? I think it's great that you do. And we're going to need your fighting spirit."

"Thank you, sir. If you don't mind, telling me...I know we're reconstituting Third Fleet. Are we going back to Roosevelt?"

"No," Jonah replied. "We're not going to go back to the old Third Fleet sector. Third Fleet is being formed as an offensive weapon to take the war to the Chinese, at least for the short term. Due to the losses in Aries and Roosevelt, the Commonwealth Navy is outnumbered by a fair amount. Within two months, we will have eight ships like this. We will take Third Fleet and try to even things up."

"Oh, wow!" she breathed. "That's not a lot of time."

"We're not going to jump right off," Jonah said. "But it won't take long. Some of the crew are already on board. The rest should be here no later than Monday. That gives you the rest of the day today and tomorrow to get ready. I want to start trials no later than 07:00 Tuesday morning."

After Captain Hayes left, Lieutenant Srp stuck her head in. "Admiral,

Captain Gray of *Centurion* has arrived and is standing by waiting for you to return his call."

Jonah returned to his office and contacted Captain Alex Gray. Gray was from Home Fleet. His background was similar to the other new captains—outstanding. Jonah informed him that ship trials would begin no later than Tuesday at 07:00. Gray gulped, then said *Centurion* would be ready.

Two weeks later, Eduardo Ramonfaur arrived to take command of *Edward I* and Margaret Tramontine took the helm of *Black Prince*. Two weeks after that, Christian DiAntonio arrived to take *Duke of Marlborough* and Pablo Rocha would captain *Theodore Roosevelt*. By the end of the first six weeks, all the captains and crews had arrived. Two captains, Tim McQuillin of *Eisenhower* and Athena Papakostas of *Elizabeth Regina*, had their crews assembled, but their ships still needed to go through reactor start-up and have their drives tuned. McQuillin and Papakostas used the additional time to begin training their crews, using computer simulations on the workstations aboard their ships. Jonah learned that *Henry V* was not the only one of the ships with a nickname. The *Edward I* was also known as *Longshanks*, the *Theodore Roosevelt* was called *Teddy* or *TR*, the Eisenhower was known as *Ike*, and the Elizabeth Regina as '*Good Queen Bess*' or *Bessie*. Apparently, the names were traditional, dating back over hundreds of years of navy history.

When *Eisenhower* and *Elizabeth Regina* were ready to begin trials, Third Fleet left the Twelfth of Never. The yard workers were already shipping out, most to Caerleon Station and the yards where the six new *Defender*-class superdreadnoughts and the ten new *Retribution*-class battlecruisers were under construction and where construction of the other new ships would soon get underway. The heavy equipment that was brought in from Aries and Roosevelt Stations would follow. Jonah was given orders to take the fleet, via a round-about route back to Caerleon. The journey would take a month, traversing multiple systems and giving the ships a chance to work out the bugs.

When they arrived at Caerleon, one of the ongoing problems Third Fleet was encountering was the general unfamiliarity with the new computer systems. Along the journey, Jonah requested and obtained a number of personnel transfers to trade crew between Third Fleet and Second Fleet. The five capital ships of Second Fleet were using the new systems much longer than the rest of the navy. Three hundred veterans of Second Fleet were spread between the eight ships of Third Fleet when they arrived at Caerleon. Within two weeks, performance throughout Third Fleet began to improve dramatically.

Jonah was busy. In this, he was in harmony with Amy, who was re-establishing the Commonwealth consulate on the German planet of New Bremen. New Bremen was captured by the Rodinans during the last war. Before that, Amy was posted to that consulate. Jonah lost his ship, *Indomitable*, helping an alliance of the usually non-aligned planetary systems in recapturing it. Though technically he was only supposed to act as an 'observer,' Jonah helped stop a Rodinan counter-attack, during which his ship was destroyed.

Jonah and Amy called one another when they could. They tried to schedule their calls at regular times, but both of them were called away to deal with urgent problems often, forcing them to miss half their calls. Still, both were happily busy despite missing one another.

Jonah developed a voracious appetite for anything the Office of Naval Intelligence sent him about the Chinese. The Chinese settled 23 planets. Five of these were marginal at best, but the other eighteen ranged from merely successful to thriving. The Chinese navy had five major bases: Líming, closest to the Commonwealth's Hercules and Aries systems; Tǔxīng, closest to the Rodninan Dneiper system; Huòxīng, nearest to Edo, Lutetia, and Rotterdam; Tiānwángxīng, nearest to the Commonwealth Avalon system; and Hǎiwángxīng, nearest to New Delhi and from there the Commonwealth Southampton system.

From the time Third Fleet left the Twelfth of Never, Jonah was relentless in conducting drills and simulations. Roughly one-third of the enlisted men and women in the fleet were inexperienced when they joined Third Fleet. Even with the solid group of non-coms with which Jonah had stocked the fleet, it still took time to train the crews. The captains were reporting that good progress was being made, but none of them were satisfied. The flagship, *Henry V*, was much further along than the rest.

In the battle sims, moving Captain Hayes into the command chair had not diminished her exuberance. In addition, she recently implemented a points system in the drills, simulations, and even normal shipboard duties that pitted the three watch rotations against one another. Results were tabulated each week, and a winner for the week was declared. Red watch won twice and Blue once since the contest began, with White finishing second all three times. The winning watch got to celebrate by having a day off with the other two covering for them. The winners also were allowed to select the dinner menu for a 'victory dinner,' and all the officers from the non-winning watches had to serve the winners ice cream for dessert at the 'victory dinner.' Captain Hayes was part of the White watch and was hungry for a win.

By the fourth week, signs and posters had begun to pop up all over the ship, supporting one watch or another. Even though the stakes were small, the crew became more and more serious about winning. Jonah even overheard one crewman berating another for doing a sloppy job and then helping him do it over again before their team was given demerits that would hurt their point total. The fourth week, White finally won and celebrated in epic fashion, with a parade through the ship with Captain Hayes on their shoulders to their 'victory dinner.'

The Christmas holiday was upon them. Jonah played Father Christmas and delivered a gift to each ship. Months before, Lieutenant Srp had found an artist who painted realistic but dramatic pictures of ships. Jonah commissioned her to paint each of the ships on large canvasses that were to be hung in the enlisted mess in attractive frames. Yet when Jonah presented each painting, the real painting was covered by a large and quite garish caricature of Jonah in wearing his circlet and the red robes of a baron.

Jonah made quite a production of unveiling the awful painting of himself. At first, it was greeted by stunned silence, but most people quickly caught on that it was a joke, booing and hissing. When the boos and hisses grew loud enough, Jonah would tear away the caricature to reveal the real painting, which was greeted eight different times by enthusiastic cheering. On *Henry V*, one of the petty officers started the crew on a 'Let's go—*Hotspur*' chant, like fans cheering their team at a sporting match. Jonah had never seen a crew so spirited.

As a joke, Jonah had sent Amy two silly presents. Since their wedding anniversary was the day after Christmas, they had agreed to combine the two. Through Laura, he had a seamstress make a scandalously short dirndl with tiny petticoats to expose her legs nearly all the way up, coupled with a cleavage-enhancing low-cut bodice, in honor of her post as consul on the German planet of New Bremen. He also sent her an obscenely small pair of bikini bottoms. Her real present, for Christmas and their first anniversary the next day, was a magnificent string of pearls he had obtained through a jeweler Laura had recommended. Amy sent Jonah a framed and signed copy of one of the topless pictures taken of her on the beach as a joke and a book of photographs of their wedding and reception as the real present. Jonah knew she outdid him. She did show him how she looked in the dirndl one night and took it off to reveal the almost invisible bikini bottom. That was Jonah's favorite present.

After Christmas, Jonah suggested to the other seven captains that they might ask Captain Hayes about her use of incentives to speed the training process. Though initially skeptical, they all adopted similar contests, and Jonah was pleased to hear they were achieving accelerated improvement. Jonah wrote Admiral Lothes about it, commending Captain Hayes. Jonah also made a point to roll up his sleeves and help dish out ice cream at a 'victory dinner' on every ship in Third Fleet during the first two weeks of January. By the end of the month, all eight captains pronounced their ships and crews fit for duty.

Jonah was keeping the Admiralty abreast of their progress. It was not a surprise when his attendance was required on a conference comm for Monday, January 31. When he connected, he was mildly surprised to see Admiral Von Geisler also on the call.

28

"Admirals," Lothes began, "today we begin the process of trying to even things up with the Chinese. We are going to attack their task force at New Delhi with Third and Fifth Fleet. Third Fleet is going to continue from there and conduct a raid on the naval base at Hǎiwángxīng. After we are done with this briefing, Admiral Lord Halberd, you are to take Third Fleet on a least-time course for Southhampton, where you will rendezvous with Fifth Fleet. At Southhampton Station, you will refuel and restock any needed supplies. Once that is done, you will proceed on a least-time transit to New Delhi.

"We do not have the transport capability to bring enough ground forces to dislodge the Chinese. As of last count, the Chinese have landed well over one million troops on New Delhi. Our objective is the Chinese navy, not recapturing and holding the system. We will be transmitting a message to that effect to the resistance groups on New Delhi after our arrival. We will encourage them not to rise up at this time since we are not prepared to support them. We fear a premature move on their part would only expose them to reprisals.

"Once we disable or destroy the capital ships in the New Delhi system, Admiral Von Geisler will eliminate all assets the Chinese navy has in place while Admiral Lord Halberd takes Third Fleet and advances. Admiral Von Geisler will return Fifth Fleet to his normal sector when his part of the mission is complete. Third Fleet will advance to Hǎiwángxīng and conduct a raid with the goal of inflicting as much damage as possible on the Chinese fleet. As soon as Admiral Lord Halberd feels he has reached the point of diminishing returns, he is to return Third Fleet to Commonwealth space.

"A patrol boat from Fifth Fleet is already in the New Delhi system and has confirmed the presence of a significant missile defense. Third Fleet, along with HMS *Fraser* and HMS *Clyde* from Fifth Fleet, will force the entrance to the system. Freighters with additional supplies of Swordfish missiles will accompany the balance of Fifth Fleet to allow the ships of Third Fleet to rearm before proceeding. A complete analysis of the Chinese assets we know are in the New Delhi system, as well as those we believe you will find in Hǎiwángxīng, is attached to your orders. Good luck and Godspeed, gentlemen."

Von Geisler sent Jonah a message immediately after. "I finally get to fight alongside you. Looking forward to it!"

Jonah issued the orders to Third Fleet to begin the journey to Southampton. He reviewed the documents attached to his orders. The Chinese navy positioned three 527-type superdreadnoughts and six 461-type battlecruisers in New Delhi, along with an assortment of escort ships. An additional seven 527s and sixteen 461s were thought to be stationed at Hǎiwángxīng. The Chinese placed just over 5,700 missiles at the normal hyper corridor exit to New Delhi. It was unknown, but suspected, that similar defenses would be encountered during transit to Hǎiwángxīng.

From New Delhi, Third Fleet would need to cross through two empty systems, L7233 and L7310, to reach Hǎiwángxīng. Both hyper corridors were short. The fleet would spend more time crossing the two systems than in hyperspace between them. Jonah convened a comm conference of his captains once they were underway and shared their orders with them.

From the time they exited the Caerleon system, it took seven days to reach Southhampton, with five of those days spent in hyperspace. Upon arrival in Southhampton, Third Fleet headed to the station to refuel and pick up provisions. Fifth Fleet was waiting for them. Jonah took the opportunity to conduct joint simulations with Admiral Von Geisler based on what they expected to encounter in New Delhi. Third Fleet, along with the two refitted dreadnoughts from Fifth Fleet, would transit first. Three hours later, the balance of Fifth Fleet would jump into hyperspace.

The patrol boat hiding in the New Delhi system gave them the position of the Chinese ships, maintaining position just inside the system from the corridor entrance. The patrol boat confirmed that the Chinese prepared a missile gauntlet of 5,760 Shark missiles in 640 pods of nine missiles each. Jonah ordered the fleet, with the two dreadnoughts attached, to enter the hyper corridor at a very slow speed, only $0.03c$, and to exit the corridor five light-minutes early. The slow speed would give the Commonwealth ships plenty of time to deal with the missiles waiting for them and make it easier for them to engage the Chinese ships.

Jonah decided to watch from his ready room with Lieutenant Srp. With the movements of ten ships to coordinate, he could not afford to be distracted by the action in the TAC. At the slow speed with which they entered, it would be slightly more than an hour until they entered the range of the missile gauntlet. Though the missiles were well-dispersed, Jonah would be utilizing the anti-matter missiles that Advanced Warfare developed. The Chinese ships were maintaining position so far. Jonah ordered the Commonwealth fleet to slow further, creeping closer.

With the reduction in speed, it took just over 90 minutes to come within missile range of the gauntlet and the Chinese ships. All ten Commonwealth ships fired three of the special anti-matter missiles at the pre-positioned Shark missiles, which fired at the same time as the Chinese ships did. The anti-matter missiles sent out a shotgun blast of tiny bits of anti-matter. When the anti-matter came into contact with the missiles, massive explosions followed.

Just over 4,300 of the Chinese missiles survived the anti-matter counter-measure. The Swordfish missile defense system had no difficulty in disposing of those. The Chinese ships began to react, accelerating to approach the invading Commonwealth fleet. They would attempt to close within range of their photon cannons, based on their experience in the Battle of Hercules. Jonah ordered the fleet to decelerate. Even so, within thirty minutes, the Chinese were within range of the Commonwealth's BFGs.

During the sixteen-minute window between when the Chinese entered the range of the BFGs and when their own photon cannons could be brought into play, the ten Commonwealth ships concentrated their fire on the three Chinese superdreadnoughts, scoring multiple hits on each one. One blew up; the other two were badly damaged and began drifting. The Commonwealth fleet began targeting the battlecruisers. Before the Chinese approached photon cannon range, all nine Chinese ships were hit multiple times. One 527 and one 461 were destroyed. The other seven lowered shields and surrendered.

Jonah ordered the different ships to employ different firing protocols. *Hotspur*, *Eisenhower* and *Roosevelt* fired their BFGs one at a time, with the shorter 15-second cycle. *Elizabeth Regina*, *Black Prince* and *Duke of Marlborough* fired two guns at a time. Jonah ordered *Edward I* and *Centurion* to fire their BFGs in tandem but with a 0.5-second stagger between the two shots. He looked forward to reviewing the damage reports to see which was most effective. Jonah ordered Third Fleet to slow, waiting for the arrival of Admiral Von Geisler and the rest of Fifth Fleet.

None of the Commonwealth ships took any damage. Fifth Fleet entered on time, traveling to the normal corridor exit at the same slow speed of $0.03c$. Jonah's ships rendezvoused with the freighters and took on Swordfish missiles to replace the ones they fired. Admiral Von Geisler brought five salvage tugs. After a brief review of which of the Chinese ships were least damaged, two tugs took one 527-type superdreadnought between them (its greater mass requiring the tractors of both) and the other tugs grappled onto three 461-type battlecruisers. They left one 461-type behind that they would need to return to pick up.

The salvage crews quickly mounted temporary Alcubierre transmitters to enable the tugs to pull the captured ships back through hyperspace. One of the 527s and one of the 461s were judged to be too severely damaged to be worth the effort. Once the crews were taken off, they would be destroyed. The personnel from the surrendered Chinese ships were loaded onto the freighters, now empty, which delivered the additional Swordfish missiles. The prisoners would return to Commonwealth space for internment.

Rearmed, Third Fleet proceeded to accelerate to the corridor entrance leading to L7233. Fifth Fleet moved deeper into the New Delhi system. They forced the surrender of three frigates and two light cruisers and confiscated the cargoes of a number of Chinese freighters. Prize crews were assigned to the captured warships and all the freighters were destroyed after their crews were removed. The frigates of Fifth fleet that joined the raid hunted down and destroyed any Chinese satellites they could find. By the time Third Fleet reached the hyper corridor, Fifth Fleet had wrapped up operations and was heading back to the corridor leading to Commonwealth space.

Third Fleet proceeded cautiously, entering the corridor at the same relative speed and position as they had entered the New Delhi system. There was nothing waiting for them when they arrived in L7233. They traveled across the system, completing their repairs as much as possible, and entered the corridor to L7310. Again, they proceeded slowly and carefully. Once again, there was nothing unpleasant waiting for them when they arrived. Several hours later, when the light-speed lag had carried the sight to them, they saw a frigate exit the system through the corridor leading to Hǎiwángxīng.

29

Wang Xhu was unsurprised when he heard the door to his house smashed open, the bang of a stun grenade followed by shouting and the distinctive snick-snap of fléchette guns firing. He sat calmly, waiting. In a matter of minutes, breathless officers of the Ministry of State Security entered.

"Am I to go with you?" Wang asked. "Or am I not leaving?"

"You are to come with us," snapped one.

Wang began to rise from his seat when he was grabbed by two of the officers. His hands were bound behind his back. They marched him out of his house and into a waiting flitter.

While on the journey to wherever they were taking him, he sat calmly. He had been waiting for this as soon as he received word regarding the Commonwealth attack on New Delhi. Dong Li did not take well to failure. She had been furious months before when Admiral Xu had failed to press home his attack. She had been chafing with barely controlled rage in the months that followed as Wang had cautiously reached out to the Commonwealth, seeking an end to the war.

When he learned of the Commonwealth's attack on New Delhi and its success, he suspected she would snap. That he had been taken from his home by force was certainly a sign. He was slightly surprised she had not ordered him to be killed immediately. He guessed that there were likely two others of the governing council she had taken or killed.

With the three of them not present, she would convene the council and force through a vote to name her chairman. Though she would ordinarily not have the support of a majority, the absence of the chairman and his two strongest supporters would communicate a not-so-veiled threat to the weaker members of the council. They would fall in line behind her. To oppose her would be dangerous. She would be confirmed unanimously.

She and Wang had seen the same information and interpreted it completely differently. The ability of the Commonwealth to thwart Admiral Xu's attack with five obsolete ships had enraged her. It had scared Wang. Wang agreed with Xu's decision to withdraw. Dong was furious that Xu had not destroyed the Commonwealth force, regardless of the cost in ships and crew.

Wang Xhu felt Xu's retreat showed that further destruction of the Commonwealth navy would only come at great cost. As a result, he had concentrated the efforts of the republics on strengthening their hold on New Delhi. He had intensified efforts behind the scenes with the politicians on Rotterdam and Lutetia who were already under Chinese influence. Given more time, he was sure he would have been able to gain control of both, with their own governments acquiescing. The longer things dragged on in their current state, the better, as far as he was concerned. Far more attractive to have Lutetia and Rotterdam join the Republics somewhat willingly, led by governments controlled by the Chinese, than to take them by force. The sullen non-cooperation they were facing in New Delhi was proof of that.

Dong Li felt Admiral Xu's retreat was a failure of will. She was not content with the gains made so far and had been pressing for further attacks against the Commonwealth. She had argued for the armed invasion of Lutetia, Rotterdam, and Edo. She cared nothing about the logistics of sending armed forces of occupation. There was no doubt that the republics could easily achieve the military objectives. The political objectives were far more resistant to a brute-force approach.

The Commonwealth's attack on the forces surrounding New Delhi was disturbing, Wang admitted to himself. The Commonwealth ships in New Delhi had all been armed with the new weapon the Commonwealth had first demonstrated in their defense of Admiral Xu's attack. Granted, the Commonwealth ships were refits of obsolete, long-retired vessels, but the upgrades made to them were impressive. They showed huge enhancement of their power plants, based on the emissions signatures, probably made necessary by the far greater mass of each of the ships. Plus, they had the new artillery weapons.

These developments gave Wang reason to pause. They had enflamed Dong, inciting her to immediate action. It was a pity their existing networks of spies and informers had all been wrecked by the new director of the Commonwealth's Office of Naval Intelligence. In the past, information had always been available for the right price. After all, it was what had gained them access to the anti-missile defense system and the enhanced computer system architecture required to use it. Time would tell who was right. Perhaps he might even live to see it.

The flitter had been traveling further into the countryside. Eventually, it reached an isolated estate, perched attractively on a slope overlooking a lake. In other circumstances, he would have been pleased to visit.

When the flitter landed, he was escorted into the house, treated more gently than he had been when they had hustled him aboard. He was taken into a library. His restraints were cut off, and he was asked politely to sit and wait.

Within a few minutes, Dong Li entered, flanked by what he assumed was a bodyguard. Wang had no weapons and was a couple of decades past the time when he would have considered any sort of physical attack upon her. He rose smoothly from his seat when she entered.

"I regret that circumstances have forced me to this," she began. Polite words, but her tone was steely.

He gave a slight nod in response.

"You will record a message for the governing council," she stated after waiting in vain for him to say something. "You will state that the Commonwealth's attack on our forces at New Delhi has shown you that you were mistaken in your approach and that you now fully support me. You will also offer your resignation as chairman and recommend that I be selected to succeed you. You regret your inability to deliver this message in person, but the strain of leading the republics in these turbulent times has taken a toll on your health, and you need to rest and recuperate for some time."

Wang Xhu nodded again.

"You will do this?" she demanded.

"Yes," he confirmed.

"Willingly?" she inquired.

"For the good of the republics," he responded. "You have already seized control of the reins of power. You hold me captive. You could easily kill me. You will become the chairman of the council whether I agree or not. Though you and I disagree on the course of action, we both want what is best for our people. I believe your plans put us on a path that leads to destruction, but for you to succeed, we must be united in purpose. Otherwise, the slim chance of success will disappear."

Her expression did not soften. She indicated the desk. "There is a statement prepared for you to read. You may have a few minutes to change the wording to your liking, so it sounds more your natural style. I will return when you indicate you are ready to deliver that message."

Dong Li turned abruptly and left the room.

30

During Jonah's transit of the two systems, he had plenty of time to review the data from the attack in New Delhi. He and Srp found that firing two shots simultaneously was the least effective in terms of causing damage. Both shots would either hit or miss, though if the paired shots hit, it would result in an almost complete elimination of the target's plasma shielding, even away from the target area, as the particle burst would overwhelm the shielding. Firing both shots with only a 0.5-second gap between them was extremely effective, but, again, if one missed, both missed. Firing on the shorter 15-second cycle was the most effective. Though there were misses, the two ships destroyed in the attack had been hit using this method.

They entered the corridor to Hǎiwángxīng. Jonah had decided to move a little faster, so they entered at $0.1c$. To compensate, he ordered the fleet to emerge from hyperspace ten light-minutes short of the end of the corridor. He expected to find five 527-type superdreadnoughts and fourteen 461-type battlecruisers. He also expected to find a missile gauntlet waiting.

Third Fleet emerged from hyperspace, activating their plasma shields and using their sensors to conduct a high-powered sweep of their immediate front. There was indeed a missile gauntlet waiting for them at the normal corridor exit. It would take 65 minutes to come within range of the missiles making up the gauntlet. Immediately behind the gauntlet was the Chinese fleet. There were seven 527s, two more than expected, and fourteen 461s. Jonah was again watching from his ready room with Lieutenant Srp.

Twenty minutes after entering, sensors on all ships reported they were about to enter a debris field. Something didn't seem right to Jonah. They hadn't passed the normal corridor exit. Debris would have been caused by some sort of explosion, but since this was past the normal corridor boundary, a ship explosion didn't make sense. Blowing up an asteroid to remove a navigation obstacle didn't make sense either.

He queried Captain Hayes. "Is the debris field expanding?"

A moment later came a different sort of answer when one of the pieces of debris exploded—a nuclear warhead pumping an x-ray laser at the nearest ship, the Roosevelt. Shit, Jonah thought, mines. No one has used mines in hundreds of years.

Jonah keyed into the captains' comm: "Debris field is mines. Target with Swordfish if possible, point defense lasers otherwise."

More of the scattered warheads exploded, with x-ray lasers hitting every ship in Third Fleet before the point-defense network acquired targets and the lasers began destroying them along the fleet's path. Damage control reports were coming in. All eight ships were hit at least three times, with *Edward I* hit five times and *Roosevelt*, six. *Edward I* suffered damage to her drives, and *Roosevelt* had huge hull breaches on its starboard and dorsal sides. The massively armored conduit powering the two BFGs on its dorsal side was severed through the hull breach. All eight ships reported hull breaches, casualties, and shield outages.

Jonah was most immediately concerned with the damage to the EM drives on *Edward I*. That had the potential to affect the entire mission. If the ship could not be repaired quickly, he would need to order her to return to safety. The rest of the fleet would need to protect her. In the meantime, they were still approaching the missile gauntlet and would be within range in less than an hour. Jonah did not order an increase in speed, so the fleet was still traveling at $0.1c$. The Chinese fleet was still lying in wait.

Edward I still had its BFGs intact. *Roosevelt*, without one of its electrical conduits, had two BFGs out of action. The two remaining would need to be monitored carefully to make sure they did not overheat the remaining conduit. On all eight ships, EVA teams were on the hulls repairing and replacing shield units and Alcubierre field generators. They would need to be recalled to safety before the fleet reached the missile gauntlet.

Jonah watched the damage control updates coming in from all eight ships. The six lesser-damaged ships, along with *Edward I*, were making good progress in restoring full shields and Alcubierre field generation capability. *Roosevelt* was not. The two holes in her hull would be unshielded and vulnerable. Repositioning the Alcubierre field generators to work around the gap in the hull would also take many hours. *Roosevelt* could not return to hyperspace until those repairs were made.

With *Edward I*'s EM drives crippled, Jonah would not be able to dictate the pace of the encounter to come. The fleet would be limited to whatever maneuvers *Edward I* could perform, at least until she could return to hyperspace and escape the system. As they approached the missile gauntlet, Jonah read that *Edward I* had managed to restore function to two of its four drives.

The fleet would enter missile range in a few seconds, but it would be another hour before they drifted far enough to re-enter hyperspace. Jonah asked *Edward I* to begin testing her repaired drives to see if a harmonic tremor had developed. He ordered the fleet to adjust course to compensate for the small changes in velocity that might occur.

When the fleet reached the missile gauntlet, the eight ships fired thirty-two anti-matter weapons to eliminate as many of the waiting missiles as they could. Over 2,500 missiles survived, but the Swordfish system was able to destroy them easily. Through the gauntlet, Jonah ordered the fleet to reform with *Edward I* and *Roosevelt* in the center of the formation. The Chinese fleet began to move towards them. Jonah ordered *Edward I* to decelerate to the limit of her capability. Captain Ramonfaur replied that they could engage only fifty-percent thrust from the two remaining drives. The other ships matched course and speed.

Jonah figured the Chinese admiral was accelerating towards his fleet to reduce the amount of time his ships would be in range of the BFGs before their own photon cannons could hit the Commonwealth ships. Jonah ordered the fleet to cease deceleration before the Chinese fleet reached photon cannon range and rotate their ships to face the 21 Chinese ships bow-on. After the initial pass, Jonah figured the Chinese would brake, reverse course, and attack his fleet again.

With the current velocities, the Chinese would be within range of the BFGs for five and a half minutes before their own photon cannons were in range. Using the fifteen-second cycle, each of the Commonwealth ships should be able to get twenty-three shots off, although *Roosevelt* might not. Both fleets would be in photon cannon range for seven minutes and 21 seconds after that. As soon as the Chinese passed out of photon cannon range, Jonah planned to begin decelerating again. The Chinese would likely wait to get out of range of the BFGs before decelerating to reverse course.

Jonah noticed that neither side was firing missiles. Since both fleets had effective missile defense systems, there wasn't much point in doing so. Jonah thought to himself that they really had entered the post-missile age.

The Chinese fleet entered the range of the Commonwealth's BFGs. Jonah ordered *Centurion, Edward I, Elizabeth Regina,* and *Duke of Marlborough* to concentrate their fire on the 14 battlecruisers. *Eisenhower, Black Prince, Roosevelt* and *Hotspur* would be targeting the superdreadnoughts. Jonah watched the display intently, hoping his fleet could whittle down the Chinese before they reached photon cannon range.

The holographic display began to show sensor blooms when the Commonwealth BFGs hit. One 527-type superdreadnought disappeared from the display before the first minute was up. Three of the 461-type battlecruisers disappeared immediately after. That still left six superdreadnoughts and eleven battlecruisers, though there was damage indicated on some of them.

In the second minute, two more SDNs began drifting, their acceleration stopped and shields down. Two more battlecruisers blew up. Another broke into multiple pieces. A fourth drifted without power. *Roosevelt* reported its remaining electrical conduit was overheating and she was going to slow to a 30-second rate of fire.

The third minute saw the explosion of two more of the Chinese superdreadnoughts, with another now powerless and without shields. Three more battlecruisers disappeared from the plot as they exploded. There were now only two Chinese SDNs and four battlecruisers. They were still over two minutes from reaching the range of their own photon cannons. Jonah wondered why they did not surrender.

The fourth minute saw one of the Chinese SDNs explode and the other drift, powerless and without shields. Two of the remaining battlecruisers blew up, the third broke into pieces and the fourth drifted without power or shields. Though he should have been pleased with such a lopsided victory instead, he was unsettled. The Chinese should have surrendered when they realized it was pointless. Thousands of lives had been lost to no purpose. It weighed on his mind along with his earlier failure to recognize the mines for what they were.

Jonah issued an order to the fleet to resume deceleration at best possible rate and to prioritize repair of Alcubierre field generators. The holographic display showed all eight of his ships were missing field generators. Jonah dismissed Lieutenant Srp and took off his ship suit.

The damaged Chinese ships were still drifting away. His fleet was still heading into the Hǎiwángxīng system but continuing to slow. Alcubierre units would be repaired within six hours on three of the ships: *Black Prince*, *Duke of Marlborough,* and *Elizabeth Regina*. Four of the other five ships indicated it would be twelve hours or less until the Alcubierre units were replaced or repositioned due to hull damage. *Roosevelt* had taken the worst damage and could not estimate when they would be able to repair their Alcubierre units. All eight lost crew killed and wounded.

Twelve hours after the battle, all the Commonwealth ships except for *Roosevelt* had repaired or replaced the Alcubierre units. Because of the size of the holes blasted in the hull of *Roosevelt*, they needed to reposition nearly all their Alcubierre units. When they were nearly finished, they found that the repositioning would not be effective in creating a complete field around the ship. A petty officer suggested cutting off sections of a beam that was broken off two decks down and hoisting the sections of the beam to the hull. She then welded the beam sections to extend into the breaches in the hull and ran the necessary electrical cables along them. She positioned an Alcubierre unit at the end of the beam.

Jonah ordered the captains of the ships which had completed repairs to their Alcubierre units to send EVA teams to *Roosevelt* to try to hurry the process of repositioning the field generators. With the jury-rigged fix and the help from the other crews, *Roosevelt* was able to complete repairs and reported she was able to generate a stable Alcubierre field, enabling it to enter hyperspace.

The EVA teams returned to their own ships. When the last shuttle had returned, Jonah gave the order to advance to the hyper corridor. Seventeen hours after the battle of Hǎiwángxīng, Third Fleet limped to the entrance of the corridor and jumped into hyperspace.

31

Because of the damage to the drives of *Edward I*, the journey back to Commonwealth space took almost four weeks. Third Fleet was ordered to return to Caerleon Station for repairs. During the long flight back to Caerleon with his damaged fleet, Jonah still felt he should have anticipated what the mines were when they appeared on the sensors. It bothered him that most of the damage and the casualties from the battle were due to what he felt was his failure. He was also bothered by the Chinese failure to surrender when their situation was hopeless. Amy could tell Jonah was ill at ease after the battle, though he denied it for two weeks. She finally got him to admit what was bothering him. The next day he received a call from Admiral Delhomme.

"Baron Cyclops," came Pierre's greeting over the comm.

"Admiral Crapaud," replied Jonah, "what urgent urgency has forced you to call from the dim, dark depths of the Hercules system?"

"You," Pierre responded. "Your delectable wife, whose near-naked picture adorns half the lockers on the lower decks in Second Fleet, told me that you're not right in the head. When I responded that this has always been the case, at least since I've known you, she told me that it's more than your usual. In which case, given that your sanity is considered by professionals to be borderline, to begin with, I thought I'd call and see what's eating you up. You're not obsessing again over how much more handsome, charming, and witty I am, are you?"

"Monsewer, that has never been the case," Jonah answered with a sigh.

"Hmmm. No witty riposte. No return insult. Something is bugging you," Pierre commented. "Spill."

Jonah sighed and then told Pierre about his failure to identify the warheads strewn in their path. It bothered him that he had just about figured it out when the first one exploded. He also mentioned how senseless he felt the Chinese had been. Pierre looked at him quizzically.

"Let me make sure I understand," Pierre said. "You're upset because an enemy did what they chose to do—something you have no control over. You're also upset because you didn't recognize a weapon that hasn't been used by any navy for over two hundred years, even though the actual weapon wasn't that but something else. How many ships did you lose on the mission? Oh, that's right, none. Did you accomplish your mission? Yes. Did you have yet another ship blown up underneath you? No. When the enemy persisted in charging into your guns, should you have stopped firing at them to give them a better chance? No. Or have you become so addicted to producing miracles that a solid, 'check the box,' mission accomplished doesn't cut it for you? Because if that's the case, then Amy is right. But you'll need professional help, and having an old friend tell you to get your head out of your ass isn't going to be enough."

"Shit," Jonah replied.

Pierre waited for Jonah to say more.

After a long pause, Jonah repeated, "Shit…I guess I'd better pull my head out of my ass then."

"That would be Dr. Delhomme's recommendation, yes."

"But I thought you were a gynecologist, not a psychologist—at least that's what you always used to tell the girls."

"Ah," Pierre remarked. "Just as a pitter-patter of little pebbles begins an avalanche, so a weak, incredibly lame crack might mark the return to sanity."

"Hey," Jonah protested, "the gynecologist crack was pretty good. I could have said proctologist, you know."

"Proctologist is more in keeping with our usual standards, you monocular mental midget."

"Is Amy's picture really in half the lockers on the lower decks?" Jonah asked, knowingly setting his friend up for another joke.

"According to my flag lieutenant, yes," Pierre replied. "He sells 'autographed' copies, and because I allow him to do it, he gives me half the take. Why? Do you think he's actually sold more, and the sneaky little devil has been fleecing me?"

Jonah burst into a guffaw. "How much?" he asked, trying to keep a straight face. "Can I get one?"

"For you, since you're a friend and all, I think I could do £10," Pierre replied, making the whole thing up.

"What's the regular price?"

"£10," Delhomme responded.

"I'm a little short right now," Jonah pretended. "Anything you'd take in trade?"

"The rights to your first-born male child?" Pierre mused. Answering his own question, he said, "Naw. The little nipper will be ugly and cranky. Hmmmm…I've got it! Give me Captain MacLeod's personal contact info."

"Right," Jonah replied sarcastically, then reconsidered. "Wait. You're serious?"

"Well, actually," Pierre answered, "I was going to ask Amy for it when I called her back to tell her the operation was successful—that I had somehow managed to extract your cranium from your rectum."

"You're serious?" Jonah said, incredulous.

"Look. I know it was over a year ago now, but at your wedding, I was having a really great night with her, and I thought there was something there, but then I got yanked off to Patagonia. I never got her personal contact info. Then after Patagonia, we were behind the eight-ball here, and then I got promoted, and it had to take a back seat for a while. For some damn reason, though, I keep thinking about her, and, well, it gets lonely out here in Hercules."

"You're definitely going to need to ask Amy for that," Jonah responded. "That would be way above my pay grade."

"Well, she owes me now," Pierre retorted.

"For helping me pull my head out of my butt?" Jonah suggested.

"That, too," Pierre answered. "I was thinking more about the £2 she gets every time she autographs one of the pictures. Quite a little nest egg it's turning into."

"Good luck, buddy," Jonah advised. "And thanks. I think the operation was successful."

"Satisfaction guaranteed," Pierre responded. "That's what I tell all the girls."

After the call, Jonah had shaken off the funk that had been plaguing him. He also wondered about whether Pierre and Elaine would make a good match. The long delay in Pierre asking for her number was going to be an interesting thing to explain. Jonah wished he could be a fly on the wall for that.

Amy passed along Pierre's request, along with his personal contact information, to Elaine. She quipped to Jonah that Pierre would now need to pay her £3 per autograph. It would be up to Elaine and Pierre now, though Amy did suggest that if Elaine were interested, she should give Pierre a difficult time in a humorous way about waiting so long. Elaine was in between relationships and had agreed that she, too, felt some chemistry at the wedding, so it might be worth investigating further.

Ten days later, Third Fleet finally arrived at Caerleon on April Fool's Day. It would take until mid-May to return six of the ships of Third Fleet to service. All had hull breaches, damaged sensors, shield outages and their Alcubierre units needed to be readjusted. *Edward I* would be another couple of weeks beyond that, repairing her drives. *Theodore Roosevelt* would be until at least mid-June due to the extensive hull damage and the need to rebuild the massive electrical conduit that had been severed. Jonah was exposed to a new set of an admiral's responsibilities, completing all the paperwork associated with the repairs. Jonah moved into quarters in the Admiralty section of Caerleon Station.

His first day back, Admiral Lothes conducted an extensive debrief with Jonah. "Between the battle in New Delhi and the battle at Hǎiwángxīng, Third Fleet destroyed or severely damaged nine Chinese 527-type superdreadnoughts and sixteen 461-type battlecruisers, with a one 527 and four 461s captured and towed back to the Commonwealth for analysis and possible repair. That's a solid success," Admiral Lothes began.

"Naval Intelligence analyzed the data from the battle in Hǎiwángxīng thoroughly. Their review concluded that what you thought were mines were instead detached missile warheads, set off remotely by the Chinese when their sensors determined your ships were in range. It's been hundreds of years since mines were an active part of space warfare since they were easy for naval warships to detect and eliminate. Intelligence considered scattering the warheads an interesting gambit. The warheads would not have remained operational for much more than a day on their own in deep space, unlike purpose-built mines, which were built to survive months or years. They are working on a programming adjustment to the Swordfish system to pick them up.

"Intelligence is still examining the captured ships. As with the ships we captured in Hercules, the computer system the Chinese are using is nearly identical to the Edoan systems. The mission to New Delhi and Hǎiwángxīng was a success on several levels. Not only did we inflict damage on the Chinese navy, but it was a public relations success as well. Your friend Lord Thorner would explain this better, but being able to strike back effectively, only a little more than a year after they hurt us so badly, has improved public morale a great deal. Though we are still outnumbered, and I am still concerned about another attack, we have shown we are far from defeated."

After the debriefing, Jonah returned to the office he was assigned. His first week on Caerleon Station was spent immersed in paperwork. Lieutenant Srp was an immense help.

On Wednesday, the following week, his comm buzzed with an incoming call from Admiral Lothes. "Admiral," she began, "we have another mission for you."

"Yes, admiral," Jonah answered, "but Third Fleet is in the yards for repair until mid-May, I was told."

"I understand, admiral," she replied smoothly, "but *Centurion*, *Eisenhower* and *Elizabeth Regina* are due to be completed no later than Friday, April 22nd. We would like you to take those three ships to Edo and assist the Imperial Navy in reclaiming their Goryeo system. As an incentive, I'm prepared to offer a week's leave on Edo at the completion of the mission."

"Admiral," Jonah protested, "it's your job to give the orders, mine to obey them. I appreciate the incentive, but it's not—"

"Jonah," Lothes interrupted, "I'm aware of what a funk you went into after Hǎiwángxīng. Times are tense and I need all my people at their best. Once you return, you and whatever ships are ready will head to Hercules and relieve Second Fleet, since they've been on the front lines the longest. It is my professional opinion you need to see your wife in-person…for the good of the service."

"Then it's an order," Jonah replied. "I have no choice but to obey. Thank you, admiral."

"For now, you need to contact the captains of the three ships and have them recall their crews from whatever liberty they've granted in time for an April 22nd departure. As soon as the three ships are cleared by the yard, you proceed to Edo. Our assistance and your involvement specifically were requested by the Imperial government. The person in charge of their end of the operation is Admiral Niimura. Until you trade kewpie pairs with him, you can reach him through the Admiralty. I am also giving you a copy of the report on the computer systems on the Chinese ships. Though we shared it through official channels, I thought perhaps Admiral Niimura would appreciate getting his own copy from you. It is an 'eyes only' copy and you need to put it into his hands personally."

Jonah thought that was slightly unusual but would do as requested and deliver the report. He suspected the version he was carrying might have additional information the 'official' report did not. Jonah contacted his captains, informing them of the new mission. He asked Captain Gray if he could transfer his flag to *Centurion* for the duration of the mission. Gray was prompt to agree. Jonah also contacted Lieutenant Srp and let her know they would be on *Centurion*.

Jonah read the material forwarded from the Imperial Navy on the situation they would encounter. Edo had maintained a patrol boat under a stealth cloak in their unexploited system. The patrol boat reported that the Chinese maintained three superdreadnoughts and six battlecruisers in the system along with escort ships, just they had at New Delhi.

The challenge for Edo is that their fleet contained only three superdreadnoughts and six battlecruisers—the same number of capital ships as the Chinese. Edo had the Swordfish missile defense system due to a technology-sharing agreement between Edo and the Commonwealth that Amy had helped negotiate. The Commonwealth, in turn, gained access to advanced Edoan computer technology.

Jonah worked well with Yoshi, Admiral Niimura. Working behind the scenes, Jonah fed information through Amy to him, which helped the trade negotiations get on track when it appeared they had reached an impasse. When Amy was kidnapped by a group opposed to closer ties with the Commonwealth, which was backed by the Chinese, Yoshi mounted the rescue.

Amy and Jonah invited Yoshi and his wife, a noted trauma surgeon, to their wedding. Regretfully they were not able to attend but offered an open invitation to the couple to come visit them at their country house. Jonah considered Yoshi and Niko good friends. Due to the time difference, it would be the middle of the night for Yoshi. Jonah would call him this evening when it would be morning in New Seoul, the capital of Edo. The Imperial Fleet, as did the Commonwealth navy, kept their ships on the same time as the capital.

Jonah then contacted Amy and let her know about his 'orders' from Admiral Lothes. As often happened, Amy already knew about it from her sources (usually her boss, the foreign secretary Brian Stewart-Crosland, or their friend Laura, Lady Thorner). Amy's post on New Bremen was only a three-and-a-half-day journey from Edo. She promised she would clear her desk of as much work as possible during the next two weeks to be able to join him on Edo for a week.

She confirmed that Elaine had contacted Pierre. With Pierre as Admiral of Second Fleet, with relatively quick access to the beaches on the planet Aries, there might be an opportunity for them to get together, though the situation at the border required constant vigilance still. Amy said that Elaine reported that their early conversations were promising. Jonah wondered if Admiral Lothes had rotated Pierre out on leave and whether he would meet up with Elaine.

32

That evening, Jonah contacted Admiral Niimura using the kewpie routing provided through the Admiralty. Both expressed pleasure in being able to work together once more. Yoshi asked Jonah how married life was treating him, commenting that his honeymoon, though delayed, certainly seemed to be pleasant. Jonah told him that Admiral Delhomme often teased him that Amy's picture was on the inside of locker doors on the lower decks throughout the Commonwealth navy and that he was selling 'autographed' copies. Yoshi teased him back by asking for Pierre's contact information so he could become the authorized distributor within the Edoan fleet.

On Friday, Jonah and Lieutenant Srp arrived on *Centurion* and moved into their quarters. Jonah was looking forward to getting to know Captain Gray. A tall, slender man with strawberry blond hair, Gray possessed a keen mind and a quick wit. Jonah considered himself quite lucky. He liked all the captains in Third Fleet, though he was most pleased with his flag captain, Catherine Hayes.

The trip to Edo would take nine days, with most of that time spent traversing systems in between hyper corridors. Jonah had plenty of time to read up on the situation and Edo's history. The government of Edo claimed two planets, Edo and Goryeo. Only Edo had been terraformed and settled. Goryeo was the planetary system the Chinese had seized.

Though the old earth countries of Korea and Japan had sometimes been bitter enemies, their relationship had begun to thaw and then warm in the 21st century. During that period, both countries became known for their prowess in the fields of both technology and heavy industry. A consortium of the leading corporations in both countries underwrote the cost of an exploratory mission that found the Edo and Goryeo systems.

Though Goryeo was the first 'Goldilocks' planet found on the expedition, it was decided by the consortium to terraform and settle Edo first. Edo was surrounded by heavy Van Allen belts, which prevented most solar radiation other than light from reaching the planet. The most advanced organism on Edo was a microscopic multi-cell body that was both plant and animal. Goryeo had Van Allen belts that were less thick, and plant and animal life had developed. There were fish, primitive amphibians, and cold-blooded creatures similar to earth's reptiles, with the largest not much bigger than a mouse.

Still, due to cultural influence and a number of ecological disasters that had befallen both Japan and Korea during the 21st century, the settlers took the responsibility of environmental stewardship very seriously. The companies who sponsored the expedition found abundant natural resources in the Edo system and encouraged colonists to move from earth with financial incentives. After the Second Great Intifada, the consortium no longer offered incentives, as tens of thousands of people desired to leave the troubled situation on earth. Extremists had exploded dirty bombs in some of the major cities of Japan and Korea, killing millions and poisoning huge areas of the countryside with radioactive fallout.

After the Third Great Intifada, Edo reluctantly severed all ties with earth as there were few people left alive on the Korean Peninsula or the Japanese Islands. The settlers conducted an extremely peaceful and orderly rebellion against the consortium of companies that owned Edo and took over the government. Since both cultures which settled Edo had a deep history of imperial government, the settlers decided to call themselves an empire, though there was no emperor or even any royal family.

The settlers found everything they needed on Edo and engaged in only limited trade with the inter-planetary powers and only on favorable terms. They were not isolationists, but relations with other worlds happened only on Edo's terms. This had begun to change recently, as relations with the Commonwealth had become stronger.

When the Chinese invaded the Goryeo system, the Imperial Navy had been there to defend it. With both sides possessing effective missile defense systems, the battle had developed into an artillery duel. The Imperial Navy fought bravely but was outnumbered. Admiral Niimura had led a fighting retreat that enabled the navy's capital ships to survive, though all were moderately to heavily damaged. There was a request for aid to the Commonwealth, but before the Commonwealth could respond, the Chinese wiped out the Commonwealth's Second and Third Fleets. There was no aid to give.

The people of Edo had a strong sense of pride. Losing their system to the Chinese galled them. Members of the minority party in the government began calling for negotiations with the Chinese. Public sentiment ran heavily against this, and the minority party's ties to the Chinese were again publicized.

They also felt a sense of moral outrage. The government strictly limited access to Goryeo to only a small number of scientists. Without government approval, it was forbidden to travel to the planet for fear that the planet's ecosystem, primitive though it was, would be irreparably damaged. The Chinese had a poor reputation as far as environmental stewardship was concerned. They already landed hundreds of people on the planet, and Edo feared they would terraform it in brutal fashion by eliminating all existing Goryeon life.

Centurion, *Eisenhower* and *Elizabeth Regina* would be joining the Imperial Navy's three superdreadnoughts, *Akagi*, *Hiryu*, and *Gwanggaeto the Great*, and six battlecruisers. Jonah had received permission to share limited information with Admiral Niimura about the capabilities of the Commonwealth BFGs. The battle would be an artillery duel. Admiral Niimura was concerned at first that the three obsolete superdreadnoughts from the Commonwealth were a veiled insult, but Jonah assured him this was not the case, as it was with *Achates*, and he would explain more face-to-face.

The three Commonwealth ships set off on the nine-day journey to Edo from Caerleon. The trip was uneventful. Jonah enjoyed getting to know Captain Gray, learning that the man was a gifted athlete in a wide variety of sports. He was also extremely well-read and fascinating to talk with.

Upon arrival, Yoshi invited Jonah to join him for dinner on Edo Station. Jonah took with him the report on the Chinese computer systems that Admiral Lothes had given him to pass along. He also took a field suppressor with him before he embarked on the shuttle to the station. They would be dining in the Imperial Navy section of the station, but Jonah hoped to go somewhere private for a more intimate discussion. He would take no chances that their conversation could be overheard.

Jonah waited until after dinner before he suggested that they leave the dining room and go talk in private. Yoshi agreed, and they went to his office. Jonah made an apologetic shrug as he pulled the field suppressor out. Yoshi nodded to go ahead, and Jonah activated it. The field suppressor would prevent anyone from listening in on their conversation. Once the green light appeared, indicating it was running, Jonah began.

"Admiral Lothes asked me to give this to you personally," Jonah told him, pulling the envelope from his jacket. "They sent a report through official channels, so I suspect this version has information not included in the other."

Yoshi frowned. "It must contain something sensitive and possibly inflammatory. I will review it carefully. Thank you. Perhaps I may have something for you to take back with you."

"You're welcome," Jonah replied, though now his curiosity was piqued, wondering what Admiral Lothes and Admiral Niimura might have been discussing. "Now, about my ships and why they are more than they might appear…"

Jonah explained the upgrades to the power plants and drives that were made to the ships, making them quicker to respond and more maneuverable. He saved the particle beam weapon for last. He even explained the 'BFG' acronym, which Yoshi found amusing.

"The gun has fifty percent longer range than photon cannons and does three times the damage?" Yoshi questioned. "I'd like to see that."

Jonah pulled out his personal comm unit. He had some photos loaded onto it that showed some of the damage the particle beam weapon had caused. Yoshi looked at them carefully.

"If your ships can do that," Yoshi admitted, "they are indeed much more than they appear."

"Yes, they are," Jonah confirmed. "They may not do the whole job, though. Our upcoming engagement might involve exchanging photon cannon fire as well. I don't expect us to come through this unscathed."

"No," Yoshi answered, thinking, "we might take some hits, but I will do my best to keep them to a minimum."

Jonah began to share with Yoshi details of his battles using the new gun. He pointed out how the Chinese were also adapting to this 'post missile' environment. The two discussed tactics and maneuvering ideas until late in the night. At 23:00, Yoshi noticed the time and returned Jonah to the shuttle.

Yoshi told Jonah to expect to run a simulated joint exercise with the Imperial Fleet at 11:00 the next day. Apparently, while they were dining, kewpie communications devices were given to the three Commonwealth ships. Since Jonah worked with the Imperial Navy in the past, he already briefed his captains on their communication protocols, so they would not need to spend time reviewing those.

When he returned to his quarters, Jonah took advantage of the opportunity to call Amy since she was now only a few hours behind him. He told her about his dinner with Yoshi. She questioned him at length about the different topics they had discussed, almost as if she were probing for something. When he had recounted everything and assured her there was nothing else, she seemed relieved. He then mentioned he was puzzled about the information Admiral Lothes had given him and Yoshi's response. Amy knew more about it than he did.

"I'm telling tales out of school, dear husband," she cautioned, "so sssshhhhh."

Jonah crossed his heart.

"I know some of this from Laura," she went on. "Remember I told you I think Laura was a spy?"

Jonah nodded.

"I'm even more certain of it now," she stated. "And some of it I know from negotiations I was part of. Regardless, apparently, there was some information related to what intelligence found in the computers of the Chinese ships that may lead to someone still in place in the government of

Edo. That information was not included in the official report because the foreign secretary felt it might be too volatile. That's why Admiral Lothes had you deliver the report to Yoshi.

"Yoshi is not allied with either party—never has been. He is as apolitical as he is respected. He wields a lot of what we like to call 'soft power'—people listen to him, and he has great influence, but he rarely uses it. The ancient Romans called it *auctoritas*—it's not authority, it's the ability to influence others to do your bidding when you don't have authority over them."

"I can see that," Jonah agreed. "But what would he have for me to take in return?"

"There are some projects that are two governments are working on together. I could tell you more, but then—"

"I know, you'd have to kill me," Jonah replied.

"Another thing is that the Commonwealth has had an extremely difficult time gaining intelligence in the Chinese republics. This is a long-time problem. We have never had the intelligence assets inside the republics that we did in the Rodinan Federation—not even close. The people we have tried to insert as agents or recruit as agents end up not surviving long."

"Is it an ethnic thing?" Jonah asked. "There are many ethnic Chinese in the Commonwealth, aren't there?"

"There are," Amy agreed. "It's not ethnic as much as cultural. Even though their genetics may make some Commonwealth citizens indistinguishable, they have been living in a different culture for a thousand years or more. The agents we try to insert end up doing something to betray themselves and get found out. Similarly, our attempts to recruit within Chinese space also end up in failure. The Commonwealth has always struggled to gain intelligence from Chinese territory.

"The only people who have had any success in intelligence gathering are the Edoans. They have had intelligence assets among the Chinese since forever. Similarly, the Chinese have assets deep within the Edoan government as well. They've played a quietly deadly intelligence game against one another from the beginning. When relations began to warm up between Edo and the Commonwealth, one of the things I tried to negotiate was access to intelligence. They pretended not to know what I was talking about and denied that they spy on anyone.

"Admiral Lothes' report might contain something so deeply buried and critical that it might open the door for greater intelligence sharing, as well as the other project. That would be a big help for the Commonwealth."

33

When Jonah awoke at 05:30, he found a message waiting for him from Admiral Niimura: "Regretfully, we must postpone our scheduled exercises for today."

No explanation was given. Jonah sent a message to the captains telling them they would be conducting exercises but that the Imperial Navy would not be participating that day. The exercises were a challenge. Director Niven set up the simulation exercise to be as realistic as possible, with the three Commonwealth ships and the Imperial Navy's nine ships against the nine Chinese ships in the system. He included a missile gauntlet and a carpet of the detached warheads at the entrance to the Goryeo system.

Jonah did not hear from Admiral Niimura the rest of the day or that evening. He contacted Amy that night. She told Jonah she had heard nothing, and her friends in the Commonwealth embassy on Edo reported that all their contacts were not returning calls. There was something unusual happening, but no one knew what.

The next morning when Jonah awoke, there was another message from Admiral Niimura: "Regretfully, we must postpone exercises again today."

Jonah had the Commonwealth forces conduct another simulation. The result was similar to the day before—the joint force prevailed. That afternoon, Amy sent Jonah a message with two news links. Jonah accessed the first article. Dated the previous day, the headline was "Defense Minister and Wife Dead in Apparent Murder-Suicide." The second article was dated that day only a few hours before and headlined "Permanent Under-Secretary of Defense Indicted for Tax Fraud."

When Jonah contacted Amy that night, she said, "Whatever is going on is of seismic proportions. None of my friends in the embassy can reach anyone. No one in the Imperial government is returning calls. Clearly, something is rotten in the state of Edo."

The third morning, Jonah awoke to another message from Admiral Niimura: "Regretfully, we must postpone our exercises one more day. I should be able to speak with you this evening. I will confirm time and place later."

Just before Jonah began that day's simulation, Amy sent him another news link. When he accessed the link, there was an article with the headline "Prime Minister Resigns Citing Ill Health."

Late that afternoon, Jonah received a message from Admiral Niimura: "Please meet me for dinner. Admiralty. 18:00."

Jonah replied in the affirmative, and at 18:00, he showed up at the Imperial Admiralty on the station, escorted by two Royal Marines in the absence of any agents of the King's Own. Yoshi welcomed him inside, and they went to the dining room. The marines were dismissed but would return to escort Jonah back to *Centurion*. Jonah noticed Yoshi looked exhausted. After dinner, they went to Niimura's office. Niimura activated his own field suppressor unit to foil any listening devices.

"The report you delivered to me was most interesting, Jonah," he commenced. "Even though it was late that night, I decided to glance through it after you left three nights ago. It was...explosive."

"I take it," Jonah replied, "that it was not necessarily about our analysis of the captured computer systems."

"Only peripherally," Yoshi sighed. "On one of the Chinese battlecruisers you captured in New Delhi, as usual, they tried to scrag the computer system when they surrendered. Damage to the ship, however, prevented the process from being completed. Your intelligence people were able to use this and have been able to hack into the Chinese navy's computer net on a limited basis.

"One of your hackers went searching for information on the new capabilities the Chinese have displayed. They found information about how the Chinese obtained the missile defense system, missile pods, and our computer. I was most interested in the section dealing with the computer. It included contacts, disguised by code names, along with progress reports and financial records.

"I won't go into the details, but while reading, it became clear to me who the people were on Edo that they had turned. I immediately called our counterintelligence agency most like your MI-5 and turned the information over to them. Things moved quickly, and my involvement, along with a few other people, was required."

"From the headlines I have read," Jonah commented, "I am guessing it involved the defense minister and the permanent under-secretary."

"It was the defense minister's wife," Yoshi commented. "As we questioned her, it became apparent to her husband what she did. She had access to her husband's computer passwords and sold the information incredibly cheaply as these things go. She was mad at her husband for having an affair. She sold the information to get back at him. Unfortunately, our agents slipped up. He had a concealed weapon and shot her, then himself. The agents were unable to stop him. The permanent under-secretary was a deeply hidden Chinese agent. She set the whole thing up. She is undergoing interrogation, but progress is slow."

"And the prime minister's resignation?" Jonah asked.

"He resigned from shame," Niimura continued, "for allowing this to happen. We call it health reasons."

"Wow!" Jonah breathed.

"Wow, indeed," Yoshi agreed. "I...we...are very grateful to Admiral Lothes for providing this report to us. It is a matter of tremendous embarrassment to us. But...the eggs are cracked. There is no putting them back together. In the meantime, we have an assignment, you and I. I apologize, but I have not been able to give it any of my attention. You have, I trust?"

"Yes," Jonah replied. "If you would prefer, perhaps we could conduct a joint briefing tomorrow with all of our captains and review the latest information from Goryeo."

Yoshi answered with a relieved sigh. "That would be advisable, my friend. I need sleep. We will all be sharper tomorrow. Let's have a comm conference at 09:00 with all the captains."

"In advance, I will send you the sensor logs of our last few battles with the Chinese for you to share with your captains. If you would provide me with the latest observations from your patrol boat in Goryeo, that would be most helpful."

When Jonah returned to *Centurion*, he found the latest report from Goryeo. The Chinese task force was maintaining position just inside the normal hyper corridor exit point. There was a gauntlet of missile pods set up with 4,500 missiles in 500 pods of nine. Jonah sent his proposed formation, entrance point, and speed to Admiral Niimura, promising to explain his reasoning in the briefing tomorrow.

Jonah suggested a formation of two rings, with the Edoan battlecruisers in the outer ring and the Commonwealth and Edoan SDNs in the middle. He also proposed entering the system four-light minutes before the end of the corridor. That would bring them into normal space short of the range of the missiles positioned in the gauntlet. He advised an entry speed of $0.1c$ or ten percent of light speed.

In the briefing, all the Edoan and Commonwealth captains appeared holographically, as did Jonah and Admiral Niimura. Admiral Niimura opened the meeting, apologizing for the delay but not explaining the cause of it. Before he allowed questions, he asked Jonah to explain why he had made his recommendations.

Jonah activated a holographic display showing the current position of the Chinese ships. He then showed where the joint task force would enter. At the speed he suggested, they would have five minutes before reaching missile range and would be in missile range for twenty-eight minutes before reaching the range of the Commonwealth's weapon. Without getting into the particulars, Jonah also explained that the Commonwealth ships were armed with a new artillery weapon with increased range. If the Chinese chose to accelerate to meet them, he estimated they would be in range of the big guns for five-and-a-half minutes before being able to return fire with photon cannons. The two forces would then both be in range of each other's photon cannons for nearly seven minutes, followed by another period of almost five minutes with the Chinese still within the range of the Commonwealth's guns.

Jonah was confident the three Commonwealth ships would eliminate the Chinese SDNs in the first five-minute engagement period. They might be able to take down some of the battlecruisers as well, but it would be wise not to assume that. Having seen the data from the Commonwealth's previous battles with the Chinese and the destruction the big guns caused, the Edoans were impressed. At the conclusion of the meeting, Admiral Niimura ordered everyone to proceed to the hyper corridor leading to system K3801 which was between Edo and Goryeo.

It took the joint force four-and-a-half days to reach the entrance of the corridor leading to Goryeo. It was late in the evening. The corridor would take eight hours and nine minutes to cross, with them dropping out four-light minutes before the end.

Jonah sent a message to Amy. "Hey, baby—we're about to jump. In eight hours, we'll be coming into an engagement. As soon as it's over, I'll let you know. If all goes well, I'll see you in a few days. Keep your fingers crossed. I love you with all my heart—Jonah."

The joint force transitioned into hyperspace and emerged eight hours, nine minutes later. The missile gauntlet and the Chinese ships were still where the Edoan patrol boat indicated. There were no mines or floating warheads that appeared on scans.

Just before entering missile range of the gauntlet, they saw that the Chinese were accelerating towards them at full thrust. The Commonwealth ships fired anti-matter missiles at the gauntlet when they reached the range. The gauntlet was well dispersed, and the anti-matter missiles only eliminated 834 of the 4,500 ship-killers aimed at them. Even so, with all twelve ships in the joint force equipped with the Swordfish defense, the remaining Chinese missiles were disposed of easily.

Neither side fired anti-ship missiles as the distance closed. Jonah allowed himself to shake his head about how much things had changed in such a short time. The two forces reached the range of the Commonwealth's big guns. In the time before they reached photon cannon range, each of the

Commonwealth ships would be able to fire at least twenty-two times.

Before the first minute was over, one of the Chinese 527-type superdreadnoughts disappeared from the plot. Captain Gray, reviewing the sensor data later, described what happened as it being "shredded." By the time 2.5 minutes elapsed, the other two 527s were out of the battle—one destroyed, the other drifting without power or shields. The Commonwealth ships turned their weapons on the six Chinese battlecruisers. Before the two forces reached photon cannon range of each other, three of the battlecruisers were destroyed and the other three were drifting helplessly.

Admiral Niimura sent a standard demand to surrender to the three helpless Chinese ships. The Chinese response was instant—all three ships self-destructed rather than surrender. Jonah was stunned. He had never seen this happen. It helped explain what he saw at Hǎiwángxīng.

Niimura issued orders for the superdreadnought *Gwanggaeto the Great*, two of the battlecruisers and their escorts to remove any remaining Chinese ships in the Goryeo system and for their marines to remove any Chinese from the planet. The Commonwealth ships and the remainder of the Edoan fleet were ordered to return to Edo. Jonah sent a brief message to Amy, letting her know he was on his way back to Edo already.

He had a conference with the three Commonwealth captains to go over the brief battle. From the sensor data, the hit/miss percentage for the BFGs dropped to just over forty percent. The Chinese were engaging in severe evasive action to the limits of their ships' performance. In looking at the data, it appeared that each Chinese superdreadnought could take no more than five hits from the BFG before being disabled or destroyed. For battlecruisers, three hits would usually incapacitate them.

34

On the return trip to Edo, Yoshi confirmed his invitation to Jonah and Amy to come visit his country house. Conveniently, the ships would be returning to Edo Station early in the afternoon on Friday. Amy would arrive that morning and would wait for them. Yoshi would take them to the house, and he and his wife Niko would be able to spend the weekend.

He suggested to Jonah that he bring outdoor clothing suitable for hiking. It was early autumn on that part of the planet, and Yoshi told him there were many beautiful trails that Jonah and Amy could explore. Jonah had none of that kind of clothing with him, so would need to do some quick shopping at the station before they departed.

When the shuttle from *Centurion* arrived at Edo Station, Amy was waiting to meet him. Agents Winchester and Lewis were just behind her. Jonah wondered why they still needed the agents. The Commonwealth was at peace with the Rodinans, so there was no longer a threat from the FSB, and the Johannsen family and all their plots had finally been uncovered. They all joined Jonah as he went to purchase clothing suitable for the outdoors and hiking. He also bought a small backpack, thinking he would use it to pack a lunch for a picnic.

Shopping complete, they proceeded to the Imperial Navy area and were met by Admiral Niimura. They flew down to the Imperial Admiralty, where Yoshi signed out a flitter, and within minutes, they were on their way to his country home. He explained on the way that Niko was already there and looking forward to seeing them again.

Niko insisted agents Lewis and Winchester join them for a pleasant dinner. Niko forbade them all from talking shop, though she did pull Jonah into the kitchen to inspect his regrown arm and leg. As a trauma surgeon, Niko had a professional curiosity. Yoshi wanted to see pictures from the wedding, and Amy happily obliged him. Niko and Yoshi both ooohed and aaahed over the pageantry of it all. Amy explained how she decided not to fight the 'wedding of the century' hoopla but embrace it instead. Yoshi made a sly comment about their honeymoon and cracked that he arranged to become the authorized distributor of 'autographed' pictures of Amy from the honeymoon. Agent Lewis, in a rare display of humor from the normally taciturn agent, commented that he didn't need a picture since he had been there.

When they retired for the evening, Amy and Jonah reconnected in the most satisfying way possible. In the morning, after breakfast, Yoshi suggested to Jonah that they take a walk in the garden. The last time they did so, Yoshi took the opportunity to share some confidential information and his thoughts on the geopolitical situation Edo and the other non-aligned planets were in. Jonah suspected he had similar information to share.

Yoshi brought Jonah up to speed on the current political situation on Edo. He confessed to Jonah what Amy had already told him, that Edo and the Chinese had been spying on one another for centuries. He explained that over time, diplomatic relations between the two had wavered between cordial and chilly. The leading minority party in the Edoan parliament was in favor of better relations with the Chinese. Members of the party were implicated in the scandal surrounding Amy's kidnapping, so their views became unpopular.

When the Chinese invaded and seized Goryeo, public sentiment turned sharply hostile towards any thought of closer ties to the Chinese. With the resignation of the prime minister, Edoan law called for new parliamentary elections within six weeks. The minority party stood to lose a huge number of seats in the upcoming elections.

Yoshi did not claim to speak for any group or faction. As Amy said, he was largely apolitical. He did mention that it was becoming obvious to all their citizens that it would be in Edo's best interests to forge better ties with the Commonwealth and that Amy had laid the groundwork for projects of mutual benefit. Jonah thought Yoshi was hinting at something he expected Jonah to know.

Yoshi mentioned that the Chinese who landed on Goryeo were rounded up quickly. Most of them had been scientists, and Yoshi believed that the Chinese would likely have begun terraforming Goryeo aggressively if they were able to maintain control of it. Except for the issue of preserving native flora and fauna, Goryeo was a near-ideal world for human settlement.

Yoshi then mentioned the situation the Commonwealth found itself in. "I must say," he commented, "that the Commonwealth's ability to absorb such a fearsome loss is amazing. Your ability to take obsolete, mothballed ships and turn them into effective weapons shows an ingenuity that is one of the things I find most admirable about the Commonwealth. Just in looking at the projects Edo and the Commonwealth have worked on together, both sides have benefitted. We on Edo have kept the rest of civilized space too far away until recently."

"I hope we will find ways to work with one another in the future. But we're not safe yet," Jonah warned. "Though things have been going our way lately, we are still outnumbered by a significant amount. We've been able to even things up some, but I worry how long we have until—"

"Until the Chinese figure out your new weapon," Yoshi interrupted. "I agree. If I were your Admiral Lothes, I would be eager to strike one more big blow before that happens. But do not despair, my friend. You may find help from unexpected quarters. Enough of 'talking shop,' as Niko says. I thought we could take a hike today. There are many trails nearby, and the scenery is amazing, a little bit higher in the foothills."

The two went inside and suggested a hike to Niko and Amy. They agreed enthusiastically and began packing a picnic lunch. Jonah mentioned it to Lewis and Winchester. After quiet discussion between themselves, they informed Jonah that they would accompany them on the hike.

The group set off and headed up into the foothills behind the house. They walked about two hours. After the first hour, they entered a pine forest. It was incredibly peaceful and quiet. The forest floor was covered with a thick carpet of pine needles. Yoshi told them there was an overlook with a beautiful view up ahead where they could stop and eat. Before they reached it, they all heard a loud 'whump!' Agent Lewis ran ahead on the trail to get to the overlook, out of the trees.

"We've got trouble," he called back.

Agent Winchester told the group, "I need your comms right now. Admiral Niimura, we're about to be attacked. If you have anyone you can call for assistance in the next ten seconds, please do so."

Winchester took the comms from Amy, Niko, and Jonah. Yoshi handed his over when he was finished sending a message. Lewis returned. Winchester took his pack off and opened it. He put the comms inside and pulled out two fléchette pistols and four folded pieces of a dull fabric in a nondescript color. He handed the pistols to Niko and Amy. Lewis also retrieved two pistols from his pack and gave them to Yoshi and Jonah. "That 'whump' was your house, sir," he told Yoshi.

Niko looked at Yoshi with a stricken expression.

Winchester handed out the pieces of fabric. "These are ponchos," he instructed. "Put them on now. They have some chameleon properties, and they will hide your heat from infrared tracking." He zipped up his pack, strapped it on, and began to jog away.

"Where's he going?" asked Niko.

"To draw whoever is following us away," Yoshi guessed, "and possibly to set an ambush if he can."

"Correct," Lewis confirmed, pulling on his own poncho. "We need to go, now. Follow me."

Lewis set off at a jog, up the slope, diagonally away from the direction Winchester had run. He stayed under the cover of the trees. No more than ten minutes later, they could hear the sound of an approaching flitter. Lewis picked up the pace slightly, now heading straight up the slope.

Simultaneously, they heard a loud whoosh and a sharp crack. Two explosions, barely separated, followed within seconds. Lewis did not stop or look around. "There'll be another," he called, "keep going."

Lewis continued uphill. Sure enough, within a minute, they could hear another flitter approaching. Lewis turned and ordered, "Put your hoods up."

When he was sure they did so, he continued uphill. They ran as best they could after him, with one or the other of them occasionally stumbling over a rock or exposed root. They could hear the flitter fly overhead but could not see it through the trees. It turned and went back the other way.

"Admiral, how many other clearings are there nearby?" Lewis asked as he ran.

"Four," Yoshi huffed. "The one we nearly reached. One the direction Winchester went. One that's another two kilometers down the trail we were on. One near the top of this foothill on the other side."

Lewis changed direction, now cutting directly across the slope. Jonah, Amy, Niko, and Yoshi were all panting. Though all were in good condition, running nearly flat out uphill was as much as they could handle. Amy noticed they had not heard the flitter for a few minutes. The terrain in front of them changed. The trees were thinner and scrawnier, while the ground underneath changed from a loamy forest floor to jagged rock. Lewis halted.

"Did you get a message out, sir?" he asked Yoshi.

Yoshi nodded in reply. "Imperial Marines," he gasped, trying to catch his breath.

"How long until they come looking for you?" Lewis asked.

"Base is a half-hour away," Yoshi replied. "They should be on their way."

Lewis nodded. "They still have to find us—before the others do. With just one flitter, whoever is after us will likely be landing back at the clearing and then track us. If they had more people, they would have landed near the top and worked their way down. You four keep going. Keep as fast a pace as you can. Stay under cover. I'm going to slow down our pursuers if I can. I'll catch up to you when I am able."

"How will you find us?" Niko asked.

"I have special…abilities," Lewis replied. "Don't worry, I'll find you. Get going."

Yoshi took the lead. It took them a few minutes to work their way across the rocky terrain, but then they were back in the forest. Yoshi picked the pace up back to a jog, continuing to go across the slope. They kept going, hoping to catch their second wind.

They were all winded. A pleasant hike in the foothills had turned into a run for their lives. No one panicked, but they were all frightened. Jonah was having trouble, getting whipped in the face by a branch occasionally because of his lack of a right eye. Fifteen minutes after leaving Lewis, they heard an explosion. Yoshi did not slow down.

Ten minutes after that, they heard the sound of another flitter approaching, deeper in tone. Jonah hoped the deeper tone was due to it being larger and perhaps containing the marines Yoshi had summoned. Still, Yoshi did not stop.

After another fifteen minutes, he called a halt and told everyone to get a drink. He and Jonah had some water in their packs. Everyone took a water bottle and drained it. When they finished, Yoshi told them it was time to move again, even though they had still not quite caught their breath. Before they could move, Lewis came gliding out of the trees. His pace was a graceful lope, but he was moving as fast as Jonah could sprint. Lewis grinned at them, slowed, and motioned for them to follow.

After another twenty-minute jog, they came across a trail. Lewis halted and turned to Yoshi. "Admiral, does this trail lead to the upper clearing?"

Yoshi nodded.

"There was a troop carrier that flew over," Lewis explained as he began to jog up the trail. "Looked like it would hold a platoon. It sounded like they landed at the upper clearing. They'll be conducting a sweep downhill. If we head up, I hope we meet them before the six who are after us catch up."

"Six?" Amy asked.

"There were eight," Lewis answered with a shrug.

They continued up the trail, but all four were clearly near their limits. Each of them fell at least once, tripping on the uneven surface. Lewis stopped suddenly, holding up his hand in a sign for them to halt. He looked around quickly and motioned them to move off the trail to the right into a dense stand of smaller trees, growing together closely in a sort of thicket, holding his finger to his lips, indicating silence.

Jonah led the group into the trees, trying to bring his breathing under control. All of them wanted to pant and gasp for breath, but they controlled themselves, staying quiet. Lewis stayed on the trail, standing motionless, with his hands in the air. Jonah and the others could not see Lewis once they concealed themselves in the trees, but shortly afterward, they heard the low murmur of voices. Jonah could identify Lewis's.

Two minutes later, Lewis found them. He moved so quietly it was as though he appeared from thin air. "Imperial Marines," he whispered. "They're setting up a perimeter downslope. I'll come get you when it's safe to move out."

With that, Lewis walked away as silently as he had arrived. The group waited quietly, straining their ears to hear anything they could. No more than five minutes passed when Lewis suddenly materialized. Holding his finger to his lips, he motioned with his other hand for them to get up and follow him.

They began walking, upslope again, but at a walking pace at least. Lewis stopped and motioned for them to drop to the ground. Seconds later, they heard the tell-tale snick-snap of fléchette rounds breaking the sound barrier. Lewis waited a few moments, then rose, indicating to them that they should stay on the ground. Lewis moved silently downslope.

Amy heard a rustle to her right. She looked over and saw two figures coming slowly through the underbrush. She nudged Jonah to get his attention as she freed her fléchette pistol underneath her poncho and flipped the safety off, moving as little as possible. Jonah saw what she was looking at. He did the same as Amy.

The two men were wearing camouflage clothing. Jonah got Yoshi's attention. Yoshi looked at the two men approaching. He shook his head slightly and mouthed, "Not ours."

In a few more steps, the men would surely see them. Amy silently mouthed to Jonah, "On three."

Jonah breathed below a whisper, "One…Two—"

Before he reached three, the snick-snap of a fléchette gun cracked twice quickly, and the faces of the two men seemed to explode. Startled, Jonah looked up. Lewis was standing there, his pistol in his hand.

"I apologize for letting them get so close, sir," he said. "We got the other four down below. These two are the last of them."

As Jonah, Yoshi, Amy, and Niko stood up, men and women in the camouflage uniform of the Edoan Imperial Marines began to appear through the trees. Their officer, a lieutenant, came up to Yoshi and saluted. The marines escorted them up to the clearing where the large military transport flitter was waiting. A smaller flitter with Imperial Navy markings arrived while they were within sight, and they were waved onto the smaller one. Within seconds they were in the air on the way back to New Seoul.

35

Once in the air, agent Lewis asked Jonah and Amy where they would like to go. He gave them two choices: the Commonwealth embassy or HMS *Centurion.* Jonah deferred to Amy. She asked, "Will we be allowed to leave either location?"

Lewis shook his head no.

"Vacation's over?" she asked.

Lewis nodded. "Lord and Lady Halberd, you have to stay in a secure location until I get backup. It will take a few days to fly someone out."

"I'm likely going to be here a few days. My people were released to go on liberty," Jonah explained. "We could recall them early, then take Amy with us back to the Commonwealth. I'm going to ask Admiral Lothes for clarification."

"Let's stay at the embassy," she said. Turning to Jonah, she commented, "If I'm going to visit your flagship, I want it to be your real flagship, *Hotspur.* No slight against Captain Gray."

"That's okay," Jonah replied. "I get to be with you—that's what's important."

"That's kind of icky-sweet," she said.

"Yeah," Jonah admitted, "I realized that as it came out."

"I'm sorry your vacation is ruined," Yoshi apologized, "and that agent Winchester had to give his life to save us."

"It's not your fault," Amy protested. "And you lost your lovely home. I'm so sorry about that."

"I wonder who they were targeting?" Niko asked. "Was it you, dear? Or was it you, Jonah?"

"When we find out more about the assassins," Yoshi mused, "we'll have a better idea. I have my suspicions. You and I had better plan on staying at my apartment in the Admiralty. I'll arrange an escort to work for you on

Monday."

The flitter was able to land at the Admiralty. Yoshi arranged for a military escort to take Amy, Jonah, and agent Lewis to the Commonwealth embassy. The Royal Marines at the embassy gate were a bit surprised to see Amy and Jonah arrive. There was no advance notice.

When they entered the embassy, Amy went to talk to the ambassador and explain what happened. The ambassador was gracious about his unplanned guests. He asked what they needed. Amy replied, "Everything."

"Everything we had with us was blown up," she went on. "Clothes, toiletries, and even our personal comms."

"I cannot allow them to leave the grounds, sir," Lewis interjected.

"I see. I'll have my secretary send someone out for toiletries," he stated. "At least for your comm, Lady Halberd, I can give you one of the units we have in stock here in the embassy. I don't know if it meets military specs, though, Lord Halberd. Write down a list of what you need. As far as clothes, you should be able to order just about anything here in New Seoul if you have your measurement files."

"Thank you, ambassador," Jonah said. "I will have my ship send me a new comm, once I can log onto a console."

"You're welcome, Lord Halberd," he replied. "Will you please join my wife and me for dinner?"

"Ambassador," Amy apologized, "I'm afraid we're not fit company. We've had a very—"

"Quite right," the ambassador jumped in. "Sorry."

"No need to apologize," Amy said. "You were being polite, and we appreciate it. If we could have a rain check?"

"Certainly," the ambassador answered, relieved.

He had a secretary show Jonah and Amy to a vacant suite and agent Lewis to a different room. Amy called 'dibs' on the shower, but Jonah ignored her and joined her. Both exhausted, with the after-effects of the adrenalin rush from their pursuit kicking in, it was not an erotic shower, more tender and reassuring. They got out and dried off, putting on guest robes. Amy started writing down a list of necessary toiletry items. There was a knock on the door. A secretary handed Amy a box with her new personal comm unit.

While Amy was busy setting that up, Jonah logged onto the console in the room. He sent a message to Lieutenant Srp and asked her to send him a new personal comm unit and some undress uniforms and underwear to him at the embassy. No sooner did he send the message when the console lit up with an incoming call from Lieutenant Srp.

He answered it, putting her on screen. "Good afternoon, lieutenant," he said casually.

"Admiral!" she exclaimed, then seeing Amy standing behind Jonah, added, suddenly flustered, "Lady Halberd."

"Yes, lieutenant?" Jonah replied as though nothing had happened.

"Admiral," Srp blurted, "the rumor mill is going crazy. What happened down there?"

"Someone blew up Admiral Niimura's house while we were on a hike and then tried to kill us," Jonah answered, as though he were describing a visit to the grocery store. "Agent Winchester sacrificed himself to buy us some time. We ran through the woods for a few hours, and then the Imperial Marines showed up. Agent Lewis saved our lives, and now we're at the embassy."

"Damn! For once, the rumor mill isn't too far off," Srp commented. "The worst rumors had you dead, though."

"Nope," Amy answered, leaning in over Jonah's shoulder. "Hi, lieutenant. I'm Amy."

"Everyone knows who you are, Lady Halberd," Srp answered, slightly flustered.

"Please," Amy protested, "Amy. I'm not feeling very ladylike at the moment."

"Lieutenant," Jonah broke in. "Undress uniforms, some underwear, and a new personal comm. Please?"

"Yes, sir," Srp sputtered. "You're okay, though?"

"We're fine, lieutenant," Amy answered. "Tired. Still trying to wrap our heads around what happened."

"Have any of the crews on liberty reported any hostility or negative reaction while on-planet?" Jonah inquired.

"No, sir," Srp responded, "quite the opposite, from what Captain Gray told me. He was prepared to bring the crew back immediately when the story broke a couple of hours ago, but the second officer reported back that the Edoans seemed outraged that this had happened and had expressed the hope that you and Lady Halberd would be safe."

Jonah ended the call shortly after. He and Amy called down to the kitchen and ordered a light dinner. After dinner, exhausted, they fell in bed.

Shortly after they woke, the console buzzed with an incoming call. Admiral Niimura was on the line. He jumped right to business.

"The people sent after us were a team of mercenaries based out of Nyumbani. My intelligence people are working with your MI-6 since the Commonwealth has a much more extensive operation there. At this point, it is unclear whether you were the target, or I was, or both of us.

"One thing is clear, however, and that is public sentiment. Polls show that people all over the planet are outraged. Coming on the heels of our successful operation to liberate Goryeo, the general public is furious, and they blame the Chinese. Whether the Chinese were behind it remains to be seen.

"Our foreign service secretary spoke with her Commonwealth counterpart overnight and approached me with a request about an hour ago," Yoshi continued. "She would like to ask you both to please stay for the week you had planned. Further, though I understand agent Lewis' firm desire to keep you in a safe location, the two of them feel that public perceptions of the relations between our two governments would benefit a great deal if you were to appear, with Niko and me as your hosts, in public, doing the sorts of things visitors to our planet would normally do."

"Normal tourist-type things, then," Amy interjected.

"Yes," Yoshi confirmed. "Normal tourist things. Seeing the sights, shopping, and, at the end of the week, attending a state dinner in honor of our successful joint operation in Goryeo. Our intelligence chief assures me that she can guarantee our safety. I believe your foreign secretary is even now trying to clear that with agent Lewis's superiors."

Amy's new personal comm buzzed then. She looked at it and mouthed, "Brian." She took the call and went into the other room.

"That was our foreign secretary," Jonah explained. "Probably about to ask us about what you were explaining."

"Talk to him," Yoshi suggested, "then get back to me."

Jonah ended that call and went to get Amy. Amy came back in and transferred the call to the console so they could both be involved.

"I was just explaining to Brian that Admiral Niimura called," Amy recapped.

"Hi Jonah," Brian greeted. "Amy explained what Admiral Niimura had requested. I spoke with Madame Ito, my counterpart on Edo, last night. Both of us see this as an opportunity to improve public sentiment further about the relationship between Edo and the Commonwealth. Things are different from a few years back when Amy was kidnapped while working as our trade attaché. Back then, though people were outraged that Amy had been kidnapped, there were still a great deal of reservations among the public regarding forging closer ties with the Commonwealth. We removed her from the negotiations because her presence would have been a reminder of both their embarrassment and also their misgivings. Her continued presence would have been a lightning rod.

"The situation now is quite different. Edo was attacked and unable to defend Goryeo. The Commonwealth came to Edo's aid, even though everyone knows the Commonwealth is still in pretty rough shape militarily. Our two governments are working at unprecedented levels on a variety of projects. In addition, Madame Ito shared with me some snap polls conducted yesterday evening on Edo. People are beyond embarrassed; they are furious that Admiral Niimura and Admiral Lord Halberd were attacked immediately after a successful joint operation to free Goryeo. They fear that the Commonwealth will abandon them as a result.

"Like it or not, Amy, you and Jonah right now are as much the public face of the Commonwealth as Edward and Celeste. Admiral Niimura and his wife are extremely well-respected on Edo as well. Having the four of you make a series of public appearances this week will demonstrate that we will not abandon Edo, that we believe the people of Edo were not behind this latest attack and that the Commonwealth is unafraid. Stiff upper lip and all that. The head of the Imperial intelligence services has spoken with the director of the King's Own, and she has personally guaranteed your safety.

"I realize what I am asking is potentially dangerous since we have not learned who was behind the attack or who their target was. I cannot order you to do it and would certainly understand if you declined. I hope, though, that you can see the potential."

"We can see the benefits," Amy responded. "Please give us a chance to talk about it between ourselves, and we will let you know shortly what we would prefer to do."

"Fair enough," Brian replied. Amy ended the call.

"What do you think, honey?" she asked. "Want to go shopping and sightseeing for king and country?"

"It's not something to joke about, Amy," Jonah answered carefully. "We don't know if there are more people on Edo that are part of the attack. The thought of deliberately exposing you to danger gives me the willies."

"I'm not trying to make light of it," Amy responded. "I am aware that there is risk. At the same time, it sounds like Yoshi and Niko feel strongly enough about the possible benefits that they're willing to take the chance. They might have been after him, you know."

"I know," Jonah admitted. "It sounds like you're willing to do it."

"At the moment, yes," Amy confirmed. "If I think about it too much, I'll probably come up with hundreds of reasons it's a bad idea, so I'd rather go with my gut feeling and commit. Once I commit, I'll be fine."

"Yoshi and Niko being willing to do it reassures me a little," Jonah affirmed. "If you want to do it, call Brian and let him know. Then we'll call Yoshi."

Amy called the foreign secretary and confirmed that she and Jonah would participate. The two of them then called Admiral Niimura.

"The deciding factor for us," Jonah explained, "was that both you and Niko were willing to do this."

"Niko's biggest problem was taking a week off work," Yoshi responded. "I tried to explain that it was dangerous, and she told me…well, it doesn't quite translate, but the English idiom would be 'Stick it in your ear,' I think. I will let Madame Ito know. She has already had the public affairs people working on it, in hopes you would agree."

36

When the Edoans exposed the Chinese plants in the Edoan government, Dong Li was angry. When the Edoans, with the help of the Commonwealth, regained control of Goryeo, she was furious. When she learned of the failed assassination attempt, Wang Xhu thought she would burst a blood vessel and have a stroke.

She blamed him for all these failures, of course. Of course, the assassination attempt was nothing he ordered or knew about. When he was chairman of the governing council, the Ministry of State Security would have informed him of such a plan. He mentioned that.

"I ordered it," she snapped.

"Then why are you blaming me for its failure?" he asked.

She just glared at him. After a few minutes of silence, during which she calmed somewhat, she also reported that the Minister of State Security also informed her that attempts to learn more about the Commonwealth's new artillery weapon had failed to this point. Their most successful agents in the Commonwealth were captured or compromised, and it would be many months before she was able to rebuild their networks.

In the meantime, Dong Li presided over the destruction of an entire battle fleet at Hǎiwángxīng and the loss of the Goryeo system along with the task force defending it. She began to discuss what to do with Wang Xhu. She had kept Wang under house arrest at the lakeside estate, though he wondered why she kept him alive quite often.

"What do you think?" she asked him. "Begin peace talks or make another attempt at destroying the Commonwealth Navy?"

Wang pondered his response carefully before delivering it. "I wonder why you ask, chairman? You already know my answer. Is it because you become more sure of yourself in opposing my views? Clearly, the time has passed when we could explore peace talks on terms that would be favorable to us.

The Commonwealth weakened though they might still be at present, would now be unlikely to grant us what we want. They likely sense they have survived the worst of the storm and that the tide might already be turning.

"Based on the two most recent exchanges between our navies, they might relish another attack by us. It seems likely that any attempt by us to bring them to their knees will likely result in bringing us to our knees as well. We would be two fighters, both punch-drunk, staggering around the ring. Who would benefit? Possibly the Rodinans, down and out as they are. Certainly, our people do not benefit from further conflict.

"Your entire strategy has failed. I regret not opposing you more vigorously. Your initial attack against the Commonwealth succeeded in rousing the anger of people who, for seven years, hardly knew they were at war with the Rodinan Federation and cared even less. The Commonwealth only became aroused in the last year or so of that conflict and that because of the actions of one man who shone more brightly because of the incompetence that surrounded him. You rekindled the fervor of the Commonwealth and even fanned the flames with your first attack."

"And you would have done nothing," she spat in reply. "You would have let this opportunity pass us by?"

"I would have preferred to let the opportunity pass us by," he answered calmly, "that is true. I allowed myself to be swayed by your eagerness and optimism. Optimism that was justified. The initial attacks against the Commonwealth will go down in history as perhaps one of the greatest victories ever recorded. Our navy destroyed over forty percent of the Commonwealth Navy in the two opening actions. Even that was not enough."

"I beg to differ," she retorted. "We are so close to breaking their backs. In spite of your loss of courage and commitment, we can still achieve the victory we seek. It requires the will to see it through. Will that you do not have. Will that Admiral Xu did not have. If he pressed the attack, this war would already be over!

"Instead, Admiral Xu's lack of will and your faint-heartedness gave the Commonwealth the chance to regroup. Now they bring the war to us!"

"Yes," Wang continued softly, "even though they are still outnumbered, they bring the war to us. What does that tell you about our foe?"

"It tells me that I must break them while I have the chance," she answered.

37

Jonah and Amy had an enjoyable week on Edo. Traveling with Admiral Niimura and his wife, Niko, they visited famous landmarks all over the planet, accompanied by the media at every step. Amy and Jonah made sure to tell the press how magnificent all the sights were that they saw and how wonderful the people were to them on their visit (which were both true).

The state dinner at the end of the week was a nice way to cap things. Amy contacted Lady Thorner, whose seemingly inexhaustible list of contacts included an up-and-coming fashion designer in New Seoul. The designer was delighted to create dresses for both Amy and Niko in time for the state dinner. Judging from the favorable media coverage the next day, the public agreed with Jonah and Yoshi that their wives looked stunningly beautiful in addition to being brilliant and capable. The press was also ecstatic that the dresses were from an Edoan designer.

During the week, they were informed that the would-be assassins were hired through a number of third parties. The Commonwealth's MI-6 was having difficulty back-tracing these third-party cut-outs to the originator of the contract. The difficulty of doing so injected some doubt into their preliminary belief that the Chinese ordered it months earlier, and the attack was aimed at Admiral Niimura. They could not rule out the possibility that the attack was planned more recently and was aimed at Jonah.

Agent Lewis was joined by Agent Remington, and the two of them accompanied Amy, along with Agent Winchester's body, on a commercial liner back to New Bremen. Jonah rejoined *Centurion*, and the three Commonwealth ships returned to Caerleon. Lieutenant Srp enjoyed visiting Edo and joined them for dinner one night. Though at first slightly reticent, by the end of the evening, she and Amy were well on their way to becoming friends.

Upon returning to Caerleon Station, Jonah transferred his flag back to

Henry V. He thanked Captain Gray and the crew of *Centurion* for being such capable hosts and for their contribution to the success of the mission. He enjoyed getting to know Captain Gray better but was still happy to be back on *Hotspur*. Every crew had its own personality, and there was something about the crew of *Hotspur* that made Jonah feel more at home.

Within hours the seven ships of Third Fleet (*Theodore Roosevelt* still undergoing repairs) began the journey to the Hercules system. They would be relieving Admiral Delhomme and Second Fleet for two months, giving those crews a much-needed break. Midway through the thirteen-day trip, Jonah called Admiral Delhomme.

"Admiral Crapaud," he greeted his old friend Pierre, "we are halfway there. I'm sure you are quivering with anticipation."

"Well, if it isn't my old buddy, the one-eyed tourist admiral himself," Pierre replied.

"Who are you," Jonah asked, "and what have you done with Admiral Delhomme?"

Pierre cocked an eyebrow in response.

"Are you feeling alright? Only the most mild of insults in your greeting," Jonah pointed out. "That's not like you."

"I'm in a good mood," Pierre explained, "and also, if I were to piss you off, you might slow down. I'm counting the minutes until your arrival, so that would never do."

"Oh," Jonah remarked. "Big plans for this leave? Going to visit Mom? Help her feed the cats, clean the litter box and take her to bingo?"

"Nope," Pierre replied smugly.

"I've got it," Jonah surmised, "going to your sister's to help her change diapers for whatever number baby she just had?"

"Nope," Pierre answered. "You're not even close."

"Well, are you going to tell me?"

"You'll probably find out from Amy anyway," Pierre sighed, "so I might as well. When you get here, I'm jumping off at what they've rebuilt of Hercules Station and catching a liner to Aries."

Jonah wracked his brain for the answer. "Would you be meeting Captain MacLeod on Aries, by any chance?"

"As a matter of fact, I would," Pierre admitted. "We've been in contact since Amy put us in touch and feel there's something worth exploring. We're going to spend a week together on the beach and see if it holds up under closer scrutiny."

"And if it does?" Jonah asked.

"We both have quite a bit of leave saved up," Pierre related. "If we're having fun and things are clicking, we'll stay longer."

"Wow," Jonah commented. "I'd love to say something snarky here, but I like you both a lot, so I hope it does work out. Good luck."

"Thanks. We'll see. Seems promising so far."

"What's going on with your responsibilities?" Jonah asked. "Anything I should know?"

"Pirates," Pierre responded sharply. "A goddamn lot of pirates. You know, I figured out the reason that you and I were so successful as frigate captains wasn't just because we were good—or in my case, excellent. It was because we were in a target-rich environment. There's something about a conflict between major powers that seems to encourage them, I think."

"I knew the Third Fleet sector was infested with them," Jonah said, "but I thought Admiral Sayyah would have helped bring that under control."

"Oh, he was better than Johannsen," Pierre confessed, "but then, one of Mom's cats would have been better than Johannsen. Sayyah was a 'by-the-book' navy regs guy. Didn't give his frigate captains much leeway."

"Still, you've got, what—twenty-one frigates and fifteen light cruisers?"

"Twenty-five and sixteen, now," Pierre confirmed. "And I could use at least ten more of each and another couple of dozen patrol boats."

"That bad?" Jonah winced.

"Oh, yeah," Pierre nodded. "They're getting better armed, too. The Rodinans are trying to raise cash, so they've been having a sale on old frigates and destroyers. They also sell munitions. One-stop shopping if you can pay cash."

"Destroyers? Those things have to be as old as…uh, my ship," Jonah remarked, gulping when he realized his flagship was contemporary with the now-disused ship class of destroyers. "Are they selling them directly?"

"They're going through 'brokers' on Nyumbani. ONI says the 'brokers' are all Rodinans, though," Pierre explained. "The munitions come in crates still closed with Rodinan navy seals."

"You sound kind of depressed about all this, old chum," Jonah commented. "C'mon. Chasing pirates was about as much fun as you could have with your clothes still on."

"If I had captains like me—" Pierre retorted, then seeing Jonah's mock stern expression, amended, "—okay, like you and me, it might be more fun. The Second Fleet guys are okay for the most part, but as soon as one shows he's any good, he or she gets promoted, and I lose them. The Third Fleet guys are all a bunch of pencil-pushers and order-takers. I can't get rid of them because they're just good enough to retain command and not good enough to get promoted. I have to wait for the promotion list, and that will take a couple of years more."

"Have you talked to Admiral Lothes about it?" Jonah asked. "Asked her for some help?"

"I've talked to her about it, but, no, I haven't asked for help," Pierre admitted. "I'm an admiral now. I thought we didn't do that."

Jonah shook his head. "Admiral, yes. Miracle-worker, no. Send me the files. After I review them, I'll tell you what you need to do to get help from Admiral Lothes and BuPers."

"Gawd," Pierre exclaimed, "if you could do that, you'd be my best friend ever."

"I thought I already was?"

"You were, but then I made so much money from selling your wife's pictures—"

"Tell you what," Jonah offered, "If I can help you, and if things work out with Captain MacLeod, name your first-born after me."

"Cyclops? I don't think she'll go for that, especially if it's a girl."

"Why do I keep feeding you these straight lines?" Jonah muttered, shaking his head.

"Because that's the system," Pierre explained. "You say something dumb, and I follow up with a witty retort. It's worked all these years—don't question success."

"Even though you're an incurable smart-ass," Jonah said, "I'll try to help. Send me the files."

"Bless you, milord," Pierre said, tugging his forelock.

As soon as Pierre sent the pertinent files, Jonah pulled the fitness reports on the frigate and light cruiser captains of what had been Third Fleet under Admiral Sayyah. He sent them to his flag lieutenant for review, figuring her time in BuPers might help provide some insight. He dove into them as well.

What he found was exactly what Pierre described—pencil-pushers and order-takers. Men and women perfectly capable of accomplishing the administrative side of running a ship who, given an order, would follow it but seemingly without an ounce of independent thought. All the personnel whose files he looked at were promoted into their current rating by Admiral Sayyah. He called Lieutenant Srp into his office to discuss them when she informed him she completed her review.

"As a group," Jonah asked, "what do you think of them?"

Srp made a face. "Yuck. They have to be the dullest, least imaginative group of lieutenant commanders, commanders, and captains in the whole Commonwealth navy. I'm surprised BuPers didn't flag it."

"After the problems Third Fleet had before," Jonah suggested, "maybe they felt anything was an improvement?"

"Admiral, when I think of a frigate captain, I think of someone like you or Admiral Von Geisler or Admiral Delhomme in your younger days, if you don't mind my saying so. Not that any of you are that old. Someone with some personality, some daring, who needs to be held back rather than pushed forward. These people," she stated, "belong back in the Admiralty doing logistics or compiling actuarial tables or something."

"We agree," Jonah confirmed. "How do we fix it? Can we rely on BuPers for help, or do I need to appeal to Admiral Lothes' good nature?"

"BuPers doesn't want to create work for itself," she counseled, "so their response would be to handle it via the promotion list."

"That's what I needed to know," Jonah confirmed.

The remainder of the trip to Hercules, when he had time, Jonah reviewed the reports from what had been the Third Fleet sector. In case after case, he saw captains who waited to be specifically ordered to investigate certain systems rather than following their own leads and gathering their own information. It appeared as though they relied solely on ONI for information and waited for it to be disseminated to them through Admiral Delhomme.

When Jonah had commanded frigates, he gathered information wherever he could. At every station they called on, members of his crew would visit the bars and saloons in civilian clothes with their ears open for anything useful. He would talk with as many merchant captains as he could, looking for leads. He made a point of visiting every Shippers Guild hall he could and bought dinner and drinks at every stop. He fed all his intelligence back to Admiral Von Geisler, who generally gave him free rein to pursue the leads he uncovered.

When they arrived at Hercules, Jonah formally relieved Second Fleet. Within moments all five of their ships were heading to the hyper corridor leading back to Caerleon. Pierre's ship lagged behind the others as he took a shuttle to the portion of Hercules Station that had been rebuilt. A liner was due to stop on the way to the Aries system tomorrow.

Now that he was formally in command of the sector, Jonah sent a long message to Pierre. The message was a request to Admiral Lothes for help which explained the problem and requested new commanding officers for the non-capital ships in the old Third Fleet sector. He told Pierre, "Put your name on this and send it before you go on leave."

38

Two weeks into their relief duty in Hercules, Pierre was notified (with a copy to Jonah as his relief) by BuPers that there would be a number of personnel transfers involving the commanders of the frigates and light cruisers in the old Third Fleet sector. Over the next month, it appeared all the commanders of those ships would be rotated out. According to Amy, Captain MacLeod and Pierre were enjoying one another's company enough that they decided to extend their vacation together to a second week and then a third.

Hercules Station was being rebuilt and was roughly thirty percent functional. Apparently, Aries Station was about as far along, if one did not consider the shipyards that had been a part of Aries. Those had been totally destroyed. It was a great stroke of good fortune that Admiral Lothes had transferred the workers and much of the transportable equipment from it to the Twelfth of Never when she did.

Elections were held on Edo, and the majority party made substantial gains, now controlling over seventy percent of their parliament. Jonah had never heard of the new prime minister, but Admiral Niimura vouched for her ability. Niimura also confirmed that the Edoan Investigative Service had been able to indeed confirm that the Chinese had been responsible for the attack on them earlier. Yoshi had been the main target: that Jonah and Amy were also present was merely unfortunate timing.

Jonah reviewed the files of his current Third Fleet captains. Ramonfaur, Tramontine, and Papakostas all enjoyed success combating pirates when they commanded frigates. Jonah realized that the experience he and Pierre shared, reporting to Karl Von Geisler, was of tremendous value. He and Pierre each built upon what Von Geisler taught them, adding their own wrinkles. Ramonfaur, Tramontine, and Papakostas also benefited from serving under knowledgeable commanders, enabling them to have solid success in curbing piracy.

Working together, they compiled a training course they called 'Piracy 101.' Once all the new frigate and light cruiser captains assumed command of the ships responsible for the old Third Fleet sector, Jonah summoned them all to a comm conference. With the assistance of Ramonfaur, Papakostas, and Tramontine, he conducted an overview of the 'Piracy 101' course. He and the three more senior captains then established a schedule to conduct more in-depth training with smaller groups of the new commanders.

When they finished with the commanders in the old Third Fleet sector, they began working with the Second Fleet sector frigate and light cruiser commanders. They led them through the 'Piracy 101' course. Jonah and his senior captains were pleasantly surprised at how eagerly the commanders approached these briefings. They were hungry for knowledge.

Jonah called Admiral Lothes later to thank her for her assistance. "Thank you, by the way, for the command changes in the old Third Fleet sector," he mentioned.

"Admiral, I smelled your involvement all the way from here," she grinned. "Did you dictate the letter to Pierre or write it yourself and have him put his name on it?"

"What letter?" Jonah replied, pretending innocence.

"Okay, be that way," she said. "Everyone who knows him knows that his one blind spot is that he doesn't ask for help as soon as he probably should. How many months do you think he waited before getting Captain MacLeod's personal contact info from you?"

"With all due respect, admiral," Jonah said with mock seriousness, "I refuse to answer that question on the grounds that it might incriminate me...but you're probably right. What's my blind spot?"

"You have to figure it out for yourself, Jonah," she answered. "Just as I hope Pierre does. Maybe our quick response to 'his' request for personnel changes will teach him to ask sooner in the future—hmmm? By the way, I heard about the 'Piracy 101' course you've been conducting with your personnel. I've picked up some very positive feedback. Please share a copy with me. We might want to look at having this documented."

"In case I get blown up?" Jonah asked.

"In case you get blown up," Lothes confirmed.

While in control of the sector, Admiral Delhomme established a regular rotation of three different patrol boats into neighboring system H2813, then through the empty system H2896 and into the Chinese Múxīng system where they would leave stealth drones. It was a seven-week round-trip for each boat. Pierre used the computer to develop a random pattern for these visits so that the time between their visits would vary. The shortest interval between visits was five days and the longest six weeks. The Chinese were more regular. They sent a frigate to the hyper corridor once a month on a predictable schedule to find and eliminate the Commonwealth drones.

Pierre was clever, always leaving one drone for the Chinese to find so that they would not look for others. Stealth drones were difficult to find in the vast reaches of space—akin to looking for a needle in a haystack. Each patrol boat left one right in the middle of the hyper corridor entrance, and the Chinese would invariably find it, destroy it, and return in-system satisfied they had done their job. Each patrol boat also released a second and sometimes a third, launched on a ballistic course to carry it out of the expected area. As a result, the Commonwealth usually had at least one stealth drone operating in the Múxīng system to give them early warning if the Chinese fleet moved through from its base on Límíng, the next system over.

On Thursday, June 16, Jonah received some good news. *Theodore Roosevelt* completed repairs and was on her way to join the rest of Third Fleet. Captain Rocha was delighted to get his ship back. By the time Captain Rocha rejoined them, they would have only another nine days of relief duty before Second Fleet returned.

He also learned, through Amy, that Pierre and Elaine had a wonderful time together on Aries and were now 'an item'. They left Aries a few days before and were on their way back to Caerleon, sharing a first-class stateroom on a commercial liner. Jonah kept his fingers crossed that things would work out for his two friends.

The next day, Friday, June 17, Jonah received some bad news when he woke. Reading his normal overnight briefing materials, flashed was a report from ONI that the Chinese had gathered a massive fleet at their Tǔxīng base. Tǔxīng could attack the Commonwealth at Automedon Station and continue to Avalon, where Fourth Fleet was based.

After reading the flash report, he took a shower. As he was drying himself, his console began to buzz with an incoming message alert. Without combing his hair, he threw a shirt on, sat down at his desk, and answered the call. Admiral Lothes was on the other end. She looked at Jonah strangely.

"Yes, admiral," Jonah prompted.

Seeming startled, Admiral Lothes replied, "I've only seen you without your eyepatch when you were in the stasis pod. Forgive me for staring."

"Sorry about that," Jonah apologized, leaning out of camera range, and grabbing it, slipping it on quickly.

"Don't apologize," Lothes said quickly. "Three thousand years ago, a Roman general named Quintus Sertorius lost an eye in battle and never covered it up. He said it was a greater badge of honor than anything the government could give him."

"Still," Jonah said with a faint smile, "I've looked in the mirror... Are you calling about the flash from ONI?"

"Yes," she confirmed, "I've received updates since the flash went out. The Chinese have gathered seventeen 527s and twenty-six 461s in Tǔxīng.

They may have already started for Automedon Station. They have a 6.5-day transit to reach Automedon and then another three days to reach Avalon."

Jonah whistled at the number of ships. "Is Edo sharing intelligence with us now?" he asked. "Just curious, since we've never had this kind of intel from Chinese space that I can remember."

"On a limited and specific case-by-case basis, yes," Lothes confirmed.

"Better than nothing," Jonah commented.

"It's a huge amount better than nothing," Lothes agreed. "Somewhat of a major breakthrough, in fact. Regardless, we need you to pull Third Fleet and head to Avalon now. To gather a force of this size, the Chinese had to pull ships from the other bases, so we believe the other sectors will be quiet. We're also having Fifth Fleet send half their force."

While she was talking, Jonah activated the astrographic maps showing systems, corridors, and transit times. "Admiral," he stated, "the quickest we can get there is 10.5 days. Given the timing of everything, Captain Rocha and *Theodore Roosevelt* can get to Avalon in time. I'm going to release him to Fourth Fleet right now. Do you have a problem with that?" Jonah asked.

"No, I agree with you. Issue the order and we'll consider him temporarily assigned to Fourth Fleet," she responded. "You're also cleared to use up to $0.25c$ entry speed on the corridors and boost at one-hundred-fifty percent the whole way. That will save about fifteen hours of transit time."

"We'll move out as soon as I type in the orders," Jonah stated. "I'll look for updates along the way."

"Godspeed for a quick crossing to Avalon," she said in closing.

39

When Admiral Lothes ended the call with Jonah, her yeoman alerted her that another call was waiting.

"It's the Rodinan Embassy, admiral," he informed her. "They say it's urgent."

Lothes connected and was surprised to see the face of Admiral Belyaev. "Admiral," she said in greeting, "to what do I owe the pleasure."

"No pleasure, I'm afraid," Belyaev said grimly. "I'm contacting you to pass along some critical information. I only hope it is not too late.

"Nearly a month ago, one of our agents on Patagonia heard through a local contact that someone was looking to hire a team to assassinate the Commonwealth consul on New Bremen. Our agent included this in her regular report, but her sector chief did not think it was important enough to flag it for further investigation. Neither did the bureau chief. A few hours ago, a clerk who is in charge of reconciling the reports came across it and made the connection that the Commonwealth consul on New Bremen is Lady Halberd.

"A courier is already on his way to your Admiralty with a hard copy of the original report. I wanted to alert you as soon as possible in the hope that it's not too late."

Lothes was stunned. "Thank you, Admiral Belyaev," she said briskly after a moment of silence. "I have some people I need to contact immediately, so must close the line. How do I get back in touch with you with further questions?"

"Please contact the embassy," he replied. "I will alert them that when you call, you are to be connected immediately." He closed the connection.

. . .

While this conversation was taking place, Amy was on her way to a reception hosted by the speaker of the house of the New Bremen planetary parliament. Amy was no longer escorted by agents of the King's Own security service. The distance between her posting on New Bremen and the Commonwealth had made logistics difficult. Reluctantly, the King's Own had allowed the Royal Marines attached to the consulate to assume responsibility for her protection.

Marines assigned to embassy and consulate duty had a wide variety of training related to all the different roles they might be expected to fill while working at an embassy or consulate. Agents of the King's Own were not trained as broadly in things such as crowd control—they were specialists. Nonetheless, the marines assigned to the foreign service were an elite group. It was rumored that they had some physical enhancements similar to those of the agents of the King's Own.

Tonight, Amy was being taken to the reception in a groundcar driven by Corporal Estella Jimenez. Sergeant Jamel Toohey was riding 'shotgun' in the front seat while Amy was in the rear. In their dress blues, the marines were not as unobtrusive as the agents of the King's Own, who tended to blend into the background wherever they went. The marines projected military force in their appearance and bearing. Amy was still getting used to the difference, though she admitted it bothered her more than it bothered the Germans on New Bremen.

Amy was engrossed in her comm unit as they drove. She had just received word about the Chinese fleet massing at Tǔxīng. She guessed that Jonah and his ships would be summoned to that sector and was trying to determine whether he would be able to arrive in time to meet a Chinese attack. The car was almost halfway along the 2.3-kilometer route from the consulate to the planetary parliament building when the street underneath the car erupted.

A huge explosion launched the vehicle fifteen meters into the air. It had been slightly off-center, so the groundcar was rotated slightly in its flight, landing on its roof and skidding forward in an additional shower of sparks. Amy and the two marines were knocked unconscious by the blast. If they had been in a normal groundcar, their bodies would have been shredded by the explosion. Fortunately, the groundcars used by the foreign service were specially armored.

Jimenez and Toohey were revived within fractions of a second by nodes implanted in their bodies that released what the marines called a "combat cocktail" into their bloodstreams. During training, all the marines chosen for duty with the foreign service had experienced the effects of the "combat cocktail" more than once. None of them were really sure what the "cocktail" included, but in comparing their experiences with one another, they were all sure that adrenalin was a significant ingredient.

The explosion had triggered an automatic distress call to the consulate.

Within minutes a flitter with a squad of six marines would lift off from the consulate roof heading their way. All Toohey and Jimenez needed to do was survive and protect their passenger until the flitter arrived.

Toohey, though his head was pounding from the aftereffect of the explosion, quickly looked at his comm, which gave him a scan of life signs in the area. The comm showed the human forms closest to his location were still or moving very slowly. It also showed a group of six running toward his location, roughly a city block away now. He gestured to Jimenez, who was on the side of the car away from the approaching group. Jimenez toggled the switch that blew the door off her side of the vehicle. She and Toohey unlatched their seat restraints, dropping onto the ceiling of the car. Both reached up to the underside of the seats and grabbed their helmets and extra ammunition magazines as they clambered out of the car.

Jimenez could see that two of the approaching group had slowed, and one was beginning to kneel. She guessed that this attacker had some form of rocket-propelled grenade, so he was her priority target. By the time she took aim for her first shot, she noticed that the pain in her skull from the explosion was already greatly lessened. She squeezed off two bursts of three shots each, at the kneeling attacker. Though she was a crack shot, she knew she would not likely kill her target. She figured the attackers would be wearing some form of body armor. She only hoped to disrupt his aim.

After those two bursts, she moved her aim to the two members of the group closest to her. They were still running towards the upturned ground car. Again, she didn't think she would be able to kill or disable them; she was trying to slow them down.

Toohey was doing the same. He turned his attention back to the kneeling attacker and his partner just in time to see the launch of the RPG. Jimenez had ruined the attacker's aim just enough. Under the influence of the adrenalin pumping through his bloodstream, Toohey thought the RPG was moving impossibly slowly. He realized right away that it would miss the car, so he continued firing.

The four attackers who had run ahead dropped to the ground. Toohey figured they would begin to use advance and cover techniques to cross the remaining distance. He continued to aim at the man he figured was carrying the ammunition for the RPG. He hoped a fléchette hitting an RPG warhead would be a game-changer.

Sure enough, two of the front four attackers rose to a crouch to move forward as the other two released a flurry of shots. Jimenez felt two fléchettes hit her body armor, but she concentrated on the crouching figures trying to advance. Toohey did the same.

After ten meters, the two trying to advance hit the ground and began firing to provide cover for their comrades to advance. Jimenez alternated between the advancing figures and the RPG, squeezing off three-shot bursts as though she were at the range. She felt a ping on her helmet but didn't flinch.

Toohey also continued to switch targets between the four men advancing and the RPG duo. Though he knew his sense of time was likely distorted because of the adrenalin, he felt as though it was taking them an awfully long time to reload and fire it. He also was struck by the eerie silence of the encounter. Because of the explosion, he could hear nothing. He felt a pluck at his cheek and knew he'd been hit. Probably just a nick, he thought, as he kept firing.

Jimenez watched as the attackers fired the RPG a second time. She and Sergeant Toohey had done their best to distract them, but this time it looked like their aim was true. As the warhead streaked closer, she and Toohey reacted simultaneously, taking a low leap back from the overturned groundcar in the hope that the explosion would not blast the car back on them.

40

Jonah quickly keyed in the orders to Third Fleet for an immediate departure. Running at one-hundred-fifty percent thrust for prolonged periods would shorten the life of the EM drives on the ships. A higher entry speed than $0.23c$ into hyperspace did not affect the transit time through the hyperspace corridor but did involve two risks. First, there was an increased risk of being ejected from the hyperspace corridor into deep space. This would make necessary a long journey at sub-light speeds. The other risk was that of a re-entry paradox. At $0.23c$ and slower, a formation of ships would leave hyperspace in the same formation as they entered. Above that speed, it was believed minute gravitational forces influenced the relative positions of multiple ships. A re-entry paradox was two ships trying to return to normal space in the same spot. The higher the entry speed, the greater risk this would occur. The risk could be plotted on a parabolic curve. At $0.25c$, the risk was still low, but Jonah would need to make sure the ships of Third Fleet were spread out further than normal distances.

Jonah entered the numbers into the astrographic program. From Hercules, Third Fleet would cross system F191, system E130, and system C0827 before reaching Avalon. Using the higher figures reduced the time to reach Avalon to nine days, nineteen hours, and thirty-nine minutes. He hoped it would be enough.

Hours later, an updated flash arrived on his comm. Jonah read it quickly. The Chinese fleet of 43 capital ships was moving out of Tǔxīng. The Commonwealth had Fourth Fleet and part of Fifth Fleet to try to block their advance. Admiral DiGiovanni was setting up three missile gauntlets between Automedon and Avalon. DiGiovanni would be waiting for the Chinese in Avalon. To oppose the Chinese force of 17 SDNs and 26 battlecruisers, he would have ten *Victory*-class superdreadnoughts, fifteen battlecruisers of which eight were the newer *Dakota*-class, the reworked *Columbia*-class

195

dreadnoughts *Yukon* and *Waikato*, and the refurbished *Regent*-class superdreadnought *Theodore Roosevelt*. Only the last three ships were armed with the new artillery weapon.

As he began his sprint to Avalon, Jonah tried to reach Amy several times while he was in normal space but was unable to get through. Her comm unit kept forwarding him to her mailbox. It had happened before that their schedules didn't mesh for several days, but she usually sent him a text or return message. With all the other things on his mind, he didn't dwell on it.

Admiral Lothes, on the other hand, wished she could avoid telling Jonah the bad news. The spectacular nature of what had happened guaranteed, however, that news of the event was traveling at unheard of speed. When she received notification that Third Fleet had entered normal space in system F191, she immediately placed a call to Jonah.

When Jonah answered, she asked if he were alone as she had some sensitive information to share. He answered that he was alone in his ready room. Lothes took a deep breath.

"Jonah," she began, then sighed. "Jonah, I have horrible news—"

Hearing this, Jonah's heart sank. He felt short of breath.

"Amy was killed in an attack just over three days ago. I'm sorry I did not tell you sooner, but you were in hyperspace."

"How?" he gasped.

"A small group attacked while she was on her way to a reception," Lothes explained. "They planted a powerful mine in the street and detonated it when her groundcar was on top of it. They then attacked the car with RPGs. Her neck was broken by one of the explosions. She would never have known what happened, as the force of the first explosion would have knocked her unconscious. Two marines died trying to defend her."

Jonah barely heard Admiral Lothes. His memory was racing through all the moments he shared with Amy. He realized the admiral stopped speaking and was waiting for him to respond.

"Why?" he asked weakly.

"We don't know, Jonah," Lothes said in a soft, sad voice. "We don't know who was behind it or what the motive was. We have leads we are pursuing but no answers yet. I'm so sorry."

Everything suddenly seemed unreal to Jonah. He felt as though his consciousness separated itself from his body. He saw himself sitting in front of the console in his ready room but from a distance. He instructed his body to say something appropriate. "Thank you for letting me know, admiral," he said without feeling. "I need to go now."

He closed the connection. He sat staring at the blank screen for some time, with his consciousness observing him sitting there. He realized he felt…nothing. His consciousness thought that was odd. When he realized he had been sitting motionless for an unusual period of time, his consciousness told his body to stand.

After he reached his feet, the adrenalin that had been coursing through his veins began to leave his system. As he started to shake, his consciousness reappeared in his body. He started to sob. Great, wracking sobs, so deep and so hard he could barely breathe. His shaking grew worse, and he grabbed the edge of the desk to steady himself.

Lieutenant Srp heard the strange sounds through the door. She knocked, but Jonah could not answer. Hearing the sounds continue, she entered. Jonah, still clutching the desk, his chest heaving with sobs, turned to her with a look of intense grief on his face. Tears were flowing in a steady stream, even from his ruined eye, where they pooled briefly behind his eye patch before finding an outlet.

"Sir!" she exclaimed. "Are you alright?"

Jonah, shaking and sobbing, could not speak. He nodded his head yes and then shook his head no. He looked at her helplessly as the streams of tears flowed down his cheeks.

Martina was terrified. "What's wrong?" she asked. "What do you need?"

Jonah could only shake his head weakly in response.

The ship's surgeon, Commander Woodworth, appeared behind Lieutenant Srp, having been alerted by Admiral Lothes. She sized up the situation quickly and crossed to him. "Admiral," she stated, "I'm going to give you a sedative."

Jonah shook his head vigorously in protest but was unable to let go of the desk or stop his sobbing and shaking. The ship's surgeon pressed a pneumatic pen to Jonah's neck and pushed the button. "Help me catch him," she ordered Srp.

Jonah's eye rolled up, and his body slumped, all control gone from his muscles. Lieutenant Srp reached him just in time to prevent him from crashing onto the deck. With Jonah's arms over their shoulders, they dragged him to his bunk. It took some effort to arrange his limp form properly.

"What happened?" Lieutenant Srp asked.

"He just learned that his wife was killed," Woodworth replied.

41

Over the next week, Third Fleet raced, trying to reach Avalon in time to join in its defense. Commander Woodworth and Lieutenant Srp kept a close eye on Jonah. He spent much of the next two days sedated and asleep. On the third day, he woke, showered, and dressed. He walked down to Woodworth's office and told her that he was fit for duty.

"And I'm supposed to take your word for it?" she asked.

Jonah stared at her. "Yes," he said firmly, with a tone of command.

"Sorry, admiral," she replied, "but that's not the way it works. I have to clear you."

"Then clear me."

"Not without some conversation first," she replied. "Sit."

Jonah sat.

"Explain how you're feeling as best you can right now," she asked. "How are you dealing with the shock you received? What's to prevent you from having another breakdown?"

"I'm not dealing with it," Jonah responded calmly. "I will deal with it later when I have the opportunity. For now, I am setting aside my thoughts and feelings about Amy's death. Putting them in a box, so to speak. After we get through the current emergency, I will open the box and process what's inside. I can't do my job and process my emotions about this at the same time. I would like to do my job. Amy would want me to do my job."

Woodworth sat quietly for a bit, steepling her fingers, as she considered what Jonah had said. She weighed his words against what she knew from his psychological profile. "Have you spoken with Amy's parents yet?"

"No," he answered. "I was planning on doing that after you and I were finished here. I know that many of my friends have tried to contact me the last two days, and I need to let them know I appreciate their support."

"Would you tell them you're alright if they asked?" she inquired.

"No, because I'm clearly not alright. It would be inhuman if I were. I will be letting them know that I will likely need their help and support after we get through this current crisis, though."

"Do you think this is a healthy response?"

Jonah chuckled softly. "Not at all. It's—" he struggled for the correct word, "— disassociative. Is that the right term?"

Woodworth shrugged in response.

"I know it would be far better for my mental health," he continued, "if I could address losing Amy now. But we are in the midst of a crisis. I am an officer in the Royal Navy—an admiral. My naval career is an important part of who I am. If I were denied the opportunity to take part in the upcoming battle, I submit that my psyche would suffer even more damage."

"Do you believe the Royal Navy will fail without you?" she inquired.

Jonah smiled for the first time since hearing about Amy. "Hell, we may fail even with me!" he quipped. "A few days before this all happened, Admiral Lothes and I had a conversation about 'blind spots.' You can tell her I figured out what mine is."

"What do you think your 'blind spot' is?"

"One of my friends told me that I had become addicted to producing miracles. He was right. I had. I'd had an uncanny string of success in preventing catastrophes in some unfavorable situations. It's very heady stuff. It changed me so that I was unhappy when I did not or could not produce one. If there's anything good to come from Amy's death, it's that I now understand this. So, getting back to your question of whether the navy will fail without me...if I'm not available to command, someone else will, and he or she will strive to do the best possible job under the circumstances. In that respect, the navy does not need me. It's the other way around: I need the navy, particularly at this point with my personal circumstances. I need to be allowed to do my job—not to produce miracles—but to serve in the role that is such a fundamental part of who I am. If I begin to feel that I cannot perform my duties, I promise I will come see you."

Woodworth nodded. "I need to make a call," she admitted, "and you have some calls to return. I will let you know soon what the decision is."

Jonah rose and returned to his quarters. Outside his ready room, he stopped to thank Lieutenant Srp for her assistance three days before. She was almost embarrassed, but Jonah reassured her that he was grateful she had stepped in.

He then busied himself, contacting Amy's parents first. They were devastated, of course, but also showed love and concern for him. He confessed to them that he was having difficulty in coming to grips with the situation but promised them that he would be back in touch soon. He contacted his mother, Geoff and Laura Thorner, Pierre, Elaine, Admiral Von Geisler, and Admiral Niimura.

When he finished, he checked the duty roster to see where Captain Hayes was. Finding she was off duty, he wandered to her ready room and knocked. When she came to the door, she immediately grasped Jonah in a hug. That was certainly not what Jonah had been expecting, but given her exuberant nature, he was not entirely surprised. While talking with her, he received a message on his comm from Commander Woodworth. "Cleared for Duty" was all it said.

42

After entering normal space in system C0827, the last system before Avalon, Jonah received the report that some of the escort ships of the Chinese fleet separated and destroyed Automedon Station, while the bulk of the invading fleet continued on a least-time course for Avalon. The sensors on the station reported that the Chinese fleet was accompanied by five military fast-transport ships. Jonah surmised that the transports were carrying additional defense missiles for the Chinese. Based on the last-reported speed and course of the Chinese fleet, Jonah's ships would arrive in the Avalon system six hours after the Chinese.

Admiral DiGiovanni established missile gauntlets at the entrances to the Automedon, C0815, and Avalon systems, using the entire inventory of Vulcan missiles in the sector. Jonah suspected it would not be enough to exhaust the Chinese inventory of defense missiles, especially with resupply accompanying them. Though Fourth Fleet had left multiple drones near the exit of system C0815 that would report the time and speed of the Chinese fleet as it entered hyperspace, escort ships of the attacking fleet found and destroyed all of them that were within range of the corridor.

DiGiovanni planned to have his ships within photon cannon range at the exact time the Chinese would be expected to exit the corridor. He took the Commonwealth fleet out beyond the normal corridor boundary, then reversed course and headed back in-system. He guessed that the Chinese would exit 30 light-seconds before the end of the corridor to give themselves a chance to launch anti-matter missiles at whatever missile gauntlet was waiting for them. DiGiovanni hoped to match course and speed with the invaders when they entered normal space.

When the drones were destroyed, he would not know whether the Chinese would continue on their last reported course and speed or change. He positioned his two dreadnoughts and *Roosevelt* slightly behind his other ships, where they would be within reach of their particle burst weapons but out of photon cannon range. With so many unknown variables at play, it would be a small miracle if the Chinese exited hyperspace within range of the Commonwealth ships.

Based on the estimates of when the Chinese would enter the corridor to Avalon, Third Fleet would arrive six hours and eleven minutes later—too late. Even worse, due to light-speed lag, they would be able to watch that battle unfold just after they entered the system, unable to help. And though the planet Avalon's position was slightly nearer to where Third Fleet would enter than the Chinese, the Chinese fleet would reach Avalon Station and the attached shipyards just under two hours before Third Fleet could. All Third Fleet would be able to do is attack the Chinese as they headed for the exit leading them home.

Forty-two minutes after entering the Avalon system, Third Fleet was able to see what had happened in the battle hours before due to the time it took light to travel the distance. Admiral DiGiovanni's guess of when and where the bulk of the Chinese fleet would enter normal space was very close. This was the only piece of good luck for the Commonwealth fleet. Seventeen 527-type SDNs and seventeen 461-type battlecruisers dropped out of hyperspace within photon cannon range of DiGiovanni's ten SDNs and fifteen battlecruisers. Moments before, however, nine of the Chinese battlecruisers dropped out of hyperspace early, within photon cannon range of the three Commonwealth ships armed with the particle burst weapons.

Jonah groaned when he saw this. *Yukon*, *Waikato*, and *Roosevelt* gave it their best, destroying two of the Chinese ships and disabling four others, but then *Waikato* exploded. By then, *Yukon* and *Roosevelt* were reduced to drifting hulks, their few remaining shields lowered in surrender. Three of the Chinese battlecruisers were still on course, moving to join the rest of their fleet.

The other part of the battle was a slugfest with both fleets in photon cannon range of each other. Shortly after this artillery duel began, the missile gauntlet prepared by Admiral DiGiovanni launched. It had no effect.

As the two fleets fired their photon cannons, ships on both sides took damage. In a short time, the greater armament of the Chinese fleet prevailed. Five of the Commonwealth battlecruisers and three of its SDNs exploded during the battle. The rest were heavily damaged, unable to carry on the fight. They lowered their shields in surrender. The Chinese lost six of their battlecruisers, but only one of their superdreadnoughts from this portion of their fleet. While Jonah was certain other Chinese ships sustained damage, they were still able to hold formation with the rest of the fleet.

But what Jonah could see all happened hours before. In real-time, through the kewpie comms, Third Fleet was receiving distress calls from the smashed Commonwealth ships. Captain Rocha on *Roosevelt*, so happy to get his ship out of the repair yard a few days ago, was able to report that he survived, but his ship would need another lengthy stay in the yards if it were ever to return to service. He also reported that Admiral DiGiovanni died when his ship blew up.

The three battlecruisers that survived from the group that had dropped out of hyperspace early to engage *Waikato*, *Yukon*, and *Roosevelt* caught up with the rest of the Chinese fleet. The sixteen SDNs and fourteen of the fifteen battlecruisers remaining in the Chinese force were heading to the planet Avalon and Avalon Station. They would swing around the planet and then around the star at the center of the system before returning to the Automedon system to reach system C0815 and then return to Chinese space. The remaining battlecruiser was taking a different course, more direct, planning to swing around the star and return before the others.

Third Fleet plotted its course to catch the Chinese. They would catch the Chinese just before they exited the system, with a two-minute, thirty-two-second window where they would be in range of the particle burst weapons. Jonah had just glanced at these figures when he received orders from the Admiralty: "Do not pursue outside of Avalon system. Render aid once enemy transits."

Not needing to slow for the entrance to hyperspace changed the equation. Jonah plugged in the new parameters. The window where Third Fleet could fire opened up to three minutes, fifty-five seconds. Each ship would be able to fire sixteen times against the thirty Chinese ships.

The Chinese swung around Avalon. They had no difficulty in destroying Avalon Station and the attached shipyard. It was after they passed Avalon on their way back past the star and towards the hyper corridor that the astrographics officer noticed something amiss. Three of the Chinese SDNs and six of the battlecruisers began slowing, separating from the rest of the fleet. Thirteen SDNs and eight battlecruisers continued heading directly for the corridor.

It became clear as the course of the smaller group unspooled that they were positioning themselves to prevent Third Fleet from reaching the other escaping ships. Jonah guessed the ships which made up the blocking force had damage to their Alcubierre units and would not be able to jump into hyperspace. If Jonah decided to push Third Fleet through the blocking force, he would expose his ships to three minutes of photon cannon fire. Third Fleet would be able to get off two shots at the blocking force from each ship with their BFGs before reaching that range. Effective as the particle burst weapons were, there would likely still be plenty of firepower left in the blocking force to damage Third Fleet substantially.

Jonah's first instinct was to follow ancient wet-navy Admiral Farragut's order of "Damn the torpedoes! Full speed ahead!" Fortunately, he did not have to make the decision now, so he took a deep breath and tried for objectivity. As he sat in thought, he realized that the tremendous emotional strain he had been under helped clarify his thinking. Blasting through the blocking force would be an attempt to manufacture a miracle.

He considered the 'butcher's bill' from the battle so far. The Chinese completely destroyed three superdreadnoughts, one of the refurbished dreadnoughts, and five battlecruisers. They heavily damaged seven superdreadnoughts, ten battlecruisers, a refurbished SDN, and a refurbished dreadnought. Fourth Fleet was effectively out of action for at least a year. Avalon Station and its shipyard were destroyed. Making repairs to the damaged ships would likely slow the production of the new ships already begun.

The Chinese lost, to damage or destruction, one superdreadnought and twelve battlecruisers so far. If the blocking force surrendered as Jonah hoped, that would increase the total to four SDNs and 18 battlecruisers. The Chinese paid a very high price to destroy Automedon and Avalon Stations and the Avalon shipyard.

While Jonah knew he would be able to get some of Third Fleet through the blocking force to damage the fleeing Chinese ships, it would cause additional damage to the most effective weapons that the Commonwealth Navy had at the present time. It was simply not the most sensible choice. Though Jonah felt the temptation to be a hero and also the desire for revenge, he found it easy to decide in favor of prudence. He would force the surrender of the blocking force without incurring additional damage to Third Fleet. With any luck, the Chinese blocking force would surrender without fuss when they saw Jonah slow to engage them.

The Chinese force of nine ships positioned themselves directly in the path of Third Fleet. They were decelerating hard, planning on reaching a dead stop in space. Jonah ordered Third Fleet to decelerate as well and come to a halt within range of the BFGs but too far for the Chinese photon cannons to reach them. As Third Fleet came into the range of their powerful particle burst weapons, the Chinese ships lowered their shields and surrendered. Their mission was accomplished: they had prevented Third Fleet from pursuing the rest of their ships.

At least, Jonah thought, the blocking force didn't force me to blow them up or, even worse, blow their own ships up instead of surrendering. Thirteen Chinese 527-type SDNs and five 461-type battlecruisers escaped. Jonah could not worry about that for long. The Chinese left five seriously damaged battlecruisers behind from the beginning of the attack, plus the blocking force of three SDNs and six battlecruisers. The marines would be boarding the surrendered Chinese ships shortly, and there were nineteen heavily damaged Commonwealth ships that needed help.

43

The next few days were busy in the Avalon system. A hospital ship arrived to take the most severely wounded. Prisoner transports arrived to take the Chinese crewmen away. A slightly better class of transport came to take Commonwealth personnel off ships too heavily damaged to make it back to Caerleon under their own power. Salvage tugs began pulling disabled ships, Commonwealth and Chinese, back to Caerleon. It would take them several trips.

Yukon and *Theodore Roosevelt* both needed to be towed back to Caerleon. Of the seven damaged Commonwealth *Victory*-class superdreadnoughts that survived, only two were able to make it back to the yards without help. Of the ten Commonwealth battlecruisers damaged, only one was able to make enough repairs to return under her own power. Smaller salvage tugs arrived and began chasing down the pieces of Avalon Station that could be re-used. To Jonah's inexperienced eye, it seemed as though quite a bit of the station survived in the form of large chunks. The shipyard, however, had been completely blasted away.

While just a couple of weeks ago, it seemed as though the Commonwealth had turned the corner, now it felt like it had at the beginning of the war. The Commonwealth had been rocked on its heels again. The Battle of Avalon, in terms of the number of ships lost and damaged, actually ended up in the Commonwealth's favor, but it certainly did not feel that way to Jonah.

With the battle over, it was harder for him to keep his grief over Amy's death boxed up. So far, he had not asked for more information about her death or who might have been responsible. He knew her body was cremated, and the ashes were being returned to her parents for safekeeping. They did not ask him about a memorial service, but he knew he needed to discuss this with them. Everyone with whom he came into contact studiously avoided the topic of Amy. No one wanted to be the person whose condolences might trigger Jonah's sense of loss. Jonah felt it was time to speak with Commander Woodworth again.

When he reached her office, she looked up. "I've been expecting you," she said with the faintest of smiles.

"I promised I would come to you if I felt I could not perform my duties," Jonah stated. "I am approaching that point."

Woodworth nodded at the chair in front of her desk. "Anything specific you'd like to discuss?" she asked.

"No. I was able to keep my feelings boxed up since there was this battle looming," Jonah said as he sat down. "The battle is over. I'm beginning to want answers to questions I haven't allowed myself to ask. I'm also beginning to get annoyed with people treating me like a bomb that might explode any second."

"Are you a bomb that might explode any second?"

"Yeah," Jonah shrugged, "I might be. I'm still keeping it together but I'm wondering how much longer I can."

"That you've made it this far is pretty amazing if you want my professional opinion," Woodworth commented. "You're not superhuman. I'll make a call, and we'll see about getting you some relief."

Jonah nodded and stood up, heading for the door.

"Admiral," she called, stopping him at the threshold, "I am extremely sorry for your loss. I probably speak for the whole damned Commonwealth Navy. Everyone in civilized space knew how you and Amy felt about one another. I cannot imagine how awful it must be for you."

Her words hit Jonah like hammer blows to his heart. They hurt, but at the same time, he welcomed hearing them. He looked Woodworth in the eye. "Thank you."

When he returned to his quarters, he found that the Admiralty had sent him a message that he and Third Fleet were temporarily assigned to Fourth Fleet's sector. Jonah accessed the files attached showing him the disposition of all the smaller ships in Fourth Fleet that were scattered through the systems in the sector. Since he had nothing better to do, he dug into the files. He noted that these commanders showed initiative and enthusiasm. Their level of activity was far higher than the commanders in what had been Admiral Sayyah's sector. Their level of success was also far greater.

After reviewing the files, he pushed back from his desk. There was a comm conference with Admiral Lothes in an hour. Pierre Delhomme and Karl Von Geisler, the other surviving fleet admirals, would be joining him on the call. He took a walk down to the enlisted mess for a cup of coffee, figuring the stroll would do some good.

A crewman approached him in the mess. "Admiral," he said hesitantly, "I'm real sorry to hear about Lady Halberd. I never met her, but I sorta felt like I knowed, uh—knew, a lot about her. She was a terrific lady, and I'm real sorry."

Jonah thanked him and shook his hand. As he went through the ship, several others of the enlisted personnel stopped him to offer their condolences. The kindness and good wishes of the crew began to rub off on him. Some of his gloomy attitude disappeared. With men and women like this, he thought, we can't help but prevail.

He entered the conference in a surprisingly better mood. Delhomme, Von Geisler, Lothes, and the director of ONI, Mtumbo Sweedler, winked into existence holographically around his conference table. Jonah winced slightly at being the last to join the meeting. He checked his watch and saw he still had two minutes before the scheduled start of the conference.

"You're not late, admiral," Lothes said. "Since we're all here, let's get started. I'll turn things over to Director Sweedler now."

Mtumbo Sweedler activated a chart that was displayed to all of them. It showed the numbers of capital ships by type immediately before the Chinese destruction of Second and Third Fleets, and the losses each side had taken since. Jonah was surprised by the numbers.

"As you can see, when the war began, our fleets were nearly equal, though the Chinese enjoyed a slight advantage, particularly in battlecruisers. The Chinese had 44 superdreadnoughts to our 43; we had 67 battlecruisers to their 85, not counting the three *Viceroys*. As of today, we have 27 SDNs to their 29, but they have suffered greatly in the battlecruiser class. We have 40 battlecruisers to their 35. Please note these numbers do not include the *Viceroys*, the *Columbias*, or the *Regents*. The Chinese have no ships like them, which gives us an advantage.

"What also tilts things in our favor is the number of captured ships. We have captured, in the Battle of Hercules, the Battle of New Delhi, and this battle, a total of five of their 527-type superdreadnoughts and seventeen of their 461-type battlecruisers. Two of the 527s and six of the 461s captured in earlier action took significant damage and will take some time to fully repair. Five of the battlecruisers captured in this battle require extensive work, and I cannot say when they will be done. The three 527s and six 461s that blocked Third Fleet from pursuing the remainder of the Chinese are only lightly damaged. They should be able to join the fleet as soon as the yards can switch their powerplants and drives and install all new electronics. They will be rechristened and commissioned in the Commonwealth Navy in six to nine months.

"There are also our damaged ships from Fourth Fleet. There are seven SDNs and ten battlecruisers that are on their way to the yards. Preliminary analysis shows that five of the SDNs and as many as seven of the battlecruisers can be restored to active duty. Those repairs will take over nine months but less than a year, we hope.

"It's not all good news, however. A little more than two years ago the

Chinese laid down keels for ten more 527s and fifteen more 461s. Those are due to be commissioned 7 to 10 months from now. If we factor in the *Columbias* and the *Regents*, we will still have the advantage of numbers, but it will be close to parity. Our new construction is still more than two years away from commissioning. Eighteen months ago, the Chinese laid down another seven 527s and ten 461s. They will be commissioning shortly after our new construction."

Lothes then took over again. "Third Fleet will stay here in Avalon until further notice. One change—we will be transferring ships around. We will be splitting up the *Regents* and *Columbias*. We don't expect another attack any time soon, but we must be prepared. Second Fleet had been the most vulnerable for some time, but these moves should correct that. There will likely be other transfers down the road to even things out.

"None of you were in your positions at the time—neither was I—but the war with the Rodinans followed a similar pattern to where we are now. There was an initial flurry of activity with significant losses on both sides, followed by several years of low activity while both sides rearmed. We believe the Chinese have exhausted their offensive capability for the time being.

"We believe the Chinese were hoping and planning to knock us out of the fight quickly. We have so far frustrated that hope. Though none of us would consider what just happened in Avalon a victory, it was equally a non-victory for the Chinese. The politicians, whose job it is to pay attention to such things, tell me that public support for the war is high, with poll numbers indicating a much more favorable opinion of the war effort than in the Rodinan conflict. We have kicked and clawed and scratched our way to an even playing field, which is a small miracle given how things started. In the meantime, we will continue to look for targets of opportunity. If an attractive target is found, we will go on the offensive. Due to our current lack of numbers, however, it will likely be on a small scale.

After that, Lothes asked for questions. There were a couple involving the timing of the ship transfers. She asked Jonah and Pierre to stay on the comm after the others clicked off.

44

Admiral Lothes turned to Jonah first. "Admiral Halberd, a courier boat is due to arrive in the Avalon system the day after tomorrow. I am cutting new orders for it, and you are to return to Caerleon on it. You are hereby relieved of duty immediately as admiral of Third Fleet and are on convalescent leave until you are cleared by the Royal Naval hospital here. Do you understand your orders?"

"Yes, admiral," Jonah replied.

"Admiral Delhomme," she said, turning her attention to Pierre, "you are hereby ordered to take command of Third Fleet forthwith. You are due into Hercules Station soon. There is a commercial liner due to transit the Hercules system shortly before your arrival. I am issuing instructions for that liner to wait for your arrival. That will get you headed in the right direction more quickly than any assets the navy has available. When you arrive at Avalon, you may establish your flag on any ship other than *Hotspur*. Do you understand your orders?"

"Yes, admiral," Pierre confirmed. "May I ask why I must choose another flagship?"

"You may. *Hotspur* has been Jonah's flagship. You're not Jonah."

"Understood, admiral," Pierre replied. Turning to Jonah, he said, "Hey, old buddy."

"Uh-oh," Jonah replied, "no opening insult. You must want something."

"Now, is that any way to greet an old friend?" Pierre asked. "Sheesh!"

"Fine," Jonah said. "Hey bro, how you doin'?"

"Not bad," Pierre responded. "You?"

"Um, been better, to tell the truth."

"You want to talk about it?"

"Yeah," Jonah said. "Maybe after Admiral Lothes is finished with us."

"Got it. So, buddy, can I ask you a favor?"

"I knew you would want something!" Jonah said triumphantly.

"Sue me," Pierre retorted. "Look, of the ships remaining, which one should I use for my flag?"

"*Black Prince*," Jonah replied without hesitation, "Captain Tramontine."

"Is she the best?"

"They are all good," Jonah answered. "I would pick Tramontine for you because she won't tolerate your sass. DiAntonio on *Duke of Marlborough* is too earnest and straightforward. He would take you seriously and end up confused. Papakostas on *Elizabeth Regina* would assume you're full of crap. Unfortunately, she'd think you were full of crap all the time instead of just most of the time. She'd end up confused too."

"Is it just me, or do I sense veiled insults in your remarks?" Pierre asked.

"Captain Tramontine would see your sass for what it is and give it right back to you," Jonah explained further, "in spades. As I imagine Captain Blutarsky does now."

"Oh! A hit. A hit. A palpable hit!" Pierre mock-groaned, clutching his heart as though wounded. "Okay," he added, more soberly, "you've convinced me. Tramontine it is."

"Good choice," Jonah commented.

"Are you two always like this?" Lothes interrupted.

"No, admiral," Jonah said flatly.

"Sometimes we're worse," Pierre finished.

Lothes groaned, then asked, "Are you two finished with the...whatever that was?"

"Yes, admiral," Pierre said smartly.

"Good. I'm thinking of promoting Blutarsky to take Second Fleet. Do you have any objections?"

"None at all, Admiral Lothes," Pierre replied. "I was hoping you would allow me to recommend him to you."

"Well, that's one thing I can cross off my list," Lothes stated. "I am finished with you both, for now."

She clicked off the comm, leaving Pierre and Jonah still connected. "You doing okay, Jonah?" Pierre asked seriously.

"Meh," Jonah muttered. "I was fine leading up to the battle and for a little while right after when things were so hectic. But now that everything is a little more under control...it's hard," he admitted, his voice beginning to crack.

"I feel awful for you," Pierre admitted. "I can't even imagine how much it hurts and how much it's going to hurt. Elaine is heartbroken too. It's just..."

Words failed Pierre. He shook his head defeatedly. "We wouldn't even be together if it weren't for you two."

Strangely enough, that perked Jonah up. "You guys serious?"

"Yeah," Pierre admitted. "I am, at least. I'm pretty sure she is too."

"You thinking marriage?"

"I've never felt this way about anyone. I keep trying to talk myself out of it, but I can't come up with any good reasons."

"I'm going to do you a favor, old buddy," Jonah said, his voice once again cracking with emotion. "I'm going to have Laura contact you. When you're done talking with her, if you want to get a ring made, she knows the right people to get it done properly by the time you reach Caerleon. If you know in your heart that it's what you want, don't waste any more time."

Pierre looked up to see tears flowing down Jonah's cheek under his remaining eye. That caused the tears to well up in his own eyes. It took him some time to be able to speak. "Wow," he said in a low tone, gravelly with strain, "that's for sure not how I thought this conversation was going to go."

"Me neither," Jonah confessed, his voice also strained.

"I want to help you out, and you're helping me out instead."

"Nah," Jonah grunted. "It's just the same advice Amy would have—"

"I know. Thanks, buddy. If she says 'yes,' I guess I'll owe you another one."

"Yeah," Jonah sighed, "you will."

45

Jonah returned to Caerleon as the only passenger on the naval courier ship. On his first day of travel, he received two calls. The first was from Mtumbo Sweedler, director of the Office of Naval Intelligence. Sweedler brought Jonah up to date on the progress of the investigation into Amy's death. He told Jonah that the Rodinans had alerted them to the possibility of an attack, but that alert came too late. Admiral Belyaev had promised that Rodinan Intelligence would cooperate fully to identify the killers and, more important, who hired them.

The other call was from a Dr. Abramovich, the head of Mental Health Services at the Royal Naval hospital on Caerleon. They spoke for nearly two hours. She asked him how he was feeling and how well he felt he was dealing with his sudden loss. The deeper they went in the conversation, the more targeted her questions became. When the conversation was over, Jonah realized that, like a good lawyer, she asked questions to which she already knew the answers. Upon reflection, that increased Jonah's confidence. Before ending the call, they established a schedule for further conversations for the remainder of Jonah's return to Caerleon.

During the subsequent calls, she helped educate Jonah on what was a normal and healthy reaction to such a traumatic event as the sudden and unanticipated loss of his wife. She assured him that what he was feeling was expected and he should not feel guilty or that he was in any way damaged for having these feelings. She also discussed with Jonah the types of things he might feel or do that would not be normal and healthy so that if he found himself acting that way, he would know to seek help.

Armed with Dr. Abramovich's advice, during the six days of the trip, Jonah allowed himself to grieve his loss of Amy. Knowing that his reactions were healthy and expected, he was able to let his emotions run their course. He was able to discuss how and what he was feeling with Dr. Abramovich.

He made a start on responding to the many messages people had left for him to people inside and outside the Commonwealth.

By the end of the journey, he was sleeping almost normally and feeling much better physically. Abramovich reminded him that his hurt and sense of loss would be with him for some time and that his arrival on Caerleon would bring new emotional stress: from seeing Amy's parents, from seeing his own mother, from deciding on a proper memorial service—especially given that the government would want to play a role in it.

He and Dr. Abramovich set up a schedule of meetings for his first two weeks on Caerleon. She advised him that everyone he dealt with would understand the depth of his emotion and that he should not try to push himself beyond his limits. "There will come a time," she warned, "when something will set you off. Don't fight it. Excuse yourself and let your feelings flow. You can return to the discussion when you're ready."

This was put to the test immediately upon arriving at Caerleon Station. Agent Remington was waiting to escort him through the civilian part of the station to the shuttle that would take him directly to the palace. While Remington and the other agents of the King's Own normally looked somewhat emotionless, today, Remington had an extremely grim cast to his face.

"Admiral, I volunteered to be the one to meet you today," Remington said with a tight jaw. "All of us are extremely upset about Amy. I wanted to pass along our condolences. We are heartbroken and furious about her death. We are sorry we let you down. If we were there—"

Jonah saw that Remington was offering his hand to shake, a gesture that none of the agents ever made before. Jonah shook his hand, looking him in the eye.

"Agent Remington, thank you and thank everyone for their kind thoughts," Jonah replied. He wanted to tell Remington that if he had been there, he would be just as dead as the two marines who tried to protect Amy but thought better of it. Instead, he simply released Remington's hand and nodded in the direction of the exit.

They boarded the shuttle and flew directly to the landing pad at the palace. Waiting for him when he exited were Geoff and Laura Thorner, standing alongside King Edward and Queen Celeste. Jonah was surprised to see the king and queen and puzzled briefly over what the proper protocol was, especially since he was carrying a travel bag.

The king gave him no time to react, crossing quickly to him and giving Jonah a hug, murmuring his condolences. The queen followed with a hug of her own, then Geoff and Laura. The eyes of all four were glittering with tears. Jonah had dropped his bag in surprise at the hug from the king. A page quickly picked it up and took it away. Queen Celeste took Jonah's right hand, and Laura took his left, and they led him inside.

They did not stop until they were inside the Royal quarters. Celeste led them to a cozy drawing room overlooking some of the gardens. Celeste and Laura guided Jonah to a sofa and made him sit between them. Geoff and Edward took seats facing them. Edward asked if anyone wanted a glass of sherry, but all declined.

"Jonah," Celeste began, "you are among friends who love you. We are all heartbroken for you and will do anything we can to help you through this."

Jonah murmured his thanks. He noticed that Laura and Celeste were still holding his hands. An oddly objective part of his mind thought that was very sweet of them.

"The next week is going to be extremely trying for you, I'm afraid," Geoff added. "Your mother is arriving this evening and the Davidsons tomorrow afternoon. Once they get here, we need to discuss conducting a memorial service for Amy."

Jonah nodded. He wasn't looking forward to it but knew he needed to deal with it. Almost at the same time, Celeste and Laura gave his hands a gentle squeeze. The objective part of his mind wanted to smile at their gesture.

"I would suspect," Edward said, "that you would prefer a small intimate service. I know I would, and I promise you that you will be able to have that, wherever and whenever you and the Davidsons decide. Unfortunately, there must also be a large public memorial. Though neither of you chose to become public figures, you are. I know you're not one to pay much attention to the media, but if you did, you would know that people throughout the Commonwealth are mourning Amy's death. In shop windows on every planet, people are posting Amy's picture surrounded by black crepe or ribbons.

"I hate to sound so cynical at a time like this." Edward confessed, "but Amy's public memorial is a political opportunity that the government must seize. We are in the midst of a war, and the outcome is in doubt. It is no different from similar speeches by Pericles in ancient Athens or Abraham Lincoln during the United States' Civil War."

"Do we know that Amy's assassination is related to the war?" Jonah asked. "I thought they were still trying to determine who was behind it."

King Edward took a deep breath, glancing at Geoff as he did. Geoff gave him a slight nod. Edward sighed heavily and waited for Geoff to begin.

"MI-6 and ONI have been working together, with an unprecedented level of assistance from whatever the Rodinans call the FSB now," Geoff began. "With their help, we learned last night that the orders for the assassination came from Sun Haiming, the director of the Ministry of State Security for the Chinese Republics. He would not have dared to make such a move without the approval of Dong Li, who is currently the chairman of the governing council. We don't know what her motive was exactly, but it really doesn't matter. We consider it a war crime. The Rodinans share our view."

Jonah felt as though a heavy weight was dropped on his heart. He suspected that it was somehow related to the war but was hoping it was something else—a kidnapping attempt gone wrong, or even somehow related to the vendetta the Johannsen family had against him. Rage swept through him, followed almost immediately by an enormous feeling of guilt when he realized Amy was killed to get at him.

He realized he had closed his eye. When he opened it, he saw all four of them watching him intently. "I'm going to need a few minutes," he croaked from his tight throat. All four of them rose.

"We'll be in another room, Jonah," Celeste told him. "There will be a page waiting outside. She will either come get us if you want to talk some more or take you to your quarters if that is what you prefer."

Jonah nodded in acknowledgment. The king and queen and Lord and Lady Thorner stood up and left quietly. Jonah waited for the door to shut. He took one of the pillows from the sofa, buried his face in it, then howled. When he stopped howling in pain, the sobbing began.

It ended up taking Jonah some time to compose himself. Thanks to Dr. Abramovich's advice, he shrugged off any feeling of embarrassment for his feelings. He asked the page to show him to his quarters so he could splash some water on his face, then requested that if it were convenient and everyone was still available if he could meet with the group again. They reconvened in the same drawing room. Once again, he was seated between Laura and Celeste, and once again, they each clasped his hands. Without mentioning the interruption to their meeting, Jonah looked at King Edward and asked, "How do you envision this public memorial service?"

46

The memorial service was scheduled for Wednesday, August 10, at 11:00 am. It would take place in Glastonbury Cathedral, where Jonah and Amy were married not quite two years before. The service would follow the traditional Anglican format. There would be two speakers: Jonah and King Edward. Jonah would speak first.

Amy's parents, Anne and Mark, and Jonah's mother, Marian, had been as loving and supportive as Jonah could have hoped. He had been worried that Anne and Mark would somehow blame him for Amy's death since she was killed because she was his wife. They quickly put him at ease on that point.

Together they had planned a small intimate memorial that would take place on the beach where Amy grew up—'her beach,' she had called it. It would be nothing like the public service. Jonah asked to excuse himself when he remembered that Amy originally wanted to get married on the beach but instead would be having her memorial service there. Anne told him to just sit right there, and she would have a good cry with him. They did.

Mark and Anne chose the hymns that would be sung in the public service. They chose "Oh God Our Help in Ages Past" and "Sing Ye Faithful, Sing with Gladness." King Edward heartily approved of both.

Jonah worked carefully on the eulogy he would deliver. He wanted to deliver a positive message reflecting Amy's wonderful personality. He would let the king deliver the more pointed, political address. When he finished writing, he asked Mark and Anne to read it. They shared it with his mother. All three of them agreed that Jonah had done a fine job. He also asked Captain Elaine MacLeod to look it over. She, too, approved. Jonah did not mention the conversation he had with Pierre.

Pierre arrived the day before the service. He promised Jonah that he would see him as soon as he could, but he told Jonah he had a pressing 'engagement' he needed to deal with first. Jonah had not heard from Laura as to whether Pierre had contacted her about a ring for Elaine, but he agreed with Pierre's priorities.

August 10 was a beautiful summer day. The weather was warm but not unpleasantly so. The sky was clear, and a light breeze was blowing. Jonah woke and read a text from Pierre. "She said YES!" In spite of what was facing Jonah that day, the message made him grin.

Jonah was waiting in a small room off the entrance to the cathedral along with his mother and the Davidsons. Pierre joined him there.

"I had a little trouble getting through the crowds," he explained.

"I'm glad you're here," Jonah told him.

"I stood up with you at your wedding," Pierre stated, giving Jonah a hug. "It's only right that I stand with you now."

They separated, still clasping each other's upper arms. Both were choked with emotion. Jonah shut his eye firmly, blinking tears away, then said, "By the way, congrats."

At that, they were shushed and told it was time to enter. Jonah's mother was to go first, followed by Anne and Mark Davidson. "Admiral Delhomme, walk with me. Jonah, you follow," the king stated.

Glastonbury Cathedral was completely full. Thousands more people watched on huge view screens set up outside. Though it was not declared as a holiday, the media later reported that most of the Commonwealth shut down to watch the service or stayed up into the wee hours, depending on where they were. Shortly after Jonah learned that the Chinese government ordered Amy's assassination, the information 'leaked' to the media. Public interest was high.

The main doors of the cathedral were shut while everyone found a seat. When they opened again for the family, the noise level dropped. When the king entered, a complete hush fell over the crowd. The king in a tasteful black suit and Pierre in his full-dress uniform started down the long center aisle. Jonah, also in full-dress uniform, followed.

When Jonah took his seat in the first pew, the archbishop began the service with the traditional words: "I am the resurrection and the life, saith the Lord: he that believeth in me, though he were dead, yet shall he live: and whosoever liveth and believeth in me, shall never die."

The service continued. They sang the first hymn. Then it was time for Jonah to speak. He climbed to the rostrum, pulled his notes from his breast pocket, and cleared his throat gently.

"We are here to celebrate the life of Amy Davidson Halberd, and it is fitting that we do so, for she lived with joy, passion, energy, enthusiasm, kindness, love, and hope. I am here speaking to you because she was my wife. Yet she also died because she was my wife.

"You know my name and my face because of my accomplishments in war. Most of you only know of Amy because she was a beautiful woman who married me. That's a pity. It's not fair, and it's not right. I'm going to try to explain why she was more worthy of your praise.

"I am a man whose greatest successes have been in war. Amy's greatest successes were in the pursuit of peace. Have any of you considered how odd it is that the two of us, with careers aimed at such different ends, would fall in love and marry?

"Diplomats rarely get much recognition for their accomplishments. They are never considered heroes. Yet the work they do, in pursuit of peace and prosperity, is much nobler than that of a warrior. Some of you, but likely not many, may know that Amy was the lead negotiator of the peace treaty we signed two years ago, after seven years of war with the Rodinan Federation. She worked tirelessly to craft an agreement that would benefit both sides because if both sides prosper, the possibility is reduced for war, bloodshed, and destruction in the future.

"She also worked to improve trade relationships with Edo. Edo restricted trade with other planets for hundreds of years. Amy was the person who showed both sides how they would be better off by working together. Already the people of the Commonwealth and the people of Edo benefit from the work Amy did. Working together, new products have been developed. New business opportunities have been created. Both sides have prospered as a result of Amy.

"Most recently, she was working on New Bremen, a planet that suffered years of occupation by an enemy. The planet's economy was in tatters, its industrial base ruined, its people without much hope. The night she was killed, Amy was on her way to a reception held by the speaker of the New Bremen parliament. She did not know it, but the reception was in her honor, recognizing her for the work she did in attracting new investment to the planet.

"Amy never sought recognition. What she did on New Bremen was find opportunities for people from the Commonwealth to work with the people of New Bremen so that both sides would be better off. She was phenomenally successful, as she was at so many things.

"So, it is right and proper that we celebrate her life and that we mourn because it was ended too soon. Not because she was married to someone, but because of her accomplishments. Her work, her passion, her ability, her talent, her love, and kindness made life better for millions of people.

"To the young people of the Commonwealth, indeed of all civilized space, I would say that there is no better role model than Amy Davidson Halberd."

Jonah returned to his pew. Inside the cathedral, all was quiet, but from the crowd outside, cheering was heard. The king rose and climbed to the rostrum.

"We meet today to celebrate the life of an extraordinary person and to mourn that her life was so brief. She captured the hearts of millions inside and outside our Commonwealth with her vitality, her beauty, and her warm personality. She married one of the great heroes of this generation. She was a symbol of the health and promise of our people and people throughout civilized space.

"There was far more to her than the simple yet romantic story of a beautiful and charming diplomat falling in love with a dashing hero. Her physical appearance, beautiful as it was, was far outshone by the beauty of her soul. Her ability was considerable; she spoke many languages fluently, she was a diligent student of different cultures, she worked tirelessly to promote the cause of peace. As you have heard, she always sought solutions where all parties to an agreement would benefit. She was tremendously successful at doing so. Despite her youth, she was already being groomed for positions of great responsibility and influence.

"She believed that the common brotherhood of man, the highest law of all our being, has united us by inseparable bonds and that the best thought of mankind has long been seeking for a formula for permanent peace. She put her considerable talents to work in the service of peace and prosperity, the heart's desire of all humankind.

"We, the citizens of the Commonwealth, are embroiled in a war. We did not seek this war. It was thrust upon us. It has been a war marked more by our setbacks than our successes so far. Amy is a tragic casualty of that war, specifically chosen for death by our enemies. What a monstrous act!

"If our enemies hoped that her death might diminish our will to fight, they will find themselves sadly mistaken. Because of what this Commonwealth is and what this Commonwealth has done and will do, we are blessed with the firmest courage and the most resolute determination.

"To those listening who live under other governments, a special word. Although I cannot be with you, I address my remarks to you just as surely as to those here before me. To those citizens of the Commonwealth who could not find a seat in this cathedral and who are standing in throngs outside, please know that I hear you. Our enemies will hear you soon enough.

"This Commonwealth seeks peace and prosperity for all mankind, but since war has been brought upon us, and has claimed the life of this bright and shining example of our peoples, along with so many other lives, I say to you, we shall not tire or fail in pursuit of victory. We shall persevere to the end. We shall fight with ever-growing confidence and strength. We shall defend our Commonwealth, whatever the cost may be. We shall never surrender.

"Our goal is not and never has been the subjugation of other nations. We prefer peace and living in prosperous harmony with all our fellow men. But since our enemies chose war, let us, therefore, brace ourselves to this unpleasant task and conduct ourselves so that humanity will say for thousands of years, 'This was their finest hour.' The battle is not to the strong alone; it is to the vigilant, the active, the brave, the resolute. Those who have tasted the fruits of peace and prosperity are not made weaker but fight all the more determinedly to return to that happy state."

ABOUT THE AUTHOR

John Spearman (Jake to his friends and colleagues) is a Latin teacher and coach at a prestigious New England boarding school. Before joining the world of academia, Spearman had been a sales and marketing executive for 25 years. In 2006 he walked away from an executive position with a Fortune 500 company to return to school. He earned his MA in Latin in a calendar year and began teaching thereafter. The Jonah Halberd series of books arose from his wife suggesting he find a hobby.

Dear Reader, if you enjoyed this book, please leave a positive review on Amazon.com or Goodreads. Since sales of these books are in the tens, rather than tens of thousands, a positive review is what keeps me going. If you did not enjoy the book, I'm sorry.

Made in the USA
Monee, IL
14 August 2022